ISBN Number: 979-8-9906448-2-3

First paperback edition: February 2025

Edited by Adrienne Kisner
Proofread by Carol Trow
Cover art by Shirley Tran
Layout by Ava Frechette and Shirley Tran
Printed by Kindle Direct Publishing in the U.S.A

Dedicated to Willow Dryden
I look for you in the trees

Author's Note

This book has been ages in the making, just like any solitary book ever written.

I think that Alone has been particularly hard because I had a very important emotion to tackle here, and I was scared to do that.

Grief is something everyone struggles with, and if they haven't yet, they will- to put it plainly.

During the pandemic, I lost my four-year-old cousin, Willow. While this was a tragedy that no one could've foreseen or fixed, it showed me that grief is so different for each person, and everyone heals in different ways, if they heal at all, which they don't- not always.

When I returned recently to editing this book, I realized something both coincidental and also mildly frightening.

You'll find, as you read, that our new royals live in a grand castle, as royals often do. But Past Ava had planted a strange detail on the castle grounds: a weeping willow tree.

This was on purpose, of course. An author never really acts accidentally, and I had put the tree there as a tribute to another character, which you'll understand once you read (see, now you *have* to read.)

But after losing *my* Willow, I realized that the tree at the palace represents so much more than beauty. It represents grief as a whole, and the idea that the people who leave you... they never *really* leave.

So, I named the royals' castle Willowood, as a tribute to my cousin, and a tribute to the trees that symbolize loss and love.

I think that grief is something so vast and so natural, I would be remiss to disregard these characters' journeys. Since the events of the last book, these kids have learned, loved, and struggled, and I wanted to show readers that grief doesn't have to hinder your healing, it can actually help it along.

I'm excited for you all to read this book, and to watch how the characters continue to become their fullest selves. Plus, a monarchy that hosts a fancy ball in a misty, coastal country never hurt anyone, right?

Turning to my younger readers, especially those who are American like me, I want to tell you that this year has been very hard. You know that, and I know that. But I hope that in times where things feel dark and despairing, you can turn to these books. Kiara, Diana, Peter, and Cameron are like you. *I* am like you. And we tell a story that proves that things can get better, as long as you fight for what's right. Things may be bleak right now, but you are strong like Kiara, you are brave like Diana, you are kind like Peter, and you are compassionate like Cameron. Hold onto those things, because that's what will get you far. Things tend to change when young people stand up for what's necessary. So stand up, and I'll be right there with you.

This wouldn't be an authors' note unless I rambled off a few thank-yous, so I'd like to start with thanking my parents. Since the release of Divided (and before) they've been my biggest fans, and my best friends throughout this process.

My brother got a whole book dedicated to him last time, so I'll skip that, *but* thank you Izzy, for always being there to make me laugh. My little sister is one of my favorite humans in the world, and I get prouder of her every single day.

I've got a bajillion other people who deserve to be thanked, but the biggest expression of gratitude has to go to my team of women who worked on this book with me. Having an all-female creative team was so important to me, and without Adrienne, Shirley, and Carol, I would not have been able to produce something that I'm so proud of. These kickass ladies (pardon the language) are so talented, and just all-around good humans.

I hope you all thoroughly enjoy Alone, and if you only take one thing from the book, remember that we all have our own paths, and emotions are valid and supposed to be felt, no matter what they are. And if you're grieving, give yourself the space to heal, because everyone deserves that chance.

Thank you all for reading, and please enjoy *Alone*.

Part One: The Taurus

Diana

Time: **12:30 PM**

What a scene.

The President, the Secretary of Security, the Citizens' Liaison, and the Secretary of Education of New America sprint down the hall of their Capitol building.

The president clutches a folder in her hand, and the polished tile floor squeaks under her sneakers as she desperately pants for breath.

It's Diana. She's the president.

And holy hell, she's winded.

Cameron is easily the fastest of the four, and he jogs ahead quickly, reaching the top of the stairs first. They all hustle down the spiraling steps as quickly as they can without faceplanting all the way down, and when they reach the bottom, they all join back together in a group, with Diana grasping the file containing the world's biggest secret close to her chest.

When they get to the doors of the Congress Hall, the two boys each take a handle and shove them open. The four run into the room as quickly as possible, startling the other four adults already seated.

"This is big!" Diana shouts, waving the file in the air and finally slowing to a stop. She puts her hands on her knees, trying to catch her breath, and feels a sheen of sweat seep into her blouse. "This is important," she huffs.

Peter grabs the folder from Diana and brings it to the large table in the middle of the room, dropping it in the center. Miriam Miller, Reginald Boone, Victoria

Brewer, and Barbara Oswald are all in their respective seats, each wearing a confused and somewhat concerned expression, eyeing the folder warily as if it might attack them. "Di is right, everyone. Apologies for the lack of decorum, but we've got big news."

They all sit, and Diana pulls the file towards herself and re-reads the passage from the top sheet, finishing with a flourish and flipping the paper around for the others to read. "-Alynthia had stayed hidden for almost seventeen years," she passes the paper to Barbara. As the older woman reads, Diana turns to the other three adults. "Did any of you know about this?"

Barbara scans the papers, including the one with the photo of the two royals on it. After a moment, her face twists into a scowl. "Henderson, that foolish-"

"What's going on, Barbara?" Ms. Brewer asks, fingers tapping nervously on the tabletop.

Kiara pipes up from her seat, where she's slumped in her chair nonchalantly as if this wasn't an issue at all. "Apparently, that one crazy guy who escaped America was the Libra Powerful One and is now the king of this country-"

"Everybody, stop," a firm voice intercedes. Everybody turns to look at Ms. Miller, whose jaw is set and eyes are closed. She opens them slowly as she speaks. "Diana, are you telling me you *found* my mother's charge?"

Diana swallows nervously. "Yes. Him and his son."

"And he still holds the Libra power?"

"I don't know that much yet."

Kiara scoffs. "The Libra Powerful One can *grow life*. Regenerate it, even. That's dangerous."

Ms. Miller nods slowly and turns to the others. "Cornelius is not a danger. Well, not that I know of. Henderson would know better than me."

"What does that mean?" Diana asks.

Ms. Miller sighs, rubbing her temples. "My mother would have been able to explain it better, but there's a... relation between George and Cornelius."

"A familial relation?" Peter questions.

It seems as though everyone is waiting on Ms. Miller's words, for they all stare at her in silent, tense attention. "Yes, a familial relation. They're brothers, if I'm remembering correctly."

Everyone, including Barbara, gasps in either shock or fear. "How?" Kiara whispers.

"Cornelius is George's younger brother. Besides the obvious age difference, they look eerily similar and very much like their father. Since Cornelius was younger, Damian focused primarily on George and got him involved in politics. Besides, when Cornelius turned twelve, he left the family anyways, since he's a Libra."

Barbara swallows. "The late queen did have the most beautiful black hair. I wouldn't be surprised if the prince looks like her, too."

"This makes no sense," Diana says, rubbing her chest as if to ease out the worry. "Why would Cornelius leave America? He could have done anything rather than betray his family and risk his life."

"The Hendersons weren't well off, and Cornelius wouldn't have inherited anything," Ms. Miller explains. "In both mine and my mother's opinions, that is a small price to pay for both power and love. He ran away with his wife, since their romance was frowned upon- well, forbidden, actually."

"He wasn't an Aries, either," Peter adds. "So he would've been split up from his family for years at that point."

"So they're not only made-up royals, they're fugitives," Kiara says, voice laced with a bitterness Diana remembered from that day on the Capitol steps. "If they're related to Henderson, they're wanted."

"They might not even know if he's still alive," Mr. Boone argues. "*We* don't even know that."

Diana takes a deep breath, then speaks aloud the thought she's most confident in, a strategy she'd been practicing since her inauguration. "We can't do anything right now, not until we know more."

"Wait," Cameron interjects, "does this mean whoever gave us these files also leaked them to the public? Because if people get wind of this-"

Mr. Boone interrupts. "Did Henderson tell you about this, Barbara-"

"Are they a threat?" Ms. Brewer asks worriedly.

Everyone starts chattering at once.

After a moment, Diana sighs. "Alright, guys!" she shouts, hushing them. "Let's try to figure this out logically," she turns to Cameron. "Cam, do you know how this file got cleared for the Capitol mail, and if so, who allowed it?"

Cameron considers. "No. I have no idea, and remember, whoever allowed it gave the mailer our personal address also. Mine and Peter's were in our bedrooms at home."

Diana nods, only pulling herself from her tornado of thoughts when Ms. Miller speaks. "Diana, do you think that's where George wound up after the battle? Alynthia?"

Diana and the others fall silent. Diana shifts her gaze to Kiara, who's chewing her lip and looking distressed. Peter, eyeing Kiara, places his hand kindly over hers. She flips her hand over and gives his palm a squeeze, a silent and subtle show of support.

Diana swallows, turning away with a shake of her head. "I don't know. But we have more important questions." Diana turns to Cameron. "Cam, this is especially big for you, being the Secretary of Security. I need a report by tomorrow morning analyzing Alynthian history. If these guys are threats, we need to talk them down before they do anything." Diana taps her fingers in front of Kiara to get her attention. "Ki, could you write me a speech for tomorrow night, and work with Brewer to get a press conference together?"

She nods, meeting Diana's gaze, her eyes filled with worry. Diana smiles comfortingly at her, mouthing "it's okay" before facing Barbara, who smiles at Diana. "What can I do, Madam President?" Barbara asks, grinning at the nickname she coined for Diana all that time ago.

"Well," Diana says, smiling back. "I need you to reap any information about Lucas and Cornelius Rutherland you can find." Diana pulls something out of her inside breast pocket and slides it across the table to Oswald. It's the key, the one that only Cameron, Peter, and herself have. "Use this to search Henderson's office. See if there's anything there that's physical evidence of their relation, and I'll search the Archives."

Barbara nods, and Mr. Boone clears his throat, his tablet clutched between white knuckles. "Diana, I hope you don't mind, but I took the liberty of changing the electric locks and getting someone to set up more surveillance at your apartment."

Diana sighs, relieved. "Thank you, Reginald. That's great." She looks at everyone in turn. "Alright, guys. I believe in all of you, okay?"

Everyone nods. Cameron, to her right, smiles, whispering so only Diana can hear. "*Vive la France.*"

Diana smiles at the table, nodding so Cameron can see and recalling her "Last Hurrah" speech (as Kiara affectionately calls it) on the monorail before they broke into the Capitol. Diana looks back up at everyone, trying to make herself seem as confident as possible. "Okay. Let's go."

Part Two: The Aries

Kiara

Time: **1:02 PM**

Diana finds Kiara deep in a pile of pens and scrap paper. "Hey," Diana says, drawing out the word as she looks around the room, her face a picture of concern. "How are things?"

Kiara looks up at her from where she's sprawled on the floor, lying on her back and reading draft number twenty-six of Diana's speech for tomorrow. Balled up pieces of paper, dead pens, broken erasers, and previous drafts are scattered around her to the point where the carpet she sits on is barely visible. Kiara stares at her. "Does it look like things are going *well*?"

Diana grins. "Uh, not really, but I didn't want to say anything." She sits down on the floor next to Kiara, brushing some loose papers out of her way first. "Is there anything I can do?"

Kiara shakes her head, rubbing her forehead as if to restart her brain. "Not necessarily. I'll do a little more tweaking, but the finished product will be on your desk by noon tomorrow, at the latest."

Diana grins. "Perfect. You're a lifesaver."

Kiara smiles back, then sighs, setting the paper on top of her desk and sitting up. "Do you think what Miriam said could be true?"

Diana chews her lip. "About..."

"Henderson being in Alynthia."

She nods, thinking. "I dunno. I always forget that he's still out there somewhere, and it does make sense for him to go to his family."

Kiara swallows. "He could be hiding right under our noses, in a fortified country with allies we don't know about."

"Have you ever thought that maybe he could be dead? You did stab him before he ran off."

"Only in the arm. And he ran off with a gang of guards, so he probably had help patching it up," Kiara responds, biting her nail and staring into the wall as if the answers will reveal themselves in the paint.

"Okay," Diana says, seeming to understand that there's no right answer, not at this moment. "What do you think we should do?"

Kiara looks over at her. "I don't know. I... I guess there's nothing we *can* do, is there?"

Diana meets her gaze. "Not right now, at least. We're prepared, and there's no way of knowing what Henderson might have. So, worse comes to worst and we deal with him again, we've got the upper hand any day of the week." She nudges Kiara with her elbow. "And besides, we've got you on our team."

Kiara smiles, and although she isn't completely reassured, she does feel better than before. "Thanks, Di."

Diana opens her arms and Kiara leans into her hug, allowing Diana to squeeze the last remnants of worry from her muscles. "Of course, Ki. I don't know what I'd do without you."

Kiara grins at her when they pull away. "You're lucky you won't have to find out."

Diana laughs and throws a paper ball at Kiara's arm. "Don't let it go to your head."

Kiara chuckles, then grabs Diana's arm, the one that's got a small scar in the crook of her elbow. "Hey," she starts, voice low, "you still haven't used it?"

Diana pulls her arm away, resting it in her lap. She casts her eyes towards the floor, as if nervous to meet Kiara's gaze. "No. There's no reason to."

"Di-"

She's cut off by Diana, who rises and snatches the draft of the speech from Kiara's desk and holds it up. "Enough stress, okay? I'm sure this is perfect," she says as she heads for the door. "I've gotta go talk to Cam a little later, but get some rest, please!" She blows Kiara a kiss and leaves.

Kiara frowns, wondering if Diana would ever really return.

Part Three: The Scorpio

Cameron

Time: **6:44 PM**

"Oh boy," Diana says as she enters Cameron's office, a few hours after her run-in with Kiara. "This is even worse than Kiara."

Cameron doesn't know *what* state Kiara is in, but he could guarantee he *definitely* has it worse.

He's turned into something of a researching packrat, and in the time Diana has been searching the Archives, Cameron has been hoarding information. Books are piled up to his waist height, papers are strewn everywhere, and the lights are off with the blinds drawn. The sun was giving him a migraine.

Of course, that has *nothing* to do with the fact he's been reading ancient, archived books for the past eight hours. Or the fact that he lost his reading glasses in the midst of hour two and decided to keep going.

Cameron looks up from where he's resting his head on an old history book, rubbing his eyes and accidentally knocking an empty cardboard coffee cup off the desk. "Uh-huh," he groans, already forgetting what she just said.

Diana moves to sit across from him, and Cameron kicks the chair out for her from under the desk. "Cam, how long have you been at this?"

Cameron bites his thumbnail. "Uh, like..." he trails off, then looks back at her. "What time is it again?"

She checks her wristwatch. "Six forty-five."

"Shit," Cameron groans. "I told Peter I'd get dinner with him."

Diana puts her hand on his wrist, and the contact startles him into focus. "Cameron, take a break. I'm sure you've found plenty on Alynthia."

Cameron grimaces, both from the headache and his lack of information. "That's the problem. I haven't really found anything."

"Anything?" Diana asks, her voice wavering.

Cameron nods, dropping his face into his hands for a brief moment of respite before looking back up at Diana. "Besides some old maps, I've got barely anything. No population numbers, or any personal information on the monarchy whatsoever."

She blows out a huffy breath. "Okay, well, let's see the map."

Cameron opens his desk drawer and removes the map he found folded in the archive shelves. He unfolds it on his desk, the yellowed paper revealing a large continent.

Cameron points to a familiar shape. "America," he says plainly. Diana nods, following Cameron's finger as it moves across the map. Cameron points to a country attached to America from the south. "Mexico."

"Right, gone now," Diana responds.

"Yeah, as far as we know." His index finger glides to Canada, and Cameron moves it in a circle around the Western part of the country. "So, I looked into these places over here. Canada had ten provinces and three territories, all but one of which were sunk."

"What about Alaska? We sunk that too, right?" Diana asks, pointing to the massive state to the left-hand side.

"Yes. The only thing left to the north of us is Alynthia." Cameron points to an island country above Sector Three. "I also did some math. Alynthia stayed hidden for exactly seventeen years before they got leaked to us. Their land used to be a country called Labrador, which- for reasons Cornelius and George have kept under wraps- disbanded the whole country in 2086. Since it was dormant land personally protected by the Hendersons, America skipped over it, and let the old inhabitants live. Enter thirty-year-old Cornelius Rutherland, who escaped America and his family at the last second and established Alynthia with his wife."

Diana nods, looking up at Cameron with full focus. "Okay, so that makes Cornelius forty-seven now, if Henderson is sixty. So Miriam was onto something with the age divide. What else?"

"Okay, well, Cornelius' power is super cool. He can grow life. Supposedly just plants, but there's no proof he hasn't tried it with... other things."

"Like... people?"

"Exactly. Anyways, a few months after the country was established as a ruling monarchy, his son Lucas was born. Ten years after that, the queen, Cornelius' wife, disappeared on the day of the prince's coronation." Cameron cracks his knuckles and looks up at Diana. "And that's Alynthia for you."

She nods slowly. "What did Henderson and the BOZ do when he disappeared?" She pauses. "How did they cover that up?"

Cameron shrugs. "We already know that Damian Henderson and his eldest son were awful leaders, but Cornelius was considerably younger *and* a Libra. I'm sure there was a falling out or some kind of animosity, but blood runs deep in this country."

"And what about the prince?"

"Lucas. He's gonna be king number two. Apparently, according to the file, Alynthia is known for a giant navy, and that *plus* this family connection makes me wonder what exactly Lucas is gonna do when his dad gives up the throne. Is he going to keep the place hidden away and secluded, ready to snap at anyone who comes too close, or is he going to turn around and ally himself with us?"

Diana seems to consider that. "Well, what is his dad gonna say? I'm assuming he still calls the shots, considering he's the current king. Plus, it would be a good idea to get Henderson's own brother on our side in case George ever returns."

Cameron grimaces. "My guess would be a big fat 'no.' Miriam says they're no threat, but I wouldn't be too sure. America really screwed the whole world over, so we can't blame the Alynthians if they're bitter about it. Add that to a brotherly rivalry, and we're pretty much screwed."

"Shit," Diana whispers. "Could we convince prince Lucas to try and change his dad's mind?"

Cameron shakes his head, getting up from his desk and pacing the office. "I don't know. Lucas, like the rest of Alynthia, has been tucked away from everyone for his whole life. I wouldn't be surprised if the kid was on castle lockdown from the moment he was born. We know very little about Alynthia, but we know even less about the prince," Cameron pauses in front of the big potted plant in the corner by the window, digging something from the small hedge and holding it up triumphantly. "My glasses!"

Diana smiles as he places them on the bridge of his nose. "Well," she says, standing and brushing herself off. "Thank you. I know today hasn't been easy." She grabs

Cameron's arm and tugs him to the door, flicking off the lights. "Now, let's go home. You've got a dinner with your boyfriend to make up."

Part Four: The Cancer

Peter

Time: <u>7:32 PM</u>

Diana and Cameron come in at half-past seven. Peter greets them from the couch, wrapped in a blanket and curled up with a book. "Hey," he calls without looking over his shoulder as Diana's light footfalls echo down the hallway in the direction of her bedroom.

Silence.

Then a beat later, Cameron launches himself over the back of the couch, landing right next to Peter. He quickly throws his arms around Peter's neck, his breath tickling Peter's skin. "Peter, I'm so sorry. I got carried away researching-"

Peter sets the book down and turns to face Cameron, pushing his glasses up so they rest on top of his head. He kisses the tip of Cameron's nose and runs his thumbs over his tawny freckles. "Cam, don't worry about it. We can have dinner any other night."

Cameron's face, inches from Peter's, shifts into a pout. "I *know,* but still."

Peter grins. "Do you want to know how you can make it up to me?"

"Yes," Cameron replies earnestly, rapidly nodding his head.

Peter lifts up his blanket and motions for Cameron to get closer. "Sit with me for a minute."

"Peter, you're a total sap," Cameron says with a chuckle. "No 'how was work' or 'what very confidential information did you learn?'"

Peter doesn't let Cameron's goading earn a reaction; instead he smiles playfully, shrugging. "I don't want to know that stuff, I just want to be near you."

With a profuse blush and a dramatic sigh, Cameron scoots up against Peter, sitting himself in between Peter's legs and reclining with his back against his chest. His fingers grope for his glasses on top of his head, and he pulls them on correctly as he squints to read the page of the book Peter is holding out in front of them.

"Peter, *how* do you read this?" Cameron asks. "The text is so small."

Peter chuckles, resting his chin on Cameron's shoulder and kissing his neck. "You need *glasses* to read, Cam. It makes sense that you can't exactly see it."

Cameron turns to face him. "Is that a subtle implication that I don't know how to *read,* Mister Simon?"

Peter kisses him quickly on the lips and smiles. "I don't know what you're talking about."

Cameron turns back around with a joking huff. "Well," he says, pushing the hand holding the book up a little further. "At least hold it up a little more so I can see."

Peter straightens the book, snuggles further into Cameron's shoulder, and smiles at this boy, this boy who is entirely his.

Part Five: The Taurus

Diana

Time: **8:29 AM**

"Have I ever told you guys how much I hate speeches?" Kiara asks as she wanders into Diana's bedroom the next morning, index cards in hand. She passes the bundle to Diana, who takes it from her place in front of the mirror that leans against the wall. "I've never written more in my life since getting this job."

"All set," Cameron says, stepping away from Diana's zipper. He studies her outfit. "Looks good."

They *do* look good. The four established an unspoken rule that they had to coordinate outfits when they did anything in public. Today, Diana was making her speech about Alynthia, and she had donned a pale yellow skirt and white blouse, with a blazer in the same shade over it. White sneakers, also, since everyone and their mother in this country knows Diana can't wear heels.

Cameron, always voted "best dressed" no matter where they went, was in a black suit with a white dress shirt, his tie a matching yellow. Peter was in chinos and a button down (in the same yellow) and Kiara was in a thigh-length dress, with long sleeves and a skirt that hugged her waist and legs. "We look like daffodils, guys," Kiara says. "Who picked these outfits, again?"

Peter approaches, standing with them so they're all in a group and ignoring the blaming finger being pointed at him by Cameron. "We still look good, though. Cam, you're escorting Diana?"

"Yes, sir," Cameron says, straightening his tie. He looks down at Diana, offering his arm. "Good to go?"

Diana runs a hand down her hair, pulled back in braids. "Yup."

They head down the hall and onto the main floor, all riding the elevator in comfortable silence as the quartet quietly fusses over their own outfits. Barbara Oswald is on the bottom floor waiting for them, in her typical navy blue, looking none too happy.

"Something wrong, Barbara?" Cameron asks as they reach her.

"Yes, unfortunately," she mumbles. Without a word, she motions with one hand to the large windows by the main entrance.

They all look. The insane mass of people outside look back.

The booing and shouting is *deafening.*

"What the hell?!" Peter whispers.

"What are they so mad about?" Diana asks, her voice growing increasingly more concerned.

Kiara groans. "Someone must've leaked the Alynthian stuff. Did anyone say something to someone outside of Congress?"

They're all quiet. Then, very slowly, Diana puts her face in her hands as something dawns on her. "Oh, no. I was talking to Barbara in my office while the staff was cleaning. They must have overheard and sold it to some media outlet."

"Who was on staff that day?" Kiara asks.

Diana shakes her head. "It doesn't matter, the public knows now. This isn't exactly how I thought the reveal would go."

"Well, we just have to come clean, I guess," Peter says with a sigh. "Let's go."

"Wait," Barbara says. "Don't mention the royals' connection to the Hendersons. That *must* stay private."

With a nod, they summon their bodyguards and race to their waiting car, where they ride in nervous silence to the Capitol. There, they enter the makeshift stage that has been set up on the steps of the building. Once again, they're met with raucous booing.

Diana grimaces, motioning with her hands for the crowd to quiet. Luckily, they do, and she steps up to the microphone before she can be interrupted. "Good morning, New America-"

"Why didn't you tell us?" someone hollers.

Diana clears her throat, heart thundering. "Everyone, please. I am standing in front of you today to ask for your forgiveness and support during this time. I can promise you that I had no idea Alynthia sat so close to us throughout the past seventeen years. As your president, my colleagues and I are going to do whatever we can to ensure that the Alynthians are not a threat to our country, to you, or to your families." Diana pauses for a moment. Everyone seems to be calming down, at least a little, which is good. "I'm still young, and I'm still learning the workings of this government. I know that is no excuse to keep things from you, but I swear to you all right now that today's conference was about announcing Alynthia to the public," she chuckles lightheartedly, putting on a smile. "But it seems like you already got the message."

Everyone laughs, and Diana turns behind her to where Cameron is standing. He steps confidently up to the microphone, grinning at the crowd and setting off a sound-barrier-breaking mass of cheering. He waves, and then lowers his hand, the people shushing instantly as if he had some sort of spell over them. "Hello, everyone, I'm your Secretary of Security."

More screaming.

"Okay, okay. Thank you for being here. I was asked by President Monroe to relay the fact that as of now, everyone is safe here. America has posed no threat to Alynthia, even throughout the Destruction, so they have no grounds of attack or instigation. As Head of Security, I'm working with the other government officials to get in touch with Alynthian communication departments so we can further gauge their intentions. As for now, please don't worry, and feel confident in your abilities to continue with your daily lives." He steps back, waving again, causing claps and cheers to echo across the Plaza.

Peter grabs his hand, tugging him close, in a visible display of affection that causes more raucous applause. "You're cute," Peter whispers, straightening Cameron's tie.

Camera shutters click all around. "You've gotta love Scorpios," Cameron whispers back.

Kiara, Peter, and Diana all simultaneously groan noises of general disagreement, and Cameron tips his head back in a bubbling laugh that immediately brings a smile to Diana's face. She turns to look at the gathering group of reporters, clutching microphones and pads of paper.

Lately, the teens have been getting a lot of publicity. According to Barbara, the old BOZ didn't get public attention like this, but because of the integration of the sectors, people had started more journalism and tabloid companies all over the country or restarted the ones that had closed. And because those who could afford them had televisions, live interviews were becoming more and more common. And Diana really, *really* doesn't like them all that much. There's nothing more distracting than getting a microphone shoved in your face every few seconds when you're trying to answer a question. Diana cringes and turns to the others. "Okay everybody, break. A couple quotes, but don't give anything important away."

"Well, it's hard to give something away when we don't *really* know anything," Kiara says plainly.

"That's... also true," Diana replies, shaking out her arms. "Let's roll."

Part Six: The Cancer

Peter

Time: <u>**9:13 AM**</u>

    The four approach the herd of reporters, bodyguards hovering close behind them. As much as Diana protests, Peter really likes talking to the journalists. Something about being able to use your platform for good would make anyone excited to speak to the public.

    "Mister Simon!" someone hollers. Peter turns to see a woman in a prim and professional-looking outfit fighting to the front of the crowd, a microphone in her hand and a cameraman behind her. Peter stops and smiles at her. "Do you have a second?"

    Peter steps closer, keeping a small distance between them. "Sure," Peter affirms as she scrambles for her microphone.

    The reporter gets her bearings after a second. She takes a deep breath and turns to Peter, holding out the mic. "Mister Simon, what's your opinion on potentially *meeting* the Alynthian royal family?"

    "Well," Peter starts, "I think meeting the royals would be a great opportunity, and I'd love to discuss their... history and foreign policy with them. I'm sure my American colleagues would say the same."

    There's a strategy for dealing with interviews, Peter's found. If you *say* that your "colleagues would say the same", it typically means that the reporter won't ask one of the others the same question. So, when a hardball question gets thrown at him, Peter sprinkles in the phrase, just to be safe. In this case, it also meant covering for the fact that these two mystery nobles were Henderson's long-lost family.

You're *welcome*, guys!

The reporter smiles and nods, apparently satisfied by his answer. "One more question, Mister Simon," she says, motioning to something behind him. Peter glances over his shoulder to see Cameron and Kiara, talking to another journalist. "Things seem to be going well between you and Secretary O'Connor. How does your public romantic relationship affect your working relationship?"

Peter smiles softly at the query, looking over at Cameron one more time. He catches Peter's eye and grins, throwing Peter a wink. Cameras click all around, and Peter grins back at him before clearing his throat and turning to the journalist.

"Um, well, it's evident that I respect Cameron a great deal," Peter says, leaning into the microphone, "and I admire everything he's done for the country. I know firsthand that his job isn't easy, and to handle what he does with such tact deserves anyone's adoration. As for our romantic relationship affecting our work, I think it helps to be so... close with each other, because you don't typically find coworkers who you trust so completely."

The reporter grins. "That's all, Mister Simon. Thank you."

"Of course," Peter says, stepping back towards the rest of the group. They reconvene towards the back of the stairs, out of earshot of anyone besides their guards.

"How did it go?" Diana asks.

Peter smiles, looking over the crowd of smiling people. "Good." He turns back to her. "Have I ever mentioned that I love this job?"

Part Seven: The Libra

Lucas

Time: **10:04 AM**

Interesting.

You know, Lucas has always heard that Americans *love* to talk. And *these* Americans are honestly pretty good at it.

He sits in the drawing room with his morning tea, watching some snotty tabloid television channel air a piece on the American press conference that took place earlier today. The actual speech was lame, but the interviews are where things get a little more intriguing.

If Lucas is being entirely honest, he has absolutely no clue who each of these people are or what they do, considering he's never left Alynthia in his seventeen years of life, but he likes watching how each of them act in front of the press.

Some are *definitely* more cut out for this than others.

For example, the ginger boy- Secretary of Security- is an absolute dream to these reporters. Tall, handsome, and charming, this kid is obviously loving the attention. He answers every question smoothly, with no hesitation or hint of doubt. Lucas suspects he could sweet-talk even the most rigid of reporters with ease. The dark-haired boy with the amber eyes is more soft spoken, but he, like the ginger, is good at keeping the press entertained, even if his method is less flashy. The dark-skinned curly-haired girl that Lucas knows as the

Citizens' Liaison answers a total of *one* question, and though she isn't shy or hesitant, she very much seems like she would rather be anywhere else. Lucas pities the reporter who spoke to her and had to be on the receiving end of her stony expression.

Then there's the blonde, wide-eyed president.

Hot mess.

Lucas has never seen anyone worse at public speaking.

When she's got her notecards up at the microphone she does fine, but with the press, unprompted, she doesn't make it very far. She stumbles over her words, hesitates, and her green eyes look almost frightened.

"Oh, darling," Lucas says with a chuckle, in the direction of the girl on the screen. "I'm *terribly* sorry."

However, something within Lucas seems to crackle with energy- anticipation, maybe- when he looks at her.

The show cuts to a different clip, of all four of the kids in a line, posing together for the cameras. The ginger is grinning widely, the blonde and brunette are smiling softly, and the other girl isn't smiling at all. Lucas silently applauds the genius behind their corresponding outfits, how they all match enough that it doesn't matter who each person stands next to. Watching them all together, almost... *united*, gives him an idea.

Lucas reaches over the arm of the couch and buzzes for a servant.

"Yes, Prince Lucas?" A young maid asks as she appears in the doorway a few minutes later.

Lucas doesn't recognize this one. She must be new. "Hello," he begins. "Do you know if my father is in?"

She considers. "I believe he went to the marina to meet with the Commander Maxon."

Lucas nods. "I see. Well, bring me letter paper and the stationary set, will you?"

She bows her head quickly, leaves, and returns with a tray in mere minutes, taking the lid off to reveal the palace stationary. Lucas waves his hand to dismiss her, leaving him alone in the room again.

He pulls out a piece of paper, dips his pen in ink, and begins to write.

After a few minutes, Lucas buzzes for the maid again. This time, a different servant appears. "What may I help you with, Your Highness?" he asks.

Lucas hands him the letter, now folded within a sealed and addressed envelope. "Please send this up to my father's office. Put it in his 'urgent' bin, and when he approves it, mail it to the address on the envelope right away."

He bows, takes the letter, and disappears. Lucas turns back to the television right as the segment on the press conference wraps up.

Lucas studies the four Americans on the screen, crosses his arms, and smiles. "See you soon."

Part Eight: The Scorpio

Cameron

Time: **3:15 PM**

Today has been a *long* day.

It's the afternoon, a day after their press conference, and all eight politicians are in the office. Cameron has mostly been doing research on the Alynthians, but he passed the brunt of it to Peter, who was far happier to stick his nose in a history book all day than Cameron was. The main focus of his office hours today was trying to find out who the hell got into their *apartment* to drop off those files, as well as search through Henderson's hoarder-style office to find any important information that was physical evidence of his relation to the royals.

Ms. Miller pops her head into the doorway right as Cameron is done reviewing security footage, to no avail of catching their burglar. The only people coming and going were the usual guards, who were all vetted by Cameron himself. Cameron looks up to greet Ms. Miller, pulling off his reading glasses and tossing them to the side. "Hey, Miriam," he says with a smile.

"Hello, Cameron dear," she says fondly. Miriam Miller always was Cameron's favorite of his adult coworkers. "Just stopping by to bring you your mail."

"Sure," Cameron says, tapping the basket at the corner of his desk with his pen. "You can leave it right here."

She deposits a handful of letters and files into the metal basket and leaves, waving over her shoulder as she disappears down the hall. Cameron grabs the mail and shuffles through, the envelopes crinkling.

Two citizens' letters, a proposal from Victoria, a letter from Lucas Rutherland, a letter from a reporter-

Wait.

A letter from Lucas Rutherland?!

Cameron drops everything else on his desk and fumbles for the gilded envelope that's fallen from his hands. He pulls at the ribbon on the front, trying to unsheathe the letter inside as gently as possible. Eventually, when it becomes evident that he's *not* cut out for royal stationery, Cameron rips the front of the envelope off completely, tearing the golden wax seal stamped with an "R."

Cameron yanks out the letter, dropping the dilapidated envelope on the desk. Unfolding it with shaky hands, he quickly gives the message a once-over:

Dear Secretary O'Connor,

My name is Lucas Rutherland, first Crown Prince of Alynthia. If it pleases you, I would like nothing more than to cordially invite you to a meeting with myself and my father, King Cornelius Rutherland. You, Secretary O'Connor, seemed to be the person to go to with this request. I believe that when discussing a setting for this meeting, the steps of your beloved Capitol building would be a grand venue. Of course, I'm sure you know that the last time an Alynthian was hosted in America was... well, never. So, as you can see, taking this opportunity to be the first nation to host the Alynthian royal family at your very own Capitol would be quite the feat. My father and I have thoroughly discussed this and we are both wholeheartedly behind this rendezvous. I await your reply.

Best,

His Royal Highness Prince Lucas Rutherland I

Holy shit.

Cameron leaps out of his chair, clutching the letter, and races out the door of his office, heading across the hall. When he reaches an office a few doors down from his own, Cameron jiggles the doorknob and pounds on the door. "Peter!" he hollers frantically. "Let me in!"

The door swings open and Cameron falls nearly face-first into the rug.

"Woah, Cam!" Peter shouts as Cameron lands on the floor. Peter crouches protectively by his side. "What the hell is the matter with you?"

Cameron sits up quickly, shoving the letter into Peter's chest. "Read this. Right now."

"Okay, okay!" Peter says, taking the letter and putting one hand on Cameron's shoulder to steady his anxious wiggling. As he reads, Cameron watches Peter's amber eyes grow wide in disbelief, and after a moment, he looks back up at Cameron. "Holy shit."

Cameron nods. "I *know*. That's exactly what I said."

Peter rises to his feet, grabbing Cameron's arm and yanking Cameron up with him. "We need to show the girls."

So, the boys race down the hall, in the direction of Diana's office. The door is open, and the two rush in, interrupting what seems to be a *very* stirring phone call.

"No, Ralph, no, that's not what I meant, I didn't mean *actual-*" she looks up as they enter. "-Oh, sorry, I have a meeting to get to. I'll call you back tomorrow! Bye!" Diana hangs up the phone and sighs. "What could you two *possibly* find this exciting right now?"

Peter slides the letter across her desk and she nabs it before it falls off the tabletop. The room falls silent as she reads, and after a minute she looks back up at Peter and Cameron, eyes wide. "Holy shit."

"I know," Peter and Cameron both say at the same time.

"What are we gonna do?" she asks. Before the boys can reply, Kiara storms in.

"Could you three be *any* louder-" she stops when she sees Diana's expression. "What's wrong?"

Diana waves the letter in the air. "The Alynthians want a meeting."

Kiara shrugs. "So, let's take the meeting, then."

The rest of them fall silent because they *didn't think of that.*

Diana huffs out a general sound of disappointment after a minute, and Cameron can only wonder what she's thinking. "I don't know... of course we *have* to do this, but I don't really *want* to."

"Diana, it might be good to at least talk to them, even if we don't propose an alliance right away," Cameron says. "Besides, I need to answer him either way, and I don't want to get them riled up by refusing."

Diana sighs, crossing her arms. "I'll... think about it."

Cameron grins at her, and Diana can't help but smile back. "Perfect."

Part Nine: The Taurus

Diana

Time: <u>12:03 AM</u>

Diana couldn't sleep.

"I missed you too," Maya says, glancing at Diana out of the corner of her eye, moonlight dancing through her blonde hair.

Maya nods at Diana, looking down at her feet. Diana follows her gaze, and she shuffles "I love you," before smiling up at her sister.

Maya whispers again, her voice fading almost as quickly as the color from her cheeks. "I haven't seen you smile in so long."

She rolls over in bed, pulling her blanket right up to her ears and squeezing her eyes shut, willing her thoughts to settle. When that doesn't work, Diana sighs and sits up straight, running her hands over her face. Her knotted blonde hair falls around her shoulders, and she sighs, looking up at her shadowed ceiling. "Oh, Maya," she whispers, blinking to clear the tears from her eyes as her hand rubs the injection scar on her arm absentmindedly. "What do I do?"

Maya would tell her to jump right in, to meet the royals. She'd agree with Cameron and the others, and then she'd give Diana one of those winning smiles that never failed to melt all her doubts away.

But Maya *couldn't* tell her that. And Diana was entirely lost.

She didn't really know why she was so opposed to this meeting. But she did know that she was torn between thinking with her head or thinking with her heart.

Old Diana would do it. She would meet the royal family, let herself fall into an alliance, and hope that everything would be alright, despite their connection to the Red Man. She would jump in merely for the experience, just to be able to meet these new people.

But this Diana had much more on the line. What happens if these people were a threat? What if they put her country in danger just as Henderson had? This Diana held millions of lives in the palm of one hand and an entire democracy in the other.

This Diana was *scared*.

And yet, this Diana felt a frightening sense of determination, an inevitability that was clenching deep in her stomach.

Diana sighs and flops back against the mattress, covering her face with her hands. Old Diana didn't exist anymore, and the one that was lying here now had to proceed with caution but proceed nonetheless. The girl that would've jumped at the chance to meet the Rutherlands died the day she was sworn into office.

Later in the afternoon, Peter, Cameron, and Kiara are all seated in Diana's office, discussing the prince's letter.

"Come on," Peter says from the chair as Diana shakes her head once again. "It was a formal, diplomatic invite."

"Peter, no," Diana argues. She runs her finger along the wood grain in her desk. "Not *tomorrow*. We need more time."

Cameron pipes up from the other chair. "Trust me, none of us *really* want to. But it looks good for us."

Kiara speaks from where she's leaning against the windowsill. "And not to mention, a successful alliance means we gain their *navy*."

"Why do we need a navy if it's literally just us and them?" Diana asks. She aimlessly shuffles some papers around on her desk and stands. "Guys, seriously. We don't know if we can trust them. I want to do more research and see if they've had contact with George."

"Oh, come on," Peter counters. "You trusted Cameron with finding me twenty minutes after meeting him and it turned out more than fine."

Cameron snaps and points at Peter. "He makes a good point."

Diana groans. "We're doing just fine on our own."

Kiara crosses to Diana and puts a hand on her shoulder, squeezing it affectionately. "You can't say you're not a little curious about the king, though?" She shoots a quick look towards Peter and Cameron, as if testing the waters. "I want to see his power."

Diana runs a hand through her hair, leaning into Kiara's comforting touch but ignoring that small jab. "...Fine," she grumbles after a moment. She goes back to her desk, stamps the envelope of the invitation with her signature to show Congress it's been approved, and then slumps into her chair in resignation. "What time tomorrow morning?" Diana grumbles.

"Nine," Cameron says. "They want to meet us here, remember, and make it a huge public event."

"Okay," Diana affirms. As much as she doesn't want to do this, an event this public *might* look good, no matter the outcome. "Head home?"

"Head home," everyone choruses.

Part Ten: The Cancer

Peter

Time: **5:45 PM**

When they get home, Diana flops onto the couch and covers her head with a pillow. The others take that as a signal to leave her alone, so Kiara crosses to the kitchen, pulling open the fridge. "Nothing good. Who wants what for food? I'll go ask the lobby to get it for us."

"I don't care," Diana groans without removing the pillow.

"Cool," Kiara says. "So, my choice, then, little Miss Bull-headed." She turns to Cameron and Peter. "Good with you?"

They boys both nod, and Kiara squeezes past them into the elevator. Cameron heads down the hall to his room, and Peter leans over the back of the couch and pulls the pillow off Diana's face.

"You okay?" he asks, disregarding the fact that she definitely is not okay.

She stares up at him with her big green eyes. "Nope. I'd rather be doing anything else than meeting these people."

Peter grins. "It'll be fine. Who knows, they might even be nice."

Diana nods, but she doesn't seem at all convinced. "Maybe." She rubs her eyes and yawns. "What time is it?"

Peter checks the clock on the wall. "Almost six."

Diana closes her eyes again. "Great. Wake me up when Ki gets back with food."

Peter nods, even though he knows she can't see it. He starts to head down the hall, but pauses when he passes Cameron's door. Peter backtracks a little and pushes it open gently, knocking on the doorframe as he enters. Cameron is sitting at his desk, feet on the table, reading a thick book. His reading glasses are on, the ones he only wears when he's trying to work. Cameron smiles when he hears Peter enter, looking up at him and pushing the glasses on top of his head.

Peter shuts the door quietly behind him and crosses over to Cameron, pulling the glasses back down so they rest on the bridge of his nose. "Leave them on, they're cute," Peter says softly. "What are you reading?"

Cameron shows him the cover: *An Encyclopedic Guide To Alynthia.*

"I dunno. Figured I should get more practice if I ever want to read with you again," he smiles and pulls Peter down to kiss him, using one hand to set the book on the desk and moving his legs off the tabletop so he's sitting normally. Peter pulls away and leans his forehead against Cameron's, putting his hands on each arm of the chair. One of Cameron's hands is on Peter's shoulder, the other instinctively goes up to mess with the curls at the front of his hair.

"How are you feeling?" Cameron asks, breaking away and pushing off the chair to sit on the edge of his bed.

"Fine, all things considered," Peter says. "You?"

He shrugs. "I think Di is overreacting. They could be nice."

Peter smiles. "That's what I said."

Cameron takes his glasses off and tosses them further up the bed, then pats the space next to him, and Peter sits so their legs are touching as Cameron twines his fingers through Peter's, looking him in the eye. Peter holds his gaze, and after a second, Cameron cracks a goofy smile. "We haven't gotten a second to ourselves in a while."

Peter smiles at him, giving his hand a squeeze. "Yeah, I know."

Cameron leans forward so their faces are inches apart. This close, Peter can see his freckles, the ones that have faded slightly with the cool winter air. As Cameron begins to close the space between them, Peter pulls away teasingly. "Has anyone ever told you your eyes are really pretty?"

Cameron groans, releasing Peter's hand and taking either side of his face. "Peter, come on," he says, his voice ever-so-slightly whiny.

Peter leans in quickly, kissing him hard. Cameron inhales sharply, and Peter runs his hands up his back. Cameron kisses him harder, and Peter parts his lips as he pulls one hand through Cameron's hair. Cameron breaks away from Peter, studying his face, and Peter doesn't know what he likes better, being kissed by Cameron or being looked at like this by Cameron.

"Peter," Cameron whispers, his voice husky.

"What?" Peter asks with a smirk.

Cameron's gaze moves to Peter's lips, and he bunches Peter's shirt in one fist to tug him close again, kissing him once more. Peter pulls Cameron tightly against him, ready and wanting, when the door opens.

"Woah, you guys!" Kiara squeals. "Lock the door next time!"

Cameron and Peter leap apart, and Peter sees he's breathing heavily, his chest rising and falling in a series of movements that cause an indescribable feeling to alight in his ribcage. Peter exhales slowly, gripping the edge of the bed as Diana appears behind Kiara.

"Can we eat- oh my word!" she shouts, covering her eyes. Kiara lets out a cackling laugh, and Cameron shakes his head, looking nothing short of horrified.

Peter brushes himself off, coughing awkwardly. "Knock much, Ki?" he laughs.

Kiara shakes her head, as if erasing the mental image. "I thought Cam was in here *alone*! I was trying to tell you I got food, and then I walk into a scene out of a-"

"Okay!" Diana shouts, her eyes still covered. "Too much information!"

"Ugh!" Kiara says with a small groan. She pinches the bridge of her nose in exasperation. "We need to get you guys a 'Do Not Disturb' sign."

"Or you could just *knock*," Peter mumbles, rubbing his eyes with the heels of his palms.

"Okay, okay," Cameron says, pointing to the door. "Kiara, out. We'll be there in a second. Make sure Diana gets down the hall. I don't think she's gonna uncover her eyes for a long time."

Kiara wiggles her eyebrows. "Sure, sure. See you two lovebirds in a second."

She leaves, making a point to shut the door. Cameron sits back down next to Peter, burying his head in his hands and breaking down into a fit of laughter. He speaks without uncovering his face. "I love them, but sometimes I want to live *literally* anywhere else."

Peter removes his hands from his face and kisses Cameron's knuckles. "Good luck with that one, Cam."

Part Eleven: The Aries

Kiara

Time: <u>6:41 PM</u>

When the boys *finally* pad into the kitchen and Kiara is done doling out their food, they all sit down at the kitchen island. Their dining room isn't used very often, and they only sit there when the other BOZ members eat at their place, so it generally remains untouched. As they eat in comfortable silence, Diana pipes up.

"So, what are we wearing to this gathering tomorrow?"

Peter leans his elbows against the table and shovels a forkful of food into his mouth. "Sweatpants?"

"*No,*" Cameron says, "because the pair you're incapable of giving back are actually *mine.*"

"Guys, what about the outfits Barbara gave us?" Kiara supplies as she dabs at her mouth with a napkin.

All three fall silent and turn to look at Kiara. "You're joking," Cameron whispers.

Kiara shrugs. "Nope. I mean, I know they're a little *much,* but if any outfit screams 'we're the infamous American leaders and you don't mess with us,' it's those."

Diana groans. "She's right, boys."

Peter nods as well. "Yeah. I guess so."

With that, they all unanimously push away from the table, falling into their traditional after-dinner routine. Peter and Kiara grab the dishes, Diana gathers dirty napkins and silverware, and Cameron wipes down the countertop. They work in a routine, companionable silence, until Diana speaks.

"I cannot believe we're wearing those in *public* tomorrow," Diana says, an airy chuckle escaping her lips. "People are going to think we're insane."

"It'll be fine. If anything, it'll scare the Rutherlands away and we never have to deal with them again," Cameron says.

A strange hush falls over the group at that, and they all mumble quiet "goodnights" to one another before heading to their rooms, an unspoken wish to be alone hanging over all of them. The clock on the wall reads seven-fifteen P.M, and Kiara changes into her pajama shirt and shorts before getting into bed and flicking on her television. They're lucky enough to be part of the group of Americans who own TVs, although they only get a couple channels. Kiara goes to the news station to see reporters flanking a sleek helicopter, where two people in almost-identical suits are getting off, guided by scary-looking bodyguards and descending a carpet-clad staircase to get down from the helicopter. Kiara recognizes the taller, older man as Cornelius Rutherland, and he looks even more terrifying in person, wearing a black suit with a white undershirt beneath it and shining leather shoes. Something about him feels familiar to Kiara and she doesn't quite know why. A black town car waits at the base of the steps, and without a word to the press, Cornelius gets into the car. The younger boy who's trailing behind him- Lucas- stops at a microphone that's being shoved in his face.

"Prince Lucas!" The reporter shouts. "How are you feeling about tomorrow's meeting with the American leaders?"

The news camera zooms in on Lucas' face. He shoots the reporter a dazzling smile, one obviously practiced, and slowly buttons the middle button on his suit jacket before leaning into the mic. He's apparently running on his own time here. "I'm feeling wonderful. I've heard lots about these Americans, and I'm elated to see what ideas we can come up with for the future of America and Alynthia as a potentially allied pair."

As the crowd roars, he nods to the reporter and gets into the car. As the door closes on him and his father, the camera follows the car down the street to a private apartment building that Kiara knows has been vacant for years. She's certain there's a penthouse in there, so her guess is that's where they're staying. It's actually just a block away from their building, and Kiara gets out of bed and crosses to her window, drawing back the curtains to spot the tall high-rise across the street. As she gazes across the Plaza, Kiara hears the reporter wrapping up the segment on the television.

"It seems that the royals of Alynthia are looking for an alliance with New America, meaning the weight of the relationship between the two countries is on the shoulders of President Monroe."

Part Twelve: The Taurus

Diana

Time: **7:00 AM**

Diana wakes up at the crack of dawn, lying in bed for a moment to listen to the rest of the apartment waking up. Cameron's shower is running, the rustling of the sheets in Peter's room tells Diana he's making his bed, and Kiara's alarm is beeping quietly. Diana rolls out of bed, discards her clothes on the floor, and heads into the bathroom.

As she climbs into the shower, Diana thinks about the events of the day. After watching yesterday's news about the arrival of the royals, her brain has been jumbled. That reporter is right: everything is on her. *She* makes the decision to ally America with Alynthia. Her heart thumps as hot water rolls down her skin.

Diana rubs her fingers through her hair, scrubbing out all the shampoo. Her eyes land on today's outfit hanging on the bathroom door, and she smiles despite herself. Barbara Oswald got them all custom outfits, two girls' and two boys', that had the American crest on it. Diana's also sported a gold pendant that marked her presidential status, while the other three had silver bands.

Diana gets out of the shower and wraps herself in a towel, finger-combing her hair and then blow-drying it. When that's done, she snags the outfit off its hook, laying it onto the bed. She puts on a bra and underwear, then groans internally as she pulls on the pencil skirt and white button-down. She shrugs into the blazer, black to match the skirt, then shoves her feet into the ugliest black wedges to ever exist.

Diana is studying herself in the mirror, pinning her badge on, when a knock sounds at her door.

"Come in!" she shouts without taking her eyes off her reflection and pointedly looking away from her left arm, which has been strangely tingly all morning.

Kiara enters, wearing the same outfit as Diana. When the girls see each other, they both burst out laughing. "You look terrible," Kiara says after their laughter dies down.

Diana smiles. "You do too. Are the boys ready?"

Kiara pops her head into the hallway, then hollers, "Cameron, Peter! Come here, quick!"

She turns around to face Diana with a smirk, and seconds later, the boys rush in, panting.

"Are you okay?" Peter asks, at the same time Cameron shouts, "Where's the fire?"

"Yes, we're okay, and there's no fire," Diana says. She studies their outfits as they regain their bearings. They look identical to her and Kiara, except instead of skirts, they're wearing black dress pants. The three of them have silver badges on their lapels, each engraved with their title and a Roman numeral. The number of lines signifies the order in which they'd take Diana's job, should she be assassinated or resign. Dark, but Barbara insisted. Diana's badge was gold, and was engraved with "President, I" showing that she was the highest-ranking position.

Cameron's badge had "S. Security, II"; Peter's had "S. Education, III"; and Kiara's said "Cit. Liaison, IV". Barbara technically ranked fifth, but Diana didn't think she'd ever seen Barbara wear her matching outfit. In true Barbara fashion, adorning the others with these gaudy clothes was fine, but heaven forbid Barbara be caught dead in them.

"Ready to go?" Kiara asks.

"If I have to be," Diana grumbles.

They head out to the elevator, but not without grabbing the last piece of equipment that goes with their outfits: matching black sunglasses.

"These are *tragic*," Cameron says, groaning.

He puts his on top of his head, same with Kiara, but Peter and Diana put them on. When they see each other, Peter holds his hand out for a fist-bump and Diana gladly accepts.

They punch the elevator button and ride it to the lobby. Through the doors, Diana can hear the screeching of the crowd.

"Holy-" Peter gasps. "We better make a good impression, or they're gonna tear us limb-from-limb."

Unfortunately for Diana's nerves, he doesn't seem *entirely* wrong.

A gaggle of bodyguards approach the four, led by a tall, muscular woman. She nods at each of them in turn, then stretches her hand out to Diana, the traditional greeting for the president.

"President Monroe, it's an honor," she says, ducking her head politely and only looking up at Diana when she accepts her handshake. "My name is Haley, and I'll be your head bodyguard for the day."

"Nice to meet you, Haley," Diana says. "Anything we should know besides the fact they might blow our eardrums out with all the screaming?" She waves a hand towards the crowd, who just reiterate her point.

Haley sighs. "Only a few things. Firstly, people will have a *lot* of questions. Don't answer them, or they'll find a way to twist your words for the media. Secondly, stick close to a guard. It doesn't matter which one. Especially with these getups, someone will try and tug your sleeves." She motions to their clothes, and Diana sees Kiara shift uncomfortably as she pulls her skirt down a little further. "And lastly, people are head-over-heels for Lucas Rutherland. He's not only charming, but he's also kind towards the paparazzi and the citizens themselves. Just this morning, he helped an old woman cross the street even though his bodyguard told him not to. The press had a field day."

All four nod resolutely. Diana shrugs her shoulders and shakes out her arms, pushing her glasses further up her nose. Cameron and Kiara put theirs on, and Diana runs a hand through her hair before giving the guards a nod. They push open the doors, and each separate guard takes the arm of one of the four in the group. The bright morning light is almost as blinding as the flash of the cameras, and the teens shove through quickly.

"Haley!" Diana calls. The lead guard turns around from where she's leading their group. "Where's the car?"

She points to the Capitol building a few blocks away from them. "You're meeting on the steps of the Capitol, remember? They wanted to make it a big event, where everyone could watch," she grimaces. "We've gotta walk."

Diana nods, and they quicken their pace. They reach a roped-off section that starts about thirty feet from the bottom step, and they pause to be let through. In the shadow of the Capitol building, Diana sees about a dozen guards, and standing shoulder-to-shoulder on the top platform are the Rutherlands. Cornelius is in a similar suit to the one he wore when he arrived, but Lucas...

"Is it just me, or does he look *way* too casual for this?" Kiara whispers to Diana.

"Uh, yeah," Diana says, pushing her sunglasses on top of her head to get a better look.

Lucas is in khaki pants, leather boating shoes, and a light-blue button down shirt that's tucked into his waistband and secured with a belt that matches his shoes. He has an extremely expensive-looking watch on his wrist, and his hands are shoved into his pockets. He's broken from his stoic father to wave to the reporters with a bright smile.

Diana feels a thrumming in the bottom of her stomach when she takes in the prince, and she shakes out her hands to eliminate the electrical tingling.

They approach the stairs, the four Americans taking the left side, across from the Rutherlands, who are hanging towards the right side of the steps. Lucas scoots closer to his father, and when all six make eye contact, Diana can *feel* the click of the camera shutters vibrate through the steps.

There's about ten feet between the two groups, and their security detail surrounds them on all sides, fanning out into a square. After a few stragglers shout questions and are shushed by the guards, the space quiets down.

"Go for it, Di," Cameron whispers.

Diana steps forward, almost exactly in the same place she gave the speech after the Battle of Zodiacs. But the girl standing here today was different than that girl six months ago, in more ways than one. Diana clears her throat, motioning with her hands for the crowd to hush.

"Citizens of New America," she starts, her voice ringing through the lofty ceiling of the Capitol stairs. "Thank you for coming here today to witness this momentous occasion. Standing with me and my colleagues are the King and Crown Prince of Alynthia, a kingdom who survived the American Destruction and are here today to help us build a brighter future." She pauses to let everyone applaud, which they do. "Today, we will be discussing foreign policy and answering your supplied questions." Diana gives the crowd her most winning smile. "So, let's begin!"

The crowd almost blows out Diana's eardrums with their raucous shouts and cheers, and she steps back to her group, turning to talk to them in whispered tones.

Someone taps Diana on the shoulder.

She turns around to come face-to-face with Cornelius Rutherland. His face is weathered with middle age, but his eyes are bright. He extends his hand without a word, and Diana takes it, giving it a firm shake, bowing her head low as a show of respect and dipping into a slight curtsy.

"Your Majesty," Diana says, keeping her voice even despite her nervous thoughts. "It's a pleasure."

"President Monroe," he says back. His voice has an accent Diana can't place, but it sounds very fancy and incredibly terrifying. "Likewise." He looks around at each of her friends. "These must be our Secretaries of Education and Security." He shakes the boys' hands and they bow just as Diana did, then the king turns to Kiara. "And you must be the infamous Citizens' Liaison." He shakes her hand, holding her gaze. "Quite the stunt you pulled with George. You're a little warrior, no?"

Kiara smiles politely at him and nods, and Diana bristles at the idea of her friend shaking hands with Henderson's own brother. "I like to think so."

He turns to Cameron next. "Mister O'Connor, do you have a moment to talk about your new police force?"

"Of course, Your Majesty," Cameron says as the pair moves to a quieter area.

Diana tunes out their conversation, looking around the roped-in perimeter. Lucas is hamming up the press again, so Diana excuses herself from the others and walks down the stairs opposite to him. As she approaches the press, they spring into action, hurling questions at her.

"Miss Monroe!" One reporter hollers. "What's your opinion on the king?"

Diana smiles at him, leaning into the mic. "The king is wonderful. I look forward to conversing with him further."

The next question comes as soon as Diana closes her mouth. "And what do you think of the prince?"

At that, Diana turns to look at Lucas, who's not-so-secretly eavesdropping. To Diana's surprise, he paces over to her, bumping her- *hard*- with his elbow as he sidles up to the reporter. He smiles at the woman, white teeth blaring, and she practically swoons. "Well, I'm glad you asked." He turns to face Diana, his smile still radiating. "We haven't been properly introduced. Give us just a moment, and I'm sure she'll have an answer for you then."

Before Diana can comment, Lucas grabs her arm and steers her back up the stairs, leading her behind one of the giant marble columns and away from the prying eyes and ears of the public. He releases Diana's arm and faces away from her, moving back about a foot while Diana crosses her arms and looks at him as he studies the crowd from their secret spot.

"I can talk to them myself, you know-" she starts.

Before Diana can finish, she's cut off by a sharp glare from the prince. Diana closes her mouth sharply, appalled by the switch that was just flipped on his bubbly, charming facade.

A jolt of adrenaline shoots up her spine, and she watches carefully as the Crown Prince pushes his shoulders back, as if disturbed by a similar feeling.

"So, you're the zodiac people," he says, glancing over Diana's shoulder where the others are still talking to the king. He speaks with the same accent as his father, and the two look exactly alike besides the fact that the king's hair is dirty blonde and Lucas' is almost jet-black. Diana can't help but wonder if his mother, the one who disappeared, was responsible for that. The prince looks back down at Diana, judgment written clearly on his frustratingly handsome face. "My father told me about you all."

Diana nods, studying his sneer. "And what exactly did he say?"

Lucas responds without missing a beat. "That your country was a mess."

Diana is thrown off for a second, but she quickly regains her vocabulary. "I presume he's speaking from familial experience."

He smirks a little, and the small action sets off involuntary butterflies in the pit of Diana's stomach and she hates both him and herself for it. "You could say that," he admits.

They both fall silent, and after a second of watching the masses of people, Diana turns back to him. "So you really are a Libra, then."

Lucas' features betray his shock, and he turns quickly to look at Diana. "How do you know that?"

Diana smiles at him, and she waits for the popping of the cameras to quiet before she continues. "Because your ego is even larger than my desire to escape this conversation."

His mouth drops open, and Diana leans forward as cameras begin to flash, straightening the barely-crooked Libra pin on his chest, which the prince notices with a snarl. She turns to walk back to her friends, but pauses briefly to look at him over her shoulder. His hand is resting over the pin, as if shocked he'd let himself be fooled by this American upstart. Diana smiles at the simple idea of pissing him off. "Good to finally meet you, Rutherland."

Part Thirteen: The Cancer

Peter

Time: **12:28 PM**

"Palpable! Truly!" Cameron shouts as he flops into his chair on the congress floor.

Diana buries her head in her hands. "What the hell is he going on about?"

"The 'evident and apparent tension' between you and the royals," Kiara replies from where her head is resting on the tabletop in front of her.

"Evident and apparent are literally the same word," Peter supplies.

Cameron shoots him a glare. "It doesn't *matter*. What *does* matter is that Diana showed them who's boss! I mean, the king *knew* you knew about the power! The prince barely even looked at you the whole morning."

"That's because he's a royal pain in the ass," Diana says.

"Get it, 'royal-'" Peter starts.

"*No*," Kiara says flatly, cutting him off.

"Anyways, I think we need to talk about what we do with the king. He's the Powerful One in question, and we need to figure out what he can do before apprehending him," Cameron states.

"No, we need to get our missing property back," Barbara says as she enters the room, trailed by Mr. Boone, Ms. Miller, and Ms. Brewer. "Cornelius belongs to us."

"No, his *power* belongs to us," Diana retaliates, lifting her head. "I seriously couldn't care less what

Cornelius gets up to as long as he's not using the power anymore."

"We don't have any idea if he's speaking to Henderson, either," Kiara mumbles. Peter frowns as he takes in her slumped shoulders: she hadn't quite been her usual self since meeting the king. "We can't forget about their family."

"Does it really matter if he has the power or not?" Peter asks, shrugging. "I mean, it's not like he's gonna use it to attack us."

"I wouldn't be too sure," Oswald counters. "Alynthia spent the time during the American Destruction building a navy. One doesn't do that if they're aiming for neutrality, *especially* someone who shares the same blood as the Henderson men."

Diana glances at Ms. Miller, who's sitting quietly. "Miriam, what do you think we should do?"

"What?" She asks, looking up at Diana.

"I want you to decide what we do with the king. It's only fair, considering he would've been under your authority had he stayed in America."

Ms. Miller thinks for a second, then sets her jaw firmly and faces Barbara. "I want to let him go. But I think we extract his power first."

Oswald thinks, then nods. "Alright then, I agree. We should discuss this with the Rutherlands, though, at a later date, when we've further gauged their ambitions."

Everyone nods, and Diana clears her throat after a long, tense beat. "Meeting adjourned."

Part Fourteen: The Scorpio

Cameron

Time: <u>8:15 AM</u>

The next few days go by in a blur, chock-full of press stuff with and about the Rutherlands.

And it's clear that Diana is *not* enjoying herself.

"Morning, everybody," Lucas chimes from the screen as his digital call connects. His face fills the large screen, where he's by himself in some giant sitting room that probably cost the same to furnish as Sector Three's entire annual budget. He's dressed in chinos, a white collared shirt, and a gray sweater over it, and he looks *far* too cheery for an eight A.M meeting, although he is fifteen minutes late.

"Morning, Prince Lucas," Cameron replies, smiling kindly at him. It's a private call, with just the four Americans and Lucas, for some leadership campaign that Barbara thought up that the prince just *had* to be present for, even if he was back home.

"Alright, let's get started," Peter says, skimming his binder. He's perfectly in his element, and it's all Cameron can do to sit and admire him.

"One question," Diana interjects, her eyes still fixated on Lucas' digital form. "Rutherland, if your dad is named 'Cornelius,' why are you named something as ridiculous as 'Lucas?'"

The prince looks up at her, smiling ruefully with a hint of pure murder behind his eyes. "Hey, Monroe," he starts, turning to look over his shoulder quickly to check that nobody's there and then turning back to Diana, "kindly piss off, thanks."

While Cameron, Kiara, and Peter's jaws go slack, Diana just smiles, turning her attention back to her folder. Cameron looks up to see Lucas' gaze linger briefly on her before he turns his face down to hide his smirk as well.

Part Fifteen: The Aries

Kiara

Time: **12:00 PM**

The four American politicians wait outside the Capitol as the helicopter they've come to know well touches down, the Rutherland crest emblazoned on the side. The stairs unfold and Lucas steps out, flanked by two bodyguards.

It's his first visit back to America since the semi-disastrous first meeting, and he's here to take some *pictures*.

It's the dumbest reason for a two-hour flight Kiara has ever heard.

Something about her gets nervous every time she sees either of the Rutherlands, and sometimes, she finds herself staring at them, trying to figure out if they shared any features with the Red Man.

So far, she'd noticed that Lucas' eyebrows creased the same way Henderson's did when he was thinking, and Cornelius shared the same green eyes and slightly crooked nose.

Shaking herself from her reverie, Kiara and the boys flank Diana as she steps up to Lucas, extending her hand. He takes it, holding eye contact and completely breaking the protocol of "don't look at the president until she's done shaking your hand."

"Alright!" The American photographer says, breaking from the handshake he had been pulled into by the Alynthian photographer, who had traveled with Lucas. "Let's get started!"

The minutes fly by, with the two photographers hustling the five kids into various poses outside the Capitol. They're dressed similarly, formally: Peter in a black, simple suit, Cameron in khakis and a dark green button-down, Kiara in a dress and simple heels, and Diana in a white dress and pearl-drop earrings, basic but perfectly put-together, exactly the look she's supposed to have. Her shoes are navy wedges, and her hair is tied back with a ribbon of the same dark blue.

Lucas is in a suit as well, a navy velvet thing, with a white button-down underneath.

As he approaches the group, his face twists into a disgusted scowl. Kiara looks at Diana to see that she's doing the same, and Kiara almost laughs out loud.

Their outfits correspond *perfectly*.

And the photographers notice too. "Ah, perfect!" The Alynthian man says as he excitedly pushes Diana into Lucas, nearly plowing both of them over. "These outfits are great."

Instructions are shouted, Cameron, Peter, and Kiara are ushered out of the shot, and after a moment, Lucas and Diana are positioned stiffly in each other's arms. Lucas' arm is around her waist and Diana's hands are clasped at her pelvis, and she's leaning into his side almost casually. The two are smiling at the camera, stunning images of young politicians.

"They look like a prince and princess," Peter whispers.

Cameron tilts his head, studying the pair. "More like President and First Gentleman."

Kiara shushes them, just in time to hear Lucas whisper through his teeth, winning smile still plastered on. "Hey, Monroe, your dress is wrinkled in the back."

Diana, without missing a beat and not breaking her perfect pose, replies instantly. "You know what, Rutherland? Find a stick and shove it *so* far–"

"Good job, you two!" The photographer says, breaking them from their intense trance and lowering his camera. They jump apart from each other, getting slightly tangled in their intertwined hands and arms.

Even though they pull apart like the other has the plague, and the group is placed for their next shot with the two leaders stuck on opposite ends of the group, any idiot could catch the stolen glances between them, filled with ire and judgement and maybe a twinge of respect.

Part Sixteen: The Taurus

Diana

Time: **3:27 PM**

Diana, Lucas, Kiara, Peter, and Cameron were walking back from their photoshoot, bodyguards trailing behind them.

Nobody spoke, and they had donned jackets over their fancier clothes due to the mid-afternoon breeze that was cutting through the Plaza.

Peter and Cameron walked fast, and Kiara had been roped into a conversation with two of the guards about something Aries-related, so Diana and Lucas were uncomfortably sandwiched between them all.

Diana's arms were crossed, but every time she accidentally brushed Lucas' elbow, she felt as though someone had shocked her. She was almost sure that if she looked in a mirror, she'd be covered in goosebumps with staticky hair.

Lucas looks around, pointing to the Capitol. When he speaks, it's not directly to Diana, which she's grateful for. "Did every president serve there?"

"No," Diana replies, because no one else does. "The old capital of the nation was a few states east."

"So why here?" the prince replies.

He could've been asking genuinely, but Diana didn't care. She was cold and tired, and sick of being zapped with that obnoxious energy every time she even dared to look at him.

"Why does it matter to you?"

He glances at her with those dark eyes, filled with so much more life than she saw in that original photo a few weeks ago, and sighs. "It doesn't, obviously. But everything else is the same as Old America, so I figured it was odd that the nation's capital was different."

It's then that Kiara moves closer to them, but to Diana's chagrin, she doesn't stop when she reaches the duo, instead continuing to move and join Peter and Cameron, but she speaks to the pair over her shoulder anyways. "Hey, some things are different. Now there's a girl in charge."

It was exactly the wrong thing to say, in Diana's opinion, because it made the prince give her a searching look, one that resulted in a small scowl settling on his lips.

"Right. We could never forget that little fact," he mumbles.

"What, ashamed that a girl can do the same job you can?" Diana asks, temper flaring although she tries to hide it behind her semi-joking tone.

"You don't do the same job as me, Monroe. Mine is much more important."

"Well," she starts with a bullshit smile, "you're just a man. In fact, a man who isn't in charge of... well, anything, actually-"

"-Just because you're a girl doesn't make you a better leader," he says, and now she realized that the emotion behind those inky eyes of his was ire. "In fact, it might make you a worse one."

She smiles again, determined not to show him just how hard of a nerve he had hit. "I think being a woman *inherently* makes me a better leader." She gets closer, and the two stop walking, lost in their mutual anger to realize the scene they're making.

They pause, both of them poised to speak, both of them clenching a hand into a fist as if itching to act on whatever was surging within their veins.

"Hey," Cameron calls, voice rising just enough to pull their gazes, "come on. We should look in the Archives while we're here."

With that, Diana turns and catches up with her friends, leaving the prince behind her.

Part Seventeen: The Libra

Lucas

Time: <u>4:24 PM</u>

The night of their photoshoot and his impromptu "girl power" argument with the president, Lucas is sitting with the American politicians on their Congress floor, waiting for a meeting to start. It was going to be another monotonous discussion about foreign policy, shrouded with the unspoken question that was 'are these two Alynthians a threat?'

Of course, neither Lucas nor Cornelius had answered this question, and neither would. The key to remaining the mysterious foreign dignitaries was never speaking on the fact that they *were* the mysterious foreign dignitaries.

The group of five was waiting for the adults to return, since the other Americans as well as Lucas' father had gone back to their respective apartments to change and get ready for the meeting. Unfortunately for Lucas, the four sitting in front of him decided to stick around the Capitol, and then they'd heard the news that Lucas was to spend the night at their apartment, to be practically babysat by these Americans while his father hosted a different meeting at theirs. So, suffice to say, not a single person in the room was particularly happy at the moment.

"So, Your Highness," the Citizens' Liaison begins, the title sounding forced and sour coming from her mouth, "how has your day been?"

The question could've very well been intended to be a kind and well-mannered inquiry, but in typical Kiara fashion it did not sound that way, and Diana warns, "*Kiara,*" under her breath through clenched teeth.

Lucas pushes his shoulders back, hoping to physically shake the awkwardness lingering in the room. "Um, I've been with you," he replies. Even to him, his accent sounds out-of-place and strange among the others.

Cameron nods. "You have indeed." He leans forward, bracing his elbows on the tabletop in front of them, and Lucas, seated across from the motley quartet, suddenly feels as if he's being interrogated. "I have a question, actually."

"Go for it," Lucas replies, because why the hell not. He presumed that he wouldn't be able to get this boy to shut up even if he tried.

"What was it like, growing up in that castle? We saw pictures in your file, and I've wanted to know ever since."

Lucas opens his mouth, then closes it again. "It was great," he says finally.

"Liar."

He looks up to see Diana Monroe reclining in her chair, arms crossed over her chest, one frustratingly perfect eyebrow raised, one frustratingly judgmental look on her face. "Excuse me?" Lucas questions.

She blinks slowly. "You're lying. Every part of how you answered that made it abundantly clear."

Lucas tilts his head, both frustrated and amused. "Really? Then how *did* I feel about growing up there, Monroe, if you can read me so well?"

She shrugs. "I mean, you were probably very lonely, being an only child. And if you were crowned when you were what, ten, you probably had a lot of pressure to perform well in front of people, right? And I'm assuming that sucked, as a little kid."

The others are silent, and Lucas nods slowly. "Well." He meets her gaze, and she creases her eyebrows in an unreadable expression. "You aren't entirely wrong."

She nods slowly, and although she mumbles her next words, they still cause a slight pang in Lucas' chest. "Well, a gilded cage is still a cage."

"That it is," he confirms quietly. After a tense beat, he glances up at Cameron once again. "How did you all do it?" he asks. "How did you live on your own, at the age of twelve? I heard rumors that when you guys are kids, they just... send you off. How did you get by?"

The Citizens' Liaison sits up a little straighter. "Well, human beings are meant to survive. We're basically programmed just to do what it takes, to keep ourselves safe. We stay away from things that hurt us and we shelter those that don't. Growing up here was a lot like that. You learn because you have to."

"And there's always help," Peter adds, causing Lucas to look over at him for the first time since the conversation began. "There's always a community everywhere. You just need to know where to look."

Lucas nods, glancing quickly at the president before back at the other boy. "Everywhere, huh?" He drums his fingers on the tabletop. "Impressive."

"How so?" Diana questions. "We did what we had to do."

"You'd be surprised," Lucas counters. "Not every random seventeen-year-old decides to go on a cross-country journey and then overthrow the government."

And he swears that he sees the inkling of a smile dance across her lips.

Part Eighteen: The Cancer

Peter

Time: **1:23 AM**

It was the middle of the night, and Peter, although sleeping, was in distress.

Most nights, no matter how comfortable and safe he was in his bed across the hall from Diana and Cameron and locked in a guarded apartment, he was plagued by nightmares about the revolt.

No, not just nightmares, absolute *terrors*. Dreams where the screams and gunshots were just as loud as they really had been, dreams where Cameron disappeared and didn't return, dreams that ended with Peter's hands slick with the blood of the others.

And consistently, every time, he woke up with a jolt, heart thundering and reminding him that he was alive and well, even though so many others were not.

Peter sits up in bed with a flash, breathing so hard his stomach churns, and he immediately buries his face in his hands.

He leaves his eyes open, because he knows if he shuts them again those visions won't go away. He's tried everything to get rid of the nightmares, but nothing worked. The only thing left to do was just simply give it time and hope that it would stitch his wounds together.

Silently creeping out of bed, Peter crosses to the door, pulling it open without a sound. Padding gently past the others' doors, he enters the kitchen, nearly jumping in fright at what greets him there.

"Hello," Lucas says with a smile from his perch at the kitchen island. "You alright?"

Peter shakes his head to bring himself back to the present, pausing to understand that what he's seeing is real and not a trick of these dreams. Lucas was in pajamas, or boxers and a t-shirt for that matter, seated with a cup of tea at the island, a magazine laid out in front of him. The only light was that of the moon outside the window and the warm glow of one of the bulbs under the countertop, bathing the prince in a halo of yellow light.

"Um," Peter begins. "I'm fine." He moves to sit next to Lucas, then reconsiders, instead leaving a stool between them. "You just scared me. I forgot you were spending the night."

Lucas hums a low agreement, then shrugs, looking at the countertop instead of Peter. "I'm not great at sleeping in beds that aren't mine."

He sounds like he's joking, but Peter gets the feeling that some part of him isn't. A glance over at Lucas makes Peter notice that his hands are clenched in his lap, his arm muscles tightening then relaxing, over and over again.

Peter just nods as Lucas speaks again. "What are you doing up?"

He starts to speak but reconsiders. Could he trust this prince, the one who made their lives hell and seemed to enjoy it? Peter knew that this boy was far too prim and proper for his liking.

But he also knew, deep down, that Lucas was broken, tortured, frightened, just as himself and the others were. He wasn't sure *how*, but he knew.

"Um, since the revolt, I've had some pretty bad nightmares," Peter replies in a small voice. "Most nights, I can't really sleep."

Lucas is quiet for a moment, and the only sound in the apartment is the ticking of the clock on the fireplace mantle. "I'm sorry," the prince says. "That must be hard." Peter doesn't fail to note the way his eyebrows crease just slightly and then return to a relaxed position, or how his mouth dips into a frown and then comes back into his neutral expression. "For a thing you created to cause such harm... I don't know how you four do it."

Peter nods. Neither boy looks at one another, but the awkward tension that had filled the room seems to have dissipated just slightly. "It is. Hard, I mean. But I can't really do anything about it."

"Have you talked to the others?" Lucas asks, finally casting a glance out of the corner of his eye towards Peter.

"No," he replies, tucking his shaking fingers into his lap. "I don't want to worry them." Lucas begins to speak, but Peter cuts him off. "Please, don't insist. I've thought about it, but they don't deserve the burden. Besides, I'm sure they probably figured it out on their own already."

Lucas nods slowly, tearing his gaze away from Peter. "I'm sure Monroe would help you."

Peter pauses, unable to decipher if his words were teasing or genuine or somewhere in between. "Maybe," is his only reply.

Lucas chuckles, more to himself than to Peter. "Or she might rain The Judgment upon you."

Peter turns to look at him. "Huh?"

Lucas meets his gaze, looking slightly confused. "The Judgment? You know, when she does that thing with her eyebrow."

"I can't say I know what you're talking about."

"That's what the people in Alynthia call it, jokingly. When she raises one eyebrow, all judgmental-like. It's absolutely lethal, and everyone over there knows that you're finished if it happens to you."

Something in Peter wonders how Lucas ever even noticed that, but another part of him thinks it makes perfect sense that he did. "I guess I've never noticed."

"Ah," the prince says with that charming smile. "That's because you've never been on the receiving end of it." Holding his mug between both hands, he looks at Peter and his gaze seems to soften. "Chin up, Secretary Simon. Remember, the sun always has a way of pushing through the clouds. Rain doesn't last forever."

Something inside Peter alleviates then, and it feels good, clearing away the dark feelings left behind from his nightmare. He smiles back at Lucas, realizing very fleetingly that maybe the prince isn't as awful as he originally thought.

Part Nineteen: The Taurus

Diana

Time: **10:42 AM**

"I don't think I like this."

Diana was standing in a line with five other people: Cameron, Peter, and three other Powerful Ones, three lucky souls who lived.

They were on the stairs of the Capitol, early in the morning, for a demonstration of sorts that would determine who would keep their powers and who would go through the painful procedure and sacrifice their powers for the good of the nation.

Jesse didn't want his, he was adamant about that. Diana realized when he had arrived that morning that his dark circles and limp handshake meant he was still haunted by a certain Virgo he couldn't save two months ago. His power was void here, anyways: he could communicate with animals, but there were none in America to communicate with, so the six Powerful Ones had agreed with his plea to rid the world of the Leo power.

This was mostly a democratic convention, Diana knew, with the six Powerful Ones being the deciding votes on whose stayed and whose was destroyed.

Claire steps down into the big, open Plaza space they were using as their arena. Diana's heart pounds and she doesn't know why she's so scared; it isn't even her power being used. She watches with bated breath as the young woman in front of her holds her hands up, palms pointing towards a black car parked nearby.

After a moment, with the Pisces girl focused intently on the large vehicle, a shimmering bolt shoots from her hands and grapples the car to her feet within moments, flinging it about one hundred yards.

Diana feels the repercussions of Claire's action, waves of power emanating towards her and the others and settling on her skin like electric snowflakes. Claire reverses her action, moving the car back to where it had been without a scratch or a dent, as if it had never happened.

She turns to the group with a shrug and a sheepish smile. "I don't really want it. There's no reason for it anymore, but I'll keep it if you all need me to."

Unsurprisingly, just as they had with Jesse, the others turn to Diana, who blinks as if stunned that they were looking to her to decide.

"Um," she starts, cheeks flushing. "What do you want to do, Claire?"

The girl considers, and Diana realizes just how much better she looks than the last time she saw her: unlike Jesse, her cheeks were rounder and less sallow, her hair was longer and healthier, and her smile seemed genuine, a far cry from what many of the others looked like. "I think I want to get rid of it."

"Okay, then we'll do that." Diana turns to the guard standing near the Capitol entrance. "Put her down for the extraction with Jesse, please."

"I'll go next," Cameron says, stepping forward.

Diana grabs the back of his shirt collar before he can move off the steps. "Nice try. We need yours at least until all the walls are down."

Cameron grumbles but complies, rolling his eyes dramatically as everyone else laughs and the mood lightens just barely.

"No offense, Cam," Peter begins tentatively. "Why are you here if you know we need you?"

Cameron scoffs playfully and squeezes Peter's hand subtly, to avoid any searching glances by the others. Diana knew they were exploring their new relationship, but she was also aware of the fact that they were still figuring out what they wanted and didn't want to do in public.

"Alright, I know when I'm not wanted, so I guess I'll go do my actual job," the ginger boy says, holding up his hands in surrender as he moves towards the goliath doors of the Capitol. "Much love to you all."

The others chuckle and wave him off, and Peter displays his power next, proving what Diana already knew: his power was worth keeping.

Diana nods resolutely as Peter launches his final projectile and it billows upwards in a spiraling column. "Yeah, Peter, let's keep yours, too. It's good in case we need it as–"

"–A weapon," Peter says, shrugging as if he knew that was the answer. "I don't disagree."

Olivia, the Sagittarius, goes next, and although her power is impressive, it wouldn't be nearly as useful as Peter's. "Olivia, that spear doesn't hit true to the mark every time, right?" Diana asks.

She nods, scarily twirling the impressive, teal spear she had formed. "No. I have to aim it myself."

"Then let's get rid of it," Diana says. "If that's alright with you."

Olivia smiles politely. "I don't mind at all."

Now there was one person left, and the other four teenagers look towards Diana as she wrings her hands together, fighting that anxious adrenaline she'd been feeling all day. "I don't... want to use mine."

"Are you going to get rid of it?" Claire asks.

Diana begins to speak, even wanting *to say yes, wanting to tell them she'd be getting rid of the destructive Gemini power once and for all, but then the face of her older sister, bruised and bleeding, flashes through her mind.*

"No," Diana stutters, blinking as if to clear the image from her focus. "No, I have to keep it. I'm just... not going to use it."

The others seem to notice her apprehension and they nod, with Claire, Jesse, and Olivia following the waiting guard to their extractions and Peter patting Diana on the arm before disappearing inside the Capitol.

Diana sits on the steps, alone, staring out at the vast Plaza with her hands tingling in her lap.

She wonders if she'll ever find peace.

Diana is seated at her desk, staring at the wall as her thoughts come back from the world they had escaped to.

She'd gotten absolutely no sleep the previous night, primarily due to the fact that one Lucas Rutherland was in the next bedroom over.

Now, this is not a good way to phrase that fact. And, contrary to what some might think, Diana wasn't wide awake because of... certain feelings.

No, she was lying awake all night because she was so, *so* confused.

It had started after their meeting, when all five teenagers had returned to the penthouse. There, they made dinner, and although Lucas had awkwardly tried to help, Peter had insisted he didn't because "guests don't do work around here."

Diana would've loved to see the Crown Prince scrub dishes, but whatever.

Instead, his job, tasked by Kiara, was to make a fire with- you guessed it- Diana.

So the two, without speaking, had busied themselves in the living room, out of earshot from the others, and Diana had begun stacking the logs in the same way she always had, perching them in the iron basket within the fireplace.

Lucas passed her another piece of wood, covered with a thin layer of bark.

And then two things happened, both of which she couldn't explain.

The first was that while Lucas was holding the log out to her, he looked away, presumably to grab a lighter, or something. But while the prince's head was turned, she noticed a leaf, poking out of the side of the log. And it wasn't a *dead* leaf, it was very much the opposite, a vibrant green that almost reminded her of her old bedroom walls in Sector Seven.

But the oddest part was that the leaf had not been there before.

All night, she wondered how she'd missed it. It wasn't a *small* leaf, and it wasn't a dull one, either, so how could he have not seen it, unless he had?

The second thing was even stranger, at least to her, which was saying something because the whole appearance of a random, inexplicable leaf was strange enough.

When Lucas had passed her the log, after her fleeting crisis over that little leaf, his fingers had brushed hers.

And it felt *electrifying.*

Yes, Diana also wanted to vomit at how stupid she sounded, but it was true. It was that recurring feeling, over and over again, the one that sparked with tension and adrenaline whenever she and the prince got close. But touching him, skin-to-skin, that close, with his midnight eyes roaming her face? *That* was a whole new level of goosebump-inducing emotion.

Suffice to say, she was awake *all night*.

Now, though, she had work to do. She was the president, after all, and she loved nothing more than sitting at her desk, elbow-deep in work that would help her country thrive.

And then her office door opens.

"Ugh," she mumbles, dramatically tossing her binder aside and rubbing the heels of her palms into her eyes. "What could you possibly want right now?"

In all his glory, there he was: the Crown Prince of Alynthia, standing in her office doorway like he was *supposed* to fit there.

Diana's emotions betray her as she rakes her gaze over him, noticing that the perfectly-put-together prince seemed... exhausted, really.

Like he hadn't slept, either.

He clears his throat, breaking Diana from her more-than-embarrassing ogling session. "If you wanted to check me out, could I at least request a more private space?"

Sometimes, she wanted to punch that smug, gorgeous face *so bad*.

"You look tired," she taunts instead. "I was just hoping you were alright."

They both know that's a complete lie, and the prince scoffs. "I was sent by the king and Grandmother Aquarius to invite you to dinner tonight," he smirks at her over-dramatic eye roll. "Seven o'clock, at Barbara's apartment. Try to clean up at least a little, would you?"

"I'll do my very best," she mumbles sarcastically.

He takes a step closer, leaning on the front of her desk, and the two stare at each other for a long moment, Diana dwarfed by his height.

She tries not to squirm under his gaze, and her brain hates the way she feels when he looks at her like this, but her body wants to reach out and touch him again, and feel that electric contact like she did last night.

"Oh, Monroe," Lucas purrs, leaning even closer, "if only your mouth was as pretty as your face."

She cannot deny the fact that her entire body floods with heat, centering in both her cheeks and somewhere near her navel. But she resists his godforsaken temptations, instead placing a hand flat on his chest, right over his jacket, and pushing him backwards.

With a smile and a shove, Diana coos, "Get out of my office."

Part Twenty: The Libra

Lucas

Time: <u>7:33 PM</u>

Lucas' favorite time of day was any time the sky looked like a watercolor painting.

That evening, he was seated with Diana Monroe and Barbara Oswald at the dining table in the older Aquarius' apartment, having a quiet and uncomfortable dinner with his father.

Nobody had talked since a little while ago, and the two Alynthians were fielding the brunt of many forced questions, mainly about the weather or other topics that were just as boring.

Lucas, completely turned off from the conversation happening around him, smiles slightly at the sight outside the window: it was a glorious sunset, as if someone had taken all the warm colors and streaked them across a canvas. The sky was layered in pinks, oranges, and yellows, and it automatically brought a smile to his face.

Barbara Oswald's apartment was slightly smaller than the Americans', Lucas noticed, probably since it was older and suited for one, rather than four. The table they were at, although grand and clean like the others', was round and smaller instead of rectangular and huge. It also seemed that she used this table more often, whereas the others' seemed untouched, from what Lucas gathered during his short stay.

Diana sat to Lucas' right, and his father sat on his left, with Barbara Oswald across from him. The other three were eating quietly while Lucas admired the view.

He hears a chair scuff on the floor next to him, and Lucas glances up, coming face-to-face with Diana Monroe.

Sitting at the small table, with their heads turned down to one another, it's obvious that Lucas and Diana underestimated just how close their faces would be, for the prince pulls back just slightly, eyes wide, and the president follows suit. Lucas can't tell if the redness flushing her cheeks was a blush or a reflection of the sky outside.

"What are you looking at?" Diana whispers, looking outside as if to see what Lucas was seeing.

He shrugs, lowering his voice to match her pitch and allow their conversation to remain unnoticed by Barbara and his father, who were now in a conversation of their own. "The sky."

Diana's eyebrows knit together, and she frowns in concentration, her green eyes following the swashes of color outside the window. "Why?"

Lucas shrugs again, not taking his eyes off the horizon. "It's beautiful."

He doesn't look at her, but he feels her eyes on the side of his head. "Huh," she whispers. Lucas glances at her out of the corner of his eye, and she looks away. "I guess I don't spend a lot of time looking at the sky."

The prince smiles slightly. "Yeah, well, maybe you should." He leans a breath closer. "They're a lot prettier here than they are in Alynthia."

She swallows, her gaze not leaving his. "I guess so."

Lucas grins, and he swears Diana's gaze flits to his lips. "I'm surprised, Monroe," he begins, "that you don't appreciate the little, pretty things," the next part comes out before he can stop himself, "being one yourself."

He doesn't exactly know how Diana will react, but she scoffs somewhat playfully and rolls her eyes, which was not how he expected her to respond. "Your flattery is much appreciated, Your Highness," she says, dramatically batting her lashes, much to Lucas' frustration, "but don't expect it to work on me."

Lucas smirks, tightening his right hand into a fist and turning back to his meal as he spits out, "Trust me, I'd never."

"Diana, did you hear me?"

Both teenagers jump as Barbara's warning tone settles over the room, and Diana turns to her. "No, sorry," she begins. "I was... a little distracted."

Barbara clears her throat. "I was just asking you to fill in His Majesty on the events that took place regarding his brother."

Diana spares a quick glance at Lucas before turning back to the king. "Well, um, he was the opposing party of the revolution."

"Wait," Lucas interjects. "Who is this we're speaking of?"

He watches as the king's face pales, and he clears his throat. "Lucas, remember the uncle we discussed?"

Lucas does remember the brief conversation he had with his father on the helicopter, the one where the king explained that his brother had been a New American politician. He didn't, however, remember the conversation where his father told him his uncle was a war criminal.

"I... no, I don't," he replies after a long beat. "Miss Monroe, care to elaborate?"

Diana seems to feel the tension rolling off him, and she swallows before nodding. "He was the Aries leader, which I'm sure you already know, and after being stabbed by the Citizens' Liaison, he fled."

"Stabbed?" Lucas whispers. "By *Kiara?*"

"Is he dead?" the king asks, his expression alarmingly neutral. Lucas wonders if he'd care at all, should the answer be in the affirmative.

"Not to our knowledge," Barbara says cooly.

Lucas turns to face Diana, who is sitting sheepishly. "You knew about this the whole time and didn't say anything until now?!"

"Rutherland, I couldn't."

"He's *my uncle*! My father's brother, and you all couldn't give us the decency to say if he's alive or not?"

"Lucas, watch it," his father warns.

With a huff, Lucas stands and pushes away from the table. "I think I'll walk back to the apartment, Father. Miss Oswald, thank you for a great night."

Barbara turns to Diana, who still seems shell-shocked. "Miss Monroe, would you walk His Highness back to the apartment?"

Well, if Lucas' night was bad before, it sure did get worse just then.

Diana nods tersely at Barbara's words, giving the older woman a stiff hug as the pair leaves the apartment.

The walk back through the now-dark Plaza is a silent one, and Lucas waits with bated breath as they reach the elevator in the lobby of their apartment building.

Reluctantly, he sighs. "Would you like a cup of tea, Miss Monroe?"

Diana smiles politely. "Sure, thank you."

Sometimes, Lucas hated his mother for teaching him chivalry.

"Thanks," Diana mumbles as Lucas hands her a cup of tea, seating himself on the ottoman a few feet away from her, all tucked up on the couch.

"Made yourself comfortable, I see," Lucas says. He tries to sound snarky, but he can't fight the small smile that creeps onto his face.

Diana shrugs and blows on her tea, steam spiraling from the mug. The two lapse into a silence that can only be described as uncomfortable, and Lucas averts his eyes from her face, from the loose hair falling over her shoulders.

"That fountain," he begins, voice wavering. "I saw that it was named after someone who... someone who has the same surname as you."

Diana meets his gaze, and Lucas is taken aback by the sudden seriosity in her frighteningly bright eyes. "Yeah, um, that would be my sister, Maya."

"Maya Monroe," Lucas whispers, turning the name over in his mouth. He glances towards the window, where the stars are beginning to gleam. "What happened?"

"I-" Diana starts, clearing her throat and swallowing what Lucas knew was a barbed lump.

"You don't have to say," Lucas says quickly, leaning forward on his knees and closing a few inches of space between them. "I, uh, I know how hard it can be to talk about."

There's silence again as the two stare at one another, and Diana speaks, her voice soft and melodic. "Your mother. The queen, she-"

Lucas nods, cutting her off. "-She died, yes."

"I'm sorry," the president whispers, her low tone making goosebumps shoot up Lucas' arms.

Lucas sighs heavily, shaking his head and squeezing his hands into fists. "There's nothing for you to be sorry for."

"I know. But still, that..." she sighs the same way Lucas did, her gentle gaze comforting him the same way a kind touch would, "that grief is never easy."

"I wish it was. You'd *think* it was, seven years later."

Diana doesn't seem to hear him, continuing on as if in her own world. "It's like a knot right in the middle of your chest, and... and eventually, it tightens so much that you forget it's there."

Lucas nods slowly, placing one of his barely-bleeding palms over his heart. "Until a loose end gets tugged and you're reminded all over again," he adds with a sad chuckle. He looks her in the eye, hoping his warm touch on his own chest could translate some comfort to her. "Grief does inexplicable things to people."

She smiles sadly, and Lucas suddenly feels like crying. "Does it ever go away?"

He shakes his head, dropping his hand to his lap and ignoring the way the president's gaze gets stuck for a moment on the stain left on his shirt. "I wouldn't know."

As Diana rises to leave after a silent ten minutes, Lucas stands without thinking and follows her to the door.

"Monroe?" He asks as she takes hold of the doorknob.

She turns around, expression unreadable. "Yeah?"

Lucas has one million questions he wants to ask her, but he settles on a milder option. "You're okay to get home by yourself?"

He realizes after a moment that he sounded condescending, but if Diana caught that, she chooses not to say anything, which surprises Lucas even more. She smiles almost sadly and nods. "I'll be okay."

Lucas takes a breath and nods back, letting his thoughts die away without acting on them. "I'll see you later, then."

As she pulls open the door, the president's eyes seem to sparkle. "Sounds good."

Part Twenty-One: The Scorpio

Cameron

Time: **11:35 AM**

A cool fall morning, the day after Barbara and Diana joined the Alynthians for dinner, all eight Americans and both Alynthians gather in front of an upscale rooftop restaurant for brunch. Very few press were invited, and the scene was painted more as a casual gathering than a foreign policy meeting. The place sits right in between Lucas' high-rise and the American team's, so at eleven o'clock, they had met in front of this place so they could go in together.

As they finally board the elevator to take them to the roof, Diana and Lucas elbow past each other for a spot. Ms. Miller, Ms. Brewer, Mr. Boone, Barbara, and Cornelius hang back to make room, so the five kids go up together.

They're in their corresponding outfits, each one with a touch of plaid. Diana was in a dress and tights, Kiara was in a sweater and jeans, and Peter and Cameron were in almost-matching button-downs. Lucas was in a bright white crew neck and tan chinos, throwing off the look *entirely*, and Cameron was almost certain he did it on purpose, having learned from the photoshoot fiasco.

As the elevator falls silent, Peter pipes up. "So, Lucas, how are you finding our country so far?"

Lucas smiles politely at his attempt to make conversation. "It's... very nice."

Kiara chuckles from where she's leaning against the wall. "And your thoughts on the president?"

Diana and Lucas share a bitter look.

Finally, and without breaking his eye contact with Diana, the prince speaks. "Miss Monroe is just a *joy* to collaborate with."

Diana visibly seethes, and she shrugs in an effort to remain nonchalant. "As are you."

The other three teenagers look around at one another, and Cameron wonders if he should interject, but thankfully for all of them, the elevator doors slide open before Diana or Lucas can say another word.

Part Twenty-Two: The Taurus

Diana

Time: **12:20 PM**

"Thank you," Diana mumbles to the waiter as her food lands in front of her.

They were nearly an hour into this insufferable brunch and she wanted to throw herself off the roof.

So far, they had exchanged the regular pleasantries and partaken in small talk ranging from the lack of Alynthian agriculture to the rise in American population trends. A few mentions of "collaboration" had been thrown in, but that mostly consisted of Alynthia sharing animals with America, or the Capitol supplying books from the Archives to the Alynthians.

The table is right in the middle of the restaurant, and the place is empty, probably on purpose. Diana guessed Oswald had pulled some strings. The air is brisk, and Diana snuggles deeper into her jacket as she glances around the table.

They aren't seated in position order. Barbara is at one head of the table, Cornelius is at the other. Next to him is Lucas, then Ms. Brewer, then Peter, Cameron, Barbara, Mr. Boone, Kiara, Diana, and Ms. Miller to Cornelius' other side.

Diana's ears perk as she finally hears what she came here for.

"We should discuss your power, Your Majesty," Miriam says, gently placing a hand near the king's to get his attention as if she were addressing a five-year-old.

"What of it?" Cornelius asks, voice hard. Diana notes the way his eyes fly fearfully towards his son before focusing on Ms. Miller, and he folds his hands in his lap rather than leaving them on the table.

"Well, because it's property of New America, we'd like to extract it and keep it here," Barbara says, voice even, testing the line of what will set him off and what won't.

Cornelius raises an eyebrow. "But your American law states I get it removed once I'm close to death. And I pick who it goes to, not you."

"Wait, I'm sorry," Lucas interjects. "Father, what are you talking about?"

"Oh, my-," Kiara whispers from next to Diana, tossing her napkin onto the table and slouching in her chair. It's unclear as to whether she's surprised or just as fed up as Diana is.

Before Diana can respond, Ms. Miller looks over at the king. "You never told your country's heir?"

"Told me *what?*" Lucas asks, voice in the same firm tone his father's held. Diana feels a pang of guilt and, remembering their awkward conversation at Barbara's, she wonders just how little he really knows about his own family.

"Son, I can explain this further back home. But for now-"

Barbara slams a hand on the table, drawing everyone's attention to her in an instant. She levels her cutting gaze at the king. "Your Majesty, we do not need difficulty here. We simply need you to agree to the extraction, and then go through the procedure. It could be done by tomorrow night if we wished it to be."

Diana glances at the prince, who looks hurt and confused. She watches his clenched fist relax, and he rests his shaking hand on the table. She swallows against the lump in her throat, straightens her shoulders, and turns to Cornelius, turning her arm down towards the table even though she's wearing a long sleeve. "Your Majesty, if I may interject. We don't want you to think we're taking this power away from you. But since we began the Integration, and we... redid the government, we want to limit the powers to the best of our ability to keep the peace. All the previous Powerful Ones have extracted their powers as well. You'd simply be one of many."

The king raises an eyebrow. "Even these two?" he asks, motioning to Peter and Cameron, seated next to each other on Barbara's left.

Peter and Cameron share a guilty look, and before Diana can intervene, the king laughs. "Just as I thought. You eight are so wrapped up in your own agendas, you didn't even consider removing the powers from these two, as that would take power away from *all* of you. And besides, you couldn't extract the power from me if you wanted to."

Ms. Brewer scoffs lightly. "Your Highness, we have completed these removals countless times successfully-"

The king rolls his eyes. "I don't mean you couldn't take it from me, period. I mean, I don't *have* it."

"You don't have the power?" Cameron asks, tone a little uncertain if not completely disbelieving. The king nods smugly, and Cameron continues. "So, then, who does?"

A long beat of silence passes. Nobody speaks, and finally, slowly, the king's eyes travel to his right.

Diana follows his gaze.

And there Lucas Rutherland sits, arms now crossed over his chest. He looks up to see all eyes on him, and his mouth drops open. He stands so abruptly his chair squeaks, and he holds out his hands, palms up, as if his own touch could hurt him. "What?!" he practically shouts.

"Lucas, sit down," the king commands firmly. Lucas hesitantly follows instructions. "Yes, it's true. The power was transferred to Lucas when he was ten, on the day of his coronation."

The prince grimaces but says nothing.

Cornelius continues. "And I *refuse* to have it extracted from him. It is rightfully mine, and I decide when to give it up."

Silence again.

Until Kiara speaks. "Technically," she says, drawing out the word as if unsure about it, "because you transferred the power to the prince, *he* decides what to do with it."

"So Lucas is the one who picks whether or not we get it back," Ms. Miller whispers.

Lucas blinks and swallows, and Diana watches his Adam's apple bob. "I..." he begins, trailing off.

"He will not," Cornelius states finally.

"Cornelius," Barbara begins, voice just as challenging, "the boy makes the choice. Not you."

"I can't decide right now," Lucas says hurriedly, voice small and unlike his own.

Ms. Brewer nods. "That's fine, Your Highness. Right, everyone?"

Begrudgingly, all eight Americans nod, eyeing the royals.

"Besides," Cornelius starts again, seemingly intent to cause problems, "Miss Monroe, I couldn't help but notice you keep rubbing your left arm." Even at a horrified look from Diana and a murderous one from Barbara and Kiara, the king perseveres. "Mind enlightening us foreigners as to why?"

"She does not have to do any such thing," Barbara says, voice firm.

"It's fine, Barbara," Diana says, willing herself to be strong under Cornelius' cold gaze. Without breaking eye contact with the king, Diana pulls up her sleeve to reveal the puncture scar from her power transfer six months ago.

As Cornelius examines the mark, Diana's gaze strays to Lucas.

The prince's eyes are fixated on hers, and his right hand rests over the crook of his elbow on his opposite arm. It's as if something in him feels the same scrutiny that was currently rushing through Diana's veins.

After another tense moment of silence, Cornelius digs a few bills out of his suit jacket and leaves them next to his untouched plate. "Well, this has been nice," he says, his voice holding no sincerity whatsoever. "Let's go, Lucas."

The pair leave, back in the elevator. Finally, after a long moment, Diana sighs. "That did *not* go as planned."

"Yeah, you could say that," Peter replies.

Barbara levels her gaze at Diana. "Miss Monroe," she says, voice firm and businesslike.

"Yes," Diana responds.

"I know that authority-wise, I am below you. However, I'd like to suggest that your next course of action is convincing our prince, Mister Rutherland, to remove his power."

Diana hesitates, then nods. "I would say the same."

"Good," Oswald replies, counting out the bills Cornelius left on the table, handed down to her by an assembly line of government officials. She smiles at the rest of the group, holding up the money. "Well, brunch adjourned. Looks like today's meal is on the Rutherlands."

Part Twenty-Three: The Libra

Lucas

Time: **6:02 PM**

"No, no, no," Lucas groans. "You have to be kidding."

He flops down on the lounge chair in the sitting room, watching his father pace the room. His tie is loosened, his shoe is untied, and his dirty-blonde hair is messy, a far cry from how Lucas normally sees him.

"Does it look like I'm kidding, Lucas?" his father snaps. "This is your fault *completely*."

"*My* fault?!" Lucas shouts. "How the hell is this my fault? I didn't even know you were some *mutant* until-"

"Until you had to go and let your guard down, and in front of those Americans no less. You looked like an absolute joke, Lucas, and rightfully so." He gets in close, his words biting. "Even the president is one of those ridiculous freaks like you are, and you should've been the authority."

"What else are you keeping from me, Father?!" Lucas yells. "First a criminal uncle, now a magical power? Next you'll go and tell me that mother isn't even dead-"

"Lucas," Cornelius warns through gritted teeth, his bright gaze piercing and dangerous. "Watch it."

Lucas grimaces. A thousand more questions and insults and fears rest on his tongue, but all he manages is "I- I'm sorry."

"You should be."

Cornelius begins to leave the room, when Lucas mumbles something else, halting him in his tracks.

"What do I do, Father?"

Cornelius turns to look at his son, sitting small and hunched on the lounge. The king's eyes are cold and unloving, and he sneers at Lucas before answering.

"Don't disappoint me."

And then he leaves.

Lucas feels empty and alone, and he's embarrassed that he aches to feel his mother's hug. He'd never known someone who could calm him down and make his anxiety disintegrate like she could. But now she's gone. She *has* been gone for years, even though it only feels like days.

He studies his hands, flexing his fingers as if willing this unknown Libra power to seep out of them. He'd only ever read of magic in books as a child, never seen it in real life. The closest thing to magic he'd ever laid eyes on were the huge blue walls that still sprang up occasionally throughout New America. But that was different from this, he supposed.

The Crown Prince rises and crosses to the windowsill, that pristine glass window that was buried in potted plants that someone used to nurture, looking out over the Plaza. A cold breeze sneaks through the cracks, dancing over the leaves and petals of the plants in front of him. Lucas traces the breeze with his fingers, gliding them over the budding white peace lily to his right.

And then one of the buds blossoms into a bright white flower.

Lucas' fingers seem to freeze, and he wonders if his eyes are playing tricks on him. But if this were a coincidence, why was energy thrumming through his whole body?

With shaking fingers, Lucas gently pinches another lily bud between his forefinger and thumb. And his eyes grow wide as his fingers shift beneath the flower, and it blooms in front of his eyes once more.

Lucas can't help but stare as his breath hitches, and he suddenly feels incredibly alone and minute in this huge room, despite his overwhelming shivers of adrenaline and power.

He rubs a hand over his face, breathing out a heavy sigh, and that's when he gets the idea. The idea that would both smite his father and protect Alynthia, all in one. He tries not to think about the fact that his little plan could benefit these Americans as well, or that it won't be anywhere close to easy to pull off.

Lucas crosses to the penthouse window, looking out over the unfamiliar American Plaza as his heartbeat begins to race. His eyes scan the street until he sees another tall high-rise, one pointed out to him earlier that morning by Mr. Boone.

He would only need five minutes to get there.

He hurries down the hall to his new bedroom, changing into more comfortable clothes, sweatpants and a long sleeve shirt.

He enters the living room, pressing the elevator button. It dings loudly, and Lucas cringes at the noise, hoping his father didn't hear. After a few tense moments where nothing in the apartment seems to move and Lucas holds his breath, he enters the elevator, the doors sliding closed behind him. He presses the ground floor button, and when he gets to the lobby, he rings the bell for a bodyguard.

"Yes, Your Highness?" the guard says as she enters the room, a confused look passing over her features. She's probably wondering what the Crown Prince is doing all alone, in the evening, in clothes fit for a common street urchin.

"I need to get to the Americans," Lucas replies, crossing his arms.

The woman raises an eyebrow. "The... president?"

Lucas scoffs at the mention of the leader. "I guess."

The guard nods slowly. "Does the king know about this?"

"No. He doesn't need to, either."

"I see," she says. "My name is Haley, by the way. I guess I'm your escort now."

Lucas stares at his watch. "Great. Well, Haley, are we going or not?"

So, the pair walk through the Plaza, drawing very little attention. Anybody who does see them presumably thinks nothing of it, and luckily, none of the bystanders are reporters. Lucas doesn't quite feel like putting on his royal facade right now.

Finally, they reach the lobby doors of the Americans' high-rise. Haley scans her fingerprint at the door, and she's waved in by two more guards, who stare at Lucas as he enters but say nothing.

"Top floor?" Lucas asks, glancing at the elevator.

Haley chews her lip. "Unfortunately, Your Highness, I can't give you access to the president-"

"Oh, please. You act like I'm trying to kill her or something. I can't stand her, but thankfully for you, I couldn't really care less about what happens to her. I just need to speak to them, and quickly."

Haley considers. "I'm gonna give you twenty minutes."

"Deal."

She sighs and punches an elevator button, which lights up under her finger. As the doors slide shut behind Lucas, she shouts to him, "No murder!"

"No murder," Lucas affirms as the elevator takes off.

Part Twenty-Four: The Taurus

Diana

Time: **7:00 PM**

The four Americans are snuggled up in the living room, a fire crackling in the fireplace in front of them. Diana is on the settee, reading the newspaper, Cameron and Peter are snuggled on the couch reading, and Kiara is sprawled on the soft rug, scribbling onto a spreadsheet.

A ding breaks them from their quiet respite, and Diana sits up to see the Crown Prince of Alynthia standing in the entryway.

"You've gotta be *freaking*-" she begins.

Kiara rises to her feet, cutting Diana off. "What are you doing here, Lucas?"

Everyone looks at him, expecting a reply, and he huffs, "Trust me, I don't want to be here anymore than you want me here. But I need your help with something."

"As *if* we would help-" Diana begins.

She's cut off again, but by the prince this time. "Jesus *Christ*, Monroe. You're acting like I just asked you for a kidney. Get over yourself. I want to bring my mother back." He meets Diana's eyes, steeling his shoulders before whispering his next words. "And maybe your sister, too?"

The others fall quiet, and Lucas raises his eyebrows, trying to hide a satisfied and somewhat scared smirk.

"What?" Cameron asks, pushing himself away from Peter and standing. He's wearing plaid pajama pants and a black shirt, and Lucas almost laughs at the goofy reading glasses perched on the bridge of his nose. "Your mother, the *queen-*"

"No, my mother the *king*," Lucas rudely and sarcastically interjects. "Just... hear me out."

Diana pushes past Lucas, her shoulder ramming his arm, heading to a phone on the wall by the elevator. She presses a button and speaks into the receiver after a moment. "Barbara, the prince is here. Yes. Something about the queen." She nods and mumbles a few more affirmations, and then hangs up the phone, turning to the others. "She's gonna be here with Miriam in ten."

Everybody nods, and Peter stands up. Diana watches as Lucas takes in his sweatpants and black hoodie, paired with the Secretary of Education's signature floppy curls. "Can I get you anything?" he asks, ever-so-kind. "Water, coffee?"

Lucas raises an eyebrow, caught off-guard by the genuine hospitality. "Um, tea would be great. Thanks."

Peter smiles and heads into the kitchen, and Cameron pads after him, footsteps muffled from his socks. Diana goes back into the living room and sits again, picking up the paper and leaving Lucas to fend for himself. She watches him carefully as he sits on the arm of the couch, looking around the room as if to avoid her searching gaze.

"Nice place," he mumbles, with no sincerity whatsoever.

Diana ignores him. Part of her sour mood was from the splitting headache and sharp stomach pain she randomly acquired about fifteen minutes ago, that she was battling along with her equal disdain for the prince.

He goes quiet again, and Peter and Cameron return moments later, the former holding a white mug with steam rising from the top. Lucas accepts the drink with a small smile and the five fall into silence.

Lucas continues looking around, and he glances over at Peter and Cameron, who are seated in their original spot again. Cameron is leaned against Peter's shoulder, and the two are holding hands, snuggled together with a blanket thrown over their laps. Diana smirks as Lucas' eyes go wide, and she can practically see the realization dawn on him.

"Sorry to, uh, interrupt," Lucas begins, "but you two are... together?"

Peter and Cameron glance at one another and smile softly, and they look back at the prince almost simultaneously. Peter holds up their clasped hands and shakes them around jokingly. "Yes, we are," he says.

Cameron appraises Lucas carefully, and Diana wonders if he felt at all threatened by the prince. "Is that... a problem?"

Lucas nearly chokes on his tea. "No!" He regains his composure in the blink of an eye. "*No*, of course not. I just... had no idea."

Diana snorts. "What, you've not seen them on TV together before?"

He glares at her. "If I had, Monroe, would I have asked?"

She shrugs. "I mean-"

"Hello, kids!" Oswald declares as she enters. She halts in her tracks as she takes in the tense scene in front of her. "Is something wrong?"

"Nothing is wrong," Kiara says, looking sternly at the prince and the president. "Let's get on with this, yeah?"

They all trot into the kitchen, where Oswald and Ms. Miller are helping themselves to seats at the pristine dining table. The others sit down, with Lucas taking a chair next to Miriam.

The Libra leader turns to the prince. "I don't know if we've properly spoken. I'm Miriam Miller, your BOZ leader."

Lucas accepts her handshake with the briefest hesitation. "Right. It's a pleasure."

She smiles at him. "Now, I'm not here to be your boss, as I would have had you been born here. Diana mentioned something to Barbara, and as the original protector of the power, I need to be here for whatever... meeting this is."

"Sure," Lucas replies. He clears his throats and tries not to fidget under the watchful gazes of these Americans. "Um, so I didn't know what my power was."

Diana raises a perfect eyebrow, but Lucas notices her tuck her left arm into her lap under the table. "What's your point?"

Lucas shoots her a glare, but continues nonetheless. "I was in the apartment, and I touched a flower bud, and it grew."

Kiara is the only one who seems unsurprised, or maybe she just doesn't show it. "Just like that?" Peter asks, leaning forward. "From your touch?"

Lucas nods. "And I... wonder if I can bring back a person."

They all fall silent, and Barbara Oswald seems to be stifling a smirk behind her bony hand. "Your Highness, with all due respect, a flower is very different from a human being."

"Yes, I know," Lucas says, uncertainty setting in, "but with the growing and all, maybe I could eventually learn to-"

"Wait," Kiara interrupts, as all eyes around the table turn to her. "Diana-"

Diana cuts in, shaking her head quickly as if to keep Kiara's mouth from opening. "Don't."

Kiara *does*, however, speaking over Diana's protests. "Diana's power and Lucas' are compatible, like Peter and Cameron's. Could they do it together?"

Before Lucas can ask any questions, Ms. Miller pipes up. "Diana's power is also incredibly *dangerous*. Warping someone's *soul* is not something to trifle with."

Lucas gasps despite himself, and he suddenly feels incredibly unsettled to be around the president. "Could someone please elaborate on what that means?"

Cameron sighs, rubbing his freckled forehead with one hand. "It means that Diana can kill someone, with just her touch."

"Or revive their soul, separated from their body," Peter adds.

They say this plainly, as if it happened every day, and Lucas' dark eyes go wide.

Barbara rises from the table without a word, disappearing down the hall. She returns a moment later with a small succulent in hand, one that, unbeknownst to Lucas, had been taken from Peter's bedside table.

She sets the plant down in front of the prince. With a navy nail-polished finger, she points to a stiff leaf, one that had snapped off the rest of the plant and left it looking slightly jagged. "Fix it," she demands, her gaze piercing Lucas' resolve.

Lucas nods slowly, setting both hands on the table as he studies the little plant. He pushes his fingertips into the polished wood of the tabletop, feeling that semi-familiar energy thrum through him. Finally, after a long moment, that adrenaline builds to a peak, and Lucas brings his fingertips to the broken leaf.

Within seconds, the plant is repaired, if not perkier than before.

"Wow," Miller whispers, looking at Lucas as if he were some supernatural being.

The only person who looks anything but delightfully surprised is Diana, whose skin is unnaturally pale and whose fingers are shaking on the tabletop, jaw clenched as if fighting the urge to cry out.

Peter, to Diana's right, takes her arm. "Di?" He asks, rubbing her shoulders gently, as if to breathe life back into her. "Are you okay?"

"No, I-" she's cut off by a ragged cough, leaning into Peter's embrace as the other Americans begin to look more disturbed.

"Miss Monroe, what is going on?" Barbara asks.

Diana finishes her coughing fit, leveling her gaze at Lucas. He can't tell if she's mad at him or sad at herself. "It's him," she whispers, voice rasping.

"The prince?" Cameron asks, casting a glance over to Lucas, who's sitting quietly at the other end of the table in utter shock.

"What did I do?" Lucas asks, feeling guilt replace the tingling of his power.

"I... don't know," Diana says, holding her hands up in front of her and studying her palms. "I just, um, some part of me knows that I'm... drained. And it... *everything* hurts."

Then it's as if everyone notices her arm at the same time.

Before, her scar had been the same as Lucas', Peter's, and Cameron's, a deep white injection mark. Now, however, as if someone had taken a chisel to a piece of marble, a long, white scar stretched from that mark down to her wrist.

"His power hurts her," Kiara says, coming to the conclusion before the others.

"So they won't be able to work together?" Ms. Miller asks, stealing the question right out of Lucas' mouth.

"They might," Peter says, still holding Diana in that protective hug, "but will it hurt her to try?"

"I'm not using it," Diana says firmly, pulling herself away from him. She looks at Lucas, and despite his hatred for this girl, Lucas can see the sincerity in her gaze as she shakily rises from her chair. "I'm sorry I can't help you, Your Highness. But this Gemini power is not to be messed with. I'm the keeper of it, not the user."

Lucas feels his heart sink, but he nods nonetheless, rising from his seat as well and taking Diana's clammy hand in his own, bowing low to her out of obligation more than respect. When he rises and their eyes meet, he lowers his voice so that only she can hear. "I understand. Thank you, Miss Monroe."

She holds his gaze for one fleeting moment, then pulls her hand from his grip.

With that, Diana turns and disappears down the hall.

Part Twenty-Five: The Cancer

Peter

Time: <u>9:45 AM</u>

Lucas joins the American government the morning after his disastrous pitch, a tray of coffees in each hand, looking exceptionally bright-eyed and healthy, considering the circumstances. One thing Peter had gathered about this prince so far was that he was very good at playing pretend.

Lucas passes out the drinks: one for Peter, Cameron, Kiara, Barbara, Ms. Miller, Mr. Boone, Ms. Brewer, and himself, pointedly skipping over Diana.

Ms. Miller's mouth drops open at the blatant sign of disrespect.

All of the others, out of status obligations more than anything, reflexively offer their cups to Diana, but she declines with a wave of her hand, the eye contact between her and Lucas burning the air around them.

"Sorry, People's Choice," he says, taking the seat across from her, "it was all I could carry." His voice, unsurprisingly, carries no apologetic tones whatsoever, and it's almost as if their chill-inducing moment from yesterday never happened.

Diana smiles calmly, folding her hands in front of her on the tabletop. She too looks far healthier than she did when their impromptu meeting was adjourned last night. "No problem," she says. "I was sure your checks would bounce sooner or later."

Lucas' eyes burn with anger, but he says nothing, instead crossing his arms, staying quiet, and letting the meeting begin.

But one thing is abundantly clear.

Something else *must* be going on.

Part Twenty-Six: The Aries

Kiara

Time: **10:30 AM**

A group of four that has now become a begrudging group of five convenes in the Capitol archives.

They were attempting to research the correlation between the Gemini and Libra powers, but Diana was adamant about not using it and Lucas was just generally clueless, both of which were annoying Kiara, to say the least.

"This has all the power correlations," Peter says, leaning back in a chair with a big book held up in front of him.

"Libra and Gemini, Cancer and Scorpio," Kiara begins. "Who else?"

"This chapter says Capricorn and Taurus," Peter replies. "The Cap can double the size of the border they're holding, and the Taurus can turn it into a weighted projectile, so double the size means a bigger mass."

"Huh," Diana hums. "I never thought of that."

"But the people in this country don't have their powers anymore, right?" Lucas asks. "Besides the three of you?"

"Right," all four Americans attest at once.

They go back to reading in silence, and after a moment, Peter whispers, "Ow."

"What?" Diana asks, protectively setting her hand on his wrist.

"I had a..." Peter trails off as he holds up his hand, which looks superbly normal, "...a paper cut."

"Christ," Lucas grits through clenched teeth. The others turn to look at him, and he's clutching his arm. A new white-hot scar has carved its way from elbow to wrist, and his face is pale with pain.

The teenagers pause; even Lucas' gasping breaths slow for a moment.

Finally, Cameron speaks, gingerly taking Peter's hand and folding it in his lap. "Diana, you healed Peter."

"But hurt Lucas," Peter confirms.

Kiara is the only one who seems uninterested in the conversation, for she picks up the book closest to her and begins leafing through the pages. "There has to be some way to harness this, you two. Peter and Cam figured it out and they never injured each other."

"No," Diana says, her voice wavering and rising at the end, as if panicked. "I really don't want to use it. It could end badly, and-"

"Diana," Peter urges, taking her hand and finally getting her to stop talking, "you don't understand. You just healed a wound with your *touch*. Think of all the good you could do."

"I would rather not get injured every time, though," Lucas mumbles, voice laced with bitterness.

"Well, it wouldn't be *every* time," Kiara begins, her head stuck in a book. "Not for long, at least."

"Care to elaborate?" Lucas replies.

She turns the book around to show an illustration of a human arm, etched in five scars that look eerily like those of Diana and Lucas. "The powers limit your lifespan."

"The prince said *elaborate,* Kiara," Cameron says.

She rolls her eyes, a flash of Aries fire in her gaze. "You can get hurt four times from each other. The fifth time, it'll kill you."

"How do we know that for sure?" Diana asks. "Besides what the book says."

"We don't, I guess," Kiara replies.

"I wouldn't be a huge advocate for testing that theory, though," Lucas mumbles.

Diana turns to look at him, studying his arm. Almost on instinct, he leans towards her, and in one fluid motion, his arm rests in her gentle hold, his knuckles hovering over her lap.

They don't seem to really notice their closeness, so Kiara says nothing and neither do the boys, and they sit in silence as Diana traces his arm with a featherlight, almost-but-not-quite touch.

"One," she whispers.

Lucas clears his throat and gently pulls his arm away, swallowing hard. "Well," he begins, voice low, "same as you."

"So, this is *dangerous*," Peter interjects, breaking the tense silence. "This could really hurt you, guys."

"What I don't understand is why it didn't happen to us," Cameron says, motioning between himself and Peter. "We've used ours separately."

"I don't get that either, but it might be because Diana and Lucas' have to do with real-life, and yours don't deal with a human or other living thing," Kiara replies.

"It's the best answer we have, I guess," Cameron says with a shrug.

"So we need to figure this out, then," Diana says, her voice shaking. Suddenly, she pushes up from the table, turning and disappearing down one of the long rows of shelves.

All the boys- even Lucas- rise as if to go after her, but Kiara stands and waves them down. "Let me," she whispers, as if even speaking too loudly would shatter the already-fragile emotions in the room.

She finds Diana among the rows of books, leaning against what appeared to be old atlases, her eyes closed and her breathing even, as if in a trance. Kiara just observes her, feeling something like regret- or maybe guilt- clench in her chest as she looks at her friend.

"Your quiet footsteps don't fool me, Ki," Diana says, a sad sort of smile appearing on her lips as she opens her eyes.

Her sharp green gaze cuts into Kiara's as she responds. "What's happening in that head of yours?"

Diana sighs. "These powers, Ki. They're otherworldly to begin with, but what I struggle with is that you sacrifice pieces of yourself to wield them, and that isn't fair."

"Explain."

That single word opens the floodgates of Diana's thoughts, and they tumble out of her mouth in a rush. "You can't get them removed, because the extraction will probably kill you. I mean, the other Powerful Ones who got rid of them after the revolt *barely* lived, and the prince and I are already weaker than them. It's as if you don't get a choice, and really, I'm even luckier than most, because I *did* get the choice. And I wonder every single day why I decided to do that to myself, and it's because of Maya. *She* should be doing this, Kiara. Not me. And I think taking this power was a way to keep myself close to her, but now-"

"-Now you've chained yourself down," Kiara interrupts.

Diana pauses, nodding slowly. "Exactly."

Kiara worries her bottom lip between her teeth, averting her gaze from Diana as a familiar intrusive question takes over her thoughts. "Diana, would you still have protected me if I had powers?"

"What do you mean?"

"Like, you and the boys have these amazing powers, and I don't. And trust me, that's the way I want it, but I can't help but think that things might have been different if I could've... *fought* more."

Diana swallows, and it's as if she's the only one who can untangle Kiara's mess of thoughts, for she mumbles, "Henderson, you mean?"

Something like a rumbling of thunder begins in Kiara's chest, and for the first time, she can't tell if it's anger or grief. "What if I was able to fight back, Di? Would that have changed what he'd done?"

"Kiara, I don't know if anyone could answer that."

"Every day, I ask myself why *I* was the kid who he hurt, and I can never come up with an *answer*, and-"

"Kiara," Diana interrupts, taking her friend by the shoulders. "Henderson is an evil person. You can't even know if it was just you, and that in itself is just... too disturbing to think about. I don't have the answers for you, and I can almost guarantee that no one else does. But Ki, never for a *moment* think that I wouldn't have protected you. Powers or no, you are important just as you are."

Kiara nods, fighting the tears that were threatening to spill over. When her eyes clear, she realizes Diana's big green eyes are misty too, and the girls pull each other into a strong, anchoring hug.

"Can you promise me something, Di?" Kiara asks as they pull away.

"Anything," her friend replies in a whisper.

"Promise that if I fight this grief, you fight your doubt. I'll try to heal, and you'll try to move forward. And if that means working with Alynthia to try and use this power for *good*, then so be it. Deal?"

Diana takes a shaky breath, then looks her best friend in the eye. "Deal."

Part Twenty-Seven: The Taurus

Diana

Time: **12:20 PM**

As they're ready to leave the Archives, Diana hangs back a bit to gather some books and papers the others left behind. Lucas approaches her, just the two of them left in the large, echoey room.

"Hey," he says, leaning against the table, a leather portfolio tucked nonchalantly under one arm.

Diana ignores him.

He scoffs. "No need to get so *emotional*, Monroe. I'm just here to give you my NDA."

Diana raises her eyebrows. "Oswald made you sign an NDA?"

"Nope. The ginger kid," he replies. "Secretary of Security, or something?"

Diana nods. "*Cameron,* but you know that. And good, thanks a bunch, or whatever, you can leave it right here," she raps her knuckles on the tabletop next to her, shuffling papers around for no reason and pointedly not looking at him.

Lucas pulls the NDA out of his portfolio and drops the thick bundle on the table, allowing Diana's previously stacked papers to flutter every which way but where they're supposed to be. She groans and drops to the ground to pick them up at the same time Lucas does, roughly bonking their foreheads together.

"Ouch," Diana groans, at the same time Lucas says, "Shit."

Diana reflexively scuttles backwards- away from him- realizing too late that his hand is hooked in the crook of her elbow. Diana tugs Lucas down with her, right on top of her, into the pile of papers.

He's... *right* on top of her.

Lucas, to avoid crushing her completely, braces himself above Diana using his forearms with a sheepish grin, and they stay in this less than ideal position for a few agonizingly long seconds. Diana's head is filled with a million thoughts, the most prominent and coherent being that the Crown Prince of Alynthia was lying directly on top of her. She wasn't really registering anything besides the press of his chest against hers and the warmth of both his breath and his gaze. After a beat, Diana leans her head back against the floor, closes her eyes, and mumbles, "Could you *please* get off me?"

She opens her eyes to see Lucas flush a deep red, rolling off her and standing up again, fixing his collar and clearing his throat. He straightens up quickly, taking a deep breath, and immediately shifts right back into that snotty monarch Diana knows so well.

"Well, Monroe, I'll see you soon," he goes to leave, turning back to face *Diana*, the *president*, still seated on the floor in a whirlwind of documents. Lucas smirks a little. "Oh, and by the way, bugger off, darling."

Diana rolls her eyes at the term, meeting his eyes and smiling back, much to her previous disdain. "Pound sand, Rutherland."

Part Twenty-Eight: The Libra

Lucas

Time: **12:45 PM**

"Would you walk with me?" Lucas asks, approaching Diana.

She turns over her shoulder, fleetingly looking him up and down. For a brief moment, he worries that their interaction that morning would make her refuse. The pair had spent the rest of the morning apart, and the others were all breaking for lunch, so Lucas knew this was his shot. After a long pause, Diana replies, "Sure."

After a small conversation with her bodyguards- where the prince explains that he'd like to converse with her alone- the pair begin their promenade through the Plaza.

They wander in silence for a moment, looking anywhere but at each other. Something like tension is passing between them, and Lucas is flat-out nervous.

"Why'd you invite me?" Diana asks eventually, giving the prince a calculating glance. "You hate me."

"Untrue, actually," he replies. "I dislike you, yes. But *hate*... let's just say the jury is still out."

"I guess I don't hate you either," she begins. Before she can continue though, she seems to stop herself. "But anyways, why are we *here* right now?"

He shrugs. "I don't know," he says truthfully, "but I'd like to know you better, if you'd let me."

She nods slowly, dodging a passerby who blatantly ogles her. "Depends on what you want to know."

"Your accent, to start," he says, their steps syncing. "It's so interesting."

She shakes her head with a small smile. "Why's that?"

"Well, people in Alynthia talk like an in-between of you and me. A British-American fusion, if you will."

"Your accent is weirder than mine, Rutherland. Besides, your father adopted a different accent when he left here, so any blame goes to him."

Lucas nods. "My mother used to tell me stories about the Destruction when I was old enough to know about this place. She was born and raised in England and moved to America at a... relatively inconvenient time." She looks confused, and he smiles, letting that boyish grin slip and break his royal façade. "Remember? When your country was blowing everything up?"

She's quick to raise that eyebrow and bestow The Judgement upon him. "Why do you think your dad changed his accent anyways?"

He shrugs. "Deniability? A chance to wash his hands of New America?"

"Not adoration for his wife?"

Lucas hesitates. "Could be that," he whispers.

"Well," Diana begins, "I like the way you talk," she continues before he can process that. "Do you have a crown?"

"I do."

"And you don't wear it because..."

He pauses, giving her jewelry a once-over. As he speaks, his fingers flit gently to each piece. "Jade earrings, gold necklace, gold bracelets." He tilts his head. "Probably a few thousand, no?"

She swallows, and Lucas forces himself to pull his lingering hand away from her wrist. "Probably."

He chuckles. "Take that and multiply it by about two-hundred thousand, and that's how much that gaudy crown costs."

"Still begs the questions as to why you don't wear it."

"I do, sometimes. My coronation, the day Kerrigan was named Second Heir, my mother's-" he cuts himself off with a sharp swallow, and Diana notices, although she's too kind to pry.

"Did you bring it here with you?"

Lucas shoves down any further emotion. "Absolutely not. Do you get paid?"

She tilts her head, then smirks. "I do, but I think talking about my paycheck with a prince would be frowned upon."

He smiles back at her, partially hating the way that this strong-willed girl has slowly tunneled her way into his brain, his breath, his being. With a quick, nervous inhale, he changes the subject, for fear of the moment lurking too long. "Do you think it's weird?" he begins, motioning with his chin to a reporter lurking nearby. "The publicity?"

She shakes her head. "I don't mind it, really. I'm not great at talking to them, but it helps to know my words can reach people."

"We don't really do that kind of thing at home," Lucas replies, voice low. "Our lives are pretty private."

She gives him an unreadable look. "Do you think- knowing what you know now- do you think that's why?"

He pauses, turning her words over. "I guess it could be. What's he like? My uncle, I mean."

"Elaborate."

"I know you guys hate him, and for good reason, from what I hear. But does he have any good parts at all?"

She replies instantly. "No." Her words weren't bitter or mocking, they were just honest.

"I see... I'm not sure my father has any good parts, either."

"Why do you say that?"

He shrugs, and although he brought it up, he doesn't want to quite elaborate, either. "I don't think any of us Rutherlands do."

"Well, I think *you* do."

He pauses, his heart giving one overwhelming *thud* to the sides of his ribcage. "You do?"

The pair maneuver through the open Plaza until they reach the edge of a fountain, where Lucas sits and looks up at the blonde in front of him. Framed by the light reflecting off the bright skyscrapers behind her, she looks like a goddess, or an angel. When she speaks, Lucas struggles to focus on her words and not her eyes. "I think that goodness isn't decided by the person who wields it, but by the person who's affected by it."

"Now it's your turn to elaborate, Miss Monroe."

With the briefest of hesitations, she sits beside him on the edge of the fountain. "Well, you might be the best person ever, but you'd never know it. The people around you would instead, because they're the ones who are affected by what you do or don't do."

Lucas chuckles ruefully. "Well, I don't have a great track record, what with my two surviving family members."

As soon as the words leave his mouth, Diana laughs. Really, *really* laughs, a loud and full sound that makes Lucas smile on instinct. "Wow, Monroe," he begins, her giggle becoming infectious, "is that laughter I hear?"

She shakes her head, her laughing fading into a blinding smile. "You *are* funny, you know. Even if you get on my nerves sometimes."

He grins right back. "That's maybe the nicest thing you've ever said to me."

"Well, I'm a speaker of the truth, Mister Rutherland."

The happy mood quiets but doesn't quite subside, and Lucas nudges Diana with his shoulder as they get up. He doesn't feel any sort of particular emotion standing out over the others, but he does feel lighter, like her presence had lifted something from his shoulders.

With another one of her trademarked glances, Diana speaks. "I'm sorry. About not telling you, I mean."

Lucas shakes his head. "It's okay. Seriously. You had your country to think about."

"Well, I also had you to think about."

He chuckles. Some part of him doesn't know if she's joking or not. "I am a small price to pay in comparison to America, Monroe."

She smiles at him, and he practically hears his blood rushing. "I think you'd be surprised."

As she starts towards the Capitol, Lucas grabs her hand. He tries to ignore the electric shock that jolts up his arm as she turns around with a heated look. "Monroe," he begins. "Thank you for this."

She smiles at him, lips quirking in that now-familiar way. "Anytime."

Part Twenty-Nine: The Libra

Lucas

Time: **4:04 PM**

Around four in the afternoon, Lucas buckles himself into the royal helicopter, leaning back against his seat.

As they take off, he closes his eyes and lets his body sink into the plush fabric. Thoughts swim through his head at a million miles an hour, and he grimaces as a migraine sets in.

After a few minutes in silence, Lucas opens his eyes and leans towards the window, gazing over what he figured was Sector Twelve based on the sea of sky blue.

"What to do about her, Lucas?" he whispers to himself. As if on cue, the president's image is projected on the side of one of the buildings, a glowing hologram of Diana Monroe.

Lucas leans forward to watch, moving with the helicopter to keep the girl's image in his sights.

"-I wished to come here... well, sort of... and announce to the Virgos that tomorrow, Secretary O'Connor and Secretary Simon will be cleared to release you all." Diana's giant image pauses, and shouts of excitement fill the air, loud enough to hear from the low-flying helicopter, and Lucas shifts all the way around in his seat to continue to watch. His heart hammers in his chest when the hologrammed image seems to *move,* and Diana's face breaks into an incredible, enlightening smile. He's never seen her smile like this, and it causes something indescribable to alight in his body. "And I will say, from the bottom of my heart, that I have never been more excited to see you all again."

With that, the image disappears, and Lucas flops back into his seat, releasing a long, shaking breath.

His leg begins bouncing up and down, and he squeezes his fists once, twice, three times, until a flash of pain from his palms makes him wince. With another heaving sigh, the prince props his elbows on his knees and buries his face in his hands.

But when he closes his eyes, all he sees is her. All he sees is the curve of her jaw, her long, incredible eyelashes, those eyes that were the opposite of his and saw right through him, saw everything within him.

"You hate her, Lucas. You hate her," he mumbles.

And he did. God, he hated the way she walked into every room like she owned it. He hated the way she ruled, the way she cowered behind her team and let them clean up this mess of a country. He hated the way she would run her fingers through that long blonde hair and let it fall across her shoulders and frame her face.

Some deep, burning part of him wished he knew her under different circumstances. Wished that her arrogance and stubbornness would leave them to just be two people and start all over. He even wished that they were commoners, not President, not Prince, and they could meet on the cliffs of Alynthia and could talk to one another for hours.

But they weren't that. They could never *be* that.

So, he would have to settle for seeing her every so often in passing over an online meeting, talking about trade networks and then logging off just to sit in the foyer for another hour wondering why his mouth was dry and his hands were sweating. He'd settle for what they had now.

"Your Highness?" the pilot calls from the cockpit, snapping Lucas from his frantic thoughts.

"Yes?" the prince responds, wincing at the way his voice cracks.

"Your father wished to remind you that the ball invitation meeting is tomorrow morning."

Lucas groans involuntarily. "What time?" he asks, even though he already knows the answer.

"Five-thirty in the morning, sir."

"Great. Thanks."

"Of course, Your Highness." With that, the pilot closes the little window between them, leaving Lucas to his thoughts again.

He sits in silence, staring out at the ocean racing below him. Until an image hits him, one that he's certain he won't be able to shake from his brain. Pressed suits, combed hair, long skirts swishing around ankles. Following that comes the question:

How would Diana Monroe perform at an Alynthian ball?

Part Thirty: The Scorpio

Cameron

Time: **5:30 PM**

"What are we looking at?" Cameron wonders aloud.

He and Kiara are standing with two men, who are both dressed in what look like bomb suits but are actually called "beekeeper clothes".

Inside a large glass jar are two dozen bees, which- as explained by the bomb men- were a parting gift from the Alynthian royals in order to begin re-pollinating New America faster.

Most, if not all, of those words were completely foreign to Cameron.

The Secretary of Security and the Citizens' Liaison were here to oversee the release of the insects in a controlled and monitored outcropping of land between Sector Ten and the Plaza.

"They're bees, Secretary O'Connor," one of the men says. "We just wanted you two to be aware of the new release and the potential threats."

"It's a bug," Kiara mumbles. "They look very un-threatening."

The beekeepers share a look. "They look that way, but they do sting, and some people may have dormant allergies."

Cameron glances at Kiara. "So what I'm hearing is this is an assassination attempt."

Kiara nods, smiling at his joking tone. "Potentially." She turns to the beekeepers. "The two of you are monitoring both the, uh, bees and the pollination routes?"

Both beekeepers nod. "We're hoping to speed up the pollination process by increasing the population. That way, we can progress faster, biologically speaking."

"Well," Cameron says, "this is good, then. Make sure any and all information goes to Kiara and me, and we get updated with any news about... these bees."

As they adjourn the meeting, Cameron and Kiara start back towards their waiting car. "If these bugs are the last we ever see of the Rutherlands," Kiara begins, "we'd be very lucky, indeed."

Cameron frowns; even with her joking tone, she sounds anxious. "Do you dislike them because of Henderson?"

She scoffs. "Of course. Cornelius is just like him, and Lucas... who knows what Lucas is like?"

"Ki, maybe the two of them are the key to figuring out where Henderson is."

"And then what? Do we imprison him? In what country? Do we kill him? We're playing tug-of-war with a criminal, and I don't have a good feeling about how this will end."

Cameron opens the car door for her, sliding into the backseat after she does. "No matter what, Ki, it *will* end eventually."

She sighs, crossing her arms over her chest and looking out of the tinted window. "That's sort of what I'm afraid of."

Part Thirty-One: The Libra

Lucas

Time: **6:17 AM**

"Next," Cornelius says, tossing a gilded envelope down the table.

Lucas yawns from where his head is resting in his hands, and he rubs the heels of his palms into his eyes, slouching down further in his chair.

"Look alive, Your Highness!" Mr. Kerrigan says as he enters, smacking Lucas on the shoulder and guffawing loudly as he sits across from the king.

Lucas groans internally.

"Morning, Lawrence," the king says, exchanging a handshake with the man, "thank you for watching over things in our absence."

Kerrigan smiles, and that very expression gives Lucas chills. "I'd do that anytime, Your Majesty."

The three, along with a few servants, were seated in the king's office, sending out invitations for the annual Alynthian Ball. They had to shuffle through the long list of nobility, one by one, until fifty invitations had been sent out. The process usually lasted from five in the morning until noon, depending on the controversy surrounding each guest.

Lucas eyes the thick stack of envelopes at the end of the table. "Fifty seems like a lot, Father," he says warily.

Cornelius ignores him, and Kerrigan interjects instead. "Who's next, Your Majesty?"

The king studies the list. "Commander Maxon and his new wife."

"What's her name?" Lucas asks.

"Riley, I believe," Kerrigan says, shrugging. "Maxon's so weak he's practically a woman. I feel bad for this new pet he's found."

Lucas rolls his eyes, and Cornelius sees. "Something to say, son?" he asks, not looking up as he slides an invitation into an envelope.

Lucas breathes deep and looks Kerrigan square in the face, unclenching his fists beneath the table. "Yes, actually. Are you implying there is something wrong with being 'womanly', Mister Kerrigan?"

Kerrigan looks taken aback, but he quickly laughs, however nervous it may sound. "Not at all, sir, simply saying that Maxon-"

"Is not in the room with us, nor explaining himself regarding his marriage. So, we shouldn't talk about him unless he's in our presence, but when he is, feel free to say these things to him. I'm sure a commander such as himself would be thrilled to hear your thoughts on *his* marriage."

Cornelius looks up at Lucas, gaze hard and eyebrow raised, and Lucas pointedly averts his eyes, instead keeping his gaze steady on Kerrigan. The prince crosses his arms over his chest, waiting for the man to respond and ignoring the pit of worry in his stomach.

"Of- of course, Your Highness. Apologies."

Lucas smirks and glances at his father, ignoring the way the king's unloving glare turns his blood cold. "Who's next? I approve of Commander Maxon and his wife, by the way."

The king ignores the comment and glances at the list. "The President, Secretary of Security, Secretary of Education, and Citizens' Liaison of New America."

"No," Kerrigan says at the same time that Lucas says "yes."

Cornelius looks between the two. "Why no, Mister Kerrigan?"

"Well, they aren't purebred Alynthians."

"They aren't Alynthian at all, in fact," the king agrees.

"Exactly. So, why should they be present at the annual *Alynthian* ball?"

Lucas pipes up, picking his words carefully. "But they're America's nobility. Having them there is good for our foreign policy and any talk of alliance."

The king considers. "Who says I wanted an alliance?"

"I didn't," Lucas says, his voice growing slightly sharp, "but even if your singular goal was to intimidate them into not bothering our country, what better way to do it than drop them into a room full of nobility?" He tries to hide the fact that the Americans being in Alynthia would *also* put them that much closer to where the late queen rested, not to mention he'd get to spend more time with Diana and the others.

Kerrigan huffs. "They're a waste of four invites. They won't even know the dance."

Lucas scoffs. "They can learn *one dance*, Mister Kerrigan. We could even request lessons in the invitation if we wanted."

"That's true," Cornelius says begrudgingly. "Okay, so they get invited."

"One more thing, Father," Lucas says, daring to push his luck, "we should offer for them to stay at the palace. An Alynthian tour."

"Lucas, I don't want them here longer than-"

"Well, it's better than them traveling to and fro, right? And, while they're here for, say, a week, we can have meetings about creating trade networks and military structures instead of just giving them bugs."

Both older men sit quietly.

Finally, Cornelius turns to a servant seated at the end of the table. "Call Mister Boone at the American Capitol and ask him to arrange hospitality measures. Tell him we can give them a week here, but any later and they must find their own place. And get me a housemaid to discuss their room assignments."

Lucas smiles softly, feeling bolstered at the idea of finally earning his place at the table. Kerrigan checks the Americans off the list and slides the sealed envelopes across the tabletop. Quietly, almost defeated, he continues. "Next. Lady Kimberly Ashton and her brother..."

Lucas tunes them out, leaning back in his chair. His heart swells with pride, and he smiles at the four fresh invitations at the top of the pile.

Part Thirty-Two: The Taurus

Diana

Time: **8:50 AM**

The next day, Peter, Cameron, Diana, and Kiara are at work, with the prince having returned to his home country about two days before. In the midst of reading yet *another* citizen's letter asking about an alliance, Diana is startled by a knock on the door.

Part of her is less startled about the noise and more startled by the fact that she'd suddenly realized her thoughts were concerned not with the letter she'd been reading, but instead remembering the way the prince had grabbed her hand that day in the Plaza, the words 'prince' and 'alliance' leaping off the page and swirling into those memories right before her eyes.

"Yeah?" she calls, voice shaking just barely.

Peter pokes his head in. "Hey," he says. "Can I come in?"

Diana nods and he enters, taking a seat in one of the chairs against the wall. Diana tosses the letter to the side and folds her hands over the table, studying him. "What's up?"

Peter shrugs. "I wanted to check in. I haven't spoken to you in a while."

Some part of Diana feels... guilty. "I'm fine."

Peter nods, and the office falls silent. After a second, he clears his throat. "One other thing. A small thing."

Diana grimaces. She's betting that this 'thing' isn't actually so small. "Go for it."

Peter meets her eyes, and Diana is once again shocked by his bright amber irises as if she hasn't seen them thousands of times before. "Oswald wants us all on the floor in ten."

Diana groans, putting her head in her hands. "Why?"

"A letter from the Rutherlands."

"*Another* one?"

Peter nods. "Cam and Ki are already down there." He stands and crosses to Diana's desk, rapping his knuckles on the table in a rhythmic pattern. "I wanted to come to get you before I let you go at it alone."

Diana sighs, standing to meet him. "Thank you. Really."

Peter opens the door and beckons her into the hall. "Don't sweat it."

The pair heads down the hall, and Diana winces as she notices her outfit compared to Peter's. "Peter," she whispers, continuing when he turns to her, "I think I'm underdressed."

Peter studies her for a second, then nods. "Don't worry about it. You look fine."

Diana nods, half-convinced. Her leggings and long-sleeve don't come anywhere close to Peter's khakis and button-down, and Diana can feel her confidence slipping away already.

When they reach the doors to the council floor and they're tugged open by the guards, the duo hurries inside and takes their seats. The floor was partially renovated when they took over, and all the chairs were reupholstered to get rid of the garish zodiac colors and were now all black, leaving the place void of much color and matching Diana's anxious mood. The setup was the same: podium and chairs at the front of the room, seats filling the rest of the place. A large, round table had been placed in the center for the chairs to be stationed around.

After a minute, Kiara and Cameron enter, coffees in hand. Kiara shakes out her hair and tucks her sunglasses into her collar, passing Diana a full cardboard cup, and Cameron hands his cup wordlessly to Peter before sitting in the second seat.

"Coffee?" Diana asks.

Kiara nods. "The meeting wasn't too long, and the briefing went fine, so we stopped on the way back."

Diana nods, and Kiara takes a seat in the fourth chair before turning to face Peter. "Peter, I wanted to talk to you about the stats on those schoolkids you gave me-"

"Hello, all," Barbara says as she strides into the room. Diana rises to embrace her before she sits, and she pauses to pat each of the others on the head or shoulder before she sits in chair number five.

Ms. Miller and Mr. Boone hustle in next, followed by Ms. Brewer. The second they all sit, Barbara produces a file from who-knows-where and tosses it on the table, and the others wait for Diana to grab it before they start to fire off questions.

"What does it say?"

"Who's it from?"

Diana motions with her hand to quiet them as she scans the innards of the file, and when she flips to the back, a gilded envelope falls into her lap. As she takes in the golden seal on the back, stamped with an R, Diana's stomach sinks.

Cameron, to Diana's right, puts his hand on her wrist. "What does it say?" he whispers.

Fingers shaking, Diana pulls on the golden ribbon to release the flap on the envelope, pulling out the invitation inside and passing it off to Ms. Brewer, who's sitting to her left. "Read it, please."

Victoria clears her throat and starts to read. "His Majesty King Cornelius Rutherland of Alynthia and His Royal Highness Prince Lucas Rutherland of Alynthia cordially invite you to a formal ball at Willowood Palace in ten days." She pauses, and Diana nods for her to continue, "among the invited are President Diana Monroe, Secretary Peter Simon, Secretary Cameron O'Connor, and the Citizens' Liaison of New America, Miss Kiara." She passes the invitation back to Diana. "That's it, unless you want me to read about the dress code and dance lessons on the back."

"No, thank you, Miss Brewer," Diana mumbles. "Barbara, the prince is no longer in America, correct?"

From her seat five to Diana's right, Barbara nods her head. "Correct, he left late afternoon yesterday, I believe, on that helicopter of theirs."

"So he's going back to Alynthia *just* to plan this ball?" Kiara asks.

Barbara nods. "I assume so. Of course, you have to accept their invite."

"Yes, but where will we stay?" Cameron asks. "Alynthia is two hours away by helicopter, and we don't *really* have the liberty of going back and forth unless they lend us transportation."

Diana shuffles back through the folder, pulling out another piece of paper. "It says here Mister Boone already discussed that with the Alynthian security team?"

Mr. Boone nods from his seat. "Yes, they called early this morning. They've agreed to let you stay a week at Willowood Palace, should you accept the invitation."

Kiara guffaws from her seat. "*That* place?" She turns to Diana. "Di, accept the invitation *just* for that reason."

Diana chews her lip. "And what on earth are we supposed to wear to a royal ball? Besides, I'm sure this is just the prince's way of getting us to agree to his little experiment."

Ms. Miller pipes up from her spot at the table. "I have some Capitol friends who can get you into their boutique. Let me make a few calls."

"Wonderful," Barbara says, "so, problem solved. I say we put it to a vote." She looks at Diana. "Madam President, if you would?"

Diana sighs, then runs through the speech she's had to deliver at all the previous council meetings. "All in favor of the four of us going to the Alynthian ball, say 'yes.'"

The voting starts from the lowest ranking person and ends with the highest, so the proposal goes clockwise around the table in a unanimous vote.

"Yes," Ms. Brewer says, followed by Mr. Boone, Ms. Miller, and Barbara.

The vote reaches Kiara. "Sure," she affirms.

Peter next. "Yes," he says, ever so compliant with the proper terminology.

Cameron is the last of the council to vote, and he smiles at Diana before giving a resounding "absolutely".

All eyes land on Diana, and she fidgets uncomfortably before mumbling, "I don't really have a choice, do I? Yes."

Part Thirty-Three: The Taurus

Diana

Time: **8:00 AM**

After receiving the ball invitation from the Rutherlands, Ms. Miller quickly booked the group an appointment at an upscale boutique, started by two women in the Capitol. Emilia was a Libra, so she knew Ms. Miller from their old sector, and her wife Grace, a Saggitarius, ran the store with her.

Diana's alarm beeps at eight in the morning, which she begrudgingly shuts off with a swing of her hand. She trods out to the kitchen to make herself coffee, and sees that Cameron is already awake, leaning against the counter and sipping from a ceramic mug. He's looking out the floor-to-ceiling window in the dining room, his gaze alert as he scans the Plaza.

"Morning," Diana says, rubbing the sleep from her eyes.

"Hey," he says back.

Diana goes and stands next to him, looking over the Plaza, which is just starting to wake up. The vendors are pulling up their grates, shop owners are flipping 'open' signs, and monorails are slowly squealing in and out of the station. Diana leans against the table and smiles as she sees a woman crouching with a child next to the fountain. They're both smiling, and the woman is pointing at a plaque carved into the concrete. It's Maya's memorial, and the woman seems to be reading it aloud to the child;

the way in which the pair smiles at one another makes Diana's chest ache, but she can't look away.

They're quiet for a second, both of them watching the same thing, until Cameron pipes up. "I've been thinking about Sector Three." As he speaks, his eyes wander to the northeast, off to where he used to live, off to where a big border wall once stood.

"Yeah?" Diana prods.

"I've just been thinking how crazy it is that I could go from there to here in just seven months," he states, his voice getting a faraway tone.

"You earned it, Cam," Diana tells him, turning to face him straight-on. He looks down at her. "You've worked *so* hard, and you're doing so many amazing things. Just three days ago, you and the Integration Team managed to clear Sector Nine for release." He smiles a little at the mention of the accomplishment, "and everything you've done has helped other people, too."

"But what if it isn't enough? How is it ever going to be enough?"

She pauses, her fingers finding that wound on the inside of her elbow. "Maybe it won't be. Not for us, at least. But isn't it nice to know that we'll do our best, and the kids who come after us will continue that on?"

Cameron nods. "Yeah, I guess you're right." He smiles at Diana, his brilliant white teeth flashing in the early-morning light.

"I know I am," Diana says, grinning back. She looks around their spacious-but-otherwise-empty apartment. "Where are the other two?"

Cameron shrugs. "Peter's still asleep, I think. Ki was in the shower last I knew."

As if on cue, Kiara comes down the hall in a gray t-shirt and black leggings, her wet curls loose down her shoulders. She looks Diana up and down, motioning a hand over her pajama-clad frame. "You might want to change."

"Huh?" Diana asks, looking down to realize she's in sweatpants and an oversized black shirt that she's pretty sure isn't hers.

Cameron nods. "We have our appointment in an hour. Also," he says, tugging at Diana's sleeve, "that's my shirt."

That explains the color. "Oh, right. Okay, give me five minutes."

As she heads down the hall, Cameron calls to Diana. "Wake Peter up while you're at it!"

Diana heads back to her room, brushing out her hair and leaving it down around her shoulders, pushing a white headband over her scalp to hold back her unruly flyaways. She changes into a light blue dress that lands right above her knees, shoves her feet into some sandals, then crosses the hall into Peter's room. He's tangled in his comforter, head buried in a pillow, dark curls sprouting every which way.

"Peter, wake up," Diana whispers, crossing to his bed and shaking his bare shoulder.

As soon as Diana touches him, Peter sits up in a flash, breathing heavily. "What?!"

"Woah!" Diana says, jumping back a bit. "I was just waking you up!"

His eyes dart around the room, as if checking for something or someone, and after a second, he calms down and looks at Diana. "Sorry. I've been... having nightmares."

Diana sits on the edge of his bed, pulling her legs up under her. "About?"

Peter plucks at the comforter. "The fight."

Diana nods slowly. They've all been struggling with the memories of the Battle of Zodiacs, each of them worrying about something different. Kiara getting caught by George Henderson haunted her, Peter was still uncomfortable being left alone, and Cameron and Diana were both wracked with guilt over Maya's death.

Diana reaches out and hugs Peter, letting her hands rest on his muscled shoulder blades. They've all found that there's nothing they could really say when someone else got like this. The only thing to do was to be close to the other person, silently reminding them that they weren't alone. "It's okay. You're okay." She pats him on the back, then pulls away. "Anyways, Cam wants you to get up. We've gotta get a move on."

He groans, rubbing his eyes, but his mouth quirks up into a small smile. "I forgot about the appointment. Something professional, or something comfortable?"

Diana shrugs. "Probably both, if you can manage that."

Diana bids farewell to Peter and goes back out to the living room, where Kiara and Cameron are sitting on the couch. Both are dressed and waiting for them, and when Diana enters, they turn to look at her. Cameron gives a joking whistle, clapping his hands slowly.

"Who's this little Virgo?" he asks sarcastically.

Diana scoffs, running her hands down the skirt of her dress. "Please. I just like the color, is all." She tugs on her skirt. "We have to agree they all got the best one, yeah?"

Cameron doesn't answer, giving Diana another once-over as his gaze grows sympathetic, eyes catching on the jagged scars stretching down her arm. "No long sleeve?"

Diana swallows, shaking her head after a moment's hesitation.

Everyone nods in understanding as Peter emerges from the hallway, and he slows his pace when he sees Cameron. "Hey," he says with a goofy grin.

"Morning, sleepyhead," Cameron says, crossing over to him and using his height advantage to kiss him quickly on the forehead. "Let's go, we're gonna be late."

Kiara rises from the couch, crossing to the door and putting on a pair of sneakers as she speaks. "No, we *are* late." She straightens up, looking at the other three with one eyebrow raised. "What are you all standing around for? Let's go." She turns and punches a button on the wall, calling the elevator.

The elevator doors open, and they all hurry in. Peter grabs a piece of toast from a plate on the counter, shoving it in his mouth before nabbing his shoes and racing in as well. "Jeez, Kiara," he says, his mouth full. "A warning would've been nice."

She shrugs, smirking. "Not my fault you decided to sleep in."

Cameron grabs Peter's wrist and tugs him towards himself, raising a hand to wipe Peter's face and brush some hair off his forehead. Peter playfully swats him away, and Cameron's laugh fills the elevator as the boys begin to converse with Diana.

Kiara checks her watch. "Does everyone know what they're doing for outfits?"

The elevator falls completely silent.

She looks at each of them in turn. "You're kidding."

"We had no time to prepare!" Peter says, raising his hands defensively.

"You had almost a week!" Kiara counters.

Peter shuts up, and Cameron laces his fingers through his before speaking. "I'm sure they'll have options, right? Di, what did Miller say?"

Diana winces. "She said we needed to tell her in advance what we're looking for," she mumbles.

"And did we?" Kiara asks, a hint of teasing in her voice.

Silence once again.

"This is gonna take *forever*," Peter groans.

The others laugh with him, and when the elevator hits the bottom floor, they're greeted by two bodyguards, who smile as the teens approach, still a mildly unnerving sight considering the guards they grew up with.

One of them steps forward. He's a huge guy, tall and wide, but he sticks his hand out to Diana and bows his head respectfully. "Hello, President Monroe, I'm Carl. Me and my partner Dan will be escorting you to the boutique."

Diana shakes his hand and smiles back. "Thank you, Carl. Anything we should be briefed on before we head out?"

Dan, the other guard who's almost bigger than Carl, silently hands him a leather-bound binder. Carl glances through it, then looks back at the group. "Yes. The public has gotten wind of the ball, and there's a few questions they may ask you." He looks at Cameron. "They want to know if the Secretary of Security is going to go with the Secretary of Education."

Both boys blush a deep red but say nothing.

Carl continues. "Fashion-wise, they're most interested in what their Citizens' Liaison is going to wear." He winks playfully at Kiara. "For the record, I'm excited to see it as well." Kiara grins at him. "And the question for their president..." he trails off, glancing up at Diana.

Diana rolls her eyes. "They want to know if I'm going to propose an alliance to the royals while we're there?"

"Correct," Carl says. "So the best plan for *all* of you is to not comment or answer their questions. The faster you get in, the faster you get out."

They all nod, and as Carl and Dan approach the heavy lobby doors, Kiara sighs. "Game faces, everyone," she grumbles.

Peter nudges her. "She means 'smile.'"

Almost simultaneously, they all plaster on friendly smiles, right as the doors are pushed open.

They're blasted by shouting voices belonging to citizens of all ages. Carl and Dan jump into action immediately, pushing them back enough to form a secure perimeter around the group. They pace forward quickly, and Diana spies the black town car waiting for them at the end of the sidewalk. As they push through the crowd, Diana catches some of the questions being hurled towards her.

"President Monroe, are you going to propose an Alynthian alliance?"

"President Monroe, who is your date to the ball?"

"President Monroe, are you satisfied with the work you've been doing?"

Diana takes a deep breath and continues walking, catching the tail end of a question angled towards Cameron from a reporter stationed nearby.

"Secretary O'Connor, are you planning on proposing *marriage* to Secretary Simon?"

Peter's eyes widen, but he and Cameron remain silent as they're ushered into the car. As the door shuts, leaving them safe behind the tinted windows, Peter buries his face in his hands while Cameron leans his head against the back of the seat.

"What the actual hell?!" Cameron groans. "I'm eighteen!"

Peter snorts from next to him. "We've gotten worse."

"True," Kiara says. "Remember? 'Kiara, is the Citizens' Liaison title a front to track down Mister Henderson?'"

"Yeah, I remember that," Diana says. "Or, when I was asked if Cameron and Peter were *both* in a relationship with me."

The boys make a face. "I remember that one too," Peter mumbles.

They ride in silence, but Diana catches Peter resting his hand on Cameron's leg, and Cameron relaxes, putting his hand over Peter's and looking at him out of the corner of his eye. The two share a look, and Peter, as if answering some unspoken question, smiles a little and tilts his head. Diana can't help but smile at the interaction, and her nerves relax just a little as the car quiets down.

Diana turns away right as they pull up to the boutique. As the car door opens and the group exits the vehicle, they're greeted by much fewer people, making it easier for them to get in. A little bell jingles over the door as they enter, and a posh-looking woman with a beehive hairdo and huge dangly earrings bustles around the corner like the noise summoned her. She claps her hands together when she sees them, clinking the massive rings on her fingers together.

"You must be the Capitol group!" she squeals, rushing forward to wrap Kiara and Diana in a hug, moving swiftly to the boys after she finishes squeezing all the air from the girls' lungs. She steps back and looks each of them up and down, finally pointing a boney finger towards Peter. "*You're* the Secretary of Education." When he nods, she squeals again. "Oh, goodie! My wife *adores* the work you do for the children." Peter blushes, and she steps up to measure his shoulders, producing a tape measure out of nowhere. He stiffens reflexively, and she clicks her tongue. "Relax, darling," she says. After a moment, and a few more measurements, she steps back. "Oh, Peter! You're breathtaking, my dear. I have some ideas."

She motions them all to a private room, filled with two plush benches that face a wall of mirrors. Sitting in front of the mirror is a small, circular platform, and there's a small curtained-off section with hangers that Diana is assuming was where they changed.

They all sit, Cameron next to Diana on one bench and Peter and Kiara on the second. As soon as she sits though, Emilia takes Kiara's hand and yanks her up enthusiastically.

"No, dearest!" she says with a laugh. "We start with you." She winks at Kiara as she opens a door that leads to another small room, and she continues speaking as she rifles through a rack of dresses. "Kiara, I've been working hard on your dress *especially*. I have two options, both of which you'd look absolutely marvelous in." She emerges with two hangers. On one is a long black dress, and on another is a dark navy dress with off-the-shoulder sleeves. She pushes the blue one towards Kiara and hangs the other on a hook on the wall, practically shoving her into the changing room. "Let me know if you need help, sweetheart!"

Kiara emerges a few minutes later in the blue gown, and she steps up onto the platform to study herself in the mirror. The dress is amazing, with a heavy-looking skirt that's patterned with shining black lace. The neckline cuts low, and the sleeves rest off her shoulder a little ways, framing her muscled arms.

"Ki!" Diana practically shouts. "It's so pretty!"

Cameron is wearing an equally appalled expression, and Peter shoots her a thumbs up. Emilia flits around her, making a few last-minute alterations, then steps back. "Thoughts?" she asks Kiara.

"I like it, but it's sort of too heavy," Kiara says, swishing the skirt around. She's right: the dress barely moves when she swivels her hips back and forth.

Emilia frowns. "Try the black one. It's a little more risqué, but it fits your character."

Kiara nods, heading back into the changing room, and when she comes out in the black dress, all of their jaws practically hit the floor, Emilia included. She steps onto the platform, putting her hands in the pockets of the dress. It's jet-black, floor-length, and has a square neckline with spaghetti-strap sleeves. A long slit runs from the floor up to the middle of her thigh on the left side of the gown, and although it's simple, it's the kind of dress that would most certainly be making the front page of a magazine the following morning.

Emilia gasps at the sight of her. "Stunning, Kiara! What do you think?"

Kiara smiles at herself, putting her hands on her hips. Her black hair matches the color of the dress, and Emilia hands her a strappy pair of black heels that she slides on, giving her an extra two inches of height. "I love it," she says, turning to Emilia. "Thank you so much. It's gorgeous."

Emilia grins, dramatically swiping at a tear that may or may not actually be there. "Of course, sweetie.

Change back into your clothes and I'll have someone package this up."

Kiara changes, joining Peter once again on the bench. He gives her a one-armed hug, then shouts in surprise as Emilia grabs him and yanks him to his feet. She reaches out with her other hand, and Cameron tentatively takes it, so she pulls him up too and shoves the boys shoulder-to-shoulder, quite roughly, as she studies them.

"I assume you two are going together, no?" she asks after a moment, not looking either boy in the face and instead supposedly continuing to marvel at the length of Cameron's arms.

"Yes?" Peter questions, looking towards Cameron.

Cameron grins, giving Peter a tender kiss on the cheek. "Of course we are." Diana notices the sneaky way he grabs Peter's hand, stilling his back-and-forth thumb movements as he turns back towards Emilia. "Why do you ask?"

She squeals for the billionth time. "Oh, goodie! Well, I made you both separate outfits, but now I can bust out the matching ones since I know you two are going as a pair."

She goes back to her small room, pulling out two suits. She hands a gray one to Cameron and a black one to Peter, along with black shoes for both boys and matching black ties. Each boy gets a white button-up shirt as well, and she shoves them into the changing room.

Peter emerges first, and he looks so formal that Diana almost gasps. His dark hair matches the ensemble perfectly, and he straightens his tie as he steps onto the platform. Cameron comes out next, matching Peter exactly, except his suit and pants are gray, highlighting his bright eyes. His red hair stands out against his white shirt, and he buttons the middle button on his jacket as he goes up to stand behind Peter. He kisses him on the cheek and leans his chin on his shoulder, brushing off his shoulders and hugging him from behind as he studies their outfits in the large mirror. "You look good."

Peter smiles, tugging on Cameron's tie. "Says you."

They lean into each other, but before they can kiss, Emilia pops up behind them, startling them apart. "Stunning, boys! Are these the ones?"

Peter laughs. "Yes, ma'am." Cameron nods as well, and they head to the changing room again.

When they disappear behind the curtain, Emilia whirls on Diana. "Now, Miss Monroe. I have a few ideas for you, but I wanted to talk to you about them first." She sits next to Diana on the bench, and Kiara comes over as well, sitting on the arm of the chair behind her. Emilia takes Diana's hands, staring much too intently into her eyes. "I was planning on making something in a neutral tone for you, but I had a different idea this morning."

"What is it?" Diana asks.

"I know it's been difficult to put Sector Seven behind you, no?"

Diana blinks. "Of course, why?"

Emilia brushes a loose strand of hair from her face. "Well, I think it would be *quite* the power move to wear forest green to this ball. Not to mention, it would give these Alynthians a sense of American nationalism and make a certain prince consider more than just an alliance." She winks at Diana, and Kiara snorts.

"Oookay," Diana says. "I'll try it on. But if it makes Lucas Rutherland swoon, I don't think I want it."

The boys come out of the curtained room as Emilia shoves a bundle of dark green into Diana's arms. She steps into the room to change, unraveling the fabric in front of herself, inhaling sharply when she sees it. The sleeves are puffy and light, with a square neckline and full skirt that billows out, covered in the same light fabric as the sleeves. It's a dark, beautiful shade of green, and when Diana looks at it, she sees the depths of her old home.

Diana changes into it quickly, and then pulls on the gold heels that Emilia gave her as well. Everything fits perfectly, and Diana pictures Emilia staying up all night to finish sewing, hunched over a table, a needle and thread between her fingers. She draws back the velvet curtain and hurries onto the platform, keeping her eyes downturned, and when she finally looks at herself in the mirror, she sees her friends staring back at her, their jaws on the floor.

"What?" Diana asks meekly, fluffing her hair and scrutinizing her outfit again.

Cameron clears his throat. "If you don't get that one, I'm going to be *severely* disappointed."

Diana grins. "Emilia, thoughts?"

When she doesn't answer, Diana turns around. Emilia is sitting in her spot on the bench, a tissue to her face, and she waves her hand around, like she's casting some sort of spell on Diana. "Oh, darling, this is it."

Diana grins, turning back to face herself in the mirror. "Yeah," she says. "I think it is."

Part Thirty-Four: The Cancer

Peter

Time: **10:05 AM**

"Come again?" Cameron asks, yanking his glasses off dramatically.

Peter nods slowly, nervously biting his lip. "Yup."

"*Dance lessons?!*"

"Specifically requested by the Rutherland clan," Peter replies, leaning against the doorframe of Cameron's office.

Cameron makes a guttural groaning noise that Peter thinks might be English words, but he can't be positive.

"Why?" Cameron whines, standing up and crossing to Peter. "Why can't we just drink champagne on the sidelines and watch the nobles waltz all night?"

Peter smiles softly at Cameron's crankiness, pulling him closer by his forearms. Cameron scrunches his nose, half-playfully, and Peter chuckles. "I think you'll be okay. It's one lesson, one dance. You don't even have to participate in anything else should you not want to."

Cameron relaxes his features and grins at Peter. "Wait, we *are* going together, right?"

Peter raises one eyebrow. "Yes?" he says, voice laced with uncertainty. "Why?"

"This means if there's a waltz, I dance with *you*."

Peter smiles and pulls Cameron flat against his chest, leaning onto the wall. "Sure, unless there's some handsome Alynthian guy you find to replace me."

Cameron smirks and considers jokingly. "Maybe. But you'll do for now."

Peter smiles and kisses him gently, heart pounding at the way he can feel Cameron grinning against his lips. He pulls away and leans his forehead against Cameron's. "You strike me as a bad dancer," he whispers.

Cameron feigns a shocked expression, and he pulls away from Peter. "You dare to claim that the Secretary of Security, the *pinnacle* of American celebrity, cannot dance?"

Peter laughs. "I don't know what you're talking about." He grabs Cameron's hands and pulls him closer again. "Besides, we'll learn together."

Cameron runs his thumbs over Peter's cheeks, giving the loose curl on his forehead a gentle tug as he pulls away. "Come on, superhero. We're late for class."

"No, no, no," the instructor shouts. "No."

The two pairs in the room break apart: Cameron and Diana, and Peter and Kiara.

They're on opposite sides of the room, and all four are dressed in workout clothes, like athletic shorts or leggings. Diana puts her hands on her hips and sighs in a futile attempt to catch her breath. This whole class had been going on for almost forty minutes, and it took place in the atrium of the Capitol, for lack of a better dancing location.

"What the hell are we doing wrong?" Diana mumbles, running a hand through her hair.

The instructor, named Damon, had flown in from Alynthia that morning. He was tall and scrawny, with a permed curly hairdo and tight workout clothes.

"Miss Monroe, you're still spinning on the wrong side. Mister Simon, *much* too stiff," he says.

"Sorry," Peter mumbles.

"I have a question," Kiara says from next to Peter. "Aren't there supposed to be a minimum of twenty people in this dance?"

The instructor, much to Peter's shock, smiles. He hadn't known that was possible. "Correct. But that's the *traditional* way. Next week, there will be more than twenty."

"How many people *will* there be?" Cameron asks hesitantly.

"Fifty."

"Oh, no," Diana whispers, covering her face with her hands.

"Explain the whole concept to me one more time?" Peter asks.

The instructor nods, pointing them to a whiteboard, which the group gathers around. "So, in the ballroom, there will be two circles. The outside circle is spaced out quite a bit, and that's made up of the twenty-five men who will be present, including Mister O'Connor and Mister Simon." He glances at the boys before continuing, as if making sure they're paying attention, "the inside circle is tighter, made up of all the women. The Alynthians take this dance very seriously, so fifty invites were intentional. They make sure there's an even number in order to do this dance."

"So, don't mess it up," Cameron says.

"Yes," the instructor confirms.

"Do we find out our partners in advance?" Diana asks, pointing at the drawing on the board. "Obviously, twenty-five and twenty-five means we get partnered up, right?"

Damon pulls his lip between his teeth. "Well, that's the problem. You four have learned the combination, which gets repeated three times. But that also means that you switch *partners* three separate times."

"What?" Diana asks.

"You begin by picking your partner. Then, as the dance continues, you switch partners twice more by moving clockwise around the inside circle."

"Okay, so we should obviously start off with one another," Peter says, looking down at Kiara.

"You two boys should be strategically placed, actually," Damon says. "So the girls have at least two partners they've rehearsed with."

Kiara looks over at him. "You're an evil genius."

Damon shrugs and returns to the front of the room. "I try. My job is to make you look good." He takes a swig from his water bottle and claps his hands together. "Back to your spots. Five, six, seven, eight!"

Part Thirty-Five: The Libra

Lucas

Time: **10:01 AM**

Lucas enters the barn at ten on the day of the ball, smiling as he comes face-to-face with Icarus.

He rubs the horse's dark snout as he peppers his forehead with gentle kisses. "Hello, darling one."

His horse titters happily, and Lucas chuckles, scratching behind his white ears.

Icarus was a massive animal, tall and muscular, the perfect steed for a prince. His coat was black and white, as if someone had taken an ink stamp to a blank canvas.

He didn't ride as much as he wanted to anymore, so Icarus spent a lot of time cooped up, which Lucas was guilty about. But he made sure to visit often and turn him out in the large open pasture when he could.

Icarus had been a gift to Lucas on his eighth birthday, so the horse was around eleven. He shared the barn with two other animals: Freya and Atlas, his mother and father's horses, respectively.

Now, Icarus may be lonely sometimes, but the barn was spacious and luxurious, a perfect home for any animal to reside. He was fed and cleaned daily, although Lucas still liked to brush out his coat when he visited, the practiced motions exactly the same as they had been when he was a child.

He fishes a sugar cube out of his pocket and feeds it to the horse, palm flat as Icarus' warm breath dances over his skin. "Who's the best horse ever? That's you, Icarus."

"How cute."

Lucas starts with fear, turning around to where Diana Monroe is standing in the entryway, arms crossed.

"Monroe," he greets, voice firm. "What are you doing here?"

She shrugs, her pale blue crewneck slipping down and baring one of her shoulders. She's wearing casual clothes, presumably travel attire. Lucas suspects the group of Americans must have arrived in Alynthia early for the ball later. "I was just wandering."

Then she does something that makes Lucas' stomach drop.

"Hello, beautiful," she whispers, turning towards Freya and running her manicured fingers down her soft nose.

To be frank, it was probably the first time that old mare had been shown any sort of affection since his mother died.

Diana catches Lucas looking at her and scoffs halfheartedly. "What?"

"Nothing," he says, voice cracking. "It's just... she isn't very friendly, that's all." He clears his throat and wills his tone to remain cold and even. "I'm surprised she isn't taking off one of your fingertips."

He had expected Diana to move away, but she inches closer to Freya, who knickers in greeting and tilts her head towards the blonde girl, her chestnut mane falling into Diana's face. She laughs and scratches the horse's coarse neck, braiding her mane together in a loose plait as she whispers affectionately to the animal.

"You don't have horses in America, do you?" Lucas asks, not looking at Diana and instead beginning to brush out Icarus' coat.

"No. We've got no animals at all," she replies, and Lucas swears her voice is sad. After a moment, she seems to reconsider. "Well, actually, now scientists have been breeding pollinators for farming." She smiles just slightly. "It's a small step, but an exciting one."

He doesn't say anything, and a few minutes pass in a semi-comfortable silence until he feels her presence at his back.

He turns to see that she's moved on from cuddling Freya and is now gazing into Icarus' big, dark eyes, her fingers scratching his chin. Lucas doesn't understand how, but he's filled with both longing to cover her hand with his own and a territorial urge to protect his horse from this heart-stealing American.

"What's his name?" Diana asks.

Lucas takes a long, deep breath, inhaling the barn's familiar woody scent. "Icarus."

"Like the myth?"

He's surprised she knows it. "Like the story."

She moves ever closer, ducking under the wooden bar that makes up the front of the stall and standing by the horse's shoulder, leaning against the animal and giving Lucas a searching look. "Myth, story. What's the difference?"

"A myth isn't true. A story-"

"-Could be," she interrupts. He nods, and she shrugs. "Well, that's neat."

He scoffs, somewhat playfully. "I think that's the nicest thing you've ever said to me, Monroe."

She rolls her eyes, and Lucas gets goosebumps. "Don't flatter yourself."

"Why would I, when you've done it yourself?"

The pair are about a foot away from each other, with Lucas still clutching Icarus' brush in one hand. Diana's blonde hair stands out against the horse's monochrome coat, and he feels something new and terrifying settle in his chest as he looks at her.

He turns away from the president and her hypnotizing gaze, instead focusing intently on his task. He knows she's still watching him, though; he can feel her piercing green eyes on the side of his face.

"You know, I really don't like you, Your Highness," she begins, removing the brush from Lucas' grip so he's forced to meet her gaze. "But I can't help but be confused by you sometimes."

Lucas can't help himself: he glances quickly at her blush-pink lips before refocusing on her eyes. "A good confused or a bad confused?"

She smirks, pulling a lip between her teeth, and he tries to focus on her words rather than how that action makes him feel. "Depends on the day, really."

Lucas steps closer, almost daring her to show him any sort of emotion, any inkling that she may feel the same frustrating emotions as he does. She doesn't move, and slowly, without breaking eye contact, Lucas moves his hand up towards her hair, his fingers sinking into her golden, wavy tresses.

Lucas' heart stutters when the president sucks in a sharp breath, tilting her head in the most miniscule of movements and pushing into the contact.

As if he'd never done it at all, Lucas smirks, pulling his hand away as he leans in close, his breath tickling her ear. "You had hay in your hair," he whispers.

She shakes her head as he leans back, but he swears her cheeks are dusted with red. "You might be the most frustrating person in the world."

As she turns to leave, Lucas grabs her wrist, turning her back around. Running his fingertips over the delicate veins there, he smiles ruefully. "Second only to you, Monroe."

With a heated glare, the president turns and leaves Lucas alone in the barn.

Part Thirty-Six: The Taurus

Diana

Time: <u>6:30 PM</u>

"Diana. Stop panicking," Peter says. "You look great."

In truth, he was right: in true Diana fashion, there wasn't actually much to worry about. The fitting had gone well, the dance lesson had gone well, and the dress Diana had chosen was altered by Emilia to perfection. Diana runs her fingers over the forest green fabric, pinching the lace between her index finger and thumb and rubbing her other hand over the soft comforter that rested on her bed. Without a word, Kiara places her hand over Diana's to stop her anxious movements.

"I just don't feel like I'm going to do particularly well in a ballroom full of obnoxious politicians and monarchs," Diana grumbles, moving her fidgety hand to rest over her scarred left arm, self-conscious about that long white etching.

Cameron turns to her from where he was looking out the window of Diana's bedroom. "We're not here to make friends. We're here to make sure people know New America is more powerful than they give us credit for."

"And have fun," Peter says from next to him.

"And drink expensive champagne until I'm seeing two of Lucas Rutherland," Kiara mumbles, rubbing her forehead as if she already had a migraine just thinking about the prince.

Diana groans instinctively. "Don't remind me."

Kiara shrugs. "He really isn't *that* bad."

Diana turns to face her, her disbelief apparent on her face. "You're kidding. *I* think he's a bad ruler."

Peter rolls his eyes good-naturedly. "He's *not* their ruler. His dad is."

"Still!" Diana nearly shrieks. "Honestly, *none* of you dislike him?!"

Cameron raises his hand. "I find him very annoying."

Diana reaches over for a high five. "Thank you."

"Guys, should we really be dissing him when he's not here?" Peter says.

"It's fine to talk bad about him," Diana says. "Anyways, all of you know that I would talk about him straight to his face."

The room goes quiet, and Diana sinks further into the mattress, willing herself to fall through the floor. She peeks through the window and clenches her jaw when she sees the large sprawling castle grounds, just as grand and imposing as Diana had once imagined them to be. As soon as she thinks it, someone knocks, and a footman dressed in a uniform opens the door, motioning them into the hall with a gloved hand. They all gather in the hall, and Peter comes up to Diana and takes her arm, Cameron taking Kiara's, and they walk towards the stairs, their voices in hushed whispers as they examine the massive, gilded paintings on the walls.

"Ten bucks they're Leos," Cameron whispers to Peter, leaning across Kiara and Diana.

"Shut up," Peter whispers back. After a moment, he adds, "and no, they're Libras. We literally covered this, Cam. In multiple meetings, with *Congress.*"

They reach the stairs before Cameron can reply, and the group congregates on the ground floor to see the main hall flooded with ball guests. Staff members wait at another set of doors, and Diana realizes people are making *entrances*. Like formal, 'everybody look at me' entrances.

"Are you guys seeing what I'm seeing?" she asks. Everyone nods without looking away from the crowd of people. "Shit, I don't have a date, I'll have to walk in by myself."

Cameron grins. "Peter and I are going first. I *have* to see you girls' grand entrances."

The boys release the girls, and Peter offers his arm to Cameron, who grabs his hand and plants a kiss on his knuckles. He loops his elbow through Peter's arm, and they head towards the staff members by the doors, talking for a moment before taking their spots in the back of the line of people who are slowly entering the ballroom, one by one or pair by pair.

Kiara looks over at Diana. "You'll be great," she says. "I'm gonna go after them, and when you're in, find me."

"Why?" Diana asks.

"Because I'll be waiting with the biggest dessert I can find."

Diana grins. "Amazing."

She goes behind the boys, running her hand over her pulled-back curls. Diana takes a deep breath and looks around, admiring the lightness and medieval feel of the hall. It truly is beautiful, as much as she hates to admit it, with a large chandelier illuminating the room and causing sparks of light to dance across the shining surfaces. From the outside- and from the picture they received- it all looks much more ancient than it is. Diana glances back over at the line just to see Kiara disappear through the doors, and she curses under her breath and races to the staff members who are closing the large gilded doors behind her.

"Excuse me!" Diana shouts. "I need to get in there."

The first staffer raises an eyebrow. "Who might you be?"

Diana pauses for a second. "Huh?"

The two footmen don't seem perturbed. "Can we see your invitation?"

Diana rolls her eyes. "I'm Diana Monroe. President of New America."

They stare at her for a second, expressions unreadable, then pull the doors open. Diana can't see into the ballroom, because the doors lead to a balcony, with a staircase leading downwards, one set of stairs on either end of the railed balcony. Diana gulps as the music changes, a small orchestra barely visible in the corner of the ballroom.

"Any time now," one footman mumbles.

Diana nods, swallowing nervously, and as the song crescendos, she steps as confidently as she can out onto the balcony.

Part Thirty-Seven: The Libra

Lucas

Time: **6:54 PM**

Lucas grimaces as he slowly rubs his fingers over the scar on his arm.

"Ah, Christ," he huffs as the touch leaves pinpricks of pain in its wake. What Diana didn't know was that his power hurt her, but for some reason, it left him in achy pain as well. His theory was that hurting her hurt him in turn, although not nearly as bad.

Curse this stupid girl and their stupid connection.

"Prince Lucas?" someone asks, knocking on the door.

Lucas pulls his bedroom door open to reveal a footman, who glances at the prince's shirtless form and gruesome scar but says nothing, instead handing him the cufflinks Lucas had requested a half hour ago. "Are you... about ready for your entrance, sir?"

Lucas raises one eyebrow. "I have thirty minutes."

The footman stares at him blankly. "You have *six* minutes."

Lucas' eyes widen, and he slams the door in the footman's face before racing to his closet. "Shit, shit, shit," he whispers as he yanks out his suit with his left hand, his right hand clenched and immobile with anxiety.

He pulls on a button-down shirt, then throws on his suit jacket, stepping into his shoes as he buttons the undershirt.

He laces the shoes, shining in the reflection of the moon through his drawn curtains, then races into the bathroom, grabbing a comb with one hand and a toothbrush with the other. Once those tasks are badly completed, he runs out the door.

The footman is still waiting at the end of the hall, and he smiles as Lucas approaches. "Perfect quick change, Your Highness."

"Thanks," Lucas says sarcastically.

"Ready?"

"How much time do I have?"

"Two minutes." He points to Lucas' wrists. "Cufflinks."

Lucas secures them to his jacket with a glare and then takes off running down the hall, thumping down the stairs, unbuttoned jacket flying behind him.

He gets to the closed ballroom doors and swears again.

"Excuse me, anybody!" he shouts, the words echoing down the hall. A staff member appears in the doorway to the servant's entrance to the ballroom. "I have to get in."

The maid nods quickly, eyes wide, grabbing the attention of two footmen, who, as the muffled violins crescendo, pull the huge doors open.

Lucas smooths his hair, flattens his jacket, and steps onto the balcony.

Part Thirty-Eight: The Taurus

Diana

Time: <u>7:01 PM</u>

"Oh, my-" Diana mumbles, taking a large and extremely impolite sip of her drink.

Lucas Rutherland, Crown Prince of Alynthia, Heir to the King, is announced by an assistant of sorts with a big, booming voice. And he steps right out onto the balcony, a minute late, with his award-winning smile and designer outfit, although it looks slightly wrinkled from where Diana is standing, but maybe that's just the light.

He works his way down the stairs slowly, waving at certain nobles and grinning at others. Charm *radiates* off him, and Diana is momentarily blinded by envy.

And then his eyes get stuck on Diana.

He lands on the bottom step and looks her up and down, taking in every seam and stitch and making her fidget under his gaze. He pulls his lip between his teeth, smirking at her for the briefest of seconds before he gets swarmed by nobility.

Trying to ignore the wild thumping in her chest, Diana turns to her companions, who are staring at her, wide-eyed. "Don't," she says, passing her empty glass to a waiter and rubbing her wrists, which are piled high with bracelets. "Alright. Let's get this dance over with."

As she says it, the apparent lead pianist stands. "If we could begin the night with the traditional Alynthian group dance."

Waiters and various staff position the men in a large circle, spread around the room. Diana watches as

Peter and Cameron are positioned seven spots away from each other, just as they had practiced. She admires everyone's outfits as they walk by, all ballgowns and pressed suits and sparkling jewels. She's never seen anything like this in America, and she tries to ignore the panging thought that tells her she's incredibly out of place here.

"Ladies, if you would pick your partners," the pianist instructs.

A few straggling gazes land on Kiara and Diana, and Kiara squeezes Diana's hand. "All or nothing," she whispers.

Diana swallows nervously. "All or nothing."

Diana pushes her way into the inner circle, facing the men, glancing around to see that literally everyone is in the dance, even the two royals. Lucas looks away from Diana as they make fleeting eye contact.

She positions herself in front of Cameron, who smiles kindly at her. He looks sharp in his suit, and Diana can't help but smile back. "You've got this," he says. "Just remember the counts."

"Yes, sir," Diana says.

The music starts, and the pairs gravitate together. The dance was technical, sure, but also reliant on the partnerships, so it was easy to let Cameron guide her, since he was certainly the best dancer out of all of them. Diana's heart thumps in her chest as she remembers she'll be paired with a stranger for the final repeat of the combination, and she won't have Cameron's familiarity to calm her racing nerves.

Cameron spins her around, and Diana takes the time to breathe deep, allowing him to take the lead once more. The music picks up speed, and Cameron barely manages a frantic smile as Diana is spun towards her next partner. She spins once, twice, seven times, until she lands dizzily in front of Peter, who grabs her hands quickly and begins the combination from the start, lowering his voice to a whisper.

"Scale of one to ten?" he asks, breath tickling her ear.

"Four and a half," she replies. "I have no idea what I'm doing."

He chuckles. "One partner left."

She nods, and he pulls her close, a few moves out from the next rotation. They dance in silence, limbs winding around one other as if it were perfectly natural. Diana can feel a few eyes on her, and she grimaces as Peter releases her into a spin.

She turns with her eyes closed, counting until she freezes, opening her eyes to take in her final partner.

"Oh, no," she groans before she can stop herself.

Lucas sighs, his eyes nearly rolling to the top of his head. "Let's just finish this, Monroe."

He grabs her hands and yanks her, more aggressively than he probably should, up against his chest. She scowls, and he rolls his eyes, giving her hands a nearly undetectable squeeze.

Diana uses their momentum to spin herself around, so her back is flat against his chest. A low sound escapes his throat, and shivers run up Diana's spine as he pulls her even tighter against her, his hands flat against her navel. "I swear to God above, you are going to be the death of me."

Diana rolls her eyes, facing him once more, their bodies centimeters away, moving as one almost automatic unit. "Sometimes, I wish that were the case."

Lucas repeats the same move Peter and Cameron had, pulling Diana's left arm straight out and running his fingers from shoulder to wrist.

But when his hand passes over that scar, Diana can't help but shiver, and to her shock, Lucas does the exact same thing. With one quick movement, Lucas brings the pair chest-to-chest and eye-to-eye.

The music ends, however, neither one moves, instead staring into each other's eyes as the other couples break apart and scatter throughout the ballroom. Lucas' eyes flit to the neckline of Diana's dress, her chest rising and falling heavily, and Diana stares at his jawline, at the sweat beading near his shirt collar. Her fingers twitch by her side, as if wanting to move and wipe it off, but she keeps her hands to herself.

Finally, without another word, Diana turns on her heel and walks back to her friends.

Part Thirty-Nine: The Libra

Lucas

Time: **7:45 PM**

Lucas heads back to his father, plucking a bourbon off a passing tray, the singular ice cube rattling against the thick glass. As he approaches, Cornelius raises an eyebrow at his son.

"Promenading with the American?" he asks, his voice passive but with a cold edge, no different than usual.

"No," Lucas says, looking away from him in hopes he won't spy the color in his cheeks.

The king studies him for a second, and Lucas holds his gaze as long as he can before he fidgets uncomfortably. Cornelius nods, as if his son's discomfort is confirming something, and to Lucas' surprise, his father says the very last thing he'd expect. "Go talk to her. We need to present a united front if we're to gauge their alliance intentions. And besides, we can't have them telling anyone anything about George."

Lucas nods, biting his tongue against the snotty remark he wants to make as his fists clench by his sides. He heads over to Diana and her cronies, noting the way all of them raise an eyebrow simultaneously as he approaches, much like a threatened animal would raise its hackles. Cameron takes a protective step towards Diana, taking the hand of the skinny brunette boy next to him. Lucas glances towards Kiara, dressed in black, then quickly looks away. She's the scariest one, without a doubt, and her dark eyes mirror his own familiar guarded expression. Then he sets his eyes on Diana. Green is certainly her color, and her blonde hair matches the gold shoes and necklace she wears. Lucas notes her pearl-drop earrings, and the way they clash just slightly with the rest of her outfit. They *also* seem to be the same ones she wore during their photoshoot, and he hopes that none of these nobles realize she's rewearing jewelry.

"Monroe," Lucas says, bowing his head quickly, which he and the others know is actually the proper way to greet her.

The president smirks, and Lucas flushes at the fact that she definitely noticed he addressed her as he should. "Why the formality, Rutherland?" she asks sarcastically.

Lucas rolls his eyes. "Trust me, I wouldn't do this if my entire country weren't watching."

She looks around, as if she's noticing the crowd of people in the ballroom for the first time, most of which are glancing their way conspiratorially. Lucas clears his throat, and she finally looks back over at him.

"Could I offer you a dance?" he asks her, trying to keep a straight face.

Diana raises her eyebrows in a genuine vision of shock. "And why would you ask *me* when I have three perfectly fitting colleagues here?" she asks, motioning behind her to where her friends still loyally stand.

Lucas gives her a warning glare. "One. Because my father told me to. Two. Because you're the president, so it would not only look good for me, but for you as well, and three. Because of your colleagues, I unfortunately think *you're* the best looking one here," somewhat on purpose, it's hard to discern by his tone if he's joking or not.

"Wow," Cameron says, sounding mildly disappointed.

Kiara leans in to whisper to Diana. "Do it. He's right, it does look good for us."

Diana glances back at Lucas, and he holds out his hand. She scoffs, almost playfully, and takes it, letting him lead her to the center of the ballroom. The crowd has emptied out, leaving the space open, which is no doubt Lucas' father's doing, so all eyes will be on him and Diana. Lucas looks towards the band as they reach the center, hoping they'll strike up a traditional, fast-paced Alynthian song that will cover up the fact this girl probably hasn't danced a day in her life, especially not in a ballroom.

After a moment, when Lucas is sure *every* sorry eye is on them, he nods to the conductor, who opens the notes of a difficult- not to mention *long*- waltz.

"Shit," Lucas whispers to himself, drawing out the word.

Diana looks at him. "Worried about me stepping on your toes?" she asks with a lift of an eyebrow.

Lucas is in no mood for her sarcasm. "No," he says, voice flat. "I'm worried about how the hell I'm going to survive this four-minute waltz with *you*."

Her emerald eyes widen. "Four minutes?"

Lucas ignores her and lets the opening notes ring out before he bows to her, low and professional, without answering her question. Diana copies him, sinking into a deep curtsy before Lucas offers his hand.

She takes it, and Lucas pulls her slightly closer, letting his feet take the lead. After a minute of blind dancing, willing his eyes to go anywhere but her face, Lucas glances back down at Diana and sees she's looking right at him, so Lucas decides to hold her gaze.

When the violins crescendo, Lucas grips her hand and leads her across the floor, sensing her eyes on his face as he looks towards their feet. Lucas looks back up to her and she smiles gently, nodding as if she understands the basics of what they're supposed to be doing. Or maybe she understands something more, he can't be sure. After a few moments of classic waltzing, Lucas decides to trust her and lets go of her hand, sending up a prayer that she can follow. Lucas walks towards one end of the floor, away from her, and as the music continues underway, he turns back to her and notices she's on the other end of the ballroom, right where she's supposed to be. Lucas starts back towards her, trying and failing to hide a smile.

Part Forty: The Taurus

Diana

He's smiling, so Diana is definitely doing this right. When they reach each other again after their trek across the room, Diana's arms work as magnets and she instinctively reaches for Lucas. When he tugs her close again and Diana feels his breath ruffle her hair, her stomach flips and she relaxes against his chest. His fingers twine themselves in her hand, and Diana feels his other hand on the small of her back. Lucas shifts his head downwards as Diana looks up at him, and their cheeks graze against one another as they make eye contact.

"You want to do something cool?" he whispers.

Shivers ricochet down Diana's spine. "Yes," she whispers in response.

They're on the far side of the room, and the walls and crowd are a blur as Lucas picks Diana up with one arm. Her dress filters down around his legs, and he turns her in a long, graceful circle before setting her down.

Part Forty-One: The Libra

Lucas

When he puts Diana down and she resumes her position against his chest, Lucas' heart betrays his brain and leaps into his throat. Every single inch of him aches and he has to ignore the protruding thoughts as he starts his best attempt to wrap up the dance. Lucas guides Diana back to the center of the room and spins her so her back is against his chest, and they continue with the steps, but Lucas is well aware that he isn't fully present in the moment.

Diana leans further into him and Lucas is having trouble focusing.

Lucas turns her back around a few beats before he should've, and Diana definitely realizes. "What are you doing?" she whispers.

"Wrapping this up," Lucas says, a little too harshly.

Lucas readjusts his hands smoothly so he's holding one of hers and the other rests on her waist, and as the last few notes of the violin ring along the lofty ceilings, Lucas pulls her as close to him as he can, reveling in the heat of her body against his own. They come to a full stop in the middle of the room and although Lucas can hear raucous applause from somewhere, the pounding of their two hearts fills his head, and Lucas sees nothing beyond her bright eyes.

Part Forty-Two: The Taurus

Diana

Lucas's dark eyes cut into Diana's. Her chest is rising and falling heavily, and when she inhales, her chest presses against Lucas'. Diana's right hand is clutching Lucas' collar while her left hand is holding his tightly, and Lucas' left hand rests on her waist. When Diana notes its presence, a jolt of electricity shoots up her spine. They're mere inches apart, worlds away from the start of the dance, where she couldn't get farther from him.

Lucas is breathing just as hard as Diana is, and Diana can feel his chest rising under hers. "You're pretty good," he says, his voice husky.

"Thank you," Diana whispers, not breaking eye contact.

Lucas' eyes roam her face, searching in the depths of her eyes for something he apparently can't see on the surface. "My mother," he whispers.

Diana coughs awkwardly. "Uh, what?"

"That's why I'm named Lucas. My mother chose the name, she didn't like Cornelius, I guess. Lucas was her grandfather's name."

Something within Diana's ribcage hammers against her chest. He remembered her question from days, no, over a *week* ago.

"Oh," Diana says. "That... um, that makes sense."

Lucas opens his mouth to speak just as the room erupts in applause. He quickly breaks apart from Diana, swallowing hard, both hands curling into fists at his sides. He bows quickly, and she curtsies back before he disappears into the crowd without a parting glance.

Diana goes back to the others, and they welcome her with gaping mouths. Diana rolls her eyes, saying nothing, and instead snags water in a champagne flute off a tray and downs it in one gulp. She bends down and unclasps her heels, stepping out of them and motioning to Kiara.

"Sit with me?" Diana asks, pointing to one of the plush benches lining the back of the room. Kiara nods, and Cameron offers Peter his hand, whisking him out to the dance floor as the girls turn away from them.

Diana sits on the bench, where they're tucked off behind the set of columns. She rubs her bare feet while Kiara looks on.

"You guys looked good," she says, her voice lined with a hint of teasing.

"I just followed his lead," Diana responds, begrudgingly putting her shoes back on.

"That lift," she says plainly.

Diana turns towards her. "What about it?"

Kiara grins. "Nothing! You guys also didn't break eye contact like, the whole time."

Diana shakes her head. "Stop. No, I know what you're implying."

"I'm just saying, you didn't look like mortal enemies just then."

Diana looks back out to the dance floor, where Lucas is talking to a group of older women who are dressed like royalty. He glances Diana's way, taking a sip of his drink to hide the visible smile on his face, and shoots Diana a sly wink.

Diana smiles back instinctively, then turns back to Kiara. "I might have been wrong." She spares one more look at the prince, who has turned back to his conversation and is smiling that smile at each passerby.

Her next whisper is more to herself than Kiara. "He's surprised me."

A few hours later, Diana approaches a well-dressed, older man who looks very, *very* rich. She remembers from their studying that he's Mr. Kerrigan, the advisor of the Alynthian army. He smiles politely as Diana approaches, but she's wary nevertheless.

"Good evening, Mister Kerrigan," Diana says, greeting him with a small curtsy. He bows his head in response, turning to her.

"Evening, Miss Monroe," he replies, not even casting her a second glance.

"I wanted to talk to you briefly about a possible security-related partnership," Diana says, forcing a smile as other people around them edge closer, eager to overhear. "I was thinking-"

He cuts her off with a stark laugh that makes her jump a little. "I'm sorry, dear. Let me interrupt." He takes a step closer to Diana, and she's suddenly hyper-aware of the sheer amount of people in the room who are listening. "Why would I consider forming a partnership with *you*?"

"I-" Diana starts.

He waves a hand at her, lowering his voice. "No, I am single handedly responsible for creating the most powerful army in the world, of which survived your country destroying every other civilization around us. And now, your people have decided a seventeen-year-old is the best choice for a ruler, the same seventeen-year-old who has decided that making each of your rabid guards a 'police officer' will help anything," he grins at Diana. "Your sorry excuse for a country is not worth my time and money, and I will certainly be telling that much to the king." He leans ever closer, his tone cutting the air between them. "Your power is void here, Diana Monroe, and everyone knows it."

Her power.

Snickers rise up around them, and Diana gulps, wanting to respond, even *feeling* the words on her tongue, but instead, she feels her face flush and she turns on her heel to shove through the crowd. Even though there are just fifty people in the ballroom, the crowd is warmer, thicker, and more stifling than before.

Diana's chest tightens, and each inhale makes her heart beat faster.

Acid rises in her throat as she spots Lucas, his back turned towards her, stationed across the room and unaware of the confrontation.

Diana blinks back hot tears as she realizes that he would probably not even bother to help anyway. He was Alynthian, after all, and deep down, he was a Henderson, too.

Someone taps her on the shoulder, and Diana jumps in surprise.

She turns to see a barely-familiar man, wearing a well-pressed suit and a kind smile. He offers his hand after bowing his head. "President Monroe," he begins, voice soft. "May I offer you a dance?"

Diana glances around the ballroom, wondering why every person was looking at her as if she were a complete fool, acrid emotions bubbling in her chest. Every part of her wants to refuse, wants to leave this place and these people, and hide away forever.

But she smiles instead, that same smile she gives everyone these days.

"I'd be delighted."

She lets the man whisk her onto the dance floor amongst the other couples. He's younger, maybe a little under forty, with shorter hair and bright eyes, much unlike Lucas'.

He whispers low to her as they begin a simple waltz. "I figured you needed a little rescuing. Forgive me for interrupting."

"There's nothing to forgive," she says, finally exhaling with relief. "In fact, I should be thanking you."

"I'm Commander Josiah Maxon, commander of the navy," he says, pulling her a little closer but keeping his touch respectful and loose, which Diana is grateful for.

Diana nods, meeting his gaze. "I did think I knew you from somewhere. That woman in the blue gown, she's your wife, no?"

He smiles so wide Diana can't help but smile back. "Ah, yes, my Beth. My other half, as they say."

"I can tell you two are very much in love. Congratulations."

"Why thank you, Madam President," he replies, meeting the gaze of someone over her shoulder. Diana turns to look, but Maxon gracefully spins her out of view. "You know, Kerrigan always has been something of a fool," he mumbles.

Diana raises an eyebrow. "Sorry?"

He sighs, looking at her as if gauging her threat level. "Between you and I, know that Mister Kerrigan means well. He's a vital part of the monarchy, and he does good work with the army. However," he tilts his head in a joking manner that makes Diana chuckle. "He doesn't like to be threatened. You, Miss Monroe, are a threat, to put it plainly."

"What do you mean?"

"Well, Kerrigan is used to being one step ahead. He's used to being right beneath Cornelius and Lucas in terms of power, and then here you are. You do know he's Second Heir?"

Something pulls at Diana's brain, as if someone had given a single strand of hair a gentle tug. "I did not know that. Thank you for telling me."

He smiles again, and Diana can't help but wonder how someone so nice has survived in this cutthroat life of nobility for so long. As the dance ends, the pair moves apart, and Maxon bows low to her. "Thank you for the dance, Miss Monroe," he starts, lowering his voice so only Diana can hear. "Keep your chin up."

Diana nods, giving him a small yet genuine smile, and turns away, coming face-to-face with a snickering group of noble ladies, who are pointing her way and wearing matching expressions of cattiness.

It's as if everything Maxon told her, all that advice, everything she knows about manners goes out the window, and Diana feels her chest get tight again and the back of her eyes start to sting.

Maya wouldn't have gotten so upset, a familiar cloying voice whispers inside her head.

Looking around the ballroom, Diana notices a hallway opening to her left, and she hurries through the archway, racing down the hall as fast as she can. The marble floors drop off into a large, ancient-looking brick spiral staircase leading both upwards and downwards. Diana hurries up, liking the feel of the cool evening air that slips through the cracked brick on her hot face, liking the hollow sound of her heels against the stone stairs. She reaches the top, coming up to a set of wooden trapdoors, and shoves them upwards to rush up the last few stairs, realizing she's inside a tower room. There's a plush futon-style bench in the middle, sitting atop a Persian rug, and two large arching windows with old and weathered glass look out over the castle grounds. She crosses to that window, looking out at the dark, sprawling gardens and that massive willow tree, and starts to cry.

Part Forty-Three: The Libra

Lucas

Time: **9:13 PM**

Standing on the far side of the ballroom, closest to the band, Lucas and his father make the rounds.

It's a political schmoozefest, and Lucas couldn't hate it more.

Lucas admits he is a showstopper in front of cameras. People love pizazz, and they love charm even more, so give them both and you're a shoe-in for the front page. And it's all fine and dandy when you're talking to someone you never have to see again, but it's another matter entirely when you have to keep up the facade with the snotty nobility who think they're so much better than you.

He knows it sounds selfish, but seriously, he's the prince. They're the 'Lord of Whatever' who hasn't attended a single political function in ten years. There's obviously an authoritative divide here.

But Lucas sucks it up nonetheless, walking with his father and nursing the scotch he was handed about an hour ago that he's taken about two sips from. It's normal to marathon drink when you've got enough money to out-buy everyone here, apparently, and Lucas doesn't like *that* part of the nobility either.

"Your Highness, how are you?" Commander Maxon asks, bowing low to Lucas as he approaches with his father.

Lucas nods, allowing him to rise again. "I'm well. And you?"

He smiles. "Splendid." He turns to Lucas' father. "Good to see you again, Your Majesty. How is everything going with the naval plan I gave you?"

"Fine," his father affirms, always a man of few words.

An awkward silence falls over them, and Lucas takes a very improper, very large gulp of his drink as a quick flash of pain in his right hand makes him wince. Every passing minute, the drunken, gossiping nobles on the far side of the ballroom look more and more inviting.

A woman joins Maxon then, winding her way around his arm. She's tall, thin, and has dark curly hair pinned in a remarkably high bun atop her head. She's dressed appropriately, too: a huge, frilly blue ball gown, and she's not wearing a tiara, thankfully. That was quite the spectacle last year when the Lady Harrison wore a tiara, since they're only meant for ranks duchess and above, which Lucas was schooled extensively on as "review" after the incident took place. Maxon takes the woman's arm and smiles widely at her, and she has to be at *least* ten years younger than him. "Ah, everybody, this is Beth, my wife. Beth, say hello to the king and the Crown Prince."

Lucas feels a surge of satisfaction as he imagines Kerrigan's embarrassed face, accidentally calling her "Riley."

Beth, Lucas supposes, says nothing, and instead sinks into a deep curtsy, waiting until he nods for her to stand again. Poor Beth; woman must be something of a trophy wife to this man. "Thank you, Beth, it's a pleasure to meet you," Lucas says with a charming and totally fake smile.

"Well," Lucas' father says, shaking Maxon's hand and nodding to Beth. "We should be off. Thank you for your time and enjoy the night."

Commander Maxon grins, all big and blinding and white. "Of course, Your Majesty, Your Highness. Thank you for inviting us."

They turn and leave, walking together to the next group, across the room. Lucas hears raised voices in the corner but thinks nothing of it as he downs the rest of his drink, leaving it on the tray of a waiter who materializes out of nowhere.

Lucas' father glances at him out of the corner of his eye as Lucas deposits his empty glass. "Don't make a fool of yourself tonight, Lucas," he says, his voice holding a threatening edge. "Alcohol does that to a man."

"Father, you talk like I'm some raging drunk. That's my first drink, and the only reason I held onto it was because I didn't want to be rude when Lord August gave it to me."

Cornelius sneers. "All I'm saying is, don't abuse the fact that you're above everyone here."

Lucas rolls his eyes before he can stop himself. "Don't worry, I won't," Lucas says, words playing with a bit of sarcasm.

The king turns to Lucas and slows their pace, lowering his voice so only Lucas can hear. "Lucas, I'm not a fool. I know that you're going to try to crumble everything I have built over the past seventeen years when you become king. But at least *pretend* to be interested in politics for tonight, will you?"

Lucas scoffs. "What do you mean, 'crumble?' I've been nothing less than supportive of you throughout my whole life, even though you *lied* and kept things from me for years."

Cornelius gets right up close to Lucas and jabs a finger in his chest. "You're *weak* compared to us, Lucas. I know that, you know that, your *mother* knew that-"

"Don't bring mother into this-"

"Alynthia is a country brought about by *war*. And God save me if I'm going to let you destroy our armies, our navy, just because you feel like playing nice." His glare is cold and unloving. "Do you understand?"

Lucas swallows hard. "Yes," he says, his voice barely a whisper.

"Good," he says, scanning the room. He points towards the entrance after a tense moment. "Your great-aunt is over there. Go speak to her, and don't leave until you've ensured her husband's support when I pitch Commander Maxon's naval plan."

Lucas nods, leaving him, wondering if Diana is under the same amount of pressure as he is.

She probably is. Right?

Wait, why does he even care?

It's probably because his father told him he *should* care.

Lucas' whole body hopes for her presence against his will.

He takes a deep breath, straightens his posture, and walks over to his great-aunt, not bothering to look around for President Monroe.

She's got her own problems, he's sure.

Lucas turns away from his great-uncle a little while later and spies three out of four of the Americans on the other side of the room, with Diana suspiciously missing from that count. Lucas aches to take a minute for himself, and he knows the perfect place to sneak away to. There's a momentary lull in conversation, and takes that moment, that *true* gift from above, to excuse himself from his conversation with his great-aunt Millie, who Lucas only ever met once in his life and who is definitely *not* actually his great aunt. As he walks away, Lucas places his half-finished drink (his second one, because even his father can't keep him from trying to forget tonight) onto a passing tray, and then slips into the hallway as quietly as he can, heading for his astronomy tower.

When he reaches the top of the stairs, Lucas considers knocking, but as he raises his hand to rap his knuckles against the wooden trapdoor, he hears quiet sobs coming from above. Lucas' heart splinters as he connects the dots, his fingers clenching and unclenching at his sides.

"Oh, God, Monroe," he whispers to himself. "What in heaven's name are you doing to me?"

Lucas shoves the doors open before he can think, letting them fall back down behind him as he pushes into the room. They slam as they latch back into place, and Lucas grins sheepishly as a teary-eyed Diana turns around from her seat on the lounge.

She quickly jumps up, swiping at her eyes. "Ugh, Rutherland! Go away!" she grumbles, her voice thick with unshed tears.

Lucas speaks before he can stop himself, blurting out the first words that pop into his brain. "Enjoying the night?"

There's a beat of awkward silence, until Diana speaks. "You're such a jerk," she scoffs, voice thick, but she's starting to smile nonetheless, which means Lucas has done his duty.

Lucas softens when he notices her disheveled appearance, and he tries not to think about how long she's been up here, all on her own. "Hey," he says, trying to sound comforting. "What's wrong?"

Diana shakes her head, sitting back down on the lounge. Lucas sits next to her, keeping a few inches of space between them. "What do you care, anyway?" she asks bitterly. "All of the people in that ballroom are just out to humiliate me and my friends."

"If I wanted to humiliate you, I wouldn't have asked you for that dance," Lucas says, smiling teasingly at her and hoping she can't hear his heartbeat.

She sighs, puffing her cheeks, and smiles softly. "You've... got me there."

"I know."

Diana looks up at him, her green eyes searing in the dim light. For the hundredth time, Lucas notices her eyelashes are amazingly long.

His heart buffers like a drumbeat.

After a heavy moment of evident consideration, she speaks. Her voice is low, and it thrums through Lucas' whole body. "You must hate me," she whispers, her voice breaking.

Lucas is caught off-guard for a moment. "What makes you think that?" He leans back against the couch, crossing his arms over his chest.

Diana shrugs, setting her mouth in a tight line, leaning back, and mimicking Lucas' crossed arms. He tries to ignore the clench in his stomach as his eyes trace her body out of instinct. "I... don't know."

When she looks at Lucas out of the corner of her eye, something crackles between them. "We *should* hate each other," Lucas replies, daring to hold her gaze. "That's what everyone else thinks." There was something both cathartic and terrifying about this moment: balancing on the precipice of danger.

Diana turns her whole body towards Lucas, and he turns to face her as well, closing another hair of space between them. "Something about you is-"

Lucas interrupts, and the two speak at once. "Different."

Diana smiles, like he'd just seen inside her brain. "Exactly."

They simultaneously turn away from each other, sharing matching, dopey grins. Her hands fidget in the folds of her dress, and Lucas scans the whole of the room, looking anywhere but at her because he doesn't know if he'd be able to *stop himself* if he looks at her face one more time. His heart thumps in his chest, a mixture of adrenaline and... something else.

Something new.

Or maybe something that had been there the whole time that both had just tried to ignore.

They settle into a positively electric silence.

After a second, and without looking at Lucas, Diana clears her throat and whispers, "Rutherland."

Her voice is soft and husky, and it sets Lucas' nerves on edge, sends his heartbeat into overdrive.

Lucas turns to face her, and she's still staring straight ahead. Her chest rises in a long, heavy breath, and she glances at Lucas out of the corner of her eye, expression filled with ache and wanting. He presumes that she saw a similar emotion in him.

Lucas raises one eyebrow, and she answers with the slightest nod.

It's enough of an invitation for him.

Both of them move like magnets, hands and legs and mouths connecting in a frenzied kiss as Diana moves to straddle Lucas' lap and he grabs her face with his hands, her fingers finding their way to the nape of his neck, sending shivers ricocheting down his spine. Heat floods Lucas' neck and face, and he realizes in a sudden flash that all he's wanted to do up until this moment was to hold her, to *kiss* her, just like this.

He's kissing the president. Holy shit, *he's kissing* Diana Monroe.

Lucas pulls away first, his hands still cupping her cheeks and hers gripping the collar of his shirt. "Monroe," he says, fleetingly leaning his forehead against hers as they breathe together in tandem. "I'm sorry, I should've, like, actually *asked*-"

Diana pulls back from him, eyes roaming his face, and shakes her head with a chuckle. "Rutherland, you're seriously the most idiotic person I've ever met."

She leans forward before Lucas can reply and kisses him again, harder this time, more insistent. Lucas pulls her against him, smiling against her lips, and pulls himself away from her mouth to kiss her collarbone. She leans into the contact, pressing a kiss to Lucas' temple as he pulls her chin towards him once again. Pulling away for the briefest moment, Diana gazes down at him with an unreadable expression, her hands on Lucas' face and her chest rising and falling heavily in unison with his.

Overwhelmed completely, Lucas whispers the first two words that come to mind. "You're stunning," he says, admiring the way the dim light casts a halo of warmth around her golden hair.

Diana meets his gaze and smiles gently. "Now *that's* the nicest thing you've said to me."

Lucas chuckles, shaking his head before looking back up at her. He can't take his eyes off her face, off her *everything*. "There's a lot more where that came from, Monroe, if you'd just believe me when I said it."

She leans down and kisses him slowly, setting his body alight. When she pulls back, she smirks at him. "I'll try."

Lucas grins, her face mere inches from his. "And that is all I ask of you."

Diana shoves his shoulder playfully, rolling off his lap so they're seated thigh-to-thigh. When she speaks, her voice is a whisper, and Lucas wonders if she meant to talk aloud. "I can't believe this."

Lucas says nothing, instead taking her hand and flipping it palm-side-up. He kisses the heel of her palm, then lowers her hand and slowly traces the initials *LR* on the middle of her palm with his index finger. "I don't know if I believe it either."

She smiles gently. "That's... understandable." Gently, she pulls her hand away, and Lucas wonders if she grazes each of his fingers on purpose. "What will people say?"

They sit in silence for a minute. "Does it matter?" Lucas asks, looking over at her.

Diana shrugs, smiling at him somewhat sadly. "For us, yes."

Lucas smiles back, and this time, it's not that fraudulent, magazine-cover smile, it's a lopsided grin that is entirely real and makes Diana want to kiss him again. "Maybe it doesn't have to matter."

Her smile fades until it's merely a wisp, and her expression turns pensive. Pensive, but content, as her eyes roam Lucas' face. "Nothing, for now?"

Lucas leans forward slowly, and she meets him halfway, their lips meeting in one more passionate kiss. He gazes into her light eyes after they move away. "You're not nothing. You'll never be nothing."

Lucas gets up to leave, and when he reaches the trapdoors, he turns back around to face her. "Bugger off, darling," Lucas whispers to her.

Diana's face breaks into a stunning grin. "Pound sand," she whispers back.

Part Forty-Four: The Taurus

Diana

Time: **9:45 PM**

After taking a couple (more like a thousand) deep breaths, alone in the astronomy tower, Diana straightens her dress and goes back down to the ballroom.

A crowd has gathered in a huge circle around the orchestra, where the string players have moved aside to make room for a large grand piano. The string players are seated to the side of it, and the bench remains empty.

Suddenly, Cornelius Rutherland emerges from the throngs of people. He claps his hands together and smiles at everyone, an unfamiliar gesture that makes Diana more than a little uncomfortable as she watches George Henderson's smile appear for a moment.

"Lucas?" he booms across the crowd. "Where's my son?"

The crowd parts a bit to reveal the prince, and Diana notices that although his clothes are fixed and straight, his dark hair is ruffled and slightly askew, a stark difference from his put-together look from earlier.

Diana's stomach does cartwheels as she remembers running her fingers through that hair.

Lucas steps forwards sheepishly, and Cornelius claps him on the shoulder. "Lucas," he starts, guiding him to the piano, "play the *Liebestraum*."

Lucas sits reluctantly, swallows, and turns to the violinist. "Sorry, darling," he says, just loud enough to hear. "Is it okay if I play something?"

The woman smiles, setting down her violin. "Go right ahead," she says, as if she had any *other* option.

Lucas rests his hands on the keys, takes a long breath, and launches into a song. His hands fly nimbly over the keys, and Diana watches the way his body moves with the music. Every so often, he closes his eyes, letting himself be completely lost in the piece.

He's really good, actually.

Diana weaves through the crowd, pushing through until she spots Cameron's red hair. They're all standing with the king, conversing in whispered tones and staring at Lucas.

Cornelius spots Diana as she approaches, and Diana curtsies quickly to him. He smiles softly, politely, and motions to Lucas. "Good, is he not?"

Diana glances towards the piano but not exactly at Lucas. "He's great. How long has he been playing?"

"Since he could sit up on his own," Cornelius responds. Something in his face is almost melancholy, almost sad, almost longing.

Diana clears her throat awkwardly and nods in Lucas' direction. "What's this song called?"

Cornelius glances at her and furrows his eyebrows, as if he *guessed* that the teenage American kids *wouldn't* know a classical piano piece. "Ah, the *Liebestraum.* A Franz Liszt piece, composed in 1850."

Peter pipes up from where he's standing behind them. "And what does *Liebestraum* translate to?"

Cornelius smiles politely at him. "It's German, I believe. It means 'Love Dream.'"

Well, shit.

The song crescendos, and Lucas' hands fly up the keyboard, a beautiful run of notes that clash ever so slightly with each other. As he closes his eyes and leans into the instrument, playing with such passion, Diana could feel the room collectively holding its breath, herself included.

She finds herself staring at his hands, and the way they seem to just *know* where to go. The confidence he radiates over the rest of the ballroom is apparent in the way he expresses the emotion of the song, the frenzy, the brokenness.

Diana swallows hard, clearing her throat and refocusing on the boy seated there as he wraps up the song and the room erupts into applause. The squirrely-looking man seated by the cello leans over to him and shouts over the noise. "Your Highness, do you know any Beethoven?"

Lucas considers for a moment, turns back around, and begins a new song, one Diana *actually* recognizes this time.

Cornelius does too. "*Fur Elise,*" he groans quietly. "He plays this one so much, he could do it with his eyes closed by the time he was ten."

Diana smiles in Lucas' direction, ignoring the king. Lucas is playing with ease, and any idiot could tell that this song was a favorite of his. Diana could see it in his smile, the same real one she had seen so fleetingly in the tower. Every single detail about him, everything she sees in front of her is perfect. Just tonight, Diana had seen a completely different prince than the one she met before. And she *likes* this version- she likes this version a lot. And the best part was that she thinks he likes her too.

A memory pangs in the back of her brain without warning.

"Take your seats, everyone," the teacher says as they file into the assembly room. "We're here to listen to the concert, so please do so quietly and respectfully."

The kids all sit as a class, and Diana waves as Peter splits off to sit with his grade, a year above her own, as she slides into a seat next to Kiara.

"Maya's over there," she whispers, pointing over the crowd to the front of the room.

Diana follows her finger until she spots Maya's blonde hair, sitting closest to the aisle in the front row. She's fidgeting nervously, and she's slouched low in her seat. A blonde boy next to her quietly clutches her hand, and she squeezes it gratefully.

The gathered schoolchildren hush, and the person on stage starts playing a song on the piano. The teacher leans across the row, whispering to the kids and motioning to the pianist. "This is called Fur Elise, by Beethoven," she turns back around to face the stage.

They sit in silence, watching the nimble fingers of the pianist fly over the keys. Suddenly, a door at the back of the room slams open, and every head turns as two guards stalk in.

The piano continues to play as someone in the front row stands.

The piano continues to play as a girl walks down the aisle, head held high to show the tears rolling down her cheeks.

The piano continues to play as she stops in front of Diana's chair. "I love you," she whispers, "and I promise that I'll see you soon."

The piano continues to play as she walks through the doors, out of the assembly hall, and into the clutches of the waiting guards.

Diana shakes her head as she allows herself to push Maya out of her mind, blinking to clear the tears from her eyes as Lucas swims into focus again. Chest constricting, Diana realizes that any minute, any moment, Lucas could be ripped from her the same way Maya was, whether it was the time eight years ago or the one six months ago. She could fly home next week and never see him again, or his father might forbid their alliance and force the pair to turn against one another. Or worse, one of them might hurt the other with their power, whether it be an accident or not.

She can't watch that. She can't *live* that. She can't lose him too.

As Lucas finishes the song, Diana watches his eyes roam the crowd, looking for someone- looking for her- and she turns away quickly, grabbing the arm of a passing butler. "Excuse me," Diana whispers, her voice thick. "Would you mind showing me to my room?"

Part Forty-Five: The Libra

Lucas

Time: **9:10 AM**

The morning after royal events are the worst. Cleanup staff are everywhere, everyone smells like expensive booze and perfume, and Lucas' father is always more than a little grumpy.

"Father, no," Lucas says, trying to keep from sounding whiny. "When am I ever going to have to *fight* someone? Isn't that what our bodyguards are for?"

Lucas quickens his pace to keep up with the king as he marches down the empty hallway. His footsteps echo around the high ceilings, and their reflections shine in the freshly-polished tile floors. Lucas groans as he doesn't slow down, and he stops where he is and shouts, "Could you listen?!"

Cornelius spins on his heel so fast Lucas flinches, and the king paces quickly over to him, grabbing his arm roughly. "Lucas Friederike Damian Rutherland-"

Lucas cringes,

"-I will *not* allow you to make a mockery of Alynthia. And trust me when I tell you, son, you're well on your way of doing so." He releases Lucas with a shove. "You and those Americans will train with our guards, and you will do so without argument. Your first class is at ten." He looks around, as if to ensure again that no one watched him break character, then back at his son. "*Do not be late.*"

Without another word, he turns and walks back the way he came, leaving Lucas standing in the hallway alone to feel that familiar ache.

"Lucas, keep up, darling," his mother says as Lucas hurries down the hall to catch up with her. She stops and turns around, her face breaking into a huge grin, kneeling down and allowing Lucas to rush into her arms and nestle his face in the lacy fabric of her royal gown. It's the one she wore for her coronation after she married his father, and she's wearing it again now.

For Lucas' coronation.

Queen Anastasia reaches up and straightens the newly-made crown on his head, kissing her son on the cheek. She pulls back to look at Lucas, and she smiles kindly as she straightens all the royal regalia pinned to his small uniform jacket. She stands, curtsying low to him.

"All hail Prince Lucas Rutherland," she says, grinning proudly and wiping at a lone tear. "I'm very proud of you, my little prince. This is a big responsibility for a ten-year-old, but I know you can handle it."

Lucas nods, happy to make her proud. Her bodyguard comes up behind her, and she turns to greet him. "Murphy, how are you?" she asks, the smile still playing on her painted lips.

He just nods, and she smiles, glancing quickly towards Lucas. "Is something the matter?"

Murphy glances at the prince before clearing his throat. "We've decided to put in place Operation Alynthian Cliffs."

Lucas' mother's eyes widen in fear, and she glances around. Lucas doesn't know what Murphy is talking about, but it's scaring his mother, which means he doesn't like it.

"Where were they located?" she whispers, her face twisted into a neutral look.

"At the prince's coronation. We believe he's the target," Murphy responds, lowering his voice to match the pitch of his mother's.

"Follow me please, Murphy," the queen says, taking Lucas' hand in a vice-like grip and marching down the hall towards his chambers. When they reach the door to Lucas' room, he goes to open it, but Murphy catches his wrist and aggressively tugs Lucas away from the door.

"Your Highness, do not touch anything. And stay in front of me, please," he says, his voice laced with fear. Lucas nods and complies, positioning himself in front of him and continuing to follow his mother down the hall. They reach a spiral staircase that leads up to the astronomy tower, and his mother points to the part of the staircase that leads down, down to the aqueducts below the castle, filled with tunnels just big enough for small rowboats to get through.

"Go, Lucas. Down there, quickly. If your father is there, go to him. If not, find a boat and follow the tunnel until you see the sunlight. Go around the back of the cliffs, far enough so the castle is out of view," she leans down and hugs Lucas, her white skirts swishing around his legs. "I love you so much, my darling little prince."

Lucas wants to protest, to bring her with him, but another bodyguard appears, taking the lead and beckoning for Lucas to follow him into the darkness below. Murphy waits with his mother, and she nods to Lucas as he catches her eye.

"I love you, mother," Lucas says, allowing himself to follow orders and trail the guard down the stairs. As they walk, Lucas hears snippets of Murphy's conversation with his mother echo off the walls.

"They have intent to kill..."

"In the palace for a week now…"

"Prince's bedroom during the night, and around the castle throughout the day…"

They reach the aqueduct tunnel, deep underground, stretching in either direction as far as Lucas can see. The tunnel is lit by lanterns, and inside are two more guards plus Lucas' father, also still dressed in his coronation outfit.

Lucas waits, fists clenched, for someone to bring his mother down, but he's ushered towards a small wooden rowboat with a lantern sitting on the seat. Lucas boards with his guard, allowing the prince to sit behind him, like a shield, and his father and his two guards board after Lucas as he waits for the door to open and his mother to walk through.

They wait in silence for one agonizing second, then two.

The handle turns, and the door is pushed open.

Lucas' mother is on the other side, her eyes wide and her mouth frozen in a scream. When the door opens all the way, her hand slips from the handle and she falls forward, putting the bloodied back of her white lace dress into view.

Plunged through her back is the royal sword Lucas was just crowned with.

Lucas opens his mouth to scream, but his bodyguard clamps his hand over his mouth as another pushes away from the concrete ledge and deeper into the tunnel, leaving his mother face-down on the boarding platform, alone.

Lucas looks at his father, but he's staring at his wife with guilt etched into his features. Then, he looks at Lucas, his frown twisting into a scowl as he shakes his head and turns away, giving the two guards stationed at the oars one quick order.

"Faster," he commands.

They're rowed down the tunnel, plunging Lucas' world into darkness.

Lucas pulls black shorts over his legs, running a hand through his damp hair and toweling it off one more time. He rings for his guard, who escorts Lucas to the training center in the east wing of Willowood, the one that nobody uses. Lucas much preferred running on the castle grounds or lifting weights in his room rather than sitting alone in the gym. On the walk down, Lucas silently drills himself on the Americans, wondering if his hangover-induced fog would allow him to remember their names and if his Diana-induced daydream would allow him to remember his manners. Kiara and Peter are already there when Lucas arrives, and Peter is dressed almost the same as Lucas, black shorts and no shirt, while Kiara is in a white tank top and red leggings. Both are in sneakers, and they're talking to each other in hushed voices. Lucas' guard goes to confer with the trainer at the front of the gym, and Lucas stands by himself until the two of them approach him.

"Your Highness," Peter says, the phrase sounding forced and apprehensive.

"Just Lucas is fine," he responds, bending down to tie his shoe in order to give his hands something to do and not bothering to look at them.

Kiara pipes up from above him. "Care to tell us why servants burst into our rooms this morning to tell us we had to go to fight training at ten?"

Lucas stands and rolls his eyes. He dislikes her the most, even more than he used to dislike Monroe, which speaks volumes. "Your guess is as good as mine."

She opens her mouth to retort when the doors open to reveal Diana and Cameron. He tries to greet her, but the sight of Diana doesn't help his brain in a futile attempt to process words. Diana is in a gray cropped t-shirt and black leggings, and her hair is pulled into a ponytail. Lucas notes that her flyaways are sticking out like usual, and he wonders if she even tries to tame them anymore. Cameron is dressed exactly the same as him and Peter, so there must have been some kind of message sent out at some point that Lucas must not remember receiving.

Cameron crosses to Peter and Kiara, planting a quick kiss on Peter's lips, the sight sending a shiver up Lucas' spine as he remembers his meeting with Diana in the astronomy tower. Lucas turns to look at her, her friends clustered a short distance behind him, and he realizes she's staring at him, so Lucas takes her in, swallowing hard, as his face gets hot.

Christ, what is happening to him?

Lucas remembers her friends are here, and he resists every urge to touch her flyaway hair or the gap between her shirt and waistband. But before Lucas can say anything to her, she brushes past him and approaches Kiara instead.

For a moment, Lucas wonders if he made up the entirety of last night and she still hates his guts, but the sight of her this close- and the way it makes him blush- makes him realize it was real. But then why is he being ignored?

Lucas turns to face the four of them, but he stops when he sees the matching stares he's getting from all of them except Peter, who's smiling apologetically as if saying sorry for some unspoken argument. Lucas wants to say something, say *anything*, but the trainer speaks up from the front of the room.

"Hello, everyone. My name is Leon." He's a big, burly guy, dressed in workout clothes that match Peter, Cameron, and Lucas, except he's got a shirt on, thankfully. "I want to start with some questions about each of you. And I will not refer to you all as 'Your Highness' or 'President.' You're all my students here." He turns to the prince. "Lucas, what do all five of you have in common?"

Lucas swallows and looks around the room, studying each face in turn. What *do* they all have in common? "Um," Lucas starts. "We're all teenagers?"

Leon shakes his head. "Yes, but that's not what I meant. You five are arguably the most important people in the *world*. Diana, you're the president of one of two remaining nations; Lucas, only heir to a throne; Cameron and Peter, adorned with magical powers; and Kiara, you ran the world's biggest antagonist out of your capital all on your own."

Lucas looks around at the others and sees them doing the same. It's like they're all seeing each other in a new light, one that makes them different people than they were before, and Lucas feels a shiver run down the back of his neck.

Leon turns to Kiara. "Who's the most important person in the world to you?" he asks.

She responds instantly. "These three."

He nods. "And the one person you want dead?"

The rest of them blink, wondering where he's going with this interrogation. Kiara grits her teeth, and her expression turns stony. Lucas tries and fails to imagine how rebels must have felt when facing her down in the American Revolt. "The old Aries leader. *If* I had to pick."

Leon nods. "George Henderson."

"You know him?" Kiara asks. Lucas wonders why she didn't just use his name, if she'd known it the whole time. He also can't help but feel a little conflicted at her answer and a little guilt at the same time.

Leon nods again. "Of course, everyone does. He practically ran the American government for the past couple decades." Without missing a beat, he turns to Cameron. "Cameron, is it? Okay, what's one goal you have for New America when you return from Alynthia?"

Cameron thinks for a minute. "The Integration. I want everyone together."

Leon nods, then moves on. "Peter, what scared you the most during the revolt?"

Peter takes a deep breath. "When I looked around and couldn't find Cam."

Peter and Cameron share an affectionate look and Leon nods, a smile playing on his face, as he turns to Diana. "And Diana, who did you lose during the revolt?"

Diana sucks in a sharp breath. "What?"

Leon asks again. "Who did you lose?" Lucas doesn't fail to note how the others received broader questions while Diana's was quite literal.

"I..." Diana trails off, blinking rapidly and shaking her head. She glances over at Lucas and then looks away quickly, and Lucas suspects he's not in on whatever secret is about to be spilled. "My sister."

The room is quiet, and Lucas' whole body aches, itching to hold her hand, knowing exactly what she's feeling- that sickening twisting pain in the bottom of your stomach- but he resists and instead looks over at her. She's looking at the ground, and she takes a deep breath before steeling her shoulders and looking back at Leon. "Why do you ask?" she asks him. Her voice barely wavers, and Lucas is momentarily jealous of her strength.

Leon smiles. "Because I want you all to tap into this hope, and fear, and grief, so you can become better fighters. So, we're going to start out with a little test. Kiara, I hear you're quite the fighter already. If you'd join me up here, please."

Kiara steps towards him, and as soon as she's within his reach, he lunges forward with incredible speed and swings a strong right hook towards her jaw. She reaches out her arm in front of her face, expertly blocking the hit, and brings her knee up into his pelvis as Leon doubles over with a laugh. "Brilliant, Kiara." She smiles and stands next to him, and he turns to the remaining four. "The rest of you are going to be partnered up."

"Why?" Diana asks. "Why can't we learn from you, or like, use a mirror or something?"

"Because, Diana," Leon says. "Each of you in a fighting situation will probably have different targets, no?" He turns to the prince again. "Lucas, who is most likely to try and attack you, the prince of a powerful kingdom?"

Lucas thinks for a second until the answer hits him like a brick. "An assassin," he answers grimly, glancing around the room instinctively to make sure no one else was lurking.

Leon nods. "And Diana, who is most likely to attack the young president of a budding new nation?"

Diana cuts Lucas a glare and answers coldly. "An assassin."

"Correct," Leon says cheerfully. "So, therefore, you two will be partners and learn more tactful moves to fight an assassin, while the boys will learn to hone their powers a little more." He levels a stern gaze at the prince and the president. "Next time, I'll just need the two of you." He points towards their arms, which Diana promptly crosses over her chest. "Interesting scars you two have. An awful lot like Peter and Cameron's."

Lucas looks at Diana, who's glaring at him out of the corner of her eye. He winks at her and the glare softens, but her arms are still crossed over her bare stomach and her lips are set in a tight line. Leon claps his hand, motioning for them to get closer.

"Peter and Cameron, back up. Diana and Lucas, shake hands, bow and curtsy, whatever. Show me what you've got, but don't actually hit or injure each other. Lucas, you play the attacker, Diana, protect yourself."

Diana sticks her hand out, and Lucas shakes it, giving it a gentle squeeze, but she doesn't seem to notice. They stand on two Xs marked with tape on the mats in the center of the room and take fighting stances. Leon shouts for them to go, and Lucas bounces forward to throw a punch at her. She barely steps back in time, but soon regains her footing as they circle each other.

"Come on, Monroe," Lucas says tauntingly. "Hit me." She scowls, and his face falls. "What's going on? Did I do somethi-"

Diana cuts him off with a sharp jab towards his neck. Lucas grabs her fist and shoves it away from him, but she recovers quickly, kicking at his left knee and grabbing his shoulder when he starts to tumble. Lucas thinks she's going to steady him, but instead she grabs his right arm, immobilizing it, and pushes Lucas with all her might. He stumbles and loses his footing, toppling to the ground, and Diana's eyes widen as she rushes over to where Lucas has quickly curled in on himself, trying to catch his breath.

"Rutherland, I'm so sorry-" she begins.

"What was that for?!" Lucas practically yells. "He said not to actually hurt me!"

"I know, I didn't..." she stops when her voice breaks. "I didn't mean to."

"Yeah, well, you did," Lucas says, turning to Leon. "Could I be excused to go get some ice?"

Leon nods. "Diana, spar with Kiara for the rest of class."

Diana nods, watching him leave. As the doors close, Lucas gets a glimpse of her guilt-stricken face, and he feels a pang of empathy that's soon covered up by sheer dizziness. With a sigh, Lucas turns his back on her and the training center as he heads down the hall to his room.

Part Forty-Six: The Taurus

Diana

Time: **11:00 AM**

"I'm such a jerk," Diana says, stepping backwards to avoid Kiara's kick.

"It's fine, he'll live," she says, following Diana's movement and twisting her around to put her in a headlock.

Diana doesn't fight back, instead, she raises her arm in the signal Leon gave them as a surrender, and Kiara slackens her grip, turning Diana around to face her. "It's just, after the ball and everything else..."

Kiara stops and looks at her. "What do you mean, 'everything else?'"

Diana blinks at her, and she feels a sudden guilt, as if she'd done something wrong. She tries to ignore the chilling sound of Henderson's voice in her head. "Nothing. I just thought we might get along better after the ball."

Kiara gets back on her X, motioning for Diana to do the same, but Diana waves her away. "I need water." She raises her hand to get Leon's attention. "Leon, can I go to the kitchen and get a drink?"

"Sure," Leon responds. He turns to the boys, who are locked in a heated-but-still-safe spar. "Actually, everyone can go for today. Good work." Diana turns to leave with the rest of the group, but Leon pulls her aside. "Diana," he says. "Make sure to go and check up on the prince."

Diana nods, wondering if he knew something she didn't. She leaves the training center, promising the others she would join them before their meeting that afternoon, then gets water and heads to her guest room. She changes into sweatpants and a baggy tee shirt laid out conveniently for her, and gets into bed, but after a moment of trying and failing to relax, she rolls over, facing the French doors leading to the balcony. She thinks about the training, the ball, and then Diana's mind inevitably wanders to Lucas. He looked so upset when she pushed him, and she really, honestly didn't mean for him to get hurt. Maya drifts into her mind like she always does when the world goes quiet like this, and after a moment, Lucas' face replaces Maya's, and Diana's brain reaches the same conclusion it did the night of the ball.

You can't lose him too.

For some reason, the people around Diana were always getting hurt, and most of the time, she was the reason why. Her actions caused them harm, and she was at a loss at how to stop it.

Diana is jolted from her thoughts when the door to her room opens, and without rolling over, she knows who it is by their careful footfalls. She keeps her eyes open but slows her breathing, hoping he'll think she's asleep.

Diana feels his weight on the vacant side of the large bed. There's a tense moment of silence, and then he sighs, and she can tell he sees right through her.

"Why are you mad at me?" Lucas asks.

Diana stays there for a moment, perfectly still, until she feels his hands grip her hips and roll her around to face him. She's busted, and Lucas raises an eyebrow when they make eye contact.

"Who says I'm mad?" Diana responds flatly.

Lucas scoffs, his cold demeanor from the ball back in a flash. "You pushed me to the ground completely unprompted." In the lazy, late-morning light, Diana can see the side of his cheeks are flushed red. He notices her gaze and puts his fingers over his face gently. "Now I have to explain to my father how I got beat up by the president of our rival country."

Diana laughs at this, and Lucas grins before it slips away and his expression changes back into a frown, and he puts his hand on her calf, still snuggled under the blankets. "Hey," he says, "please talk to me. It hurts to see you upset."

Diana frowns too but says nothing. She's too stuck in her own thoughts.

"If you don't want to be with me, please just say so, so I can get on with my life," he says, tilting his head in a sort-of-teasing-sort-of-genuine pout.

"I..." Diana starts, looking up at him. "I've been thinking about you a lot."

He smiles a little. "Me too." Diana tries to ignore how those two words make her feel.

Diana rolls onto her back, looking up at the high ceilings. Sometimes even being in this colossal room isn't enough to make it feel real. "And I've been thinking about Maya."

Lucas's face twists in confusion. "Who's Maya?"

Diana frowns at the ceiling. "My sister."

He nods, putting the pieces together. "The one who passed in the revolt. The fountain..." Diana nods, saying nothing, but Lucas notices the way her eyes begin to shine. He looks at her out of the corner of his eye after a moment, and in a flash, his shoes are off, his shirt is off, and he's sliding under the covers next to her.

"Rutherland!" Diana gasps. "What are you doing?"

Lucas smiles at her, all big and boyish. "It's not fair that you're the only one who gets to be cozy."

Diana groans halfheartedly but lets him snuggle in about two feet away from her. They're both lying on their backs, looking up at the ceiling, with nothing but their elbows touching, and after a few moments of silence, he speaks.

"I lost someone a few years back."

Diana turns to look at him, but he's still staring straight up. "Your mother?" she asks. She thinks back to that night in his apartment, the hot tingling of the mug in her hands just as vivid as the grief-stricken face of the prince who used to be a stranger.

He doesn't move a muscle. "Seven years ago."

Diana remembers and nods, looking away from him, because if she looks at him, she's worried that she'll feel too much- maybe even regret. "Do you want to talk about it now?"

Lucas shrugs, and she can't tell if he's pretending to be nonchalant or if he actually felt that way. "It was the night of my coronation when I was ten. Her guard said that we needed to leave, that assassins had been hiding in the palace for over a week, ready to target me." He looks at Diana out of the corner of his eye. "They were hiding in my bedroom the whole week, and they slipped right under our noses."

"Rutherland, I-"

He's not done. "And so we went into the evacuation dock, located-" he pauses, "actually, I can't *legally* tell you where it's located, but my father and I waited for my mother and after a second, someone- the assassins probably- pushed her body through the door." He flinches. "My father just gave them the order to row us out of there, and we didn't return until the danger was gone and she was too."

The room falls silent, and Diana props herself up on her elbow and looks down at him. He looks goofy from this perspective, and the put-together prince from last night, all decked out in his royal garb, is gone. He's replaced by this tan-skinned, dark-haired teenager, looking up at her through his dark eyes, his chin just slightly doubled from the angle he's lying at. Diana decides she likes this version of Lucas Rutherland much better.

His face gets serious again. "I moved rooms shortly after. I couldn't stand being in my old one. I was terrified, especially because we never found out who sent the assassins after me in the first place."

Diana nods. "Well, that's understandable, you were ten." She looks around. "How did they get into your room, anyways?"

He talks without missing a beat, his eyes locked on Diana's. "The guards think they grappled up the balcony and came through the French doors that led onto the veranda."

Diana stares at him, and then her eyes get wide with realization as she glances towards the French doors on the opposite wall. "Rutherland!" she gasps, her voice lowering in a panicked whisper. "I've been sleeping in here alone for days!"

Lucas nods as if he understands her fear. "I can't even come in here on my own."

She studies him. "You did when you came in just now, though."

He looks at her, his face filled with seriosity and something else Diana can't quite place. "Because I knew you were in here." He looks away from her, but his right arm, the one closest to Diana, relaxes a little and he unclenches his fist. Diana hadn't even noticed his fingers were furled until that moment. "I, um, have a lot of scarring on my palms. I clench my fists when I get anxious." Diana catches a glimpse of the white-pink scars, and her breath catches in her throat. "I only started doing that after my mother died. I know it's a bad habit, but..."

"But sometimes it's impossible to stop," Diana whispers. Slowly, gently, she sits up, and Lucas follows suit. She takes his hand in hers, running the very tips of her thumbs across the scarring on his palm.

Lucas swallows, and his fingers curl slightly, making an electric contact with her thumb. "Exactly. Um, I never really struggled with my anxiety until then. Sometimes, I wish that my mother was still alive, because she's the only one who would be able to understand," he chuckles sadly. "She'd know what to do."

Diana smiles a little, flopping back down onto her back and shoving her worry for him out of her gut with a sigh. "I guess it's my turn to talk, huh?" He nods. Diana doesn't see him do it, but she feels it against the pillow. She squeezes her eyes shut, taking herself back to that day, the one she tries so hard to avoid. "She was fighting, we all were. Peter put a border around her, and Cam, without knowing, dropped it when he fell by accident. The guard who meant to shoot Cam shot her instead, right in the stomach." Diana pauses, swallowing hard. "There was nothing I could do. So, they gave me her power, even though I'm a Taurus." It goes quiet again, and before he can speak, she rushes her next words out. "I tried to push you away because I know how dangerous our lives are, *especially* with these powers. I mean, you were targeted by assassins as a ten-year-old. I don't want to get close to you and then lose you too. There's too many variables, too much that could go wrong. When I left the ball last night, all I could think about was how Maya... she wouldn't have ran away."

Lucas is quiet, then after a few agonizing seconds, he speaks. "You didn't run, though. You... you reassessed. You recalculated. That's who you are, Monroe. You're smart."

Diana wills her cheeks not to burn, and she shrugs. "Well, not really, I-"

"-I said last night that you need to start believing me when I compliment you."

She sighs. "I remember."

"Good. Because *my* Monroe is all those things I just said."

Diana bites the inside of her cheek to keep from smiling. "Yours, huh?"

Lucas doesn't respond, but his eyes darken the way they did in the astronomy tower for one fleeting second. "Can I tell you a story my mother used to tell me?"

"Sure."

He turns to face Diana, and she turns to look at him too. His gaze travels her face before he speaks. "Once upon a time, there was a scientist. A crazy one, who everyone thought was just totally bonkers."

"These are your mother's words?" Diana asks with a grin.

"Shut up, Monroe. I'm paraphrasing." He shakes his head with a smile before continuing. "Anyways, the villagers told the scientist that unless he could come up with a cure for a deadly disease that had been killing the townspeople, they would banish him. So, the scientist decided to research the disease, because he obviously wanted to stay in the village. Then he found out that the disease was incurable, unless someone ate a specific flower, called a 'rossom blossom,'" he smiles at the rhyme. "The flower was incredibly poisonous, and no one who ate it had lived to tell the tale. The scientist debated with himself, knowing that leaving the village would be easier than risking the citizens lives by using this dangerous plant. There were too many variables to risk it." He looks pointedly at Diana.

"What did he do?" Diana asks, slightly embarrassed at the way she was hanging on his every word.

"He decided he would test it on himself. If it worked, it worked, and he'd get to stay and help more people. If he died, at least he wouldn't have to live all on his own." He frowns slightly at the thought of being all alone, with no one to turn to. "So, he purposely infected himself, then he ate the blossom."

"And?" Diana whispers.

"And... I don't know," he confides. His dark eyes get cloudy, like a thunderstorm in the middle of the night. "Mother never got to finish telling me."

Diana nods slowly, processing his words. "So, what's your point?"

Lucas props himself on one elbow, and Diana does the same. "My point is that he took the risk. He took the risk not only for his own good, but to help those around him." He eyes Diana's right hand, splayed on the white sheet between them. "He didn't want to be alone."

"No one *wants* to be alone," Diana responds.

Lucas watches her for a moment, and the two share a similar look as they did after their waltz. Finally, he smiles sadly. "I guess you're right." He gets out of bed, pulling his shirt back on, and as he heads for the door, he looks back over at Diana. "I'll be around, if you need me." He can't hide his smirk. "Icing my ribs, probably."

Before Diana can respond, the Crown Prince leaves her room, shutting the door gently behind him.

Part Forty-Seven: The Scorpio

Cameron

Time: <u>12:55 PM</u>

Cameron is walking down the hall towards his room when he hears a door shut behind him.

He turns to see Lucas gently closing the door to *Diana's* room.

He watches as Lucas puts a gentle palm on the door, leaning his forehead against his hand and closing his eyes. After a stalker-esque moment, Cameron raises an eyebrow and clears his throat.

"*Ohmygod-*" Lucas spins around and smiles. "Secretary O'Connor, hello."

Cameron doesn't fail to notice the way the prince jumps a little and slowly shuffles away from Diana's door. "What are you doing?"

Lucas rubs the back of his neck. "I, uh, was trying to get Miss Monroe to meet with me before the conference later, but she was sleeping. So, I guess I'll just talk to her after the meeting with my father."

Cameron nods slowly and shrugs. "Well, I have to head that way anyhow. You can walk with me, if you want."

"Perfect," Lucas says hurriedly, jogging to catch up with Cameron. As they walk in silence down the hall, Cameron notices Peter's door is open, and as he glances inside the empty room, he sees that Peter's favorite book is sitting out on his bed, bent back at the cover to hold its place.

"One second," Cameron says, huffing. Peter *always* leaves his books like this when he's in a hurry. He enters the room, crosses to the book on the bed, and pulls his handkerchief out of his back pocket, folding it into a small square. Like routine, he sticks it into the marked page and closes the book, leaving it neat on Peter's nightstand.

Cameron leaves, shutting the door behind him, and rejoins Lucas.

After a long moment, Lucas speaks. "Secretary Simon seems like the person to do that often."

"Huh?" Cameron asks, glancing at the prince out of the corner of his eye.

Lucas shrugs. "It isn't necessarily a bad thing. But he's always doing *something*, and as someone who also enjoys reading but never has time for it, let's just say I break the spines on my books more often than I should."

Cameron smiles despite himself. "He... is certainly lacking in the bookmark department."

Lucas smiles back and nods, and the two fall into a more comfortable silence than last time.

They reach the meeting room, at the very end of the hall, and Lucas tries the handle. It doesn't budge, and the prince groans. "Early. Father hasn't unlocked it yet."

Cameron shrugs. "That's okay." He glances around at the empty, echoey castle. "Got any ideas on how to kill some time?"

Lucas thinks for a second. "Garden?"

The pair heads through the ballroom to the veranda doors. Lucas pushes them open, and the boys seat themselves under the balcony overhang at a well-kept table. Around them are sprawling lawns that extend into a garden of trees, hedges, and flowers.

"It's so nice out here," Cameron says, surveying the land.

Lucas nods, seemingly pleased with the comment. "I've tried to have our staff keep it up as best they can, especially now that it's getting a bit colder."

"What, your dad doesn't do that stuff?"

Lucas looks sad for a moment, but his face quickly softens into his usual neutral facade. "No. He doesn't quite care for the gardens as much as me and my- as much as I do."

Cameron nods, opening his mouth to say something else, when something small and blue lands on the table.

Cameron's mouth drops open, and Lucas follows his shocked gaze. After a moment, Lucas bursts out laughing.

Cameron tears his gaze away from the... *thing* for a brief moment to see the prince absolutely losing it. "What the hell *is* that?!" Cameron whisper-shrieks.

Lucas wipes his eyes, snorting with laughter. "A bird."

"A *what?!*"

"A bird. A blue jay, to be exact."

Cameron studies the creature perched on the edge of the table. It's small, and blue, as Lucas' supplied name suggests, with little feet and wings. Cameron tilts his head and the bird does the same. "What does it do?"

Now it's Lucas' turn to look shocked. "What the hell do you mean?"

"What is its purpose?"

"It's... just a bird."

"Well, I *know* that now, but what does it do? Is it like the bees?"

"It flies, I guess? Nests? I don't know; they're all over here."

"Really?!"

Lucas chuckles. "You're acting like you've never seen a bird before."

"I *haven't.*"

Lucas turns slowly to face Cameron. "Never?"

"No! I wouldn't have asked if I knew what it was!"

Lucas shakes his head, turning the information over in his head. "Okay, well, you... you *do* know what an animal is, right?"

Cameron scoffs as the bird begins wandering about the cobblestoned veranda, pecking at crumbs. "Obviously. But we were only shown pictures of the important ones, like cats and horses and stuff," he glances at the prince. "And I know bees."

"Okay, so basically, a bird can fly. And there are a bunch of different kinds of them. Some are big, some are small, and some are different colors, too. They eat crumbs and stuff. Bugs and plants too, I guess," he pauses, thinking. "This is super hard to explain. Okay, they make nests. And lay eggs."

"Eggs?"

"Baby birds hatch out of eggs."

"Woah."

"Wild, I know. Anyways, that's basically it. We get a lot of blue jays here, so sometimes, the staff sprinkles seeds out to feed them when it starts to get cold, so they have food for winter."

Cameron smiles. "That's... really nice."

Lucas smiles gently. "My mother told me that blue jays are signs of protection and selflessness. If you see one around, it means there's someone looking out for you."

The redheaded boy chuckles softly, never taking his eye off the bird flitting around. "Who would be looking out for you?" He motions to the jay. "This bird here. Who is it?"

Lucas swallows as he thinks over the question, then turns to Cameron. "Not sure," he lies. "Who's looking out for you?"

"Someone... dead?"

"...Yeah."

The other boy replies immediately. "Maya, then."

Lucas nods, leans back in his chair, and folds his hands over his chest. He wonders just how big of a hole Maya's loss put in this group but speaks before he can come to an answer. "I've always loved birds. It's a shame you never got to see them."

Cameron shrugs one shoulder, glancing at Lucas out of the corner of his eye. "They aren't the only animal I've missed out on, I guess."

Lucas glances at him as the bird flies off, headed towards the palace's namesake willow tree in the garden. "Do you... not have animals in America?"

"Not anymore."

"Well, what happened to all of them?"

Cameron shrugs. "Some ran off to other places when the weather and air started to change because of the Destruction. Most just died during the battles. Radiation, smoke, fires, the works. And house pets, like dogs, were killed and eaten when things started getting bad. Eventually, we had none left. They couldn't keep themselves alive."

Lucas frowns. "That's so sad."

"Yeah," Cameron says, nodding. "I kind of wish we did have animals. It would be nice to know that the country could sustain them again."

"Well, you guys are fixing things. Bees are back."

Cameron chuckles. "Thanks to you guys."

"Evolution does crazy things." Lucas nudges Cameron gently with his elbow. "Should you ever need any more, Alynthia has a pretty good-sized bounty of woodland creatures, as you well know."

Cameron chuckles. "I might just get Di to take you up on that."

Lucas laughs, and then gets serious again. "Wait, have you ever seen a dog?"

"No," Cameron says, sort of tuning out the conversation as he watches the jay flit from tree to tree. "A picture, when I was super young. But never in person."

Lucas nods, smiling to himself ever-so-slightly. "Gotcha."

Cameron doesn't respond, instead glancing at his left wrist, the one with the fancy watch, to check the time. He stands and brushes himself off. "Meeting time?"

"Meeting time," Lucas responds, rising to his feet, "although I'd say you learned more just now than you will in any government meeting."

Cameron laughs as the two boys re-enter the castle.

Part Forty-Eight: The Aries

Kiara

Time: **2:09 PM**

"You're late," Kiara whispers to Diana as she sits down next to her.

"Sorry," Diana whispers back. "I was taking a nap and forgot to set an alarm."

"You do remember what we talked about?" Kiara whispers.

Diana nods conspiratorially. "Of course."

They're seated in a big conference room, around a circular table that's probably older than Barbara Oswald. Diana sits in between Kiara and Cameron, Peter is on Kiara's other side, and Lucas walks through the door to take his seat next to Cameron, who's shrugging off his jacket. Diana suspects he must've been late as well.

"Afternoon, everyone," he says with a smile, sliding into his chair. He nods to Cameron on his right. "Long time no see, Mister O'Connor."

Cameron smiles at him. "Just Cameron is fine."

Lucas smiles as his father enters with another semi-familiar man. "Everyone, this is Mister Kerrigan, Head of the Alynthian Army," Cornelius says as he takes his seat next to his son and Kerrigan sits to Peter's right. "He's going to be discussing an alliance with us today."

"And Second Heir to the King," Kerrigan adds with a forced chuckle, casting Lucas a much too obvious glare.

Kiara feels like causing problems, and she already dislikes this middle-aged upstart. "What exactly does that mean?" she asks innocently, batting her lashes dramatically.

Kerrigan, unsurprisingly, doesn't seem to realize that she's being completely satirical. "Well, should His Highness Prince Lucas be unable to take the position of sovereign, I'll do it," he says, slamming a hand onto the table with a forced guffaw. "Isn't that right, Lucas?"

Lucas' lips are set in a tight line, and Kerrigan would have to be a complete fool to miss the murderous look in his dark eyes. "That's 'Your Highness,' thank you."

Kerrigan ignores the boy, instead steepling his hands and staring Kiara down. "Kiara, is that right?" he asks.

Kiara nods. "Yes, why?"

"No last name?" he asks, looking at her with an over-exaggerated expression of confusion.

Kiara bites back a snide remark and shakes her head. "In our country, they don't tell us our last names."

Both the king and Mr. Kerrigan look mildly disturbed. "Oh," Kerrigan says awkwardly. "Well, no matter. It obviously doesn't seem to affect anything you do publicly."

Before Kiara can respond to the underhanded insult, Kerrigan pulls out a leather-bound folio, leafing through the pages until he finds the one he's looking for, which he rips out and slides over the table to Kiara. It's an itemized list of agreements, along with a spot at the bottom for a signature, one she's seen before thanks to Diana's sleuthing.

Kiara clears her throat and prepares to lie. "What is this?"

Kerrigan grins triumphantly. "Well, if your leader forges an alliance with Alynthia, I'd like to buy you out of your duties. I mean, what does a Citizens' Liaison even do? I can find someone from Alynthia to cover that position, and you can head a section of my army." He shoots her an unnerving grin. "You'd be the first female to ever hold an Alynthian Command."

The table falls quiet. "So," Kiara begins, her voice never wavering. "You want me to resign?"

Kerrigan leans back in his chair. "Well, yes, but you'd receive a large sum of money for doing so."

Kiara looks over the list again, noting some of the more... *radical* requests.

> *Don't speak of your previous duties to anyone, noble or common man.*
> *Should Mr. Kerrigan ask, any and all confidential files will be released to him.*
> *An official resignation speech must be made upon your return to New America.*

Kiara looks back up at him, sliding the paper back across the table. With a deep breath, she sits up straighter, forcing herself to eke out a little more confidence. "I'm interested."

"Kiara-" Peter starts, voice shocked.

"It's Kiara's choice," Diana says, voice warning and her stern look focused on Peter.

Kerrigan looks hungry, like he's about to snap up a prize. "Is the money giving you hesitation? I can up the ante, give you two million instead of-"

Kiara shakes her head, cutting him off. "No. I'll do it for the money you've already offered."

Everyone, even the king, looks completely shocked. Diana, however, just has a small smile on her face, as if Kiara hadn't just betrayed her and their entire country.

"Kiara, *what* are you doing?" Cameron asks. Kiara turns to him, and her heart breaks slightly at how hurt he looks. "You can't just *leave*."

Kiara swallows, fighting the sudden urge to cry. "I can, though."

"Ki," Peter says, sounding almost angry. "Why didn't you say anything?"

She shrugs, knowing if she spoke she'd probably crack. Diana speaks instead. "Peter, I know you're hurt-"

"-And you aren't?" he replies.

Diana continues as if she didn't hear him. "But Kiara has to be the one to choose what's best for her career," as if she got the final say in the matter, she turns to Cornelius. "I believe next we should discuss the alliance?"

The king clears his throat awkwardly. "Yes." He turns to Diana. "Unfortunately, as much as your friends and yourself have made a good impression here in Alynthia, I have yet to see anything of note that would make your country a valuable asset besides the bringing of Kiara onto our team."

Diana looks confused, and she opens her mouth to speak when Lucas interrupts. "Father, I don't think it's a bad idea. We're the only two countries left, so why wouldn't we ensure peace?"

"Well, Lucas, that's just the thing," Cornelius smiles menacingly. "Should things come to blows, we don't want to be stuck in a peace agreement."

Kiara doesn't fail to note the triumphant smile on Mr. Kerrigan's face, and she can practically hear his words coming from the king's mouth.

"So you're *planning* to attack us somewhere down the road?" Cameron interjects. Kiara bets that the anger that was for her was now being redirected to the king.

"I never said that. I'm simply wanting to ensure that we don't end up reconsidering later on down the line," the king replies, waving his hand in a so-so manner, "and besides, the only other thing that could bind our two countries is a marriage alliance, and that will *never* happen."

Lucas and Diana make a small, strangled choking sound simultaneously, which Diana hides behind a nonchalant hand to her mouth and Lucas turns into a coughing fit.

"Well," Kiara supplies as the prince is quickly handed a glass of water by a waiting servant, "if we're having a disagreement, and things get bad enough for a declaration of war, couldn't we just rewrite the agreement?"

"That would take months of legal action," Cornelius says. "It's easier to just be civil now, and remove the legal binding."

Peter turns to Diana. "What do you think? If you propose something today that says we'll be civil for say, three years, and Cornelius signs it before we leave, that gives us a little more moving room if it comes to a war declaration."

Diana turns her head down towards her portfolio, and Kiara glances up quickly to catch the prince staring intently at the top of her head. She looks up, straight at Cornelius. "I don't *want* this 'civil agreement.' Actually," she pulls a thick stack of papers from her binder and shoves it towards the king. "This is a document proposing a *formal* alliance. And I'm going to give you until the end of our time here to sign it. If you do, we've officially aligned our two countries, and if you'd like to declare war, which we have no intention of doing the same to you, then you can go back on the document. And yes, you'll have to wait for the 'legal action,' because *this* agreement won't be undone with a snap of your fingers." She raises one eyebrow and leans back in her chair. "Sound good?"

The room falls silent, and Peter leans over to Kiara. "I didn't know she even *wrote* an alliance proposal."

Kiara smirks, eyes trained on Diana. "Neither did I," she lies.

Cornelius flips through the paperwork, then pushes it off to Lucas. "Read this," he demands through gritted teeth.

Lucas glances at Diana before clearing his throat and reading out loud. "This alliance is legally binding, and therefore proclamations, instigations, or threats of war will not be tolerated unless both parties have agreed to terminate the alliance." He looks over at his father. "Why does this matter?"

"Because," Cornelius snarls, "she's got us in checkmate."

Diana nods. "Yes, you're right." She stands up behind her chair, pacing the room. "Should you sign on, you won't *ever* be able to declare war unless we-" she motions to the other Americans in the room, "-agree to it. Of course, Alynthia is a powerful nation, and I'm almost positive that you must know your military is significantly larger than ours. But, if you don't sign, you don't get any of the benefits of our alliance."

Kerrigan snorts. "Like what?"

Diana considers, tilting her head to the side a little dramatically. "Agriculture, for one. When was the last time Alynthia was able to trade for farmed goods, again?"

"Increased trade networks," Cameron adds with a smirk.

"Private security benefits," Peter states, quirking an eyebrow.

"And you've got me." Kiara deals the final blow.

Kerrigan and Cornelius clamp their mouths shut.

Finally, Cornelius sighs. "Well, what about Lucas? When he's king, does he have to terminate the alliance should he want to declare war as well, or does it reset as soon as I'm done ruling?"

"He won't declare war," Diana says at the same time Lucas says, "I won't declare war."

The two share a barely detectable look.

After a second, Diana clears her throat. "Well, I'll let you think about it. The document requires yours and Lucas' signature, because he's next in line for the crown." She grabs her binder and taps the back of Peter and Cameron's chairs. "Let's go."

As they head for the door, Diana pivots on her heel and faces the prince. "Your Highness, would you want to join us for dinner?"

Lucas smiles as Cornelius stands. "I don't think so, I need to speak to my son-"

"Actually, Father, I think I'm going to go with them," Lucas says, grinning at the king. "I'll see you later."

Part Forty-Nine: The Taurus

Diana

Time: **3:23 PM**

Diana and Kiara meet in Diana's bedroom later that afternoon.

"I hated that," Kiara mumbles as she enters, shutting and locking the door behind her. "The boys are furious. They've barely even looked at me all afternoon."

"I know, and I'm sorry," Diana says, rising from her perch at the foot of the bed and embracing Kiara, "but this is the only way to keep you on the inside."

Kiara runs her hands over her face. "I feel like this isn't a good idea."

The pair sits up by the bed's plush pillows, and Diana pulls out a box of chocolates from under one of the throw blankets. "For comfort," she says with a chuckle.

Both girls sit shoulder-to-shoulder, picking through the box as Diana explains. "Okay, so since the ball, I've had a bad feeling about Mister Kerrigan. I think he knows about all the powers, and his whole 'Second Heir' act is-"

"-Really freaking weird?" Kiara finishes, mouth full.

"Really freaking weird," Diana confirms. "But I can't investigate alone, and they don't like me. So, *I* can't be snooping around in their castle or else they'll completely ice us out."

"How'd you get them to offer me the army job?"

Diana shrugs, chewing and swallowing before speaking again. "I think they already wanted to poach one of you, and they weren't about to trifle with powers they know nothing about, so I made sure that they saw you as an asset." She glances Kiara's way apprehensively. "And I trust you."

"More than the boys?" Kiara's tone sounds like something near disbelief.

Diana tilts her head in a so-so manner. "The boys need each other, and that's fine. But I need someone right now who will handle this with discretion and tact, and I can't have Cam and Peter doing that together. Besides, they'd never agree to staying here."

Kiara puts down the other half of the sweet she'd picked up, suddenly feeling nauseous. She snuggles into Diana's pillows, and Diana notices the way her hand flies to her scarred arm. "I wish it didn't have to come to this."

"Ki, you don't have to do this if you don't want to."

"No," she protests. "I already said yes. And I *do* want to help, in any way possible." She looks at Diana out of the corner of her eye. "But Di, why do you care so much about all this?"

Diana opens her mouth to respond, but no response comes to mind. After a long pause, she shrugs. "I don't really know, but some part of me does care," she replies finally. "No matter what that part is."

Kiara nods, seemingly satisfied enough with that answer. The two girls share a look, one full of hope and grief and every emotion in between, and finally, Kiara breaks the silence. With a lopsided smile and a quick move to pick up the half-eaten box of chocolates, she gives Diana a nudge. "Let's polish these off, yeah?"

Part Fifty: The Libra

Lucas

Time: <u>7:30 PM</u>

Lucas is led by the hand through a pitch-black palace hall.

He's shaking, but not from the cold.

All he can see in his head is his mother's body, her powdered face forever screaming.

She'd *always* believed that Death came when it was supposed to.

But this? This was too early.

He hadn't seen his father either, not since they'd returned to the palace after their evacuation. The assassins had been caught, and it was safe for his two guards, including Murphy, to bring him back to his bedroom.

"Murphy," Lucas whimpers, feeling foolish to be holding the man's strong hand at the old age of ten. "I don't want to stay in that room anymore."

The guard seems exhausted, and guilty, which Lucas recognizes because he feels the same. "We can arrange for you to move to a new room, Your Highness. First, we need to do one thing."

Lucas doesn't have time to ask what that thing is, because he's ushered into the Westing Room, where another guard and an unfamiliar doctor await. On the large table is a needle, and a vial with a blue liquid and a few ruby drops of blood.

"Murphy-" Lucas starts, voice rising in fear.

He's interrupted by the new guard, the one standing with the doctor, moving closer and grabbing him by his *skinny arms. He kicks and thrashes, but to no avail, as the doctor moves closer with a long syringe that glints in the evening sunset.*

"Stop!" Lucas screams, too many emotions to name flooding his body, the most primary being violent grief, "Father, help!"

"Hush, Your Highness," the doctor says, moving closer with a wicked grin. "This will be painless."

He doesn't get to ask what's happening, because the needle is pushed into the crook of his elbow, and two breaths later, the young prince is completely unconscious.

"I'm *panicked*, is what I am!" Lucas whisper-shouts.

"Okay, calm down," Cameron says from his seat.

The five teenagers are seated in the garden, spread out around a latticed metal table, waiting for the dinner gong. Lucas is up and pacing the cobblestoned veranda, whereas the Americans are all sitting comfortably with the tea and biscuits they had been served.

"I literally cannot calm down," Lucas replies, borderline snapping at him. "My father is going to bring it up and I'm going to have to tell him. He's going to find out we've been working together somehow."

"Jeez, Rutherland," Diana groans. "Just tell him you didn't say anything to us."

"And how do I explain *this?*" Lucas wails, yanking up his sleeve to show his jagged, spider-web like scars.

Kiara cuts him off. "Okay, so that *might* be a problem."

"Where is the king now?" Peter asks, turning to Diana.

She swallows the sip of tea she had taken and shrugs. "I don't know. We'll have to talk to other palace staff."

Lucas' eyes widen considerably at her tranquility. "So *do* that, please!" He feels a sharp sting of pain from his hands and reminds himself to unclench his fists.

"Stop being such a drama queen! I will! You need to calm yourself for *five* minutes and let me do my job," the president replies, although she doesn't meet Lucas' gaze.

Lucas huffs and plops into the only open seat, which happens to be next to Diana. The two share a very blatant look before Cameron interjects.

"Lucas, what's the deal with that Kerrigan guy?"

The prince rolls his eyes. "Oh, you mean Mister Lawrence Kerrigan, Second Heir to the King?" he scoffs, his hands in fists under the table as he fights his flaring temper. "He's quite literally the worst. My father's right-hand."

"Why is he so... awful?" Peter asks.

Lucas shrugs. "He's always around, somewhere. Even when my mother was alive, he was still the next person, after me. I'm surprised that the bastard hasn't tried to kill me just to take my place in the line of succession."

"When do we go home next?" Diana asks, changing the subject after sharing a barely-noticeable look with Kiara.

Peter thinks for a moment, scratching his finger across the tabletop. "We're supposed to check in with Barbara in the Capitol in two days. So we'll fly out tomorrow afternoon, probably."

"If you guys need help packing," Kiara begins gently, "I'm around."

Cameron shakes his head, and it seems as though a little anger has subsided. "I can't believe you're staying."

Kiara begins to speak when Peter interrupts, setting a hand on Cameron's arm. "Hey, it's fine," he says, voice even. "It's what she needs to do for her career."

Everyone nods awkwardly as Lucas looks around at all of them in turn, and his chest aches against his will when he thinks about how quiet the castle will be without this full, rambunctious group of Americans. Out of the corner of his eye, he sees Diana uncross her legs under the table, and he realizes he's fighting a hot feeling throughout his whole body as his gaze traces up her leg. Slowly, looking around to make sure none of the others see, Lucas reaches over and places his hand on her thigh.

He watches as she looks down first, noting his presence, and then she glances at him out of the corner of her eye. Lucas' fingers squeeze ever-so-slightly, and Diana's lips part as she sucks in a sharp breath. The hair on the back of his neck stands up at the heat in her gaze, and very quickly, Diana rises to her feet, pulling Lucas with her by his arm.

"If you'd excuse us for one second," she says hurriedly. She begins to head for the door, Lucas' wrist clutched in her grip, when Kiara interrupts.

"Where are you two going?"

Lucas and Diana glance at each other as she drops Lucas' arm, and Diana turns back to Kiara with a stiff smile. "The prince and I made a meeting with the band from the ball. I wanted to arrange them to play for Barbara's birthday, and he said he'd introduce me."

She books it towards the door, walking at the speed of light and once again dragging Lucas with her. They disappear through the veranda doors, leaving Peter,

Kiara, and Cameron sitting at the table, more than a little confused.

Peter and Kiara shrug it off, resuming their conversation, but Cameron smirks as he remembers that Barbara's birthday is months from then.

Back in the hall, Lucas is dragged by Diana through the castle. "Where are you taking-"

"Shut up, please."

They reach a door, a small one, that Lucas knows leads to a broom closet. "Why are we-"

He's cut off again by Diana practically shoving him through the door. "Please be quiet."

They enter the cramped, dark room, and Diana shuts the door behind them. Before Lucas can say anything, she grabs him by the arms and pulls him towards her, covering his mouth with hers.

Lucas swallows the words rising in his throat and smiles.

After a long moment, Lucas pulls away. As he speaks, he runs his hands up and down Diana's sides. "So, you wanted to get away from *them* to be alone with *me*?" he asks teasingly.

She looks up at him from under those long lashes and Lucas fights to keep his eyes from wandering. "What, you're not happy about it?"

He kisses her again, hard enough that she gasps, and pulls back just enough to whisper, "Who said I wasn't happy?"

Diana pulls him in for another searing kiss, gripping Lucas' arms and tugging him flush against her hips. Lucas pulls away, planting kisses on her jaw and neck, and her fingers work their way through his hair as their chests rise and fall in unison. The way Diana's manicured nails tug at his hair makes Lucas' brain short-circuit and all he can think about is kissing her harder.

"Rutherland," Diana whispers, pulling his chin up to look at her. He studies her face, her eyes. She's gorgeous, and he can't think of anything past that.

"What?" he whispers back, running his fingers through the hair hanging past her ears.

"I..." she trails off, looking down at the floor. After a moment, she glances up again, making searing eye contact with him. "I don't want to leave tomorrow."

Something besides lust burns in Lucas' chest and he kisses her again. She parts her lips and sighs, and he lifts up her shirt just enough so that his fingertips brush the small of her back. He leans his forehead against hers, and when he speaks, he realizes he means his words sincerely. "I don't want you to leave tomorrow, either."

She smiles gently, running her thumb across his cheek. It's a more subtle show of affection than the ones they've shared before, but it makes Lucas' heart pound all the same. "I guess we knew we'd have to go at some point, right?"

Lucas shrugs, kissing her temple and looking back at her. "It's not like we won't see each other again."

"Yeah, well, not for a while."

Lucas smirks and pushes further into her, causing her breath to catch in her throat. "What, sad that you won't have someone to pull into broom closets?"

Diana quickly regains her composure and smirks. "Not even that. Just sad I won't have *you.*"

Lucas swallows, his breath escaping in a shaky sigh. "You have no idea what that means."

Part Fifty-One: The Cancer

Peter

Time: **8:27 PM**

"Is everything arranged?" Peter asks as he and Kiara pace down the hall. Diana and Lucas had disappeared, so it was just the two of them on this little stakeout.

"I think so," she replies, holding a folder to her chest. "Decorations, music, venue."

Peter nods as the pair reach the end of the hallway and begins to climb the spiral staircase there. "How did Diana find this place, anyways?"

Kiara shrugs. "Dunno. Probably just exploring, or something."

Something about that doesn't quite sit right to Peter, but he nods nonetheless. "Uh-huh. And where is Cam right now?"

Kiara glances at him out of the corner of her eye as Peter focuses on unlatching the wooden trapdoor above his head, the rough wood scratching his hands. "Jeez, Peter. Any other questions from you?"

Peter chuckles. "I just want to make sure everything is perfect." He steps into the tower room and offers Kiara a hand, shooting her a grin. "Besides, who doesn't like a good party?"

Peter is caught off-guard a few moments after he leaves Kiara by Diana, who grabs his arm and yanks him into her room.

Before he can voice his surprise, she shuts the door with a gentle thud and points towards her bed. "Sit," she commands, using her president voice and making Peter comply instantly.

"Di, what's going on?" he asks, crossing his arms as he notices her turbulent expression. "Is everything alright?"

"I need to confess something," she mumbles, not meeting his gaze as she begins to pace back and forth across the floor.

Peter's heart batters nervously but he ignores it. "Alright?"

After a deep breath and a few more anxious trips across the floor, Diana stops, slowly meeting Peter's gaze. Her dark lashes accentuate her downturned expression, her lips pulled into a frown and her forehead creased. "Kiara and I have a plan." Before he can say anything, she continues. "She's staying here to investigate the royals, not to work for the army."

Peter can't help himself; his eyes grow wide and his mouth falls open. "What?"

She nods, running a hand through her hair. "I think that the assassination of the queen was intentional, and I think it was someone on the inside here."

Peter shakes his head, letting out a scoff of disbelief. "Kerrigan."

She nods. "Exactly. He knows more than he's letting on, and if we want to make an attempt on the prince's plan, he needs to be out of the way."

"You *have* to make sure nobody is hurt," Peter says evenly, refusing to take his eyes off his friend. "This can't cause a scandal."

Diana bites her lip, turning her gaze to the floor, and nods. "I knew you wouldn't say anything, and I had to tell someone. I knew if anyone would take this to their grave, it would be you."

Peter nods slowly, standing up and crossing to her. Gently, like she might shatter, Peter wraps Diana's hands in his own. "You're right," he begins. "I won't say a word. But what are you going to do first?"

Diana looks up at him, and her green eyes are filled with that look that Peter knew well, the one that meant she had a plan. "I think I have to tell the Crown Prince," she whispers.

Something cold settles in Peter's stomach, even though he knew that's what she'd say. "Okay. But don't tell the king."

"Or anyone else," Diana affirms. "I would never."

Peter squeezes her hands gently, releasing her and taking a long look at the scars on her left arm. "It'll be okay."

Part Fifty-Two: The Taurus

Diana

Time: <u>**9:17 PM**</u>

Diana is walking down the hall a few hours after dinner when she hears the music.

It was coming from the ballroom: someone was playing the piano.

Diana had talked to Peter a few hours before, and for reasons she wasn't allowed to discern to anybody else, she had to be awake for the next handful of hours, so she was on her way to the kitchen to make herself a cup of coffee.

She creeps to the doors that lead to the balcony of the ballroom and notices they're open a crack, so she pushes them open as gently as she can and slips inside. Quietly, she walks to the railing and peers over at the grand piano in the corner, the only remnants of the orchestra from the night of the ball. Lucas had mentioned the old piano, the one that sat vigilantly in the ballroom, watching over it day in and day out.

Now, Lucas happens to be sitting there, eyes closed, fingers dancing across the keyboard. The lights of the stars from the big windows outside and the lit candles on the walls make a halo of shadows around his dark hair, and the addition of his gray shirt makes him look almost ghostlike.

Diana smiles to herself as Lucas begins another song, a slower one than before, and to her surprise, the prince begins humming along with the chords. His voice floats through the rafters, clean and beautiful. After a few more moments, he opens his eyes and spots Diana watching from the balcony, and her heart leaps as he smiles at her. "What are you doing?" he asks, taking his eyes off the keys even though he continues to play.

Diana shrugs, smiling back. "Just listening." She watches as Lucas glances back down at the keyboard briefly. "What is this song called?"

He shrugs one shoulder. "I don't know."

"You don't know?"

"Yeah, I'm kind of just making it up."

Diana's eyes widen. "Woah."

Lucas laughs and begins moving his fingers a little quicker, speeding up the melody. "I've been doing this for a long time. Sometimes regular songs just get boring."

Diana begins down the stairs as he looks back to his hands, and she approaches the piano slowly, as if it were an unfamiliar animal. Lucas, without looking at her, scoots over, making a spot on the bench. "Sit," he commands.

Diana does, crossing her arms, and Lucas nods down to the keys. "You can play, too."

She scoffs playfully. "I don't know how."

"Sure you do. Playing piano is just making music. So if you do that- doesn't matter how well- you know how."

Diana, after a very evident moment of consideration, plunks her index finger onto a key, and a singular low note rings out over Lucas' practically perfect melody. But the prince just grins at her. "See? That was good."

Diana can't help but laugh, and Lucas' smile somehow gets wider. The dark-haired boy removes his hands from the keys and takes Diana's waist, scooping her up like she weighs nothing and sitting her between his legs. Then he moves his hands to her wrists, positioning her fingers over the keys. "Okay, so your left hand starts on this one." He rests his hands on top of hers and pushes down on her left index finger. "And your right hand plays this black key right here." He demonstrates again. "Here, put your hands on top of mine."

Diana complies so that Lucas' hands are on the keys. "What now?" she whispers.

Lucas doesn't respond, he just launches into the song, and Diana's hands travel with his. He plays in silence, and when the song finishes, his hands rest on the keys once again as Diana hooks her fingers through his, turning to face him.

Lucas' face is inches from hers, and Diana's heart skips a beat. Without breaking eye contact, Lucas flips his hands so the pair's fingers are intertwined. "What song was that?" Diana asks, glancing briefly at his perfect lips before back at his dark eyes.

Lucas swallows and gives her fingers a squeeze. "Uh, it's from a Tchaikovsky ballet."

Diana shrugs and smiles gently. "We don't learn about those in America, unfortunately."

Lucas chuckles, turning his head down even though Diana can see the blush dusting his cheeks. "It's a required class here." He releases her hand and leans his forehead against hers. When he speaks, his voice is a whisper, meant only for her. "I'm doing a very bad job of not falling for you."

"I can tell."

He pulls away and smiles. "You're impossible."

Diana smiles. "Thanks."

Lucas opens his mouth to speak, then pauses. "Monroe, what do you think?"

Diana raises an eyebrow. "You mean about your wild idea?" Lucas nods. "We... haven't made a final decision yet." She moves so she's seated shoulder-to-shoulder with him again. "Why?"

Lucas shrugs, but Diana sees him move his shaking hands from the piano and fold them in his lap. "I don't know. I just... I kind of worry about what's going to happen with it. Between the public finding out, and my father."

"All of those things are problems, yes."

Lucas glances at her, and this nervousness seems different than usual. "And... have you thought at all about your sister?"

Diana swallows as her stomach flips uncomfortably. "I... you mean about bringing her back, too?"

Lucas nods. "I don't expect you to decide, but I know you've thought about it."

"I... I don't really know what to do."

Lucas squeezes her hands again. "You don't need to have it all figured out, Monroe."

Diana nods slowly, then rises from the bench. "Well, I'll see what we can do about it."

Lucas smiles at her, and the expression of pure relief that passes over his features makes her feel more guilty than anything else. She opens her mouth to tell him about her and Kiara's plan, but he speaks before she can. "Good. Thank you."

Diana just nods and turns away, hurrying back to the stairs before he can ask her another unanswerable question.

Part Fifty-Three: The Scorpio

Cameron

Time: **11:00 PM**

Cameron wakes up with a quiet gasp as his bedroom door creaks open.

He hears gentle footsteps enter the room, and he stills his breathing as much as possible, willing his body not to move.

The door shuts quietly, and Cameron hears the *lock* slide into place.

The first thought he has is that he absolutely will be getting murdered.

His *second* thought is interrupted by someone grabbing his arms and rolling him over onto his back.

Cameron tries to scream, but this mystery attacker stifles the noise with their hands over his mouth.

Frantic, Cameron closes his eyes, flailing wildly until a voice cuts through the darkness.

"Cam! Cameron, relax."

Cameron opens his eyes to see that it is not, in fact, a murderer, but instead his *freaking boyfriend*.

Peter is dressed in a gray suit with a white undershirt, and his hair is combed and parted down the middle. His hands are still pressed over Cameron's mouth, and Cameron yanks them away, sitting up with a gasp.

"What the *fuck*, Peter?" he whisper-shouts. "I thought I was about to be assassinated!"

Peter shifts so he isn't kneeling over Cameron and is instead sitting in the middle of the bed, and he grins and shrugs. "It was funny, though."

Cameron's eyes grow wide, and he shakes his head as he pulls the sheets up to his face and hides himself in them. "No, it wasn't!" he groans from within the white fabric.

He feels Peter pull the sheet down, and Cameron looks at him with raised eyebrows. "You were trying to give me a heart attack, weren't you?"

Peter laughs. "Whatever makes you feel better."

Cameron whines, all high-pitched and dramatic. "You're not helping."

Peter ignores him and stands. "Get up and get dressed."

"It's eleven at night."

"And?"

Cameron is caught off-guard, and he smirks at Peter, who is standing with his arms crossed at the head of Cameron's bedside. Suddenly, Cameron is less scared and more focused on the boy in front of him. "Demanding."

"Well, we have to go."

"Go where?"

"Can't say."

"That is *not* fair, you almost just killed me."

"Don't be dramatic, Cam. Let's go."

As Cameron watches, Peter crosses to his dresser, pulling out socks and a pair of boxers. He throws them at Cameron, who catches them and grins. "You look *really* good, by the way. Very distracting."

Peter holds up his middle finger in Cameron's direction and walks to the closet. He grabs two jackets on hangers and holds them out, turning back to Cameron, who is now sitting on the edge of his bed in just socks and underwear. "Which one?"

"Navy."

Peter hangs the black jacket back up and grabs pants and a button down, laying those far more gently on the edge of the bed. In front of the door, Peter grabs Cameron's favorite brown dress shoes.

Cameron shouts as they hit him in the arm. "Jeez! Why are you so angsty tonight?"

Peter crosses back to the bed and takes Cameron by his bare shoulders, leaning over him, and Cameron grins as his carefully-parted hair falls in front of his eyes. "Cameron, I need you to just stop talking for one night, please, and get dressed."

"Tell me where we're going."

"No."

Cameron holds up his undershirt. "Will there be pictures?"

"Not professional ones."

"So I don't need to comb my hair?"

Peter glares at him and Cameron sighs, pulling on his pants. As he zips them up, he points to his bedside table. "Can you hand me my belt?"

"Black one?"

"No, Peter. These are *navy pants*. The brown one." It smacks him in the leg and Cameron rolls his eyes. "It is very obviously not Cancer season, is it?"

"Screw you."

Cameron laughs, buttoning up the undershirt as Peter heads into the bathroom and emerges a few moments later with deodorant and a comb. Cameron takes them and goes to the wall mirror, precisely parting his hair.

"I don't *love* the hard part on the side, Cam."

Cameron chuckles. "I like what *you're* doing."

"Well, we're doing something important tonight. I need to look good."

Cameron tosses the comb down, finished with it, and turns to Peter as he pulls on his jacket. "Please tell me."

Peter smiles. "No."

Cameron sits back on the bed, pulling his shoes on. "At least a hint?"

Peter thinks for a minute. "It's not just us in attendance."

Cameron reaches forward, beckoning Peter into his outstretched arms. Peter allows himself to be pulled in, perching himself on Cameron's knee. "Bummer, I don't get sassy Peter to myself tonight."

Peter runs his thumbs across Cameron's cheeks, following the movement with his amber eyes. He looks up at Cameron and smiles. "Yeah, sucks for you."

Cameron rolls his eyes, but before he can say anything, Peter is kissing him. Cameron leans into him, wrapping his arms around Peter's waist, and Peter pulls back after a long moment with a smirk. "Ready?"

"Are you joking?"

"Nope. Let's go."

Peter stands, but Cameron grabs his wrist. "Let's just stay here. It's too late to be out, anyways."

"Come on, Cam. We're late already."

"Late to what? Come *on*, superhero. You know you want to tell me."

"You would know already if we could get a move on."

Cameron stands and threads his fingers through Peter's, smiling. "Okay, let's go, then."

Peter raises an eyebrow. "Changed your tune, didn't you?"

Cameron shrugs. "I just want to see what it is you've been hiding."

"One more thing," Peter says, pulling something small and black out of his pocket.

"What the hell?!"

"Please? You can't see where we're going."

"I'm not wearing a *blindfold,* Peter!"

"Cameron, come on. Ten minutes, if that."

Cameron groans. "Give me *one* good reason why I walk down the hall *blindly* for ten minutes."

"I will hold your hand the whole time."

Cameron, after a long moment of consideration, yanks the blindfold from Peter's hand, much to Peter's thrill. Cameron puts it on, and his world is swallowed up by darkness.

He feels Peter's fingers around his wrists, and he's guided forward. The door lock clicks and squeaks open, and after a few more moments of walking in silence, Cameron can tell they're in the hallway because of the way his footsteps echo off the walls.

"You look so dumb right now."

"Shut up, Peter."

They continue down the hall for what feels like forever, until finally, they come to a stop and Peter lets go of Cameron's hands.

"Oh, hell no. Come back."

"One second."

Cameron stands there nervously as Peter's footsteps recede, and after a moment, he hears a loud groaning sound as large doors are pulled open. Moments later, Peter reappears at Cameron's side, the warmth of his body alerting Cameron of his presence. He grabs

Cameron's wrists and leads him further forward, and they enter a cold room.

"Holy crap, it's freezing." Cameron's voice echoes off the walls, bouncing back at them. "Woah! It's so echoey. Echo, echo-"

Peter's hand covers Cameron's mouth. "Ugh, Cam, you're gonna wake the whole castle."

They continue on for t-minus five seconds until Peter speaks again. "Uh-oh."

"Uh-oh, what?"

"Uh-oh, stairs."

Cameron groans. "Let me at them."

"A lot of stairs. Like, minimum of forty."

"Hm. Okay, that might be trickier."

Peter goes around Cameron so his chest is pressed against Cameron's back. "Okay, ready? Step."

Cameron steps blindly and lands down a stair. "Nice," he says, grinning.

"Step."

Cameron complies, and he lands successfully again.

"Step."

Eventually, they get to the bottom of the stairs, and Cameron lands shakily, both feet planted and arms outstretched.

He hears Peter come down behind him, and soon, his gentle hands are around Cameron's wrists again. "Good to continue?"

Cameron nods, tilting his head in the direction he thinks Peter is. "Yup. How much further?"

Peter hums low in his throat as he thinks. "Not that far."

They continue in a straight line, and Cameron listens around their surroundings. He notices that every so often, his shoes squeak on tiled floor, or that his footsteps echo louder this time, or that the room is cold, and feels vast.

He whispers to himself as he tries to work it out. "A big room... cold... stairs?"

Peter chuckles softly. "How is that going for you, Cam?"

"Pretty well, superhero, thanks for asking."

"Don't bother trying to figure it out. We're practically there." They stop again, and Peter laughs out loud this time. "More stairs."

"Up or down?"

"Up."

"Okay, tell me when."

Peter flits around Cameron, positioning his feet at the base of the first step. "Step."

They repeat their process from before, up almost thirty creaking, wooden stairs until Cameron bangs his head against something. "Ow, shit."

"Oops. Forgot to tell you about that." Cameron feels Peter's presence at his shoulder, and he feels as Peter reaches up, grunting softly at the force of pushing something open. Two loud banging noises sound against cobblestones, and Cameron can swear he hears shushing noises before the world around him goes silent.

He can't feel Peter anymore. "Peter?" he calls, trying to keep his balance on the stairs. "Where did you go?"

His familiar voice chuckles from somewhere. "Okay, Cam. I'm gonna give you some instructions, and I just need you to follow them."

He nods. "Okay."

"Step up."

Cameron does. He's in a new room now, a warm, semi-stifling one.

"Turn like, ninety degrees to your right."

Cameron does and is met with silence once more. "What next?" he asks, voice growing concerned.

"Take the blindfold off."

Cameron gladly obeys, and his heart leaps into his throat as he takes in the sight.

"Happy birthday, Cameron!" Kiara, Diana, Lucas, and Peter shout at once, blowing party horns and throwing confetti in the air.

Cameron laughs, forgetting the blindfold and dropping it on the ground. "You guys, what is this?!"

"A surprise party!" Diana says, rushing towards him to wrap him in a hug. She's wearing a dark green velvet dress and strappy sandals, and Cameron thinks she looks stunning; like a goddess of this green Alynthian landscape. "Happy nineteenth, Cam."

Cameron hugs her back and smiles at all of them. "When did you plan this?"

He looks around the room he's in: it's an astronomy tower, made of wood and cobblestones. It's old and dusty, that's for sure, but the place feels alive with energy, much in part to the streamers and fairy lights hanging around the place.

"Well, we knew your birthday was coming up fast. It was Peter's idea to throw a party, but we didn't know we'd be in Alynthia for it. That's when Lucas volunteered the tower," Kiara says, motioning around.

"It's amazing," Cameron whispers, looking around the room again. He looks back at his friends to see them looking at him expectantly, all in a line in front of him. "It's really, *truly* amazing. You guys are..." he trails off as emotion rises in his throat, and he laughs, looking down at the ground. "You guys are too good to me, really."

"It's nothing less than you deserve," Diana says, shrugging. "Really, Peter organized it, from the cake to the dress code to the decorations. We just got the orders to be here at ten-thirty."

Cameron grins at Peter, who steps forward with his arms outstretched. Peter's cheeks are dusted with a blush that's also creeping up his neck, and Cameron steps into his embrace. "Thank you, Peter," he whispers, "for everything."

Peter smiles against Cameron's skin and squeezes him tighter. "I wouldn't do it for anyone else," he pauses for a long moment. "Cameron, I-" he pulls out of the hug, glancing at the others, before looking back at Cameron with an unreadable expression. "I think we should open your gifts."

Cameron raises an eyebrow at the way Peter fidgets nervously but brushes it off as Kiara and Diana pull him towards a chaise lounge in the center of the room. They practically shove him into the seat, and as soon as he sits, a wrapped gift box is planted in his lap.

"Guys, I don't want gifts-" he starts.

"Oh, don't give us that," Kiara says, rolling her eyes and sitting on the floor in front of him as Diana, Lucas, and Peter follow suit. "Open them."

So Cameron opens the box, laughing out loud at what's inside as he pulls out a roll of gauze, antibacterial wipes, and anti-infection cream. He holds them up for all to see. "Thank you, Ki," he says after a moment.

She salutes him and grins. "For next time."

"I don't get it," Lucas whispers to Diana.

She smiles and shakes her head. "That's a story for another day."

Lucas hands him another gift from the pile. "Here's mine."

"Thank you," Cameron says sincerely. He opens the gift, pulling out a delicately engraved pin. It's silver, with a shield on it, and inside the shield in carefully carved lines is the New American Capitol dome.

Before Cameron can say anything, Lucas interjects. "Let me explain. Basically, when I was crowned, I got all kinds of pins for my jacket. An Alynthain one, a royal crest one, the Libra symbol, you name it. And I know you guys don't have portraits yet, not like the ones we have here. So with this pin comes official portraits, that you guys can then hang in the Capitol if you want, and that's a badge for the Secretary of Security. If you want to wear it, of course."

Cameron turns the pin over in his hands, smiling. "This is amazing. Thank you so much."

Lucas grins, a different grin than the one he's seen on television, and Cameron can't remember the last time he saw that, if ever. "Yeah, of course."

"Me next!" Diana says, clambering over Lucas to grab a gift bag. "Here, Cam."

Cameron pulls the gift out of the bag. It's heavy, wrapped in tissue paper, and he unwraps it to see a framed photograph of five people.

It's the photo all of them took in the Plaza, a few days after they had met Lucas. They're all in their formal outfits, Cameron's green shirt, Peter's suit, Diana's white dress. They're in a line, and Cameron grins at all the smiling faces in order: Diana, Peter, Cameron, Kiara, Lucas. He runs his thumb across the frame and looks up at Diana, eyes growing misty. "Diana, this is beautiful. Thank you."

She blushes and shrugs. "I figured you could put it on your desk at work."

He holds the picture to his chest. "This is going on my bedside table back at the apartment. I love it."

She smiles and nods as Peter helps himself onto the lounge next to Cameron. "I *do* have something for you, but it's not here."

"We know what *that* means," Kiara says, earning a laugh from Lucas that sounds eerily similar to Kiara's own.

Peter rolls his eyes and turns to Cameron. "I can give it to you later."

"You're not helping yourself, Peter," Diana says in a sing-songy voice.

Peter laughs and Cameron loves the way his whole being seems to glow in the warmly-lit room. Lucas stands, brushing himself off, and puts out his hands, helping Kiara and Diana up as he turns to Cameron with a grin. "Okay, I got the kitchen staff to bring cake and top-shelf booze."

"You're cut off after two drinks," Diana says to everyone, looking sternly at Lucas and Kiara in particular.

Lucas crosses to the table that was set up with drinks and cake, and he grabs a bottle with amber liquid inside and holds it up. "Only brought one bottle, Monroe," he says with a smirk, "although Cameron *is* of age here in Alynthia."

Cameron rises and places a hand on Diana's shoulder, smiling comfortingly at her. "Don't worry, Di."

She smiles back, taking the bottle from Lucas and putting it to her lips. She wipes off her mouth and passes the bottle to Peter, glancing at Cameron. "Who says I'm worried?"

A few hours later, the group of five is standing at the end of the hallway, looking into the ballroom.

"Okay," Cameron says with a huff, laughing at nothing, "on three?"

They look much less put-together than they did before: the boy's shirts have been untucked, ties were undone or in Peter's case missing, and once-combed hair was tangled and unruly. Diana and Kiara were barefoot, heels long since abandoned in the astronomy tower, and Diana's hair is tied back, with none other than Peter's missing tie.

"On three," Lucas echoes, laughing as well.

Now, they were all fairly buzzed, and full on birthday cake. The plan was that they make a break for it across the ballroom floor to avoid being seen, although nobody was going to be there at one in the morning *to* see them.

"One," Peter says, leaning back on his heels.

"Two," Kiara yells, her voice bouncing through the room.

"Three!" Diana shrieks.

The five take off running, laughing and tripping over one another. Their footsteps pound across the tile, and the first one to absolutely eat shit is Lucas.

"No, Rutherland!" Diana shouts dramatically as she drops to her knees next to him. "You guys go! Leave us!"

Peter, Cameron, and Kiara continue to run, and they stumble up the stairs, gripping the railing and each other.

They reach the top landing, and begin down the main hallway, laughing breathlessly as they reach a door. "This is me," Kiara says. She leans on the door, chest rising and falling heavily. "Love you both. Goodnight, Cam. Happy birthday."

She disappears behind the door, shutting it gently behind her, and Cameron stares at it until he feels Peter's hand wind its way around his own. He glances over.

Peter is gazing at him affectionately, his cheeks rosy and hair tousled. "Come on, Cam."

Cameron nods and lets Peter tug him down the hall, jogging (more like stumbling) until they reach the door to Cameron's room. Peter pushes it open, both boys chuckling and shushing one other, which just makes them laugh harder.

Cameron gasps when he sees his bed. "Oh, my God, I missed you!" he yells, yanking his suit jacket off and collapsing onto the mattress facedown. Peter laughs, shutting the door, and crosses to the bed, pulling Cameron's shoes off before taking off his own. He unbuttons his own undershirt, pulling it off so his chest is bare, then heads to Cameron's dresser, digging through the drawers for pajama pants as he starts to undo his belt with one hand.

Cameron sits up and watches Peter, so comfortable in his bedroom. Peter pulls out a pair of pajama pants, stepping out of his dress slacks. He stretches his arms over his head, muscles chiseled and taut, and Cameron imagines running his fingers along those curves in his back or his chest. Peter changes, grabbing an extra pair of sweatpants and crossing to Cameron.

Without saying anything, Peter reaches down and unbuttons Cameron's undershirt, pulling it off gently as Cameron unhooks his belt, pulling it free from his waist, and wriggles out of his pants. Peter passes him the sweatpants, and Cameron, with great difficulty, manages to get them on.

Peter rolls Cameron over and gets into bed next to him, covering them both with the fluffy comforter. Peter props himself on his elbow and studies Cameron.

"Hi," Cameron whispers.

"Hi back."

"You're my favorite person, like, ever."

Peter chuckles. "Thank you."

Cameron pulls Peter forward, and their lips meet in a gentle kiss. Peter tastes like alcohol and chocolate, and Cameron gravitates closer, hungry for more.

Peter deepens the kiss, sloppy and rushed due to their drunken state but caring nevertheless until he puts his hands on the sides of Cameron's face and breaks away from him. "You are wonderful. Okay? So wonderful. And like, I think when you kissed me for the first time, I didn't really know if I was bi or not but then you did that and something very not straight happened to me. So thanks."

Cameron laughs, cheeks smushing under Peter's hands. "Peter, what happens if we aren't together in like, eighty years?"

"We will be."

"How do you know?"

"Because I want to be with you forever, and eighty years is less than forever. So it'll be way longer than that."

"Okay, good. I want to be with you for that long too."

Peter kisses Cameron again, smiling against his lips. "We should go to bed."

Cameron sighs, running his hand down Peter's side. "Yeah, probably."

"Snuggle me."

"I was planning on it."

They dissolve into sporadic, boyish giggles.

So, the two situate themselves, Cameron nestling his chest into Peter's back and wrapping his arms around Peter's waist as he buries his head into Peter's hair. After a moment, he snorts with laughter, muffling the sound in Peter's curls.

"What?" Peter whines.

"We are *hardcore* spooning, Peter."

"What of it?"

"Nothing! You're just so cute."

Peter grabs Cameron's hands and kisses all over his knuckles. "You are too, but you *have* to go to bed."

"Okay," Cameron closes his eyes, but before he begins to doze, he plants a kiss on Peter's neck. "Goodnight, Peter."

"Goodnight, Cameron," Peter whispers in response, snuggling further into Cameron's chest. "Happy birthday."

Part Fifty-Four: The Taurus

Diana

Time: **6:00 AM**

Diana and Lucas arrive at the gym early the following morning, pounding headache and all.

Besides themselves and Leon, two other things sit on the floor.

One is a potted plant, an orchid.

The other is a small animal Diana doesn't recognize, and- to her horror- it lies dead on the floor.

Diana freezes in the doorway, heart hammering. All of a sudden, the last thing she wants to do is train, especially here, in her present company.

"Welcome," Leon says. His tone isn't light and joking as usual, instead, it's calm and even. "We've got work to do."

Lucas approaches the plant as if drawn to it, kneeling down beside it, while Diana, however, stays stock-still two steps from the entrance.

"Miss Monroe," Leon says. "Please come here."

Diana does as she's told, moving to stand in front of Leon but staying a suspicious distance away from the dead animal on the floor.

Leon studies her carefully, ignoring Lucas, who is still seated on the ground. "Diana, I was told by the prince about this... plan to try and bring the queen back to life."

Coming from someone else's mouth, the entire thing sounds ridiculous- and maybe it was. "Okay," Diana whispers, feeling chilled with fear.

"I won't let you two try this without training first. The strange thing about the two of you is that you hurt each other while managing to somehow channel life into some other being. And something could go horribly wrong if you two are unprepared."

Diana nods shakily, her gaze flitting towards the creature on the other side of the room. "What is that?" she whispers.

"It's a bunny," Leon replies, matching the low pitch of her voice. He seems to sense how scared she is, for he rests his hands on her shoulders and forces her to meet his caring gaze. "And you're going to bring it back to life."

Something in his words alights that energy and electricity Diana has tried so hard to tamper down, and she nods after the briefest of hesitations. "Okay."

"Lucas," Leon starts, turning to the boy on the floor who is still somehow enraptured with the stunning plant in front of him. "If you'd do your whole... thing."

Lucas nods without even thinking, so it seems, and rubs his hands together. After a moment, he pinches one of the orchid buds between his fingers, and it blooms into a vibrant, purple flower.

Diana watches, and then after a moment, a sharp pain digs into her side, right beneath her ribcage. She gasps in pain, her hands flying over the site of the stabbing feeling, and Lucas leaps to his feet, moving to Diana as the pain worsens and a gruesome, white scar etches from her injection point down to her wrist.

"Ow," she hisses between clenched teeth. "Shit."

"Hey," Lucas says, finally approaching her and placing his hands on her shoulders. "Are you okay?"

Diana doesn't answer.

Because suddenly, in a jolting flash, the pain is gone.

Diana looks up at Lucas, who's gazing at her with genuine fear in his eyes. When he notices her shock, he raises an eyebrow but doesn't move his hands. "What's going on?"

Diana takes a step forward towards him, pushing the two of them back towards the plant. To Lucas' shock and fear and absolute ardor, she kneels next to him and clutches one of his hands in hers, motioning with her free hand towards the orchid. "Do it again."

Lucas looks over at her, and Diana's heart skips a beat when he gives her hand a squeeze, and she puts her other hand on top of their joined ones. "Rutherland, do it again," she demands before he can disagree.

Lucas doesn't say a word, instead using the hand not wrapped in Diana's to once again pinch a broken stem between two fingers. Diana watches with bated breath as the stem regrows itself with Lucas' power, and she realizes with a jolt of delight that she feels absolutely fine.

"Rutherland," she whispers as he looks towards her. "It didn't hurt."

Leon clears his throat, and it's as if the two teenagers completely forgot he was in the room, for they spring apart in shock. "It's his touch," the older man starts. "You won't hurt Diana if you touch her, Lucas."

Lucas' eyes grow wide, and he glances towards the dead bunny sitting on the other side of the room. Diana's pulse leaps into her throat as Lucas gingerly takes her hand again, shyly, carefully, as if he'd never touched her before. "Should we try it?"

Diana's fear mounts, and she wants nothing more than to shake her head, but she forces herself to focus on Lucas' touch and instead nods slowly.

The pair moves towards the small animal, and Diana's eyes immediately well with tears as she gets close enough to really take it in.

It's what Leon and Lucas are calling a "bunny," and it's a tiny little creature with long, floppy ears and big feet. Its fur is a dusty white, and when Diana gingerly runs her fingers over it, she's shocked at the pillowy, soft texture.

"Diana," Leon starts, kneeling in front of the two others and the bunny. "I believe that you and Lucas should try what you did with the plant, but it's *you* touching the subject, instead of him."

"Okay," Diana whispers, her voice wavering and watery.

Lucas wordlessly takes her hand, tilting his head towards the small animal. "Go ahead, Monroe," he says, voice soft.

Diana takes a deep breath, and then gently presses three fingertips against the animal's stomach.

All three wait, holding their breath, but nothing happens.

"Come on," Diana whispers, pressing down harder as her eyes begin to sting with tears and her stomach roils at the bunny's skin caving under her touch, "please."

Still, nothing seems to work, even though Diana's grief is almost outweighed by the thrumming of adrenaline and power in her veins.

"Come *on!*" Diana urges to no one in particular, pulling her hand from Lucas' grip as she presses both palms flat against the tiny bunny.

Buzzing electric energy flows through her, and it blocks out Leon's pleas for her to stop and Lucas' sudden cry of pain.

After a moment of frantic, panicked motion, Diana suddenly feels hands on her waist, yanking her backwards and forcing her to drop the animal in her hands.

"Monroe!" Lucas' voice and intimate touch pulls her from her frenzy, and Diana gasps as he pulls her between his legs, wrapping his arms around her waist and keeping her completely still.

"What... what was that?" Diana whispers, wiping tears off her face that she hadn't even known were there.

"I don't know," the prince replies. "You just... panicked. Your powers weren't working, and you-" he gasps in pain as one of his hands flies to his side, "-ah, goddamnit."

Diana turns, shifting to her knees to look Lucas in the eyes, placing her hands on his arms. His left arm now looks similar to hers: a new scar has bloomed, as if it had been there the whole time. "I hurt you, didn't I?"

Lucas shifts uncomfortably, obviously forcing himself to pull his hand away from the painful area. "You didn't mean to."

"But... I still did."

Lucas shakes his head, motioning back towards the bunny. "We're doing this again," he says, voice firm and similar to how it sounded the first time Diana met him. "I won't leave here until this thing is alive again."

Diana just nods, and when she turns back around, she sees that Leon is cradling the dead animal with a look of uncertainty. But Diana's fears are dissipated just enough when Lucas pulls her close again, his chest to her back, and wraps his arms around her, clutching her tight as if she'd float away. Her heart leaps when she feels him rest his head on her shoulder, whispering into her skin. "You can do this." Diana is almost certain that she wasn't meant to hear his words.

She cups her hands and puts them out, and Leon places the bunny into her hands. With a level gaze, he speaks just to Diana. "Remember, Diana. So far, you have only believed that the Gemini power is one that *destroys* life, but you must remember that you can also *grant* it, too."

Diana's heart pounds, but she nods. Without a word, she closes her eyes, focusing on three things: the soft fur of the bunny in her hands, Lucas' arms around her waist, and that familiar intensity that sets her skin aflame.

Diana doesn't know how much time passes. Ten seconds? A minute? Five?

But finally, she opens her eyes.

And that tiny bunny is looking back at her, eyes alive and alert.

Part Fifty-Five: The Scorpio

Cameron

Time: <u>7:43 AM</u>

While Kiara slept in, Peter and Cameron were in the parlor with Lucas and Diana, talking quietly over tea as the fog outside slowly rose off the dewy grass. The pair had just returned from their practice session with Leon, and the other two boys were being regaled with the tale of their resuscitation.

It serves as a good distraction, since Cameron was feeling a multitude of emotions regarding their leaving Kiara, and he had to focus intently on Diana's voice and not his impending tears.

"It was... incredible," Diana says from her spot on the settee, teacup in hand. "I've never felt anything like it."

Cameron was seated next to her, while Lucas and Peter were opposite them in two large, plush chairs. "It's that adrenaline, right?" Peter asks, looking between the two newer Powerful Ones.

"It's that buzzing feeling," Lucas begins, looking at the ground, his expression alarmingly neutral. "It shoots through your whole body, like you're being electrocuted." He takes a sip of his tea, shaking his head in the smallest of movements. "It's no wonder my father wanted to get rid of this power. I wouldn't wish that feeling on anyone."

Diana looks mildly concerned at that, and she shrugs half-heartedly. "I dunno. I think it can be thrilling."

"So are you glad you tried, Di?" Peter asks.

Diana tilts her head in a *so-so* manner. "I guess. I feel really tired now, though. Not in pain, but just... drained."

Cameron scoots to the edge of the settee, trying to get Lucas' attention. "Well, you figured out the touch thing. That's pretty cool."

"I read about you two," Lucas says, finally looking at something other than the floor and motioning between Peter and Cameron. "How you can almost... telepathically communicate." He finally meets Diana's gaze, and Cameron watches goosebumps shoot up her bare arms. "I wonder if we could ever get to that point."

Peter shrugs, and Cameron stifles a smitten smile as the early-morning light catches his dark curls in a shining halo. "Do the two of you feel like this all the time?" he asks, pointing at Lucas' arms. The prince holds them up, and, to the others' surprise, they notice his skin is dotted with goosebumps just as Diana's was. Peter continues talking as Diana and Lucas share a heated look. "I know for me and Cam, especially when we first met, the air would feel thick with that electricity you talked about, mostly when we'd touch. But after we..." he trails off awkwardly, casting a look at Cameron before continuing, "...became more, um, *intimate*," he perseveres through Diana and Cameron's groans of protest. "It went away, for the most part."

Diana and Lucas can't take their eyes off each other, and Cameron suddenly feels as though he and Peter are interrupting something. When Diana speaks, her voice is just above a whisper. "Every time I look at him, pretty much," she begins, tearing her eyes from the prince. "I feel it."

"Every sense is heightened," Lucas says, leaning back in his chair and finally looking slightly more comfortable. "I thought it was completely normal, until I met you all. The world is just..." he trails off, searching for the words.

"More vibrant," Cameron interjects.

Lucas looks up at him, and Cameron is momentarily taken aback by how dark his irises seem. They almost match Kiara's. "Exactly. More vibrant."

Their words hang in the air for a moment, until Peter finally rises from his seat, setting his teacup onto the small table beside them. "Well, you two," he says, giving Diana and Lucas a smile that's teasing and sympathetic at the same time. "You'd better get used to it."

Part Fifty-Six: The Taurus

Diana

Time: **8:11 AM**

Something hasn't been sitting quite right in Diana's brain.

Multiple things, actually.

From the very first time Diana entered the Alynthian ballroom and conversed with the Head of the Army, something hasn't been right. Lawrence Kerrigan was a supreme fool- and a complete asshole- but that wasn't it.

That wasn't *all*.

She was seated in a room she had found empty after leaving Lucas with Peter and Cameron, labeled "The Westing Room" by a brass plaque hanging above the door. Inside was a large table, with a massive vase of flowers and a long, embroidered table runner.

She'd taken with her a piece of paper and a pen, shut the doors behind her, and dismissed the strange looks the servants were giving her.

Sitting at the head of the table, Diana tried to recall what she'd been told by Cameron a few weeks ago, when they conversed in his office about Alynthia for the very first time. He'd said that seventeen years ago, the nation had established a ruling monarchy. Seven years ago, Queen Anastasia Rhea Rutherland had disappeared, and now Diana knew it was foul play that spurred the loss of the country's queen.

She begins sketching a timeline, one that starts in the year 2120, and puts a mark at the year 2130, the year Anastasia was killed.

She knew from asking around that Lawrence Kerrigan was pretty much a crucial part of Alytnthia's upbringing. The king, who was forty-seven, had two men at his side who helped establish Alynthia's massive military force. First was thirty-seven-year-old Josiah Maxon, Commander of the Navy, and second was Lawrence Kerrigan, Head of the Army, who was forty-three.

The king is ten years Maxon's elder, and so, naturally, he was closer with Kerrigan, who was just four years younger. But Diana couldn't help but wonder why Maxon- being younger and more inexperienced- was the head of Alynthia's infamous navy, while Kerrigan was the leader of the smaller, less important army.

Most people, Diana presumed, brushed it off to the fact that Maxon could be more talented at commanding the navy than Kerrigan. And that could very well be true.

But Diana didn't think that was the case. And she and Kiara were set on figuring this out.

Marking two more lines on her chart, Diana puts "Kerrigan" in the year 2126, and "Maxon" in the year 2129. She'd gathered that those were the years that the two men were hired, and immediately, Diana sees the hole.

Cornelius Rutherland was no saint. Not even close, and Diana supposed that it was probably impossible, considering his family circumstances. But Diana did know that he was smart, smarter than she originally gave him credit for. If Kerrigan was brought on three years before Maxon, that meant that something had changed.

She had a hunch what that was.

Diana rises from her seat and begins pacing the room behind her chair, putting the pieces together in her head.

Alynthia was a nation revered for its navy. Cornelius, being the king, wouldn't leave said naval fleet without a command, and if Kerrigan was hired *before* Maxon, that meant Kerrigan was the first Commander of the Navy.

And then his closest friend, the King of Alynthia, replaced him for a younger, more savvy commander.

It sounds like a motive, to Diana.

But Kerrigan wasn't just the Head of the Army, he was also the second heir to the throne. Diana can't help but wonder if that little title was given as a consolation for his demotion from the navy.

A man like Lawrence Kerrigan was no idiot. Well, he was, but he was also vying for a higher station, and Diana knew from experience that men who hungered for power rarely let things get in their way.

If she were a scorned noble with no title, a job with no fame, and one rung of the royal ladder below sovereign, she wouldn't let a seventeen-year-old boy get in the way either.

She may even be so inclined to hire a group of assassins to try and help her get ahead.

Diana knew she could be jumping to conclusions, but some part of her thought she was also entirely right. Kiara used to tell her that her intuition would never fail her, and looking at her homemade timeline, Diana realizes that if she were wrong, she wouldn't have circumstantial proof laid out in front of her like this.

But she needed more evidence. She needed to catch him red-handed.

The only question was, how would she do that?

Part Fifty-Seven: The Cancer

Peter

Time: **11:32 AM**

"I just... don't know what to do."

Cameron sighs and gently pulls Peter out of the way of a group of servants by his elbow. "I can't think of anything either."

Peter rubs his eyes as Cameron drops his arm. "I can't believe Reginald never told me sooner."

"You're the Secretary of Education. This is a job for Diana." The pair turn a corner and Cameron glances at Peter out of the corner of his eye. "Disease control would be her job, not yours."

"It's *my* home sector."

Cameron stops them in their tracks in the middle of the hallway, right outside the training center where they were due to be two minutes ago. He takes Peter's bare arms and looks down at him, pushing a couple stray curls from his forehead, and Peter can't help but smile at his sparkling eyes and slightly pursed lips. "Superhero, I know that. But you heard Reginald, there isn't anything you *can* do right now." He glances at the double doors leading to the gym. "So let's just see what the Alynthians have in store for us right now, and then we'll go from there. Okay?"

Peter takes a deep breath and sighs, long and heavy. Finally, he looks back at Cameron. "Okay."

Cameron smiles and pulls Peter into a hug, smiling against his cheek. As he pulls away, he plants a soft kiss on his temple. "I *will* kick your ass, though."

Peter laughs and shakes his head as he tugs open the door. "You wish."

"Okay, we're gonna do something new today," Leon says as he walks up and down the line of the five teens.

"Like?" Diana questions from her place at the end.

Leon gives her an indecipherable look. "You're going to fight each other."

Kiara mumbles something under her breath, and then looks up. "Do Peter and Cam get access to a border source?"

"Yes."

"So how do we contend with that?"

Leon shrugs and smiles. "You'll need to figure it out." He goes to the front of the room and picks up a big cube-shaped item covered in a sheet. He yanks the sheet off and a blue glow shoots through the room, so bright that Lucas shields his eyes. Once the light settles a bit, Peter realizes it's a cube of the border material. "I was loaned this by a Miss Barbara Oswald," he says, smiling, "for the two of you to use at your discretion."

"Who's first?" Lucas asks. He's shirtless again; Peter and Cameron were both in t-shirts. Peter thinks Lucas might just be enjoying the way people's gazes catch on the scars on his arm and then inherently travel to his muscled torso.

Leon considers, then claps his hands together. "Lucas and Kiara."

"Oh, for God's sake," Lucas mumbles.

The two take their spots on the taped marks on the floor. Leon raises his hands, and they both take up fighting stances. "Don't go easy on me, Trust Fund," Kiara says, winking at the prince.

Lucas shakes out his hands and huffs out a short breath. "I think anything I could throw at you would be considered 'easy.'"

Leon lowers his arms and the two lunge at each other.

It's over in three minutes. Kiara has Lucas flipped over and pinned on his back, legs and arms pinned down.

"Ah, okay, okay!" Lucas says between gasps of pain. "I yield!"

"Very good, Kiara," Leon says as Kiara releases Lucas.

"As if we didn't see that coming," Lucas says with a chuckle as he pulls himself up.

"On a scale of one to ten, how much do you want to do this right now?" Diana whispers to Peter.

He watches as Kiara and Lucas share a reluctant and awkward high five as they grab their water bottles. "A solid negative three."

"Alright, next is Peter and Cameron," the instructor says.

The ginger boy barks out a laugh and turns to Peter. Holding out his hand, Peter takes it and squeezes. "Ready for an ass-kicking, superhero?"

Peter shakes his head with a grin. "You bet."

The boys take their marks, and Leon smiles. "Alright, a bit on this. You two need to work on your speed as well as your fighting. So, the border source is going to be in the center of the room. You two will start on opposite walls, and when I say go, you begin. It's universally known that whichever Powerful One gains control of their source-"

"Has the upper hand," Peter finishes.

"Exactly. So the best strategy is to-"

"Control the cube," Cameron says in a joking, spooky voice.

The others laugh, and the instructor nods. "Precisely." He waves his hands outwards, motioning the two boys towards the walls on either end of the room. "Ready?"

Cameron pulls off his shirt and tosses it to the side. Peter just nods.

In one sweeping motion, Leon lowers his hands and both boys take off running towards the cube. They reach it around the same time, and Peter lunges for the glowing material. But in one fluid motion, Cameron sweeps Peter's legs out from under him.

He hits the ground with a grunt and laughs. "Jeez, Cam."

Peter reaches out with his hand and grabs at the cube, rolling away from it with the last of his strength. He pushes himself to his feet, holding a piece of the border in an open palm.

Cameron is standing in front of the cube, and Peter remembers in a fleeting thought that if he touches it, the whole thing will disappear. But until the cube is gone, Cameron could work his way out of any hold Peter puts him in.

"Let's make some moves, you two," Leon shouts.

"I hate this," Cameron mumbles with a smirk. He takes a few steps towards Peter, who backs up nervously. As if that answers some question, Cameron turns to Leon. "Why don't you four fight us, then?"

Peter's eyebrows practically hit his hairline.

Leon grins. "Fine." He waves to the other three. "Let's go, the rest of you. Change of plans."

He steps forward, and Peter and Cameron, almost on instinct, fall back next to each other. Peter nudges Cameron with his elbow. "Ready?"

Cameron elbows him back gently and nods. "Don't worry, superhero. I'll protect you."

Peter laughs and shakes his head, angling his aim towards the instigator on the end of their little clump: Diana. "If only I needed protecting."

Within seconds, she's swallowed up by the border material. She shrieks, and Lucas' attention is diverted just long enough for Cameron to throw a punch. The two of them engage while Peter turns towards Leon and Kiara.

"Cam, you there?"

Peter feels Cameron's back press against his own. "Yup. Lucas is out."

"You'll take Kiara?"

"Yes, sir."

So they break apart again, with Cameron heading towards Kiara nearer to the cube. The two are relatively evenly matched, with Cameron's height working to his advantage sometimes and other times knocking him off balance sooner than Kiara. Peter turns to Leon.

The two circle each other, fists raised. "Do you enjoy fighting eighteen-year-olds?" Peter asks with a playful grin.

Leon laughs. "Only when they have God-like powers."

Peter throws a punch, but Leon grabs his wrist and flings him to the ground. Peter wriggles out of his grip, scooting backwards. He rises again, glancing around the room.

Lucas is leaning against the wall, having yielded to Cameron. Diana is stuck behind her shield, arms pinned to her sides to avoid touching the blistering blue wall.

Cameron and Kiara are still sparring, and Peter works twice as hard to tear his eyes away from them.

He couldn't beat Leon on strength alone. And the border source was right behind the burly instructor. So he needed something else.

Just then, Cameron reappears. "Welcome back," Peter says, squeezing his hand.

"Thank you. Need help?"

Leon begins moving toward them. "I need a distraction."

Cameron nods. "Say no more."

So, Cameron races towards Leon. Peter watches for a moment, noticing that while Kiara fought like a clean, well-trained soldier, Cameron fought dirty: he punched where he shouldn't, went for the legs, and certainly didn't show the well-practiced restraint that Kiara did.

Peter shakes himself out of his stupor and races to the cube, grabbing a piece from it. As he's kneeling over the source, a shadow falls over him and he rolls out of the way right as Cameron hits the ground next to him, groaning. The sound of him in pain makes Peter's heart skip a beat, and the ball in his hand extinguishes to match his piqued fear.

Leon has Cameron pinned to the ground, with one of his hands bent at an unnatural angle that makes Peter's stomach turn. With a grunt of effort, Leon shoves Cameron's hand towards the cube.

"No!" Peter shouts as Cameron's palm presses flat against the blue source. Peter counts one second, then two, and finally, it fizzles out and disappears.

Cameron lets out a groan of frustration and lets his head fall against the mat. "I yield."

Leon rises and lets Cameron push himself off the ground. He's disheveled and sweating, and he looks at Peter apologetically as he limps to the wall to join Kiara, Lucas, and a now-freed Diana. "I'm sorry, superhero," he gasps, putting his hands on his knees. "He just- he..."

"It's okay, Cam," Peter says, taking his eyes off Leon for a moment to see Cameron slide down the wall into a sitting position. "You're okay."

But *he* wasn't. He had no border source anymore, and no partner. How could he win now?

Leon pauses, studying the anxious fidgeting Peter was doing. "Peter, may I ask you a question?" he asks as he starts taking slow steps towards Peter.

Peter stops moving, clenching his fists. "Sure."

"When someone is aiming at you, when they have you lined up in their view, certain to fire, what do you do then?" He takes a step closer, and then another. "Give up?"

Peter swallows. "No."

Leon is three steps away, two. "Then what do you do?"

Peter looks him up and down. And then he has a plan. A last-ditch plan, sure, but a plan nonetheless.

"You dodge."

And then he swings his fist, full force, into Leon's stomach. When he stumbles backwards, Peter kicks out, connecting with Leon's kneecap and sending him tumbling to the ground. With a burst of energy, he pins Leon's arms behind his back and shoves him face-first into the mat.

After a moment of struggling, Leon laughs and stills. "Okay, okay! I yield!"

The other four cheer as Peter rolls over onto his back, panting like a dog. After a moment, his friends' faces appear over him.

Lucas holds out a hand and hauls Peter to his feet. "That was badass, Peter."

Diana claps him on the shoulder. "I'm so proud of you."

Peter hugs her briefly and then realizes how sweaty he is. "Thanks, Di."

She smirks. "Even though I didn't love being trapped in your death cylinder."

"It won't happen again," he says. "Probably."

Kiara passes him a water bottle. "You might be better than me."

He laughs. "I hope not."

Peter moves through his shroud of friends and approaches Cameron, who is still slouched against the wall. "Hey, soldier."

Cameron grins. "Hey. Sit."

Peter complies, burying his head in Cameron's shoulder. They sit like that for a long moment, their heavy breathing the only sound. Finally, Peter speaks. "You're sweating really bad."

"I just fought three people."

"You vaporized the source!"

"Not *consensually*."

Peter raises his head and moves closer to Cameron, so close their noses almost touch. "Thank you for everything. I would've been dead in the water without you."

"Thank you for finishing the whole thing." He leans in and kisses Peter slow and soft. When he pulls away, he leans close to whisper in Peter's ear. "And for looking really good while doing it."

Peter laughs and pushes him away as Leon approaches. Both boys stand, and Leon puts out a hand towards Peter, who shakes it.

"That was a formidable fight, Peter," he says, "but a very obvious last-ditch effort."

Peter shrugs. "I had no other option."

Leon laughs. "No, you didn't." he turns to the group. "Class dismissed. Great job, everyone. If anybody needs me, I'll be icing my knuckles."

They all gather their things to leave and exit the training room together. As they go, Leon calls out to the group. "And Peter?"

"Yeah?" he calls, turning around to face the trainer.

Leon smiles. "You're one talented kid. Don't let anyone take that part of you away."

Part Fifty-Eight: The Libra

Lucas

Time: **1:33 PM**

Lucas rolls over in bed with a dramatic groan, throwing down his flashcards.

"My little prince, can you try to focus?" his mother asks with a chuckle. She's seated at the large desk in his room, and nine-year-old Lucas is snuggled under the covers of his large four-poster bed.

"Mother, I'm tired of geography," the boy whines. "I want to go see Father."

Queen Anastasia chuckles, rising from the desk as her long day dress sifts around her ankles. "Alright, my darling, let's first see where he is."

So, Lucas and the queen travel together down the hall, hand-in-hand, until they reach the large adorned door that leads to Cornelius' office.

Anastasia smirks playfully, placing her ear against the door, and Lucas follows suit with a grin. He can hear two muffled voices: one is his father, and the other is a man Lucas has known for about three years: Lawrence Kerrigan, Commander of the Navy.

Lucas and Anastasia listen as the voices begin to rise, Kerrigan's drowning out the king's.

"No, Cornelius, you listen. I have done nothing but excel in this position, and you're handing the command to a twenty-year-old child?"

"I am doing no such thing," Cornelius begins.

"-Aren't you?" Kerrigan interrupts. "Alynthia isn't known for its army, it's known for the naval fleet. And

Josiah Maxon is no better at leading the command than I am."

There's a pause, and Lucas wonders what his mother is thinking as he glances over at her. She's still focused intently on the door, as if watching the exchange rather than just listening to it.

"I'll make you a deal," Cornelius starts, his voice calmer and less frazzled than before. "If you accept the position of Head of the Army, then I'll make you Second Heir."

Lucas doesn't know what that means, but the way in which his mother's eyes grow wide leads him to believe that she does.

"Second Heir?" Kerrigan asks. "You mean my rank of succession is below a nine-year-old's?"

"Of course it is," Cornelius responds with a scoff. "Lucas is a pureblood member of the royal family. He will always be Crown Prince, no matter what. The throne is his birthright."

"His birthright that you invented."

"So what?"

"All that holds up this monarchy is your whim to be royalty, Cornelius. Nothing else."

"And yet Alynthia thrives."

"So, if Lucas abdicates, then I take the throne after you?" Kerrigan asks. Lucas almost doesn't catch his next words, and he wonders if Kerrigan even meant to speak aloud. "Or if something else were to happen to the Crown Prince, I'd serve in his place-"

Lucas doesn't catch the rest, for his mother takes him by the arm and pulls him away from the door. "Come, my little prince," she says, voice just slightly shaky. "Let's go find a sweet in the kitchen."

"Mother," Lucas asks, looking over his shoulder at the office door. "What does Kerrigan mean, what does 'Second Heir'-"

"Hush, darling," Queen Anastasia replies, her voice kind but stern enough to make Lucas realize the conversation is over. "That's enough now."

Diana finds Lucas in the barn.

"Hey," she says, voice barely above a whisper. "Can we talk?"

Lucas turns away from Icarus, hanging up his sleek leather halter on a hook near the stall. When he pauses to look at her, he smiles on instinct. She's dressed in black shorts and a simple white sweatshirt, her hair pulled back in a loose braid.

"You look beautiful," he says without thinking.

She laughs half-heartedly. "I look a mess, thank you."

He shakes his head, almost too nervous to approach her. "No," he replies. "Beautiful."

Diana blushes and moves towards Icarus, busying her hands in his mane and not meeting Lucas' gaze.

"Monroe," he says, heart thumping. "What's wrong?"

"What makes you think something is wrong?"

"I just know."

She hesitates, sparing a glance at him. "I need to tell you about something I did."

He can't help but shoot her a lopsided smile. "Uh-oh. Murder? Arson?"

She shakes her head, her expression not changing in the slightest. "It isn't funny, Rutherland."

"Hey," he says, suddenly nervous. "Talk to me."

She turns away from him, leaning her forehead against Icarus' for a fleeting moment. "Kiara is staying here because I told her to, not because of the army job."

"What does that mean?"

She looks at him, moving so swiftly Lucas is caught off-guard. She takes both of his hands in hers, her emerald eyes startling him with their intensity. "I think Kerrigan and your father were in on the assassination, and if we're going to try to bring the queen back and undo what they did, we need to stop them first."

Lucas freezes, taking a moment to study her gaze and ensure she's not joking. "You think my father was behind the plot to kill me?"

"Think, Rutherland," she says, voice on the edge of pleading. "Why else would he dislike you so much?"

Some emotion that rages within Lucas' ribs causes him to drop her hands. "My father might hate me, but he doesn't want me dead."

Her sympathetic look causes grief and a shock of anger to flash through Lucas. "How can you know that?" she whispers.

Lucas walks a few paces away, shaking his head. "Monroe, I don't know what you think you're doing here, but it isn't going to go over well."

"I've already started, Rutherland."

"And you didn't tell me?"

She sighs. "I couldn't. I didn't want to put you in danger, and I needed to get the ball rolling before Kiara and I said anything."

Lucas shakes his head, rubbing a frustrated hand over his face. "By sluething in the monarchy, you've put *everyone* in danger. And you never asked to investigate my *family*."

"Don't you want to know?"

"No!" Lucas shouts, the floodgates of emotion finally open. "My mother is *dead,* and we can bring her back *without* blaming my father for her death!"

She stalks closer, mirroring his anger with her sadness. "I'm not blaming anyone, not until I know more. I just want to help."

"You could've helped some other way."

She nods slowly. "I'm sorry you feel that way. But I have to look out for my country."

"All this stuff- with my uncle and the assassination and the powers- is ridiculous enough. I thought you understood that."

"How could I not?"

He scoffs, but he feels his anger dissipating as he turns over her words. "I wish you'd just talked to me."

She pulls a lip between her teeth and sighs. "I know. And I'm sorry for keeping it from you."

"Can you promise me one thing?"

"Of course."

Lucas closes the distance between them, placing both hands on either side of her face and staring into her eyes. "Please be careful, Monroe. I need you to do this safely."

She nods, and Lucas pulls her into a crushing hug, his cheek against her hair. His voice is a whisper, even though he knows she hears. "I really can't lose you."

Diana just hugs him tighter.

Part Fifty-Nine: The Taurus

Diana

Time: **1:10 PM**

If there was one thing Diana was good at, one trait that she inherited as a Taurus, it was her ability to logically solve a problem.

She was also incredibly stubborn, which lended itself to this situation, in her opinion.

For the past few days, Diana had been researching.

Snooping, actually, was the better word.

Due to a well-timed meander down the Southern Hall, the president had accidentally run into Lawrence Kerrigan when he was on his way out of his suite, headed to a meeting with the king and Commander Maxon.

"Accidentally" being the key word here.

So she knew where he lived, and she knew that every other day, those three men met for a cigar and a meeting after lunch.

Using her Taurean logic, Diana had come to a very obvious conclusion, one that she was sure any fool could figure out.

At one o'clock, Lawrence Kerrigan was not in his suite. Thus, the empty rooms would be prime and ready for Diana to do some sleuthing.

Today, during this little cigar meeting, Kiara would be present, to "discuss negotiations" of her new position and also naturally stall in case Diana needed more time. There were six points on the agenda, and Kiara was prepared to argue every single one.

She reaches the large double doors that lead to Kerrigan's suite, pulling them open and slipping through. She shuts and locks them behind her, turning to face the foyer, with a door to the bedroom on one side and the bathroom on the other. In the foyer, resting against the far wall, is a huge desk, piled high with papers.

Wonderful.

Diana crosses to the desk and begins shuffling through countless documents: draft papers, fort plans, prison warrants.

She didn't exactly know what she was looking for. She didn't even know if her hunch was right, and she guessed that Kerrigan wasn't foolish enough to leave a handwritten note reading "I sent assassins after the Crown Prince" lying around.

Diana also didn't really know why she cared. Anytime she'd try to figure that part out, she'd get as far as "I owe it to Lucas" and then her train of thought came to an abrupt halt.

Today, after her and the prince's somewhat disastrous conversation in the barn, Lucas retired to his bedroom, presumably to process it all on his own, which Diana wholeheartedly understood. The minor issue was that the Americans were going back home that same evening, which meant that she had about an hour to find evidence that would pin Mr. Kerrigan to his crime before she left Kiara to go at it alone.

Any guilt, regret, or further emotions would have to come back later. She owed the Crown that much.

Diana pulls open the first drawer, which is just as disorganized and cluttered as the desk's surface. Pulling things out, making sure not to disturb the area too much, she scans the pages, words pulling her eyes from paper to paper.

War draft.
Fort Kizis.
Blockade.
March.
Third Regiment.

Nothing here, *absolutely nothing*, is incriminating in any way, and Diana's breath starts to quicken as she realizes that she may have made a huge mistake.

But that panic is replaced with a sudden jolt of fear as she hears a key in the lock.

Dropping the papers back into the drawer and slamming it shut, Diana dashes into the next room as the main door opens. She hurries into Kerrigan's bedroom, sliding quickly under the large bed and letting the velvet bed skirt hide her from view.

Just in time, too, as Lawrence Kerrigan enters the bedroom, sighing dramatically as he sits down on the bed, the mattress caving under his weight and pressing uncomfortably down onto Diana's back.

She holds her breath as she looks out from under the bed skirt, peeking through the crack between floor and fabric. It's only when she shifts her leg in a miniscule movement that her foot grazes something.

Turning her head slowly- and as best she can in the tight space- Diana examines the box she kicked. It's a hatbox, an old one, weathered with time, and on a tag tied to the handle, a cursive font reads "L. Kerrigan."

Perfect.

Stretching awkwardly, Diana reaches for the box, fighting the straining groan that attempts to escape from her lips. Pulling it closer with two fingers, she holds her breath, willing Kerrigan to leave the room or at least rise from the bed.

Slowly, quietly, she removes the lid on that old hatbox, gently pulling out the contents of the box.

A phone rings in the other room and she jumps.

Mr. Kerrigan curses under his breath, rising from the bed and moving towards the foyer. Diana gasps with relief as the mattress realigns itself and she fills her lungs with a full breath of air, and she gathers the papers she pulled from the hatbox and army-crawls closer to the edge of the bed.

"-Yeah, sure. Yes, I'll be right there. Tell him not to start without me," Kerrigan is saying into the phone. After a second, Diana hears the tell-tale sound of the phone hitting the cradle, and she waits for a long minute, then two, until the door slams closed.

She slides out from under the bed, clutching her papers in hand, and races through the foyer to the front door. Peeking out into the hall to ensure the coast is clear, Diana makes a mad dash back to her bedroom, only daring to exhale with relief when her door is shut and locked behind her.

Dropping the papers onto her bed and spreading them out, Diana examines each one carefully, heat rising in her cheeks and excitement mounting with each new page.

The first of the three things is a photograph of four people. On the back of the picture is a date: 2128. A year where Kerrigan was still Commander of the Navy and the nobility hadn't even heard of Josiah Maxon.

Lucas is eight, standing in between a woman Diana can only assume to be Queen Anastasia and a much younger, much kinder looking Cornelius. On the other side of the queen is Mr. Kerrigan, and all four people are smiling wide, dressed to the nines, posing in a line for the picture with their arms around each other.

The second thing is a program, an order of events, even, with the date printed in calligraphy at the top: September 27, 2130.

Lucas' tenth birthday, and his coronation as Crown Prince.

And the day Queen Anastasia was murdered.

The list of events seems normal enough, Diana thinks, although she's never been to a royal coronation and has no idea what it entails. Greeting, anointing, crowning, exit, dinner. But in faded red pen, the word "exit" is circled, and so is Lucas' name, which is beneath the king and queen's in the exit procession.

The third piece of paper in the hatbox is a handwritten receipt.

On it is Kerrigan's signature and a written promise of four million dollars in return for proof of the Crown Prince's assassination.

Diana gasps, heart racing and fingers shaking. In her hands was proof, *real* proof, that tied Lawrence Kerrigan to Lucas' assassination attempt and the murder of the nation's queen.

The only question now was how she could fix this.

Cameron raps his knuckles on Diana's slightly ajar bedroom door thirty minutes later.

"Come in," she says.

After one last training session, Peter, Cameron, and Diana had to come to terms with the fact that they were headed back to America. Oswald and the others decided it was best to return for a few days, to just update the people on what their next step was in regards to the Alynthian alliance, the one had Diana proposed the previous day. Cornelius still hadn't signed the proposal, even though Lucas had signed practically as he was leaving the room, so they were going to eventually return to this foggy northern land to try and convince the king, as well as see how Kiara was faring in her new role. And at the bottom of her suitcase, Diana had nestled three pieces of paper she'd pulled out a hatbox twenty minutes ago, biting back a confession that was sitting on the tip of her tongue.

"Done packing?" Cameron asks as he enters, eyeing the clothes strewn about the room.

Diana turns around to face him, tossing the shirt she had been folding onto the bed next to her. "Nope," she groans. "I'm never gonna get this done."

Cameron moves to her, pulling her into a hug. "How do you feel about leaving Ki?"

"I... feel a little better," she says honestly. "I'll miss her, but this will be good for her," she lies.

Cameron nods, smiling, and picks up a pair of jeans, beginning to fold and pack away Diana's jumbled mess of clothes. The room falls quiet, and they work in a comfortable albeit slightly heavy silence until he speaks.

"So. Lucas Rutherland."

Diana freezes, her hands involuntarily dropping the dress she was holding as that nervous, guilty feeling returns. She clears her throat and shakes her head. "Huh?"

"Are you guys official yet?" He smirks knowingly at her.

Diana swallows hard and tries to ignore her hammering heart. "I... I have no idea what you're talking about."

Cameron laughs. "Di, come on. I see the way he looks at you." He smiles to himself. "It's exactly the same way I'd look at Peter when he wasn't paying attention."

"Ugh," Diana groans. "Fine." She's surprised at how easy it is to admit her feelings for the prince.

Cameron grins wickedly. "What the hell happened between you two? You seemed like you hated each other!"

Diana flops onto the bed, covering her face with her hands. "*I know.*"

"Cute," he says, drawing out the word. "You're getting so big! Growing up so fast." He grabs Diana's arms and drags her into a hug, cradling her the way he did all that time ago in Kiara's bedroom in Sector One. "How are things?"

"They're good," Diana says, not bothering to go into further detail. "I'm nervous, though, about what Kiara will think."

He studies her face. "She doesn't know?"

Diana shakes her head. "And Lucas... Lucas is Henderson's nephew."

"Di," Cameron says, taking her hand, "relax. Kiara trusts you to do what's best, and Lucas isn't the murderous psycho his uncle is."

"Cam," Diana says, "please don't tell Ki and Peter. I still don't know where the whole relationship is going, and I don't want it to be a big deal."

Cameron nods. "Your secret is safe with me."

"Monroe, I swear to God I'm going to-" Lucas says angrily, entering without knocking. When he sees Cameron, he stops, his face getting red, and he clears his throat in the same panicked fashion Diana did minutes ago. "I mean, um, Madam President, um, I brought you the, uh, papers you gave me." He looks down towards the floor, his face a mixture of guilt and embarrassed glee.

Diana notes the way his top button was slightly undone, and she recalls asking him to stop by when he had the chance. She takes a step towards him and grabs his forearm, kissing him on the cheek in an intimate gesture that surprises even her. "It's fine," she whispers. "He knows."

"Oh, thank God," Lucas says, crossing to the bed and sitting down. The way he seems to instantly relax in their presence makes Diana's heart skip a beat, and she's suddenly sad to leave all over again. "That was scary." He looks around at the disheveled room. "What's happening here?" He picks up a sweatshirt and unfolds it, studying the front and then holding it up against his chest. "Also, is this mine?"

"Packing," Diana says. "Leaving tonight, remember?"

"Right," Lucas says, frowning despite himself. "I forgot." He folds his sweatshirt back up and puts it back in the suitcase to his right. "Promise you'll come back, though?"

Diana smiles gently at him. "Of course."

"Here's an idea," Cameron says, piping up from where he's reorganizing Diana's shoes. "How about Lucas comes with us? Make it an American tour for the shiny young prince. People will eat that up, and you guys won't have to be away from each other." He grins at the pair, as if knowing the plan were a good one.

Lucas and Diana share a look, and then Lucas springs up from the bed and rushes from the room without saying a word, returning in two minutes and panting hard. "Cleared by my press team for an American tour." He crosses to Diana, cupping her face in his hands and lowering his voice so just she could hear. "See you on the helicopter, darling."

Diana tries not to show him how badly his words hurt.

Part Sixty: The Cancer

Peter

Time: <u>1:37 PM</u>

"Okay, but we have to make this quick," Cameron says as Peter tugs him down the hall.

"It will be."

"Like, quick quick. We leave in twenty minutes."

"I know, Cameron. I need five of those twenty." The two reach the door to Peter's room, and Peter grabs Cameron by the shoulders. "Are you ready?"

Cameron raises an eyebrow and studies Peter. "For...?"

"Your birthday gift."

Cameron grins, leaning against the doorframe. "Oh, yay. Finally getting my gift," he smirks playfully. "I was beginning to think it didn't exist."

Peter rolls his eyes. "It only came a few hours ago."

"What does that mean?"

Peter grins and nods towards the door. "Open and find out."

So, Cameron cautiously pushes the door open, revealing Peter's dark and empty bedroom. He looks around nervously. "Superhero, there's nothing here-"

Suddenly, a crash sounds from the bathroom, and out trots a four-legged, furry creature holding a roll of toilet paper in its mouth.

"Woah!" Cameron says, sinking to his knees and outstretching his arms. The animal walks into his waiting embrace, huffing and whining lightly, wiggling around as Cameron scratches his back. Cameron looks over at Peter, unable to suppress a giant grin that makes each and every one of Peter's nerves alight with adoration. "What the heck is this, Peter?"

Peter takes the toilet paper from the little animal and sets it on the bed, reaching over so he can pet it as well. "A puppy! Lucas told me about a woman in the town whose dog had a litter, and they were looking for one more home for this little guy." Peter sits next to Cameron, nudging him with his elbow. "I figured we could take him in, if you want."

Cameron studies the puppy, a platinum-haired thing with droopy ears and big feet. It flops over and rolls onto its back, yipping at Cameron, who scratches his belly. "Of course, Peter. This is amazing."

Peter kisses Cameron on the cheek and pats the dog's head. "I have all the food and training things." He picks up the puppy, pulling it into his lap and giving Cameron a playful pitiful look that matches the dog's. "Now he just needs a name."

Cameron smiles, playing with the dog's paws as he curls up in Peter's lap. "Hm. How about... Finnigan?"

Peter grins and nods, kissing the puppy on the head. "I love it."

"Hello, Finny!" Cameron says, bringing his voice up a few octaves to speak to the dog.

Peter laughs and stands, cradling Finnigan in his arms. "Alrighty. I think it's time Finnigan saw America, yeah?"

Cameron pulls Peter closer, sandwiching their dog between them. "Absolutely."

Part Sixty-One: The Taurus

Diana

Time: **1:56 PM**

When the four kids board the helicopter together, it's just about two in the afternoon. The pilot, a close friend of the Rutherlands', sits up front, with Peter and Cameron on one bench and Lucas and Diana on the one across from them. They buckle up, checking with the pilot that their stuff was packed away, and then take off, with Finnigan curled up at Cameron's feet, tired from all the attention he'd received from Diana and Lucas.

They all sit in silence, everyone packed in like sardines sitting shoulder-to-shoulder and thigh-to-thigh. Every so often, Lucas nudges his leg against Diana's, or stretches his hands out, making whatever contact with her that he can. Cameron shoots Diana a knowing look, and she rolls her eyes in his direction.

"Okay, guys," Cameron says. "Game plan for when we get there? We haven't really made any good headway with Old Man Rutherland." He winces as he glances at Lucas. "Sorry."

Lucas smiles politely. "It's fine."

"Um, I guess I could talk about Kerrigan?" Peter says. "We discussed education curriculums briefly last Tuesday."

"What do you mean, 'briefly?'" Diana asks, heart rate speeding up against her will.

Peter grimaces. "Um, I mean I physically ran into him in the hallway and we chatted for about fifteen seconds."

The helicopter falls silent again.

"I have an idea," Lucas says as everyone turns to face him. "What if we said something about the ball?"

"What about it?" Cameron asks.

"Well," Lucas starts, reaching awkwardly into his back pocket and producing a piece of paper. As he speaks, he unfolds it, holding it up for the others to see. "This looks a lot like the beginnings of an alliance, no?"

The photo is a tabloid cut-out of a candid shot of Diana and Lucas dancing. Both of them are grinning at the other, eyes locked on each other and hands clasped together. Diana feels her chest tighten with emotion, not to mention everyone's eyes on her.

Including Lucas'.

"You kept that?" Diana whispers to him, not actually caring if everyone else hears.

"Of course I did," Lucas whispers back, glancing at the picture. "I always keep it with me."

"I like it," Cameron says, interrupting. "We should publish it as soon as we get back."

Everyone nods, and Lucas methodically folds the picture again, smiling to himself as he tucks it into his back pocket. Diana watches his every movement, and when he's finished, he rubs his hands down his legs as if drying them off, and then he catches Diana looking at him. "Something wrong, Monroe?" he asks with a goofy smirk.

"No," Diana says back, fighting a smile. "Quite the opposite, actually."

Part Sixty-Two: The Aries

Kiara

Time: **2:30 PM**

Kiara had watched from the guest room balcony as the helicopter had left, carrying her friends back home without her.

Her schedule that day was chock-full of contract negotiations, fort tours, and armor fittings, so she was certainly busy, but she still felt very alone.

Kiara was alone when she had lived in Sector One, but she had prepared for that. This last-minute plan was a very different kind of adjustment, but she knew she had to try, at least.

As she exits the guest room, a frazzled staff member notices her and huffs. "Commander Kiara, we've been looking for you everywhere. It's almost time for your first meeting with the king and Mister Kerrigan."

Kiara just nods, following the footman down the hall and crossed her arms over her chest. Today of all days, it felt like that garish scar was more pronounced than normal.

"Morning, commander," Cornelius greets as Kiara enters the Westing Room.

"Good morning," she replies, sitting down next to him and across from Kerrigan.

"So, let's get started-" Cornelius says, pulling out the same contract Kiara had seen at their previous meeting. Before he can continue, though, the same footman that found Kiara in the hall barges in.

"-Your Majesty, you're needed in the study," he begins, "the phone is ringing."

Cornelius sighs, rising from his seat. "Just give me a moment."

Then he leaves Kiara with Kerrigan.

"Well," the older man says with an awkward chuckle, "how do you feel?"

"About leaving my country to work for you guys?" Kiara says sarcastically, not bothering to hide her ire. "Great, thanks."

"I know you may dislike the situation, commander," Kerrigan says, leaning forward just enough to intimidate. "But this is what's best."

Kiara shakes her head with a mirthless chuckle. When she speaks, it's quiet enough that she knows Kerrigan doesn't hear. "I'm sick of men telling me that."

To her surprise, Kerrigan pulls a flask out of an inside pocket and leans back, tipping his chair so he can rest his legs on the weathered tabletop.

Kiara is blatantly disgusted, but she fights to hide it as best she can. "You know, Kiara," he says, taking a swig. "I wish you could've seen this monarchy at its heyday."

"Explain."

"When the prince was crowned, there was this incredible ceremony. There were countless Alynthians there, nobles to commoners to soldiers. The ballroom was grand and filled with people.

"The prince was terrified, of course, but he only ever had eyes for his mother, who calmed him like it was magic."

"You were there, I assume?"

Kerrigan laughs aloud. "God, no. Those kinds of events... they aren't for me. I was involved in some of the planning, though."

Before Kiara can ask any other questions, the king re-enters the room. "Ah, Cornelius!" Kerrigan says, hiding away the flask and sitting normally quick as a flash. "I was just telling our newest commander about Lucas' coronation."

Cornelius grimaces, but it quickly fades to a polite, neutral smile. "Well, the only thing missing from that day was you, my friend. My Anastasia did a wonderful job with the planning, Commander Kiara. It really was a grand event."

Kiara squints at the men as they pull out their papers again, all business. But something doesn't sit right with her.

She assumes if Diana were here, it wouldn't sit right with her, either.

Part Sixty-Three: The Libra

Lucas

Time: **5:15 PM**

"I forgot how nice this place was," Lucas says as they enter the American's apartment about two hours later. He looks around at the marble counters, high ceilings, and ginormous windows and can't help but admire the modernity of it all, so different from where he was raised.

Lucas watches as the trio disperses, almost instinctively, helping each other with their bags and unpacking everything. This group is truly something special to each other, anyone could tell, and something inside Lucas aches with longing. He waves away the footmen as they finish dropping off bags, and after a few minutes, Diana comes down the hall and silently motions for Lucas to follow her.

Lucas takes his suitcases and follows her down the hall to a guest bedroom, the sound of their footsteps echoing across the floor. When they enter, he puts all his bags on the bed and looks around, unable to find any sort of imperfection at all, as if the room was usually in a constant state of cleanliness. When Lucas turns around, he notices Diana is still standing there, watching him intently.

He can't help but smile at the awkwardness. "You okay?"

"Um, yeah," she says, motioning with her hand in the general direction of his waist. "That's smart, to keep that picture. In case people ask about the alliance."

Lucas smiles a little, his heart fluttering at how perfect she looks in the hazy afternoon light. "I keep it because I love the picture. Not in case someone asks about the alliance." He takes it out of his pocket, unfolding it and admiring the captured scene. "You look so happy. And I like looking back on how this whole thing started," as he begins to re-fold the picture, he mumbles something he's sure she hears. "This is about a lot more than an alliance to me."

Lucas looks up to see that she's smiling at him. "I think you're something special, Rutherland."

Lucas tilts his head playfully. "Better than what you felt for me at the time this was taken, no?"

Diana laughs. "For the record, you still annoy me sometimes, too."

He crosses to her, wrapping his arms around her waist and admiring the way she fits perfectly into his arms. When he speaks, his voice is gentle and soft. "And I still think you're a little scary."

Diana leans into him, resting her head on Lucas' chest and reaching her arms around his neck. Lucas grabs her hand, kisses her palm, and traces his initials onto it, and Diana plants a soft kiss on the scars on his hand. The gesture makes Lucas' stomach flip with both nerves and adoration, and he yearns to say something romantic, but his thoughts are cut off by Diana pressing her lips to his.

"Monroe," Lucas whispers, pulling away just far enough to speak but still close enough to feel the warmth of her breath. "You…" He's lost for words, and Diana smiles gently.

"What?" she whispers back.

Lucas feels a melancholy ache in his chest that's quickly replaced by infatuation for the girl in front of him. "I said before that my mother would be the only person to ever understand me. But you..." he kisses her slowly, gently, in hopes that all he was feeling could be known to her. "*You* understand."

Diana nods slightly, her eyes searching his face, and Lucas feels so *seen* under her gaze. "I always have, I think."

Lucas smiles wider, pulling her in for another kiss but first making sure to whisper, "You always have."

Lucas is the first to pull away, but Diana shakes her head as her fingers work their way through Lucas' hair, making him feel weak in the knees. "Kiss me again," she demands, smirking at Lucas the same way she always did when she was looking for a challenge.

Lucas shakes his head with a wolfish grin and backs Diana into the wall closest to them, his hands gripping her waist. "Yes, Madam President."

The two connect in a kiss that causes the both of them to gasp, and Lucas pushes as close to her as he can, her hands exploring the planes of his chest and his pulling at her waist. She smells like jasmine and lavender, and the scent paired with the softness of her lips makes Lucas dizzy and hungry for more.

Before he can ask for anything else, though, she pulls away. "Can I show you something?"

Lucas nods, and they cross wordlessly to the window. He watches as she draws back the curtains, and he blinks against the glare of the sunlight. "Those stones, by the fountain?" Lucas nods, and she continues. "The ones with the engravings? Those are where the six Powerful Ones are. Maya included."

Lucas hums in acknowledgment, then looks down at her. She's staring out at the Plaza, where those large tiles shine in the dimming light. "What are you saying?"

"I'm saying that I don't think I want to bring them back."

"You could, though. You know you could bring them *all* back."

She inhales shakily. "When they engraved those stones after the memorial, it took weeks. Weeks where I grieved, along with the rest of the country. I lost my sister, but people lost their spouses, their parents, their children, too. And Maya... we fought before she died. A really awful fight, and I never got the chance to apologize to her. But I think that she would want me to keep moving on."

"She'd want you to move forward."

"Exactly. And I know that it doesn't make sense to bring her back, because then, all that she taught me would be for nothing. She always wanted me to grow up and be independent, and to trust myself more."

Lucas reaches down and takes her hand. "I remember my father telling me that she was part of your group. She sounded like she was really brave."

Diana nods, squeezing Lucas' hand but still not looking at him. "She was." Something seems to change in her expression then, and her eyebrows knit together for the briefest moment. "But we all were."

Lucas smiles, and his heart swells as he listens to her *finally* give herself credit. "Will you regret not bringing her back?"

She shakes her head almost immediately. "No. Dying is part of living, and Maya was proud of the fact that she gave her life to the country. I can only hope that she's proud of me too, somewhere."

Lucas takes her shoulder and turns her to face him, cradling her face between his hands. "I wish everyone were as wise as you, Monroe."

She smiles and exhales, although her eyes are a little misty. "You realize you helped me, too?"

Lucas nods, brushing his thumbs over her cheeks. "I'll always be here to help you."

It's like both of them realize that there's no way for Lucas to keep that promise, and Diana gently pulls away from him, changing the subject. "Come on. We shouldn't keep Barbara waiting."

Lucas nods, pushing down any rising worry. "She's the old- um, the Aquarius, right?"

"Yup. Fifth in line?"

"Right," Lucas says, remembering the old woman. "Can I talk to Miss Miller, maybe?"

Diana smiles and nods. "I'm sure she'd love that."

She leads him out into the main entrance, where a familiar, scary-looking woman is standing by the door. She wears a pencil skirt, white button-down, and matching blazer, and a pair of tortoise-shell glasses rest on her head.

Lucas would be genuinely terrified of her, had it not been for the three American kids all rushing up and hugging her at once.

"I missed you too," she says with a laugh. When they pull away, she looks Lucas up-and-down and suddenly Lucas feels *very* aware of his plain white t-shirt and khakis. "Ah, the Alynthian Prince." She extends her hand, a stark difference from the bows Lucas receives back home. "Good to see you again."

Lucas smiles and shakes her hand, and the gesture feels foreign and strange. "You too. These guys have given me a lot of stories about you since I've seen you last."

"All good things, I hope."

"*Only* good things," Lucas affirms.

Barbara crosses to the window and studies the Plaza. "So, Lucas, a letter came in from your father this morning."

He nods slowly, feeling color rise in his cheeks. "I see."

Barbara looks over to him, turning away from the window. "I didn't open it, of course. And as much as I hate to say it, I need to take these four from you for a few hours." She motions to the three Americans.

"Wait, why?" Diana asks. "I- I mean, *we,* -were gonna show the prince around."

"We've hit a snag with the release of Sector Six, and we need our resident Powerful Ones to bring down the border. Diana, you need to oversee it."

Lucas watches the mood in their faces change, shifting into those of politicians and leaders. Sometimes, it's hard to remember that these teenagers are in charge of this whole country.

"Oh," Diana says, looking at Lucas out of the corner of her eye. "Sorry, Rutherland. We'll be back by dinnertime."

"No problem," he says, trying to hide his disappointment. "Good luck out there."

"Thanks, Lucas," Peter says as he heads towards the elevator. "Let's roll, guys."

As they leave, Barbara hands the prince a gilded envelope that's part of the palace stationary. "Your father's letter," she whispers, pausing before she leaves. "You're a very good kid, Mister Rutherland."

And then the four of them disappear.

As Lucas opens the envelope, he takes a seat at the kitchen island, since he definitely doesn't want to mess up the almost pristine-looking dining room. He also wonders what the hell Barbara could've meant by her cryptic comment.

Lucas snaps the wax seal with shaking fingers, pulls the paper out of the envelope, and starts to read.

Lucas,

I wanted to thank you for informing me about your galivant to America. Oh, I forgot. You didn't inform me. Remember, your press officer knowing is far different than the king knowing. These rash decisions are not fit for the Prince of Alynthia, Lucas. When I hired Mr. Kerrigan, I told him: 'one mistake and you're out.' I couldn't count how many mistakes you've made, even in the past year. So I'll give you this, Lucas. One more mistake and the crown will no longer rest upon your head when I pass. Mr. Kerrigan is Second Heir, and let me tell you that I would much rather Alynthia fall to him than to you at this very moment. There has never been a less deserving prince in the history of worldly monarchies, Lucas, and your mother would be extremely disappointed in your actions.

One more mistake.

Signed, His Royal Majesty King Cornelius Rutherland.

It feels like the air has been sucked out of the apartment.

Without thinking, Lucas crumples up the letter and tosses it across the kitchen, and it bounces off the refrigerator and onto the floor. His brain is a jumble of incoherent thoughts, and the only thing that comes to mind is the picture of his mother in the aqueducts the day he was crowned, the white dress, the dank tunnel, the glaring stain of blood, the weight of the sword and the crown that Lucas never asked for.

Beneath the counter, Lucas' leg moves up and down, and he runs his hands through his hair once, twice, three times before he jumps from his chair as if he's been burned. Somehow, his thoughts were racing and yet he knew nothing besides his wild heartbeat and sweaty palms. Without thinking, Lucas digs his nails into his palms as hard as he can, trying to feel something, anything.

He turns around, towards the cabinets, shuffling through plates, cups, and silverware.

He spots something on a high shelf, grabbing it with his now-bloodied hands and reading the label.

Lucas cracks the top of the bottle and sits back down.

Part Sixty-Four: The Taurus

Diana

Time: **8:25 PM**

Diana punches the button on the elevator an hour later, heading home alone.

Turns out, they didn't *really* need her in Sector Six. All she had to do was make a quick, reassuring speech and then she was good to go, and make sure she angled herself in pictures so that the suspicious spiderweb-like scar on her left arm was hidden from view. So, she left everyone there and went home to spend time with Lucas. As the elevator rises, so too does her excitement to see the prince, which she tries to combat to the best of her ability.

But when Diana enters the apartment, he's nowhere to be found.

"Rutherland?" she calls from the entryway, shrugging off her jacket.

"In here," someone slurs from the bedroom.

Shit.

As Diana starts to head in the direction of his room, her foot kicks something across the kitchen floor. It's a balled-up piece of paper, and she uncrumples it to reveal a letter. As her eyes skim the page, Diana feels her blood boil, and her cheeks heat up with anger at someone who isn't even here. Some guilty part of her wonders if she could've revealed a certain secret and prevented this before it even began.

Without a thought, she shoves the letter into a drawer and continues towards the direction of Lucas' voice, which is now humming a jaunty tune from somewhere down the hall.

When Diana enters his room, she's hit with the smell of sweat and scotch. "Oh, Rutherland!" she groans. "It reeks in here!"

Lucas sits up from where he's wrapped in a bundle of sheets and blankets on the bed. "Monroe!" he shouts excitedly. "I found your booze. Since when do you drink, naughty kid?" He flops back onto the bed with a manic laugh.

Diana groans and picks up the empty bottle of scotch that's lying by her foot. "We *don't*. It was a gift from Boone after the Integration Bill got passed." He's shirtless and shoeless, wearing nothing but boxers, and Diana sighs. "Rutherland, you're drunk."

"I'm perfectly functional, thank you."

Diana sets the bottle on his bedside table and starts unraveling him from his blankets. "Nooo. Don't take me from my cocoon, Monroe, I'm chilly," he whines.

"Sorry, but it's gonna get a lot colder," Diana says, grabbing his arms and hauling him from the bed. Lucas flops onto the hardwood, his skin squeaking as it's dragged across the floor and into the bathroom.

She helps him into the bathtub, wincing at his disheveled appearance. "Sorry," she mumbles quietly, before cranking the shower head onto the coldest setting.

It's probably one of the highest pitched screams Diana has ever heard.

She turns the water off after a long, agonizing minute, and looks down at where Lucas is sitting like a shamed puppy, soaked through, hair matted and teeth chattering. Diana grabs a towel from the rack and holds it open, allowing him to step into it and for her to wrap him up like a swaddled baby.

Lucas stumbles back into the bedroom, sitting on the floor with his back against the foot of the bed. "My head," he groans, shaking the water from his hair with his fingers. Diana notices that his palms are red and bleeding, and her stomach sinks a little.

"What's the matter with you?" Diana asks, already knowing the answer.

Lucas looks up at her, his dark eyes filled with sadness, and her heart breaks in two. Without any word or warning, his bottom lip quivers, and Diana quickly rushes down onto the floor to wrap him in her arms. "My father," he whispers, crying silently into her shoulder. "All I wanted to do was impress him."

"Rutherland, you're more than what your father thinks," Diana whispers back, her clothes getting wet from his damp chest.

He shakes his head, pulling away from her. "No, he's right. I'm literally a royal screw-up. Hell, I couldn't even be *assassinated* correctly as a kid," he grimaces, and Diana is almost positive it's not from his headache. "And stupid Kerrigan is gonna take my crown and I'm going to have *nothing*."

Diana winces, bracing herself for what she's about to tell him. "Rutherland, I really need to tell you something-"

He holds up his hand. "No, don't say I'm more than them. I'm not, Monroe, I'm *not*. My job is not to be *more*, my job is to be *exactly* like them," as he speaks, he shakily stands up, and Diana does the same. "I'm always going to be what they think of me. And I'm *nothing* unless I've conformed."

"Trust me, you haven't done *anything* wrong-"

He scoffs, and suddenly the person in front of Diana is the same prince she met on the Capitol steps.

"Haven't done anything wrong? You out of all people probably know what I've done wrong. You've never messed up *once,* Monroe, and now you're stuck with me, a prince who can't even get a letter from his father without getting drunk and wallowing."

Diana rolls her eyes. "Enough with the pity party, Rutherland. That's what makes a good leader, messing up. Everyone does, it's part of life."

Lucas buries his face in his hands. "No, no, it isn't. Not when you've got all this pressure to be perfect."

Diana is officially tired of this, whether "this" is Lucas' complaining or the way his words make her feel guilty all over. "Rutherland, you don't get it. You talk to me like I'm some little kid, but what you're forgetting is that we both have pressure on us. If anyone should relate to you, it's me."

"Don't do this, Monroe. Don't make this some kumbaya moment where we sit around and mope about our shared problems."

"Isn't it? That's sort of exactly what you're doing right now."

"No, you're the one making it all about yourself."

"Oh, please. If one letter is enough to set you off like this, maybe you *don't* have enough responsibility to be king."

Lucas doesn't even seem to hear her, instead, he's staring down at the floor. "Maybe we're too similar."

"What?" Diana asks, exasperated.

Lucas' eyes meet hers. "We can't keep doing this, going back-and-forth about who has it worse. We... we shouldn't even bother."

"So, you're...we're through, then?" Diana asks, crossing her arms as if that's going to keep herself from falling apart. "Is that what you want?"

Lucas nods, and Diana thinks she might have imagined the brief moment of hesitation.

"Fine," Diana says, heading for the door and willing herself not to fall apart in front of him. She turns back to him after a moment, hoping the shine on his cheeks is just water rather than tears. "Good luck."

Part Sixty-Five: The Scorpio

Cameron

Time: **12:10 AM**

Cameron, Peter, and Finnigan get home *late* that night.

"Jeez," Peter huffs, flopping onto the couch as Finnigan curls up next to him. "Why did that take so long?"

Cameron sits on the coffee table in front of him, burying his face in his hands and saying nothing, and Peter puts his hand on his shoulder. "I'm sorry, Cam. The Geminis weren't exactly nice to you today."

He moves his hands away from his face. "It's fine, that's the job. People are still riled about Maya and Oliver, anyways, and I can't really blame them. They lost two important Geminis in the same breath, and that would hurt anyone."

"Back to Alynthia tomorrow already, also," Peter replies from his horizontal position. "I can't believe Kiara told us to come back so soon."

"We probably need this alliance more than ever," Cameron says. "It's all on us, Peter. We've all gotta convince Kerrigan and Maxon that we're not a joke."

Peter sighs. "I know."

Finnigan leaps off the couch, heading down the hallway, his nails clacking on the floor, and Cameron sits where he had been sitting, looking down at Peter, who cracks one eye open. "Yeah?"

Cameron smiles. "You were good with those little kids today."

"Thanks. You did most of it, though."

Cameron sits on the edge of the couch, running his fingers through the curls on Peter's forehead. "We both did it."

Peter nods, closing his eyes again, but only briefly. His amber irises sparkle in the light of the moon drifting through the window. "Cam?"

"Yeah?" Cameron responds, his fingers still playing with Peter's curls.

"Look at me."

Cameron does.

"Your eyes," Peter whispers.

Cameron chuckles a little. "What about them?"

"They're so pretty."

"Thank you. I could say the same for you."

"I love them," Peter says, making eye contact with Cameron.

Cameron blinks, and he suddenly feels sick to his stomach. "Huh?"

Peter reaches up, halting Cameron's hand that's messing with his hair so the focus is entirely on him. He presses a kiss to Cameron's knuckles before speaking. "I love *you*, Cameron."

Cameron is quiet for a moment. Nobody, not even his mother, has ever said that to him. Not in this way, at least. He struggles to swallow the anxiety in his throat. "Are you- are you sure?"

Peter laughs, a deep belly laugh that makes Cameron's heart leap. "Am I sure?!"

"Well, yeah."

"Cam, I've been sure." He grabs both of Cameron's hands and sits up. "You want to know when I realized?"

"Do I?" Cameron whispers, heart thumping nervously.

"Remember when we had to meet with the king, on October thirtieth?"

"Kiara's job offer meeting?"

"Exactly. You came in late, and when I asked you why afterwards, you said it was because you were walking past my bedroom and saw that my book was on my bed."

"Yeah, I know, you had left it open. All I did was put a bookmark in and close it, so you didn't lose your spot or break the spine. You do that *all* the time."

Peter smiles. "Right. You were late to an official meeting on your *birthday* because you stopped to fix my book." He rubs Cameron's knuckles with his thumb, and the movement helps slow down Cameron's frantic heartbeat just slightly.

Cameron shrugs. "It's your favorite book." He squeezes Peter's hands. "Peter, you know I've never-"

"Never said that to anyone, not really. Yes, I know. And I don't expect you to say it back. Just... when you're ready. I just really wanted you to know how I felt."

Cameron leans forward and kisses Peter's forehead. "Thank you."

Peter makes a fake gagging noise. "Ew, Cameron, go shower. I take back everything. You reek."

"We've been outside all afternoon!" Cameron says, laughing and standing up.

"No excuse, gross!" Peter pushes at Cameron's leg, flopping back down. "Goodnight, Cameron."

Cameron smiles at him, even though Peter has already closed his eyes. "Goodnight, Peter."

As Cameron heads down the hall, he notices Diana's door is open a crack and her lamp is on, the warm beam of light cutting through the opening in the door. Cameron pushes it open a little ways, enough to see her hunched over at her desk, head in her hands.

"Hey, you okay?" he asks quietly.

She turns to look at him, and Cameron so nearly grimaces when he sees her swollen cheeks and puffy eyes. "Nope."

Cameron sits on her bed. "Do you want to talk about it?"

She moves and sits next to him, sighing a watery sigh. "It's over. For good, I think."

"What?" Cameron asks. "Why, what happened?"

"He got a letter from his dad. It was awful, he basically threatened to kick him out of the line of succession if he kept screwing up. And then he got drunk, and we fought, and now it's... over."

"Yikes," Cameron whispers, eyebrows knit together in concern. After a moment, he shrugs. "Well, is he okay?"

Diana looks at him, raising an eyebrow. "Is *he* okay? I just got broken up with."

"Yeah, well, he did too, technically. And I mean, he must be super upset about his dad." Cameron nudges her with his elbow, pulling her into his arms. "I know you're stronger than this, Diana. It hurts, it *really* hurts, but it will get better for you. Lucas, on the other hand, *needs* your forgiveness. Because when we go back there tomorrow, and we're just having little luncheons and meetings, he has to face his dad again. The *only* family he really has."

She thinks on that for a moment, then sighs. "You're right. *Ugh*, you're right, it just sucks."

"I know. And I can't pretend to know how to fix it, but all I know is that even if you guys were never meant to be, it doesn't hurt to have him in your life. Because... if you have him now, don't let him go."

Diana studies him for a while, pulling herself out of the hug. "Cameron, I have a confession to make."

"Okay, go," Cameron replies.

She sighs, and when she speaks, her voice is barely above a whisper. "I think I might be in love with him," she whispers, her mouth turning up into a confused smile. She seems to trail away for a moment, eyes going somewhere else, and then quieter, and more to herself than to Cameron, she whispers again. "I might be in love with him."

"You think?!" Cameron says back, probably a little too loudly. "Trust me, he feels the same. Any boy who carries a photo of the two of you in his pocket is definitely in love with you."

She sighs, resignation appearing on her face once again. "But I'm not ready to hurt him, or myself again, so it might just be better to... let him go."

Cameron nods. "That's okay too, though. You have to do this on your *own* terms, Di."

Diana smiles gently and hugs him again. "Thank you, Cameron."

Cameron squeezes her tight, trying to show her as much support as he can muster. "Of course."

He leaves Diana's room, whispering a quiet goodnight, and heads into his bathroom to take a shower. He changes into pajamas, brushes his teeth, and crawls into bed, staring up at the ceiling as minutes tick by. Cameron hears a door down the hall click shut, and he can just sense that it's Peter, going to bed as well. Cameron closes his eyes, tries to sleep, but his words from his talk with Diana play through his head at full volume.

"If you have him now, don't let him go."

Cameron gets up and leaves his room.

When Cameron gets to his door, he knocks softly.
"Come in," Peter whispers.

Cameron enters, crossing to Peter's bed and sitting down. "Hi."

"Couldn't sleep?" Peter asks, sitting up. His hair is messy, and his chest is bare, and Cameron notices the choice of pajamas tonight were his sweatpants, the ones Peter hasn't given back. Cameron's heart warms at the sight, and Peter pats the pillow next to him. "You can stay here if you want." Without waiting for an answer, he begins to slide over, making room for Cameron on the side of the bed that was normally Peter's.

Cameron smiles, shaking his head. "No, it's not that."

Peter, mid pillow-fluff, tilts his head with a confused look. "So, what do you need?"

Cameron studies Peter's face, his amber eyes, his curls. And now he knows. "I love you."

Peter's face splits into a huge grin. "Really?"

Cameron nods. "Yeah."

"Are you sure? I don't want you to feel pressure-"

Cameron takes Peter's hands to silence him. "Peter, I'm sure. You're the best thing that's ever happened to me." He swallows against the lump of unbridled emotion that's rising in his throat without his permission. "Peter, I love you *so* much. You're all I think about, you're the only person I want to see at the end of the day, and you're the kindest, brightest, most heart-stopping person I've ever met in my life." Cameron gives Peter's hands a squeeze and grins jokingly at him. "Want to know when *I* knew?"

Peter smiles back. "When?"

"Well, I think it was when you were taking care of my ankle." Cameron wiggles his foot out from under him and Peter groans, shoving it away. "Do you remember what you said when I woke up that one time?"

Peter considers. "Not really. I typically try not to remember that chapter of our journey, unfortunately."

Cameron runs his thumb over Peter's knuckles. "You said 'survive tonight and we can go from there,' and I realized that *my* version of 'going from there' was spending the rest of my life with you."

Peter stares at Cameron, eyes big and round, and then he grins. "The rest of your life."

Cameron groans. "I knew I shouldn't have told you this, Peter, you have to go and ruin it-" Cameron goes to get up, but Peter wraps his arms around Cameron's legs and tugs him back down, laughing. Peter pulls him into a huge hug, and Cameron can feel him smiling into his shoulder.

"I love you so much, and I promise I'll be the best boyfriend ever." Peter pulls away, still grinning.

"You already are." Cameron ruffles his hair and gets up to leave again, to let him sleep, but Peter tugs him back down by his wrist.

"Excuse me, you're not going anywhere." He pulls open the covers and motions for Cameron to lie down. "Come on. I just want to hold you for a while."

Cameron gets in bed next to him, wrapping his arms around Peter's waist and allowing him to snuggle into his chest. It's quiet for a moment, until Peter speaks, his voice soft and gentle. "Thank you."

Cameron props himself up on his elbow, looking down at Peter with a confused expression. "For what?"

Peter stares up at him. "For everything. If I hadn't met you, who knows where I'd be. But I did, somehow, and now, whenever I even bother to think about the future, you're there, right by my side, and it makes everything way less scary." He smiles a little. "So thank you."

Cameron leans down and kisses him affectionately. "I'm not going anywhere."

"Ever?" Peter asks with a sly smile. Cameron can tell he already knows the answer.

Cameron grins back down at him. "Ever."

Not long after, Peter is fast asleep against Cameron's chest. Carefully, he kisses Peter's jaw and sits up, looking down at him.

Nights with Peter are Cameron's favorite thing *ever*.

His room has a big window, and the moon cuts right through the blinds. When they moved in, they all got blackout curtains for the sake of privacy, except Peter, because he said he wanted to be able to see the stars from his bed. Tonight, the moonlight casts shadows across his pale skin, and it takes everything in Cameron not to trace the pattern of the constellations across his neck and collarbone with the tips of his fingers.

His dark hair is matted against the white pillow. Ever so gently, Cameron reaches across and twines a loose curl around his finger, his favorite thing to do during the day, when they're both caught up in different tasks, or reading on the couch at home.

And his hands: one rests by his stomach, the other is in a loose fist, right against his lips. His hands, which spend all day writing proposals, flipping through ledgers, and taking notes. But these are also the same hands that cook breakfast for all of them on early days, hold babies for magazine pictures, and silently comfort Cameron with small touches.

And his heart, God, Cameron has never met anyone with a bigger heart than Peter. Someone who is so utterly selfless, who will run away from the only home he's ever known to see his childhood friend, who will sit for days and take care of someone's wound, who will wait and talk to his coworkers for hours about things he *really* doesn't want to talk about, just to be nice. His smile, his sharp wit, and his brilliant ability of just knowing what to say; Cameron could talk about him forever.

I love you, Peter Simon, Cameron thinks, *I always will.*

Part Sixty-Six: The Taurus

Diana

Time: **2:10 PM**

Diana and the boys arrive back in Alynthia in the early afternoon.

She's greeted at the entrance to Willowood Palace by Kiara, who shrieks excitedly and races to wrap Diana in a hug.

A hug, to most, but when the girls embrace Kiara whispers, "We've gotta confront him, *today*."

Diana nods and pulls away, making room for Peter and Cameron to hug her, as Lucas trails awkwardly behind them, just giving Kiara a nod before entering the palace.

Without a word, they're ushered in by Kiara, who guides the boys to their familiar guest rooms before pulling Diana aside at the ballroom entrance.

"Listen, Di. I found out that-"

"-That Kerrigan ordered the assassination," Diana finishes. "I know, I found the receipt in Kerrigan's room. Did he confess?"

"Sort of," she replies, casting a glance around the empty hallway as if someone were listening in. "But I know we can get him to if he's goaded the right way."

"The boys are elsewhere?"

She nods. "The royals are in the ballroom, all together. So it's now or never."

"But Lucas is in there-"

Kiara gives her a look. "I know you want to spare him from this. Why, I'm not sure, but we have no other choice."

Diana nods, swallowing her fear, and Kiara pulls open the ballroom doors.

Once her and Kiara sneak onto the ballroom balcony, Diana realizes that she hadn't thought this through in its entirety as she watches Cornelius, Kerrigan, Maxon, and Lucas plan an event.

The two girls watch as the four men move around the ballroom, with Maxon occasionally jotting things down on a clipboard while the other three point things out along the room, presumably the location of a few banquet tables, from what Diana could overhear.

Quickly retrieved from her suitcase on the helicopter and now clenched in her hand were two things: the receipt and the program for the coronation.

Kiara is empty-handed except for a dagger.

Before Diana can make up her mind and truly decide how they're going to tackle this, one of the four men turns around and spots the pair.

"Ah, President Monroe, Commander Kiara," Maxon says with a friendly smile. "How are the both of you?"

Diana blinks as the others turn around, and she can't help but flounder for words as Lucas and the king look at the two girls with confused and slightly annoyed expressions.

Then she notices that Mr. Kerrigan is glaring at her, and suddenly, she's possessed by the spirit of someone much bolder.

"Something wrong, Lawrence?" she asks with a fake smile.

"That's 'Mister Kerrigan' to you," he replies. "And yes, I happen to be missing the contents of an important private box." He raises an eyebrow. "Do you two happen to know anything about that?"

"Watch what you accuse her of, Mister Kerrigan," Kiara warns. Her possessive and protective tone bolsters Diana just slightly, and she gives Kiara's free hand a thankful squeeze before continuing.

"No, Kiara," Diana says dramatically with a batting of her lashes, "he's right."

With that, she holds up the pages in her hand and watches the color drain from Kerrigan's face.

"What is that?" Cornelius says, squinting up at the balcony. "Come closer, you two."

Diana and Kiara do, taking the stairs slowly, partly in fear that they'll lose control of the narrative when they reach the bottom step. "Well, I may have stumbled upon a plan of attack created by our dear Mister Kerrigan, and a receipt, one offering four million dollars in exchange for the assassination of the Crown Prince, and Kiara was here on the inside to do a little more digging on behalf of New America." She hands the papers off to a shocked Cornelius and continues, "And what we've found makes it concrete that Kerrigan was the one who sent the killers to the coronation and is responsible for the death of Queen Anastasia."

Lucas, Cornelius, and Maxon are wearing matching expressions of shock, and Kerrigan is pale-faced, fists shaking at his sides. "Why on earth would I wish harm upon Prince Lucas?" he acts, his tone feigning innocence. "He's been like a nephew to me."

Diana raises an eyebrow. "Second Heir is quite the motive, is it not? And, with just a ten-year-old boy in the way, you must have thought you had the sovereignty at your fingertips." Kerrigan takes a menacing step forward and Kiara reflexively inches closer to Diana's side. "But the queen was smarter than you thought, and she knew how to protect the prince-"

She's cut off by Cornelius. "-Miss Monroe, are you trying to tell me that my closest friend and confidante was responsible for the death of my wife and the attempt on the Crown Prince's life?"

Diana weighs her words, meeting the king's gaze. He seems strong, but deep in his eyes, Diana sees the grief there- that grief she knows all too well. "Yes," she says, lowering her voice, "I am."

"And when I talked to Lawrence, he admitted to me that he *was* involved with the events during the coronation. But photos I found from the event and the king's word show that Kerrigan wasn't even there, so he must have been involved some other way," Kiara adds.

Cornelius looks over at Kerrigan, who has moved closer still, but to Lucas rather than one of the girls. "Lawrence, is this-"

He doesn't get to finish his sentence before Kerrigan moves in a flash, shoving Lucas to the ground and pulling a gun from his jacket. Diana, Maxon, Kiara, and Cornelius begin shouting protests when Kerrigan yells wildly.

"If anyone moves, I pull the trigger." He levels a glare at Diana. "You of all people wouldn't want that, would you?"

Diana shakes her head slowly, extending a hand in an expression of surrender as the gun's safety clicks off. "Hey, I don't want you to do anything rash-"

"The crown is *everything*, President Monroe. You may not understand that where you're from, but there are some who are fit to lead and others who are not. Anastasia was an unfortunate repercussion of a necessary act to protect the monarchy-"

Lucas interrupts from where he's frozen on the ground. "Taking my mother's *life* was beneficial to the monarchy?!"

Maxon steps forward, a sympathetic smile on his face. "Lawrence, think about this-"

Kerrigan turns, levels the gun at Maxon's chest, and pulls the trigger in one fluid motion. Diana gasps as Maxon crumples to the ground and Kerrigan once again turns the barrel towards Lucas, Maxon's gasping breaths threatening to shatter her resolve. "You always meddled where you weren't wanted, Josiah," he says, voice now slightly manic, "and you deserve to pay for that."

He looks down at Lucas, and that same murderous glare flashes through his eyes just as it did before the trigger was pulled on Maxon.

She'd seen that look before, the same look shared by the guard who had pointed that gun at Cameron seven months ago and taken Maya's life in his stead. And Diana was just as scared now as she had been before, but she had to do *something*.

She refused to just stand frozen again.

Diana moves before she can stop herself, throwing her weight into Kerrigan and bringing them both to the ground.

Lucas scrambles to his feet, racing over to Maxon and throwing his hands over his chest where that gruesome gunshot wound is rapidly worsening. Diana turns towards Kerrigan, who is struggling against her hold, knuckles white in a vice-like grip around his revolver as Kiara rushes to assist her.

"Monroe!" Lucas calls, grabbing Diana's attention although she doesn't look towards him. "Use your power!"

"I can't!" she replies, struggling to grab the gun. "I don't want to hurt you!"

"Do it, Monroe," he pleads. "You can do it, and then you'll help me heal Maxon. Come on, quickly!"

Diana nods, and, without a second thought, presses her palms into Mr. Kerrigan's back. She barely notices Kiara racing over, metal dagger glinting in the white light.

She doesn't think too hard or too much, focusing on the grief she saw in Cornelius' gaze and how she felt exactly the same when she saw that guard kill Maya in cold blood. She ignores the almost-matching screams of pain that Kerrigan and Lucas produce, letting the ringing of her ears take over.

After a few moments, she moves her hands and slowly, carefully, stands up.

Kerrigan is stock-still, and Diana uses all her strength to roll him over.

"Di," Kiara says, "before you say anything-"

Diana watches Kiara hold up her now-bloodied knife, and she's shocked that *relief* is her overriding emotion.

Kerrigan's skin is eerily pale, and his eyes are wide and unseeing. A thin line of blood runs from the corner of his mouth and down his chin, and a long, messy slash near the base of his throat is proof of Kiara's addition to the fight. Before she can think about anything else, though, Diana turns around at the sound of a pained groan.

It isn't Maxon, it's Lucas, who is using one hand to press down on the commander's bloody chest and the other to clutch at his arm, which now has another scar from elbow to wrist. When he looks over at Diana, though, the pain on his face is replaced with pride. Diana has to fight those recurring feelings all over again, coldly reminding herself of their fight in her bedroom. But when Lucas speaks, her instinctive response is to move closer to his side.

"Get over here, Monroe," he jokes through gritted teeth, "and give a guy a hand?"

She quickly goes to kneel by his side, pulling his hand from the crook of his elbow and taking it in hers. Holding his teary gaze, she presses a kiss to his knuckles, despite her better judgment. "Do it, Rutherland."

Lucas closes his eyes, squeezing Diana's hand as his power begins to heal Maxon's wound. She feels his adrenaline in her veins and gives herself up to the strong thrum of his power.

After a long moment, Maxon sits up with a gasp, fingers clawing at where his wound used to be. He looks at Lucas and Diana, eyes wide, thousands of emotions swimming behind them, and grips their shoulders, his fingers digging into their skin. "You... I owe you two my *life*. Thank you. Dear God, *thank you*."

He rises shakily and moves to Kiara, wrapping her in a hug, which shocks Diana more than anyone else. Then her gaze turns to Cornelius, who is standing to the side, shellshocked and agape. With an unreadable look towards Lucas, he turns and begins climbing the stairs, letting the ballroom doors slam behind him.

Diana looks over at the prince, who is panting for breath and covered in Maxon's blood. The two share a look, a look that's a blame and an explanation and an apology all in one, and then Lucas throws his arms around Diana, anchoring her with a hug.

Part Sixty-Seven: The Libra

Lucas

Time: **3:00 PM**

Lucas still can't seem to catch his breath.

The events surrounding the aftermath of Kerrigan's death and attempted attack were a blur, and all he remembered was servants entering and whisking Diana away from his side, fussing about some kind of afternoon event that she just had to attend, even though the figurative blood of a noble was still fresh on her hands.

Lucas and Kiara stayed there, assisting with cleanup, although multiple staff members asked them not to. He felt guilty, felt ashamed- less about Kerrigan's death and more about his father's grief-stricken face. And he knew that Kiara didn't want to inflict any more pain, because he felt similar. It seemed as though the two shared the unspoken urge to fix the problem in front of them.

He and Diana still hadn't talked since, and, technically speaking, they were still broken up. And Lucas was still very much angry about the fight that unfolded back in America.

But she risked her life to protect him, without even thinking twice.

And that fact procured a strong and strange feeling in Lucas.

Now it's around three, and Lucas is taking tea in the garden. Alone. The sky is gray and cloudy, and it looks like rain, but he asked the cook to bring his food out here, so he could eat in the garden. Whenever he's alone, this place makes Lucas feel close to his mother, and today of all days was one where he needed to be nearer to her. His chest aches with sadness, and he watches a scarlet cardinal soar towards the palace's namesake willow tree.

As the bird lands within the branches, out of Lucas' view, he wonders about the tomb that sat near the edge of the castle lawns, and whether or not it would ever be opened now that he and Diana were through. Lucas wished that he could do this on his own, but of course, even the supernatural aspect of life had to shackle him to the President of New America. He just couldn't win, it seemed, and he runs his fingertips aimlessly down the new scar that Diana's power had created earlier that day, his fingers tracing each white mark, *one, two, three.*

Thunder rumbles across the sky, and a shadow falls over the ground as the sun sinks behind a storm cloud. In front of him, the grass is a gentle green and the hedges look bright and vibrant, considering the season, as they rustle in the wind. Lucas studies the erratic movements of the fountain as he raises his cup to his lips.

Someone clearing their throat behind him makes Lucas jump, sloshing a bit of tea into his lap. He sets his cup onto his saucer as gently as he can, trying to calm his pounding heart.

Lucas turns around and comes face-to-face with Cameron and Diana.

Lucas catches Diana's eye and she holds his gaze for a second before waving her hand towards where his table and single chair has been set up. "Excuse us," she mumbles, her voice a mixture of embarrassment and ire.

Cameron grabs her hand and pulls it to her side, and the action makes Lucas' chest involuntarily constrict with envy. "What she means is, can you point us in the direction of the barn?"

Lucas laughs out loud before he can stop himself. "The-"

Diana rolls her eyes in a gesture that could certainly strike down the bravest knight. "-The *barn.*"

"No, I heard you," Lucas says, "but why?"

Cameron shrugs. "That's where our photoshoot is." He glances at Diana, who's staring at the stone floor. "They... didn't want to cancel."

Lucas gives Diana a searching once-over. "Don't remember how you got there the first two times, Monroe?"

Cameron looks confused, but Diana meets Lucas' gaze with the smallest of smiles. "No, actually, I don't."

Lucas points through the garden. "Go straight until you reach the hedge maze. A good shortcut is to go into the maze and keep taking rights until you get out. It'll be about a hundred yards from there, you'll see it right away."

"Thanks," Cameron says, at the same time Diana says, "a hedge maze?"

Lucas clears his throat and studies Diana closely, but her guarded expression gives nothing away. "Yes, Monroe, the hedge maze. Is there something wrong with that?"

She stares right back at him. "I don't think I said there was anything wrong, no?"

Lucas smirks a little. "You didn't have to."

"Oookay!" Cameron says, putting a hand on Diana's back and steering her towards the garden. "Thanks, Lucas!" he shouts as they disappear into the hedges.

"You're welcome," Lucas mumbles, turning his face back towards the darkening sky.

About thirty minutes later, the two of them still haven't returned. Lucas had changed out his tea set with the local news, and by that he means a raunchy little tabloid that's plagued Alynthia for years. It's a new issue about the royals' foreign guests, and plastered on the cover is Diana and the Americans in their ball outfits, posing for the photo. Lucas is desperately searching for quotes from the other nobles about him, wondering if anyone had gotten word of Kerrigan's sudden lack of appearance.

A splatter of precipitation on the page startles Lucas out of his reading, and after a few seconds, rain is coming down steadily in the garden, beading on the tabletop and the branches of the willow. Lucas throws the magazine on the table, shaking the water out of his hair, and when he looks up, Diana is standing in the entrance to the maze, Cameron nowhere to be seen.

"Where's the ginger?" Lucas shouts to her as he shrugs off his jacket, leaving him in just his pants and his white button-down undershirt. Lucas' eyes wander to the hem of Diana's red dress, plastered to the middle of her thighs from the rain. The rain gets heavier and heavier, and the sleeves and bodice stick to her skin. Her blonde hair is stringy and brown because of the general wetness, and Lucas fears that his hair doesn't look much better.

"We finished early," she shouts back, expression clouding. "I just... wanted to be alone; hang out with Icarus for a bit."

Lucas looks at the clouds as he pushes up his sleeves, and as if on cue, thunder rumbles again. He turns towards the door of the castle, considering leaving her in the rain, but then he curses his chivalry and nabs his wet jacket, jogging over to her under the arch of the hedge maze. Without a word, Lucas holds the jacket over Diana's head, blocking a good portion of the rain and casting a shadow over her features.

"Rutherland, what are you doing?" she asks.

Before Lucas can respond, she interjects, taking the jacket from him and shrugging it onto her shoulders. "Actually, I know what you're trying to do. But trust me, a little act of chivalry isn't going to solve anything. This is all too... complicated for me."

Lucas rolls his eyes as frustration grates on his nerves. "God, Monroe, what do you want me to say? I've run out of ideas on how to fix this."

Diana turns to him. "I don't want you to say anything. For once, Rutherland, I want you to *stop* talking."

She starts to walk back towards the house, Lucas' jacket still draped around her shoulders. Lucas steps out from under the cover of the hedge and shouts to her, ignoring the immediate buffet of rain. "Monroe, wait!" She turns around, and Lucas takes that as his sign to continue. "What is your problem with me? Why do you insist upon controlling my every move?"

She scoffs so loud Lucas can hear her from where he's standing about fifty yards away. "Controlling you? Rutherland, trust me. I couldn't control you if I tried."

"So then tell me what's going on!" They're full-on yelling at each other now, and Lucas suspects that if no one in the castle has heard before, they certainly will soon.

"Fine!" Diana yells, taking a few steps towards him. "You have *everything*, Rutherland. And yet you insist upon throwing it away to get totally drunk and almost cause a scandal for not only you, but me as well!" She comes closer still. "I almost just killed a man, Rutherland. For *you*. Do you get that? Do you know how hard it is for me to live a life without wrongdoing when you're taking every opportunity to drag me down with you?!"

Lucas shakes his head, feeling his cheeks flush with anger, a stark difference from the chills the dampness was causing all over the rest of him. "I have this entire monarchy on my shoulders, Monroe! I have *no one* to guide me, and sometimes I can't be as high and mighty as you! My mother-"

Diana paces closer, cutting him off. She's close enough for Lucas to reach her in a couple more steps, close enough that he could cross this distance now or back up even further and both would be definitive resolutions. "Don't use your mom as an excuse, not again. The last of my family *died* in my arms, and I won't be responsible for feeling that way again!" Her words are dripping with bitterness, and Lucas takes a step towards her when she holds up a hand to stop him in his tracks. "Rutherland, you said so yourself that we can't keep doing this. We just can't, so if there's no way for this to work, we shouldn't even try." She pauses, looking down at her scarred arm and then at his. "What happened earlier was just me trying to help you and your father, alright? Nobody deserves to go through a loss without answers, and things got out of hand. Now we have a much larger problem, one that *I* have to fix. So just... let me fix it, and things will be better for you again."

Diana turns on her heel and starts trudging back towards the palace, and Lucas shouts to stop her. "Monroe, wait!"

She freezes, and Lucas can *see* the calming breath she takes before she turns around. "What?" she asks, facing him square on.

Lucas pauses for a moment. Her flyaways, the ones he loves so much, are plastered to her forehead, the raindrops are rolling down her cheeks, and Lucas notices her lipstick, almost the same maroon color as her dress, is matted from the precipitation. If he could do one thing forever, it would be to notice Diana in this way. Even if she was angry, even if she was upset, he could still only see the beautiful parts of her, which were always so incredibly abundant. Something hot burns in Lucas' chest, and it isn't anger, it isn't power, it isn't even simple desire.

It's love.

Lucas swallows before he continues talking. "We have to make this work."

"What?" she asks, stepping closer. Lucas can't tell if she's asking for clarification, or if she genuinely couldn't hear him over the rain.

"I said, we *have* to make this work."

No, she definitely heard him this time. "What is that supposed to mean?"

Lucas runs his hands over his face, suddenly embarrassed, feeling a chill from the rain or the nerves run down his spine. He looks back up to see Diana has moved a little closer, and with a deep breath, he finally says it. "We have to make this work, Diana, because I'm in love with you!" His shout rings loud and clear over the rain and the rooftops, and it's as if every other sound seems to stop.

Diana's eyes widen, and her mouth drops open a little. Out of the corner of his eye, Lucas sees that all her friends are on the veranda of the guest bedroom, looking just as shocked as Diana was.

Speaking of Diana, she still hasn't responded. Lucas turns back to her, throwing caution and proper vocabulary to the wind, because he's done holding back. "God, do you need me to say it again?" Lucas yells, louder than before. "I love you, Diana Monroe! I love you, and I have since you took that first step into my ballroom. Since you wore that stupid outfit to meet me for the first time. You're the *worst* mistake I *ever* made, and I love you endlessly for it."

God, Lucas, you're an idiot. Keep going.

"I love your bravery, and your selflessness, and the way you always look at me out of the corner of your eye when you *think* I'm not looking but I *always* am because I can *never* not look at you, Diana and- please, say something. Because I just yelled that in front of not only my entire country, but also your friends too, and I'm feeling sort of ridiculous-"

"Okay!" she shouts, interrupting him and sounding more than a little flustered. "Okay- ugh, Rutherland! What do you want me to say here?"

"I don't know!" Lucas yells back to her. "Maybe that you feel the same way, or that you forgive me?! Just say *anything*, Diana!"

A strangled, frustrated noise escapes from her throat and she paces a few feet closer. "You are seriously the most idiotic person I've ever met. You think I'm *not* in love with you, Lucas? You think I *couldn't* fall in love with the rude, charming, arrogant, *frustratingly* perfect prince who literally waltzed into my life and has somehow decided he's staying *right* where he is, *right* in front of me and yet so far out of my reach it drives me *insane*?!"

"Monroe-" Lucas starts.

She isn't finished. "You honestly think that I didn't love you?! Every time I wake up in the morning, Lucas, *you're* who I think about. When I go to bed at night, it's thoughts of *you* that keep me awake for hours-"

"Monroe!" Lucas shouts again, trying and failing to hide a delirious laugh.

"Oh, my *God*, what?" Diana shouts, *finally* shutting up.

Lucas stops in his tracks, about ten feet away from her. Rain pounds the earth around them, and her chest is rising and falling heavily. Lucas can't help but grin at her angered appearance, and at the fact that she definitely does not understand the impact her words have just had on this whole situation. "Diana," Lucas says again, his voice dropping to an almost-whisper. "Di, you just told me you loved me." Lucas tilts his head in a so-so motion. "In... one way or another."

Diana is painstakingly quiet, unmoving, and then in a flash, she's crossed the last few steps to Lucas and wrapped her arms around his neck. She puts both hands on either side of Lucas' face, leaning her forehead against his. "You're *seriously* the worst, Rutherland."

Lucas leans into her touch and smirks. "Not according to what you just said."

Diana shakes her head with a laugh and leans in, kissing him deeply and passionately. Lucas smiles against her lips and kisses her once more, pulling away and tugging her into a fierce hug. He scoops her up and spins her around in the rain, and she laughs, and it's a beautiful sound that Lucas would listen to eternally if he could. He puts her down, keeping his hands on her waist, refusing to let her go in fear that he was dreaming. "I'm never leaving you ever again," Lucas whispers to her, "I promise," he sighs against her wet hair. "I promise."

Diana grins at him and starts to pull him in again when they're broken apart by the sound of slow, sarcastic clapping.

Diana, not looking away from Lucas, smiles. "Ki, make fun of me all you want-" She turns to face the sound and freezes, her eyes getting wide in fear. She quickly separates from him, and Lucas turns to see what could be freaking her out so badly.

It's not her friends. It's his father.

Cornelius stops clapping and crosses his arms. "President Monroe. I had high hopes for you." He turns to his son, gaze raking up and down Lucas' form. "Although, Lucas, you've only given me more reason to be disappointed in you."

"Father, I can explain-" Lucas starts, but he pauses when Diana holds up a hand.

"No, Lucas, please," she starts. She turns towards his father, and Lucas notices her friends disappear from the balcony, leaving the three of them completely alone on the lawn. He focuses back on the scene in front of him, where Diana is now a few steps from the king, and they're staring each other down with a fierce intensity.

"Diana, he's not worth it," Lucas says, his hands circling into clenched fists at his sides.

She whirls to face him. "No, Lucas, he is." She turns to the king once again. "Your Majesty, with all due respect, you've been nothing but cruel to not only my companions and me, but to Lucas as well. And I'm sick of it. All I have ever done was try to help your country- in fact, I solved your wife's *murder* for you, and I wasn't even given the decency of a 'thank you'. I gave you all a chance when your closest relative tried to *destroy* my country." She's moving ever closer to him, and Lucas resists every urge to pull her back. "And this is how I'm repaid?"

Lucas feels the presence of someone at his side, and he turns his head to see Diana's friends have approached him. "Is everything okay?" Kiara asks.

"No," Lucas says, not taking his eyes off the confrontation, "but she's handling it."

"Madam President, what exactly do I have to thank you for? You brought scandal and ruin to the monarchy, and now a business trip to discuss an alliance with your country has resulted in you sleeping with my son and killing the second heir?" He grins as he delivers this blow, obviously knowing he's getting under her skin, and Diana grits her teeth and scowls, forcing Lucas to step forward.

"Father, you have no right to talk to her that way," he interrupts.

Diana nods in his direction. "Lucas is right. And I'm *sorry*, I didn't think that me dating your son would make you throw a temper tantrum."

The king's face betrays a vision of shock at this, and Lucas can hear Cameron stifle a laugh behind him. "You have no right to speak to me like that. I am the king," he growls.

"Really?" Diana asks, crossing her arms. "And I'm the president, so one would presume you don't have any right to ask about my sex life, either."

Lucas' father turns and stalks away, pausing before he reaches the door. He addresses Diana once more, and the two glare at each other in equally cold fashions. "President Monroe, good luck getting a political career off the ground." He turns to Lucas. "And son, I don't think I have *anything* more to say to you."

With that, he leaves, and Diana sighs and turns back to the others. Her face falls for a second, then brightens as she recalls something. "I cannot believe I just said the word 'sex' in front of the king, who also happens to be my boyfriend's father."

Her friends laugh, and Lucas grins at her. "Sorry, your what?" Lucas asks, voice just low enough for her to hear.

She catches his eye with a smirk. "I don't know what you're asking, Rutherland."

Lucas reaches out his arms, and she steps into them. She reaches out her hand, and her friends take it, piling their palms on top of hers. "I love you guys."

"We love you too," Kiara says, looking at Lucas. "We *all* do, apparently."

"Kiara," Diana begins, words hurried, "I know what you're probably thinking, but Lucas is different than-"

"-Di," Kiara interrupts, and Lucas thinks this might be the first time he's seen her smile. "I know. And I'm okay with... all of this."

At that, her friends turn to pin a look on him. "I'm sorry?" Lucas suggests.

"It's fine, Lucas," Cameron starts, "besides, we all pretty much knew."

"We did?!" Peter says, spinning to face him. "You didn't tell me?"

"Peter, where have you been?" Cameron says with a smile. He pulls Peter closer, planting a quick kiss on his lips. Lucas takes the cue to tug Diana gently away from them, nestling his head into her hair.

Lucas kisses Diana on the head as her friends continue chatting. She looks up at him, and Lucas smiles down at her, his fingers working instinctively to brush her wet flyaways off her forehead.

"You're beautiful," he whispers to her.

"Yeah, I know," she says back, scrunching her nose a little and holy *hell* that's the cutest thing Lucas has *ever* seen. She turns to the others. "I think we need to try again. We revived that bunny, and we healed Maxon."

The other four, Lucas included, look confused. "What are you talking about?" Cameron asks.

Diana, still wrapped in Lucas' arms, gives the prince an appraising look before continuing. "I think we can bring back Queen Anastasia."

"Woah," Peter whispers. His shocked and mildly disturbed tone makes Diana look over at him anxiously, and Peter's eyes grow wide when he sees everyone staring at him. "Sorry, it's just... that's such a cool coincidence."

"What is?" Lucas asks.

"Anastasia?" Peter says. When everyone continues to look confused, he sighs. "It's Greek for 'resurrection.'"

The others let that sink in, and then Kiara hums low in her throat. "Wow."

Lucas shakes his head. "Diana, what made this come about?" He takes her arm, holding it lengthwise against his own. Their jagged white scars, like cracks on porcelain, create an irregular and craggy puzzle. "If it doesn't work, it hurts us both. You know that."

"I do," she agrees, "but we tried once, and it didn't kill us. Maxon and Kerrigan didn't kill us. And I think... now I think we can do it." She runs her fingers down his arm, then her own. "You've got three scars; I've got three scars. Which means we still have room to try."

She doesn't have to say it, but Lucas knows that something within her has shifted due to their tryst in the rain and everything before it, because something within him feels different, too. Before, he believed he was shackled to the president, but now, he had voluntarily tied himself to her. And somehow, some way, his power knew that.

"Alright," he says finally, "before you go home tomorrow, we'll try again. One more time."

The others nod, and Lucas extends his arms to beckon all the others into a group hug. "Thank you, guys," Diana says from where she's smothered in Lucas' chest and packed like sardines between the others. "We can do this."

Lucas pulls her close again as the others separate from the couple. "Wanna get out of here?"

Diana smirks. "What are you implying?"

Lucas chuckles quietly, his chest thrumming beneath hers. "I'm *implying* that you're soaked through and there's extra blankets in the upstairs broom closet."

She nods, her green eyes glittering in the rain, which has subsided to a light drizzle. Lucas takes her hand, waving farewell to her friends, and starts to tug her inside.

She pauses in the doorway as Lucas takes off his shoes, her eyes searching the ballroom as if seeing it differently. When he straightens up, she hugs him from behind and traces her fingertips across his stomach. "Lucas," she says, her voice echoing slightly off the grand walls.

"Yeah?" Lucas responds, taking her hands and spinning her to face him. She twines her hands around his neck and Lucas puts his on her waist, rubbing the fabric of her dress between his forefinger and thumb.

Diana stands on her tiptoes and pulls his face down to her lips, planting a kiss on his cheek. When she leans back, Lucas notices her eyes are misty. "I'm sorry."

"For what?" Lucas whispers, kissing her ever so softly on the lips.

She shrugs sadly. "For hurting you earlier."

Lucas chuckles. "For the record, I asked you to."

"Yeah, well..." she trails off, motioning to the space where Kerrigan was killed. "I didn't want to hurt *anyone*."

"I know," he replies, pulling her closer, "but you saved us. No matter what my father says, you and Kiara cut the rot out of the monarchy. He should be thanking you."

She shrugs, and Lucas is relieved when she finally smiles softly. "I guess so."

Lucas kisses her again and squeezes her tighter against his chest. "You remember how I said you were different? The night we first kissed?"

She chuckles and nods. "Yes?"

"I really love that different."

An hour later, Lucas knocks on his father's office door, fingers shaking and blood rushing in his veins.

"Come in, Lucas," Cornelius mumbles from the other side.

Lucas takes a deep breath and pushes the door open, stepping into the room and closing the door behind him. He hesitates when he sees the photo his father is holding in his hands.

The king speaks without looking up at his son. "The nobility has been informed of Kerrigan's death."

"Okay?"

"Of course, I didn't say that Kiara killed him. He died in a freak accident regarding a new artillery shipment for Fort Kizis. And Kiara has been released from her new position here and given the order to go back to America, because of cultural differences that misalign her career goals with ours."

"Okay," Lucas says again, his jangling nerves calming down just slightly. His father wasn't saying it explicitly, but he knew his words meant that this situation was void and would no longer haunt them unless he let it.

The king looks up at Lucas then, eyes dark. "You know that I loved your mother, Lucas."

"I- I know," Lucas whispers, studying the photograph of his parents, holding a small infant, his mother laughing at something his father said. The sight of his mother's wide smile makes Lucas's hands shake, and he digs his nails into his palms.

"And all I ever wanted was to watch you love someone the way I loved her." He finally meets Lucas' gaze, and Lucas swallows the lump rising in his throat as he watches Cornelius' eyes fill with tears.

Lucas sighs shakily. "I do love her."

He shakes his head. "No. You're children, you're... too young, too naïve." He looks Lucas in the eye, raising one eyebrow dangerously. "She can't be queen, Lucas. You would never be able to ask that of her."

"I ask her to be president. I ask her to continue doing the job that she loves to do," he replies. "I would never demand anything more than that."

The king sets the photo gently, delicately, onto the desk, as if his white-knuckled grip would shatter the frame. "Explain to me how you think you're in love with this girl."

Lucas crosses to the desk and grabs the picture, studying his mother's kind face and eyes. "Because I grew up watching you and mother. I watched you go off for *days* on work trips, and yet still return to her open arms. I watched you walk her around ballrooms and smile at her as if she was the only person in the room." Lucas blinks back tears to no avail. "And then she was *gone*, and you changed. You got... mean, and bitter. And you became that way because you had *no one* to love anymore."

"I had you, did I not?" he asks, his voice dripping with the exact bitterness Lucas was describing.

Lucas shakes his head. "No. Because I reminded you of her. So you pushed me away because you were too sick of dealing with your own grief that you couldn't even *look* at me anymore. Do you know how many times you spoke to me in the entire year after she died?"

"How many?" Cornelius asks, voice growing smaller, ever so slightly less confident.

"Only twice. Once on the day she passed, telling me to get out of my lifeboat, and the other when you told me to leave your office when I asked you to play with me."

The king is quiet, almost pensive.

"Father," Lucas says, his voice finally breaking. "I know I love Diana because what we have is what love is supposed to look like, and I know what it's supposed to look like because I've *seen* it before. You ran away from the only home and the only family you ever had because of her. And the *last* thing I want to do is lose Diana and end up like you have."

Lucas' father looks down at the desk, and when he glances back up at his son, tears are streaking down his cheeks. "I can't do this anymore, Lucas," he whispers. "I've tried."

Lucas nods, wiping his cheeks with the heel of his palm. "I know."

"But I truly loved your mother."

He nods again. "I know." He wants so badly to admit what they were planning, but he bites his tongue. The last thing he wants to do is fail under his father's watchful gaze.

"I wanted you to be strong, so you didn't get hurt like I did. Because as soon as she died, I was *weak*. And I saw so much weakness in you that I needed to fix you before you made a mess of everything."

"It's not weakness," Lucas says. "It's empathy. It's *kindness*. And I got it from her."

He nods solemnly. "I know you did. That's another reason I wanted to get rid of it."

Lucas walks forward slowly and places the photograph gently on his desk. "You told me on the day of the ball that I was going to destroy Alynthia, but you're wrong. There's nothing in this world I care about *more* than Alynthia. And you can rule however you want, but know that the day you pass, I'm coming back here, taking the crown, and turning this place into a kinder country, one that mother would be proud of." Lucas turns and heads to the door. "I'm going to go, and let you think about her, and I hope that someday I can walk back in here and you'll be the father I used to have." He pauses. "Diana lost her older sister in the American Revolt, you know. She said that she recognized your grief, and that's part of why she did what she did earlier." He moves towards the door, not bothering to look at the king. "So you may hate her for it, but she was only trying to help us heal."

As he opens the door, Cornelius speaks. "Where are you going to go now, Lucas?"

Lucas turns back to face him. "America. All four of the others have invited me back with them. So I'll see you soon, maybe. And I wish you luck."

With that, Lucas turns and leaves, shutting his father behind him.

Part Sixty-Eight: The Cancer

Peter

Time: <u>4:15 PM</u>

Peter and Diana are walking side-by-side down the hall to Diana's room in complete silence. Both are relatively soaked through from the rain, and both are feeling the awkwardness of the situation they found themselves in. Suddenly, Diana's voice cuts through the tension.

"Peter, I'm sorry I didn't tell you," Diana says, stopping in the middle of the hall.

Peter turns to her, eyebrows creased in confusion. "What?"

Diana looks on the verge of tears, and she doesn't meet his gaze. "I'm so sorry I didn't say anything. Cameron knew because he guessed, and I couldn't say anything to Kiara because of Henderson, and then everything happened with Kerrigan, which you know, and I-"

"Diana," Peter says, crossing to her and taking her hands in his. He swears her fingers are shaking, and he gives her hands a squeeze. "Di, do you think I'm... *upset* that you didn't tell me?"

"You have every right to be," she begins, voice wavering. "I was a bad friend."

Peter grins despite himself. "You were the opposite." He shakes his head with a chuckle. "Diana, you were dating the Crown Prince of Alynthia. Of *course* you'd keep that a secret."

Diana sighs. "I should've trusted you. Every single day, I wanted to tell you. But for some reason, I was so scared."

Peter cups her cheek with his hand, and she leans into the contact. "Di, it's okay. Please trust me when I tell you that." He jokingly gives her head a gentle shake. "Ugh, you think too much."

"I could say the same to you," she says, finally allowing herself to laugh.

Peter shrugs one shoulder as they continue walking. "Besides, it's understandable that Lucas wouldn't tell me. He might be threatened by me, being your best friend, and all."

Diana laughs at his sarcasm. "Very true. You know, no romance will be able to top our fleeting childhood fling."

Peter shakes his head, trying to keep his expression as serious as possible. "How could it?"

The two dissolve into laughter, and Peter pauses in the hall once more. Diana turns to face him as he smiles down at her, resting his hands on her arms. "Di, I am so proud of you. Of everything you do for us, for America, even for Alynthia. Every day I remind myself of how lucky I am to be your best friend, and if things go wrong tonight, I want you to know that."

Diana wraps him in a hug, closing her eyes and breathing in the smell of fresh linens. "I love you, Peter."

"I love you more, Di."

Part Sixty-Nine: The Scorpio

Cameron

Time: **5:30 PM**

Peter, Cameron, Kiara, and Diana wait for Lucas with bated breath, scattered about Diana's room. She's standing by the veranda, Peter is picking at the bedspread, Finnigan lying down next to him, Kiara is seated at the vanity, and Cameron is pacing the middle of the room.

The door opens and they all spin around to face him.

The prince is standing in the doorway, head hung low. "I spoke to him," he mumbles.

"And?" Diana asks.

Lucas looks up at them and swallows. "It doesn't matter what he said, because I told him what *I* was feeling. And that's enough."

"So, are you coming?" Cameron asks.

"Yes," Lucas responds with a smile. "Even my father couldn't keep me from you guys."

The others whoop and cheer and wrap Lucas in a big group hug. "Congrats, Lucas," Peter says. "You deserve a little freedom."

Lucas pulls away from them and studies their faces. "Thank you, everyone. I don't know how, but you all have become almost my... family these past few weeks."

"Well," Cameron says, giving his arm a friendly squeeze, "you *are* family."

"Partly because you and Diana-" Kiara starts.

"Okay, Ki, thank you!" Diana shouts over her, sending the room into a fit of laughter. She looks around the room, then turns to Lucas. "Rutherland, are there any extra blankets or pillows around here?"

Lucas studies her. "My room, probably. Why?"

"Go get them," she says with a smile. "We'll have a slumber party in here before we leave tomorrow morning. It'll be something nice to come back to."

Part Seventy: The Libra

Lucas

Time: **9:01 PM**

As soon as twilight settles, and mist curls across the castle lawns, the five teenagers make their way towards the large marble tomb at the edge of the property.

The others had seen photos of Queen Anastasia Rhea Rutherland's tomb, but nothing would have prepared them to see it in real life. It was a magnificent structure, made of blinding marble that seemed to glow in the pitch-dark night. The door sat between two large pillars, and carved above the door was an inscription of the queen's name.

"Wow," Peter whispers as the rest of them fall into place beside Lucas. "It's stunning."

"It's what she deserves," Lucas whispers. Peter looks over at him, but the raven-haired prince is standing still, eyes fixated on the tomb. Cameron, to his right, wonders if his eyes are filled with tears, or if it's just the reflection of the moon.

Kiara approaches the door, which is bolted with a large metal beam that's latched horizontally over it. She tries to lift it, but it stays completely stuck.

Lucas steps into place beside her, and as he examines the tomb, he notices something on the walls. With a glance over his shoulder, he waves Diana to his side, and the couple seems to step towards the door, but Lucas instead moves towards the old, reaching ivy that grows across the walls. Taking Diana's hand in his, he places his free hand against the scraggly plants.

The others watch with utter shock as the plants warp and grow beneath Lucas' touch, and they twine themselves around the bolted door, pulling the heavy piece of metal clean away with just a flick of Lucas' hand.

With a groan of metal, the door creaks open, revealing the inside of the tomb, dark and dusty.

"Shall we?" Cameron whispers.

"What, grave rob on a Tuesday?" Kiara says with a snort. She heads towards the now-opened tomb, tossing a look over her shoulder. "Let's get on with this before someone knows we're here."

As the group enters and their eyes adjust to the dimness, Lucas takes a good look around. The walls are etched with carvings of forests, flowers, and majestic birds. The ceiling is arched above them, and Lucas notices there's a skylight that peers up into the starry night sky. In the middle of the room, on a marble dais, is the queen's gilded coffin, with the Rutherland crest engraved into the lid.

"Have you ever been in here, Lucas?" Diana asks as she wanders around, fingers tracing a large carving of a phoenix on the far wall.

"Once," he says. He feels much calmer than he did outside, as if the closeness of his mother's spirit was relaxing him.

"Let's do this," Peter says, approaching the coffin. "Cam, Lucas, help me get this lid off."

Cameron heads to Peter's side, but Lucas hesitates. To everyone else's evident surprise, Kiara moves to Lucas and places a reassuring hand on his shoulder.

"Hey, Trust Fund," she begins, motioning to the large coffin. "If you don't open the lid, you won't ever get her back." She shoves him towards the other boys, but her voice remains soft and encouraging. "Go."

So, the three boys each grab a part of the lid, straining and grunting as they lift it off and set it carefully on the floor. When the group of five gathers around the now-open coffin, the tomb grows completely silent as they take in the sight.

Queen Anastasia Rhea Rutherland lies beneath them, and Lucas' stomach roils when he realizes that her body is not entirely decomposed. After eight years, her skin and clothes have started to disintegrate, but one thing remained almost completely unchanged in the cool, stale air: her face.

Sure, it was much more... dead, Lucas supposed, but the queen was still somehow a picture of grace and poise, even eight years deceased.

And she looks exactly like Lucas.

Speaking of, Lucas is sure that the others see the fear in his eyes and the resolve in his features. Without a word, he moves to Diana's side, whispering in her ear, and although quiet, his voice is the only sound in the hollow tomb, so his words echo against the walls.

"We can do it, Monroe."

Diana nods, and although her face is a picture of calm, when Lucas takes her wrists, he can feel her pulse racing beneath her skin.

"What if it doesn't work, Lucas?" she whispers as the other three move to the opposite side of the open coffin.

Lucas moves to trace the long scars on her arm, his fingertips flitting across her skin. "Then it hurts. And she doesn't come back. But we will survive, and we'll get through it either way."

Diana nods, and without a second glance at him, she turns towards the queen. Lucas moves to stand behind her, placing both of his hands on her shoulders and letting his fingers dance their way down until his warm palms rest near her navel.

The others watch as Diana and Lucas take a deep breath in unison, and Diana reaches out both hands, placing them on Queen Anastasia's embalmed chest.

Lucas isn't sure how much time passes, breathing in dust and wallowing in fear and grief, before a memory strikes him.

"Isn't it beautiful, my darling?" Anastasia asks, pulling Lucas to her side, settling on the mattress of her huge four-poster bed.

Lucas studies the photograph in her hand. "What is it, mother?"

The queen shifts but doesn't remove her arm from around his waist. "My tomb."

The young prince, being nine, doesn't quite understand her words. "What does that mean?"

"It's where I'll rest when I die, Lucas," she replies, standing and moving to her large vanity. "Hopefully not anytime soon," she adds with a lilting chuckle.

Lucas stays put on the bed, watching as his mother, in her satin night robe, removes her earrings and sets them in the porcelain bowl beside her. "I think it's silly that it's already built," he says.

She gives him a familiar look, one that means I'm the queen. *"Well, so is your father's. It's a rite of passage, my little prince."*

Lucas' eyebrows knit together, and he scoots to the edge of the bed. "Mother, I'm not sure I understand."

The queen sighs and moves to sit next to him once again, taking his hands in hers. "My darling, sometimes it is okay to not understand. There are children in other places that are far less fortunate than you, so if that means you do not know the reason behind royal tombs until you rest inside one, then that is okay."

"I suppose," Lucas says, "but what do you mean, 'less fortunate?' Isn't Alynthia well-off, mother?"

Anastasia doesn't bat an eye, and looking back, it's no wonder Lucas didn't find out about America sooner. "Well, Alynthia is very well-off. But you're lucky that you have myself and your father, and the Crown, and this beautiful home."

Lucas nods, and the queen pulls him into a warm, comforting hug. "Mother," he begins, willing his voice not to crack as some unknown emotion settles over him. "I don't want you to ever die."

"Oh, my little prince," she says with a soft laugh. "When I die, you'll be far older, and you won't need me anymore. You'll have Willowood, and your father, and you'll be wonderfully okay."

"But still."

"Darling, trust me. Whenever I die, you will be ready, and I will be ready. That's the most important thing. Whenever Death comes around, Lucas, it's important to remember that you'll always be ready." She stands, moving to the bed and pulling the covers back as she continues to speak. "Death is not something to argue with. When you pass, my darling, it's meant to be, as hard as that is to reckon with. Do you understand?"

Lucas nods, and, although he's young, he really does understand. "Yes, mother."

She grins, and Lucas' nerves dissipate. "Good. Now, come read with me, my little prince."

Lucas startles back to the present, refocusing on the scene in front of him. Diana's magic is working, and working powerfully, for life seems to be slowly seeping back into the queen's features.

Suddenly, as Lucas watches his mother grow nearly to life in front of him, something constricts in his chest. He isn't in pain, and it isn't from Diana's power, but he's overwhelmed with grief and an unrelenting ache that makes him shiver with fear.

"Stop!" he shouts without thinking, pulling away from Diana. As soon as he does, his body alights with pain, and he gasps as his hands fly to his stomach. "Ah!"

"Lucas!" Diana says as she spins around, finally taking her hands off Queen Anastasia's chest and racing to him as he crumples to the ground. "No, what did I do?"

Lucas sucks in a sharp breath and looks towards his left arm, where a fourth, white-pink scar is carving its way through his skin. He groans in pain, curling into Diana's arms as tears spring at his eyes.

"What's going on?" Peter asks as the others hurry towards the pair.

"I don't know," Diana says, voice frantic, "but he just moved away all of a sudden, and I hurt him on accident."

"Why did you move, Lucas?" Kiara asks. "It was working!"

"That's exactly why," Lucas huffs out. "I can't do it."

"Lucas," Diana starts, cradling his face in her hands, "what do you mean?"

He shakes his head, and he suddenly registers the hot, wet tears on his face that were now beading on Diana's fingers as she held him. "I don't know, I just... she's ready to be here. I can feel it- I know she's fine. And *I'm* fine. She's resting, and I have to let her. Just like you said about Maya."

The others share a look, and Diana nods after a long moment. "Okay, then. Cam, Peter, can you two put the lid back on without him?"

"No, I'll help," Lucas says, beginning to rise to his feet. Diana pulls him down, however, resting his head on her shoulder as Kiara moves to help the other two boys.

"Lucas," Diana whispers as soon as the others are out of earshot, "I'm proud of you. And I know Anastasia is too."

Lucas smiles and closes his eyes, breathing in her jasmine perfume, even though it's slightly muddled by the smell of dust. "She would've loved you," he whispers, "just as much as I do."

Part Seventy-One: The Scorpio

Cameron

Time: **11:56 PM**

The group gets back much later that night, and they move to their blankets and sleeping bags that are scattered on Diana's bedroom floor. Lucas and Diana get in bed, and Cameron notices that Lucas is asleep within minutes.

"He must be exhausted," Cameron says, frowning slightly at the prince and Diana, who is sitting up and running her fingers through his ebony hair.

"Poor guy," Peter whispers.

Diana nods, looking down at his arm, which rests on top of the blanket. "That's crazy," Kiara whispers, pointing to the couple's matching left arms, "the scars, I mean."

Diana shrugs. "I just can't hurt him in the future, or..."

"Are you feeling okay about all of this, Di?" Peter interrupts as he pulls his pajama pants over his legs. "You've had a pretty ridiculous day."

She nods, pulling her lip between her teeth. "I'm okay. I feel tired, sure, but I just want Lucas to feel okay about all of it. I know everything wasn't... emotionally easy for him."

The alarm clock on the bedside table strikes midnight with a flash of light, and Diana stretches and yawns.

"Okay, guys. Lights out for me," she says, flopping back on the bed and snuggling under her covers as the conversation draws to a close. "Love you all."

"Love you too," everyone else choruses.

"We should *all* go to bed," Peter says. He spreads out his blankets on the ground and nestles into the pillow pile they made.

"Goodnight, everyone," Cameron whispers. Diana flicks off the lamp, plunging the room into darkness. Kiara rolls over on her blanket, her fingers nestled in a sleeping Finnigan's fur, and Cameron taps Peter on the shoulder.

"Yes?" he whispers. Cameron can hear his smile in the dark.

Cameron rests his chin on Peter's shoulder, wrapping his arms around his waist. "Can I lay with you?"

Peter turns around, kissing Cameron slow and long. "Uh-huh. You don't ever have to ask."

Cameron lays down with him, kissing his temple gently as he threads his arms around Peter's waist. They breathe in unison, and Cameron smiles into his shoulder blade. "I love you, superhero."

Peter's hand finds its way over Cameron's, and he gives his fingers a squeeze. "I love you too, Cam."

Cameron peppers his neck with gentle kisses. The intimate way in which Peter was rubbing his fingertips over Cameron's hands made his stomach flip. "You're my favorite human, do you know that?"

Peter nods. "I do, yes," he states sarcastically.

Cameron chuckles, muffling the sound in Peter's shirt. "Don't be a jerk. You know I don't do emotional speeches."

Peter rolls onto his back so he's looking up at Cameron. "I also know *that*," he says with a sly grin.

"Peter, you're asking for it," Cameron says, smiling back because he can't help himself when it comes to Peter.

"Okay, fine," Peter groans. His eyes flick to Cameron's lips. "Kiss me again."

Cameron grins and complies.

Part Seventy-Two: The Taurus

Diana

Time: **8:10 AM**

"I thought you never wanted to see me again," Diana says as she enters Cornelius' office, fighting to keep her tone from sounding bitter.

The king arches an eyebrow, and the expression is frighteningly similar to Henderson, if not exactly the same. "I figured you would want more information on my brother before you left, no?"

She pauses. "What do you mean?"

Cornelius leans back in his large chair, clasping his hands in his lap. He motions to the chair across from him, a framed photograph of the Rutherland royals conveniently placed on the desk for all to see. Diana sits as the king speaks again.

"I admit that I kept a few secrets over your time here, Miss Monroe," he begins, his steely green eyes cutting into Diana's own. "And there's more to the Henderson story than just myself and Lucas."

The two study each other for a brief moment until Cornelius smiles gently. Something about that smile unnerves Diana, and she realizes with a jolt of fear that it's George Henderson's smile. "He's thirteen years my senior, you see," the king starts, "and that wasn't easy growing up. George was just being introduced to your country's politics, so my mother and I spent much time alone."

"What was she like?" Diana asks apprehensively.

"Well, she was very gentle. Very much like my Anastasia, in a way."

He doesn't continue, and Diana doesn't wish to push any further, so she changes her line of questioning. "And George? Was he a good brother?"

Cornelius tilts his head in a so-so mannerism. "He resented me, I think, just because I held more of my mother's favor. Besides, being the second son means that you don't bear the pressure of an inheritance. But he did love me, too."

Diana raises an eyebrow. "Those two things go together?"

The king nods, that familiar assessing look boring into her. "That's the case with family often, is it not? Love and hate in the same breath?"

Something weighted settles in Diana's ribcage. "I suppose it could be."

"George was rather distant, but never unkind to me."

She laughs bitterly before she can help herself. "That doesn't sound like him."

Cornelius continues without replying. "Well, I guess that must be true from where you sit. But he was very family-oriented, and when he married-"

Diana sucks in a sharp breath. "Henderson never got married."

The king looks confused, and Diana's pounding heart drowns out her ability to tell if he's lying or not. "He did. His wife was quite the same as him, in a way, what with the 'Aries traits' your people all speak of."

Diana swallows hard, fighting to keep too much emotion from showing on her face. "He... uh, she's never made herself known to us."

Cornelius tuts sadly, even though it doesn't sound sincere. "She passed away, actually. Childbirth complications."

Now it's as if Diana's heart drops and her blood runs freezing cold, and this time she can't help the look of terror and shock that springs onto her face. "What?" Her voice comes out a whisper.

The king doesn't seem to realize, seemingly consumed by a memory of this distant family. "Yes, my niece was born... oh, probably not long after you and my own son. Maybe a few years either way, but the exact date escapes me."

"Is she with you all?" Diana asks, both scared and eager to learn anything. "In Alynthia?"

"No," Cornelius replies, and Diana doesn't know if she's glad or disappointed. "I've never met her. George spoke of her less and less as time went on, and she very well could be dead now. He always said she was the spitting image of her mother, though, and I think her name started with a 'C,' or maybe a 'K,' like Clara or Kaylie..." he pauses. A full, weighted pause that is entirely intentional as the king's faux-confused look changes into an evil, sadistic one. "Kiara, maybe?"

Diana stops listening, the king's voice fading into static in the background of her racing thoughts. She feels like her brain can't hold this information, like her heart can't harbor it, like the very notion of knowing this secret was poisoning her body.

She rises abruptly, startling even herself. "I need to leave."

"Sorry?"

She clears her throat, reminding herself to tread carefully. "I, uh, have to pack, I'm afraid," she lies, "but thank you for telling me this."

"She's royalty, you know. And she's the daughter of your greatest enemy-"

"-That's enough." Diana says firmly, although she feels a little surprised when Cornelius complies.

The king nods slowly, and it seems that a little animosity has faded just slightly, to Diana's shock. "You're welcome. Thank you for re-sealing the tomb, by the way."

Diana hesitates, and she didn't know it was possible for her heartbeat to get any faster. "What?"

"I do know what happens at Willowood, Miss Monroe, and I'm not a fool. I didn't want to intervene, but... it pleases me to know that you gave her the respect she deserves."

Diana swallows and nods slowly. His words didn't feel like an attack, they felt like genuine gratitude. "I wouldn't dream of treating her as any less than her given station."

The pair shares an unreadable look, and then Diana turns and leaves, pulling the office door shut behind her.

As soon as Diana hears the latch click into place, she lets herself cry.

Part Seventy-Three: The Cancer

Peter

Time: **12:00 PM**

They get to the apartment at noon the next day, eating a late breakfast at the cafe, allowing multiple reporters to snap candid shots of all five of them, and not really caring when citizens come up and ask questions.

"So," Diana says over her meal, "are we going into the office today?"

Peter, Cameron, and Kiara nod. "We should," Kiara says, mouth full. "We've been gone for long enough that Barbara is probably sick of covering for us."

So, they wrap up breakfast and walk to the Capitol, all of them dressed casually and without bodyguards. Peter has never seen everyone so happy, which makes him happy in turn. Lucas looks *thrilled* to be away from Alynthia and their fumbled experiment, Kiara is obviously loving the fact that she's home, and Cameron, based on the way he doesn't let go of Peter's hand for the whole walk, is deliriously overjoyed as well. But something seems off with Diana, and he isn't sure what.

Ms. Miller and Ms. Brewer are standing by the entrance when they get in, and both practically squeal with excitement when they see Lucas.

"Our little prince is back!" Ms. Brewer says, wrapping Lucas in a huge hug.

Lucas laughs and hugs her back. "The very same."

Ms. Miller shakes her head with a chuckle and releases Cameron from the one-armed hug he'd been roped into. "Sorry, dear," she says to Lucas as she squats down to pet the dog. "We Americans aren't ones for royal manners."

Lucas grins, and Peter realizes all over again how different this smile is than the one he's seen in tabloids, and how different it is from his father's. "No, it's refreshing. I've had far too much experience with royal manners for one person's lifetime."

"Ah, they're home," Oswald says as she glides down the stairs. "No hugs for me?"

Everyone except Lucas races to give her a hug, and she laughs as they barrel into her.

"How are things here?" Diana asks as she pulls away, her voice strangely even.

"Fine," Barbara affirms. "One sector left to be released."

They all give a little cheer, even Lucas, even though anyone could tell he has no idea what he's cheering for. "Which one?" Cameron asks, rubbing his hands together as if his power was just aching to be used.

Oswald sighs. "Sector Five. It's the disease, we can't risk its spread."

"What, and nothing from the doctors there?" Peter asks. For a while now, Sector Five had proved problematic when it came to its release, because of the disease that continued to linger within its walls.

"Not yet," she replies.

Suddenly, Mr. Boone races down the hall. "Hello, everyone," he says, then he turns to Barbara. "Oswald, we've gotta get everyone on the floor."

"Why?" Barbara and Diana ask at once. Barbara sounds confused, but Diana sounds... scared.

Mr. Boone chews his lip and eyes the others. "Because, we've got new information on the disease," he smiles awkwardly and bows to Lucas. "Your Royal Highness."

The group falls silent. "Well," Barbara says finally. "You heard the man. Everyone on the congress floor in five."

The group scatters, and Lucas plants a kiss on Diana's head. "I should go," he says. "I'll wait at your place, I- I don't want to get in the way of you guys."

Oswald shakes her head and waves the prince closer. "No, no, Mister Rutherland," she says. "You're something special to these kids, which means you're something special to all of us. When I said everyone needed to be on the floor in five, I meant *everyone* needs to be on the floor in five."

Lucas beams at her, and he nods. "Yeah, okay. Sure," he replies sheepishly.

So, they all splinter off in their familiar directions, and after five minutes, they reconvene in their seats around the table on the congress floor, right where they fit best. Peter notices a chair that had been put into a ninth spot, where Lucas sat.

"Okay, Reginald," Diana says. "What's this news?"

Mr. Boone sighs and runs a hand through his thinning hair. "Well, one of the doctors got back to me. Doctor Charles is a friend, and he's reported that the cases have doubled in the past twenty-four hours."

"Doubled?" Peter whispers. His heartbeat seems to still for a moment before coming back even faster.

Everyone sits in silent thought.

Finally, Peter turns to Lucas. "Are there any doctors in Alynthia we could bring in?"

The prince thinks for a minute. "I think I could pull some strings, maybe get someone to fly down. I wouldn't gamble on a lot of help, considering the whole business with my father."

"Okay," Diana starts. "Reginald, ask this Doctor Charles if he'd want to come to the Capitol to help us figure this out." She turns to Lucas. "Rutherland, get in contact with any doctor you can get a hold of from Alynthia."

Lucas and Mr. Boone nod, and Peter reaches across the table to tap Diana on the wrist. "Di, maybe I could do something over the television that airs around the country, just showing support for Sector Five, since it's my home sector."

Diana beams at him. "Absolutely." She turns to Ms. Miller and Ms. Brewer. "Do we know what the stats should be before we send Cam in for release?"

Ms. Miller flips through her ledger. "I'd say the cases need to be lessened by about forty percent. Herd immunity could be reached, but it's a risky gamble to take."

The others nod, and Diana turns to Peter. "Well?" she whispers.

Peter looks at her, eyebrows creased with worry, and shrugs. "There's not a lot we can do right now, is there?" He swallows hard. "Meeting adjourned?"

Diana nods, her face a picture of worry, and turns back to the others, raising her voice louder now. "Meeting adjourned."

Part Seventy-Four: The Libra

Lucas

Time: **4:15 PM**

"On air in three, two..." the cameraman nods at Lucas and he begins to speak.

"Good afternoon, New America," he says, putting on what used to be a phony smile but was now fully genuine. "I'm Lucas Rutherland, Crown Prince of Alynthia."

He was seated in the living room of the American's apartment, in a big white chair in front of the fireplace, which housed a roaring flame. He was in a white sweater and khakis, and positioned in front of him was a cameraman and his rig. Airing live on televisions all over the country, at that very moment, was this exact press conference.

"I wanted to speak with you all today, from the comfort of my new home." He winks at the camera. "A few folks who work in your Capitol are letting me stay for a while. Aren't they kind?" He shakes his head with a chuckle, letting his arms rest on the chair and his fists unclench. "Anyways, I'm here in New America to help assist the president and her team with foreign policy. I'm also here because..." he trails off, thinking to himself. His heart hammers in his chest, but there's no going back now. "Because I wanted to announce that the Kingdom of Alynthia is officially allied with New America as of this afternoon. We have declared peaceful intentions and set up a three-year alliance program, in which we support each other through trade and commerce as well as military strength." He smiles again, ignoring the sweat trickling down the back of his neck. "So thank you, citizens of New America, for convincing us Alynthian nobility that you're the cause we want to support. Know that I will fight for you, although my heritage isn't the same as yours. Know that your success is my success, and your pain is my pain. I am here for you, President Monroe is here for you, Secretary Simon and Secretary O'Connor are here for you, your Citizens' Liaison is here for you. We fight for *you*, New America. Thank you, and have a good night."

The camera clicks off and the lights that had been set up around the room are unplugged. Lucas leans back in the chair, sighing with relief, waiting for the other shoe to drop.

The phone rings and he grimaces.

As the cameraman packs up and heads for the elevator, Lucas enters the kitchen and picks up the receiver with shaking hands. "Hello?"

"Lucas Rutherland, you are a *disgrace* to the Alynthian crown. I *never* agreed to this alliance, and I would *never* let you go about telling the country that when it is *not* true-"

"Let me stop you right there, Father," Lucas says, leaning against the wall and willing his voice to keep steady. "First of all, as kindly as possible, screw off. I'm the prince, and I *am* going to take the crown. If you have *such* a big *issue* with that, pull me from the line of succession. I have a nagging feeling you *won't*, since you honor 'family ties' more than anything and you know as well as I do that there's no longer a Second Heir."

"I could ask Maxon-"

"-And he'd say no."

"Lucas-"

"I'm not done. I did a little research, and I found out from my friends here in the American Capitol that only *one* reigning monarch needs to agree to an alliance. Sure enough, I went to the archives. There's a neat book there, you should check it out. It's called 'An Encyclopedic Guide to Alynthia.' Anyways, it said that a prince or princess could be the deciding vote on an alliance, should they have been officially crowned. Well, do you remember the day I officially became *Crown* Prince, Father? I sure do. So, *I* made the choice to ally ourselves. You're welcome, by the way, since agricultural, medical, and educational support are clauses in the contract and you're benefiting from any goods shipped to Alynthia, not me."

"Well, I can just terminate the alliance," Cornelius says, voice growing cold.

Lucas smiles at the empty room. "Sure, in three years? Knock yourself *right* out."

"You're lucky I don't disown you."

"Go right ahead. We'll both be better off with it in the end, won't we?"

The line clicks, a sure sign the king had hung up on him, and Lucas knows he should feel sad, or guilty.

But when he crosses to the window and looks across the American Plaza, he can't help but smile.

Part Seventy-Five: The Taurus

Diana

Time: **10:15 AM**

The morning after Lucas' alliance conference, everyone is gathered in the Capitol again. Cameron is in the Plaza, getting lunch with Ms. Brewer and Ms. Miller, Peter is in his office, prepping for a radio interview, Kiara is talking with Barbara about relocation for sick citizens, and Lucas is sprawled on Diana's office floor, flipping through a portfolio.

Diana, however, was sketching a tentative family tree on a blank piece of paper.

"Monroe," Lucas calls from the ground. "Come look at this."

Diana gets up from her desk and crouches next to him, and he holds out the sheet he's reviewing. "These are stats from the kids in the Sector Five children's hospital. Look at that spike."

He traces the line on the graph with his finger, starting low to the axis and slowly but surely rising. "How is it spreading so fast?" Diana asks as Lucas' other hand rubs her back soothingly.

Lucas shrugs. "I don't know. It might be something with weakened immune systems in the young kids, but it still doesn't tell us how to solve it."

Diana gets up and starts pacing the room. "I mean, we could quarantine the sick people, but that wouldn't even matter because they're already stuck where they are. We've stopped the monorails, we've postponed the border drop, and the only people allowed in or out are doctors."

Lucas sits up, propping himself on his hands as he leans back. "What about sectioning off the hospitals? Anyone who's sick has to go to a specific place, so they don't risk infecting the entire hospital."

"That could work, but what about the people on the outside? Maybe we could limit or stop any hospital visitation unless it's absolutely necessary."

"Yeah, that would help slow the spread from outside the hospitals. Then comes the matter of developing a method of healing the disease."

Diana chews her thumbnail. "I have no idea what that entails. We need to wait for Doctor Charles to give us the medical side of it. Honestly, I don't even know what the disease *does* to you once you're infected."

"Hey," Peter says as he enters the office. "What're you guys looking at?"

"Children's hospital," Lucas says, passing the papers to Peter, who flips through them intently.

After a second, Peter looks up at Diana. "Di, what if I *went* there? Not now, obviously, but once the curve starts to flatten a little bit. I could even bring Cameron, in case we decide we could release the sector."

Diana leans against her desk, tilting her head as she turns over his words and blocking her little project from view. "I don't know, Peter. I wouldn't want you guys getting sick. Especially because your powers weaken your immune systems more than normal people."

Peter puts the papers down and sits in one of her chairs. "Yeah, but we'd be careful. Limited public appearances, we'd bring a team of doctors, and I could make a speech on the new regulations you release."

Diana sits down, flipping through the planner on her desk. "Okay, fine. But listen, I'll give you a train a week from now, and I want you back in the Capitol by noon four days later. That gives you six days to prepare."

Peter grins. "That sounds great. Am I making the itinerary, or should I ask someone else?"

"I'll give Miriam a call," Diana replies. After a moment, she grabs a pencil and writes down the dates on a piece of paper, holding it out to Peter with a tired smile. "I know what you're waiting for. Give that to Cameron and tell him he's going with you."

Peter pumps a fist in the air. "Awesome. We'll be careful."

"I know you will," Diana says back.

Peter turns to leave when Lucas pipes up from the floor. "Hey, Monroe. I think Peter should stop at this children's hospital while he's there."

Diana blinks. "But the cases are crazy high there. I'd be putting him in direct danger."

Lucas shrugs, standing up and looking over the graph one more time. "Well, it could start to decline a bit in a week, and obviously, he won't be *interacting* with the kids, but he is the Secretary of Education. It would look good for us, and I'm sure the kids would be delighted just to see him, even from behind a safety screen."

Before Diana can respond, Peter nods. "Please, Di?" he asks, hands clasped dramatically. "Lucas is right, the kids would love it."

Lucas glances at Peter and mimics his clasped hands, so now both of them are pouting and begging. Diana laughs and shakes her head in a sign of defeat. "Ugh, you two are awful together. Fine, I'll write to the hospital and let you know what they say."

Both boys cheer, and Peter heads for the exit after an enthusiastic high-five from Lucas. He turns to face

Diana when he reaches the door. "Thank you, Di," he says with a grin.

Diana smiles back. "You're welcome, Peter. Have fun, and *please* be careful."

Peter gives her a two-fingered salute. "Aye aye, captain."

Epilogue: Two Weeks Later

Peter

Time: **9:20 AM**

Peter loves snowy days.

It might be something about being back in the Capitol, or something about growing up in the South, but snow during the late winter months like these are easily his favorite kind of weather. The falling flakes have a way of soothing his worries and reminding him that he's entirely human, no matter his powers or job.

"Morning," Diana says as she enters his office, Lucas close behind her. She's in a casual outfit, just leggings and a puffy jacket, and Lucas is in khakis and a sweater, both of their noses red from the chill. Diana sits on the edge of Peter's desk, and Lucas in one of the chairs against the wall. "What are you doing?"

"Wrapping up the Sector Five stuff," Peter says. "It's taking a lot longer than expected."

A little over a week ago, Cameron and Peter had gotten to Sector Five to do some digging on the disease down there. As much as they tried to stop it while they were there by putting some quarantine measures in place, it was still continuing to spread across the sector, leaving the boys unable to drop the walls in fear of it spreading across the whole country. So, they've been in further correspondence with medical professionals from all over, and Lucas had put them in touch with some doctors from Alynthia as well. Peter tries to ignore the pang in his chest every time he thinks about the sick citizens he saw there, or the fact that he woke up every morning just to find out that things had gotten worse.

"Ugh. That puts a damper on things," Diana says, turning her head to read over his shoulder at the skyrocketing numbers of diseased people.

"Yup. The Cancers are *still* the only sector still cut off from the rest of us," Peter says with a frown, willing himself not to become consumed with the anxiety and sadness that was plaguing him.

"Any word from the Alynthian doctors?" Lucas asks. "I know back home they've been trying to figure this out."

Peter shakes his head, and Lucas' face falls as well. This past week had been tricky for all of them, with the Sector Five issues, Lucas' father trying to interfere, and for the past two days, the public had been getting more and more agitated with the fact that the Cancers were still isolated. Diana had been off, too, ever since they'd returned from Alynthia.

"Peter, you okay?" Diana asks, breaking him from his daze. "You look pale."

Peter laughs halfheartedly. "I'm always pale."

She shakes her head with a smile. "No, paler than usual." She presses her hand against his forehead and rapidly yanks it away. "Peter, woah. Go home!"

"What?" Peter asks, standing up and taking a cautionary step back. "Why, what's wrong?"

"You're burning up!" she says, hopping off the desk and backing away from him ever so slightly. "You shouldn't have come in if you had a fever!"

Peter presses the heel of his palm against his forehead. Sure enough, he's hot and sweaty, but for some reason, the rest of his body is chilled, even under his long sleeve shirt.

Diana ducks her head out of the office and hollers down the hall. "Cameron! Kiara! Come here!"

Kiara and Cameron enter moments after, and for some reason, as soon as they see Peter, they both look equally disturbed. "Jeez, Peter," Kiara says. "Sit down."

Peter sits.

Cameron passes Finnigan off to Kiara and crosses over to Peter, kneeling in front of his chair. "Hey, are you okay?" he whispers, putting both hands on Peter's knees and rubbing them up and down his legs in a comforting motion that doesn't comfort Peter at all.

"I don't know!" Peter whispers back. "Everyone is saying I'm sick?"

"Well, you look it," Cameron says with a chuckle, "why did you come in today?"

"I didn't even know I had a fever," Peter says. "In fact, I'm actually pretty cold."

Cameron looks taken aback, and he slowly turns to the others. "Di, is Doctor Charles still here?"

"Yeah, why?" she says. After a moment, her eyes widen. "Cameron, you don't think-"

"No, I don't know. But it doesn't hurt for him to get checked out," he says, motioning to Peter.

"They *were* in Sector Five recently, Di," Lucas says, taking her hand. "Cameron is right."

Diana nods and leaves, returning minutes later with Doctor Charles, an older Gemini who had been brought in by Mr. Boone to help with the crisis in Sector Five. "Peter, hello!" he booms in a deep, welcoming voice. "Feeling sick today?"

"Uh, I guess I am, apparently," Peter replies.

Charles crosses over to him, taking instruments out of his bag. He was a nice guy, loud and tall, who—although he hadn't solved the mystery in the Cancer sector yet- was, in fact, pretty smart. He takes Peter's temperature, his blood pressure, and checks his eyes and ears, and then sits back with a frown.

"What's wrong?" Cameron asks, hovering nervously behind Charles' shoulder.

"Well, I'm not sure. That's the problem." He turns to Peter. "Peter, I'm going to ask you a series of questions. I just need yes or no answers, okay?"

"Okay," Peter replies.

"Any itchiness this morning?"

"No."

"Alright, how about rashes or bumps anywhere?"

"No."

"Vomiting?"

"Nope."

Charles eyes Cameron. "And when was the last time you two-"

"Woah," Cameron interrupts, flushing a deep red. "We've never- just continue."

"Okay," Charles says with a cheeky grin. "How many people did you interact with when you went to Sector Five?"

"Um, no adults, but I visited a children's hospital for a press release," Peter replies.

"How many of those kids had the disease?" Charles asks.

Peter looks over at his friends, at their nervous and knowing faces, and swallows. "All of them."

"Oh, no," Diana whispers, burying her face in her hands.

Peter looks up at Charles. "Is this bad? Do I have that disease?"

"Well, I have to say you must. You're most at risk anyways, considering you were born in Sector Five, and since you have powers, your immune system is weaker than normal peoples'. It's very possible you had a strain from your younger years that flared up when you revisited."

"So, how bad will this get?" Cameron asks. Peter wonders if it's just the lighting in the office that's making Cameron's eyes shine.

Peter looks at Cameron's face, at the small, barely-there wrinkles in the crease of his eyes, his hands fidgeting nervously. He catches Peter's eye, and Peter smiles shakily and mouths "I love you" to try to calm him down.

Cameron smiles, somewhat sadly, and mouths it back.

"Well, I'm not sure. In normal patients, the disease acts like a regular flu, until it isn't," Charles replies.

"What the hell is that supposed to mean?" Kiara asks.

"Well, we've found it follows three stages. Stage one is where Peter is now, just a fever, chills, and he'll probably develop a rash sometime soon. Stage two is vomiting and diarrhea, with all the same symptoms as stage one as well."

"And what's stage three?" Lucas asks, his voice even, regal, as if he turned on this part of himself to avoid feeling any emotion. His fists are clenched and his knuckles are white.

Charles tilts his head. "That's where we've been hitting some roadblocks. Stage three is exactly the same as stage two, except rather than puking up the contents of your lunch, your body is relieving itself of... mostly blood."

"I'm gonna throw up," Peter whispers, his stomach churning with the concept of this newfound knowledge.

"Please don't!" Cameron shouts instantly, his voice sounding increasingly concerned.

"So, wait. His organs become infected, and we don't know until he starts barfing up blood?" Kiara questions.

"How do we fix it?" Diana asks, ignoring Kiara. She's chewing her thumbnail, glancing at Peter nervously.

"We don't know yet. But Peter is highly contagious, meaning all of you are in danger, Cameron especially." The doctor motions to the group. "So, everybody out."

"Wait!" Peter shouts. "Where will I stay? I mean, I don't think I should go home."

"You're right. We'll turn this office into a hospital room. And of course, Peter will be the first to be administered a vaccine or antibiotic as soon as we discover one," Charles nods at his own idea, gently and methodically packing his tools back into his bag.

"No," Peter says immediately.

Everyone looks at him like he's crazy. "What do you mean, 'no?'" Diana asks. "You *don't* want the medicine if they find it?"

"Of course I do, but there are so many other people, though," Peter says, remembering the sick kids lying immobile in Sector Five. "There are people who were infected before me, so they should get healed before me. That's what's right."

"But-" Cameron starts, shaking his head. "Peter, this could kill you."

Peter nods, trying to look more confident than he feels. "I know. But I would feel so awful if other people missed out and I didn't just because of my title."

"Don't you think that's a little foolish, Peter?" Dr. Charles asks.

Peter speaks without missing a beat. "I think it's fair."

The room falls silent.

"Okay," Diana whispers. "Okay, let's get a head start on this. I'll make a speech, saying that Peter is unavailable for the next little while. Ki, help Charles get Peter's office set up. Lucas, talk to your dad and tell him that until Peter gets better, you should stay in America to avoid bringing strains back to Alynthia. Cam-"

"I'm staying with Peter," he interrupts, crossing to Peter and taking his hand gently.

"Cameron, no," Peter says. "You're at just as high a risk as I am. Our immune systems are the weakest out of the group," Peter gives his hand a squeeze and releases it.

"Peter is right," Charles says. "Cameron, we could possibly set up occasional visitations, but you can't see him head-on."

"But-" Cameron persists.

Peter shoots him a serious look.

"Fine," he huffs.

The group disperses without another word, and within the next half hour, Peter's office has been set up like a quarantine station. He gets assigned a nurse, and Charles as his personal doctor. Charts are plastered all over the wall, and he's hooked up to I.Vs and plopped into a movable hospital bed.

"Can I go by the window?" Peter asks his nurse. Her name is Ms. Butters, and she's loud and kind, with a big, bubbling laugh that fills the whole room, just like Charles'. She'll be in charge of enlisting more nurses if needed.

Let's hope they *don't* need more nurses, because they all know what that means.

"Of course, dear," Ms. Butters says. She gets Peter situated in one of his office chairs by the window, away from his bed, which is tucked against the far wall. Peter looks out the window, to where a crowd is starting to gather. Diana, Kiara, Cameron, Lucas, and Charles are stationed on the top step.

"Good afternoon, New America," Diana starts, no notecards or prompts visible anywhere. She's improvising, which makes Peter nervous on her behalf. "As we know, Sector Five has been unable to be released, because of the disease we now know is spreading through the sector. One of my very close-" she pauses, "no, my very best friend Peter is from Sector Five. He works closely with all of us in the Capitol, and you all know him better as the Secretary of Education. Unfortunately, Peter has come down with this- as of now-incurable disease."

She pauses, swallowing, and Peter watches through the window as her shoulders start to shake. Lucas grabs her elbow and gently tugs her towards him, passing her the handkerchief he'd previously had folded in his chest pocket. Peter bites his lip, watching as Lucas whispers something to Diana, something that makes her nod and wipe her eyes. Kiara and Cameron turn to each other, whispering fervently, and the microphone at the edge of the top stair is left deserted.

"So what does this mean?" someone shouts from the crowd, loud enough for Peter to hear through the weathered windowpanes.

Silence. Even the nervous chattering stops.

After a brief pause and a nod from Diana, Cameron steps up to the mic.

He looks up to Peter's window, and the boys make eye contact. Peter sees the sadness, the worry, and most importantly, the unspoken love swimming under his gray eyes. Peter forces himself to smile a little, although he feels no happiness whatsoever, and Cameron doesn't smile back.

Cameron turns away from Peter and out towards the crowd, his broad shoulders straightening in false confidence. With a deep breath, Secretary O'Connor speaks, his voice slow and calm.

"It means the Sector Five sickness has infiltrated the Capitol."